## STARBRIDGE
### by A.C. Crispin

The first book in the series takes you to a distant asteroid, where StarBridge Academy begins its mission of extra-terrestrial contact . . .

"A great success . . . an adventure novel with some thought in it."

—Vonda N. McIntyre, author of *Enterprise: The First Adventure*

"Crispin's aliens are a diverse and fascinating lot . . . She'll be the leading candidate for the title 'the Norton of the 1990s'!"

—*Dragon*

★　★　★

## STARBRIDGE: SILENT DANCES
### by A.C. Crispin and Kathleen O'Malley

Deaf since birth, Tesa is the perfect ambassador to the alien Grus—whose sonic cries can shatter human ears . . .

"Plenty of action and drama . . . *Silent Dances* entertains and does so while enlightening its readers about the cultural meaning of deafness."

—*Gallaudet Today*

"Four stars . . . *Silent Dances* shows the growth of a woman who finds her place in the future worlds." —*OtherRealms*

*The STARBRIDGE Series*

STARBRIDGE by A.C. Crispin
STARBRIDGE 2: SILENT DANCES by
A.C. Crispin and Kathleen O'Malley
STARBRIDGE 3: SHADOW WORLD by
A.C. Crispin and Jannean Elliott
STARBRIDGE 4: SERPENT'S GIFT by
A.C. Crispin with Deborah A. Marshall
STARBRIDGE 5: SILENT SONGS by
A.C. Crispin and Kathleen O'Malley

*Also by A.C. Crispin*

V
YESTERDAY'S SON
TIME FOR YESTERDAY
GRYPHON'S EYRIE (*with Andre Norton*)

# STAR BRIDGE
★ ★ ★ ★ ★ ★ ★ ★ ★ ★ ★ ★ ★ ★ *Book Five*

# SILENT SONGS

## A. C. CRISPIN and KATHLEEN O'MALLEY

ACE BOOKS, NEW YORK

This book is an Ace original edition,
and has never been previously published.

SILENT SONGS

An Ace Book / published by arrangement with
the authors

PRINTING HISTORY
Ace edition/June 1994

ISBN: 0-441-00061-4

ACE®
Ace Books are published by The Berkley Publishing Group,
200 Madison Avenue, New York, NY 10016.
ACE and the "A" design are trademarks
belonging to Charter Communications, Inc.

PRINTED IN THE UNITED STATES OF AMERICA

10 9 8 7 6 5 4 3 2 1

Dedicated to the memory of
Louis Cain
We all miss you, Uncle Louie
—K. O'Malley

"Will we let ourselves be destroyed ... without a struggle, give up our ... country bequeathed to us by the Great Spirit ... and everything that is dear and sacred to us? I know you will cry with me, 'Never! Never!' "

—Tecumseh of the Shawnees

"When people come to trouble, it is better for both parties to come together without arms and talk it over and find some peaceful way to settle it."

—Spotted Tail of the Brulé Sioux

# Prologue

First-in-Conquest Atle grasped the sides of the hydro-sleeper and pulled himself out of the nutrient broth with an effort. He lingered drowsily in the tank, his long legs folded tightly under his narrow pelvis, as the warm, sweet liquid lapped against his broad-chested, red-blue mottled torso.

This resting stage gave his body time to synchronize with its forebrain. That organ, the one that made decisions and took risks, still had to wait for the tiny hindbrain. A small cluster of glands and nerves, the hindbrain was the seat of instinct and bodily functions. Safely tucked away in his short, thick, triangular tail, only it could signal the end of estivation.

The need to breathe came suddenly, as the First inhaled the cool, oxygen-rich air of his ship, the massive Exploratory Ship *Flood*. He coughed, tasting sweetish, viscous fluid. As his thoughts cleared, he clambered stiffly out of the tank, his long, narrow feet hitting the deck with a splat. His hands and feet had evolved from the need to grasp tree limbs, and had two long digits in the front and two more extending from the heel.

*Something must have happened*, he realized. *Something important*. The readout on his tank said that it'd been three years since he'd last been brought up.

Gazing down the stacked rows of hydro-sleepers, he paused to stare lovingly into the one nearest his. It held his mate, Dunn.

*So beautiful*, he thought, leaving a wet smear on her sleeper from his hand. Their four children had been perfect, too.

The First's large, round, protruding eyes—marbled with the same red and blue pattern as his skin—roved the expansive estivation chamber. Reluctantly he moved to the communications station, drying his hands before activating the console.

The music of his language filled the air as the computer spoke. "Greetings, First-in-Conquest Atle, Captain of the *Flood*, First of all the Chosen."

*I know who I am*, he thought wearily, wishing the machine had not been programmed by rank-jealous bureaucrats.

"There is important news from Home," the computer continued, "and the reports of robot probes that you must screen alone."

"I am alone," he confirmed. His song vibrated from his throat, making his vocal pouch swell; his mouth remained closed. "Give me the news from Home, first." He requested this hesitantly. It wasn't like the ship to wake him for news releases—they'd been gone more than ten years, so whatever happened back Home now had little relevance to them.

*Such a long time, ten years.* A male matured in five, and bred in ten. Atle himself was forty. Few lived to be sixty.

"One year ago," the console sang, "the Exploratory Ship *Deluge* discovered a planet with atmosphere. But the air is thin, and the water underground. Colonization will be expensive."

*Won't it, though,* Atle thought grimly. A dry world would not take the pressure off Home.

"Two years ago," the computer continued, "communications with the Exploratory Ship *Monsoon* were abruptly terminated. It is considered lost."

He swallowed and closed his eyes while the computer droned on with all that had been done to reestablish contact. Atle listened for a respectable time, then asked for the next item.

"It is with profound regret," the machine began, "that your Government must address you with sorrowful news."

The First stood rigidly, gripping the console with both hands, his two forefingers and two opposing thumbs clamped tight. He knew that phrasing—it preceded the announcement of a family death that came about through Government service.

"The Exploratory Ship *Pluviose* was destroyed when two of its reactors malfunctioned. Your son, the Glorious First-in-Conquest Dunner, valiantly struggled to save his ship and crew but was killed in the ensuing explosion. Your daughter, Stalwart Second-in-Conquest Alta, courageously staffed the lifeboat station to ensure that all producing females were loaded into sleeper ships."

*She escaped,* Atle silently wished at the machine. *Tell me she escaped and is out there, waiting for rescue.*

"Unfortunately, ship's communications ended abruptly, and simultaneously all lifeboat beacons ceased. It is believed that the reactors exploded, destroying the ship and lifeboats, which would not have had time to get beyond lethal range. Your Government grieves with you in your loss, Glorious First."

Atle's moan of despair whistled through silent corridors, past the endless rows of sleepers. His legs buckled; only his grip on the console kept him from falling.

"I *begged* them not to go on the same ship," he sang. "My children . . . ! My children . . . !"

The pain was like drought, like fire, parching his organs, squeezing his heart. His hindbrain, understanding only struggle or escape, flushed his smooth skin, making his already brilliant colors painful to the eyes. The small yellow patches on his upper arms flared, sweating the deadly poison his species was named for. He turned back to Dunn's tank, grief-stricken. How could he tell her? What would he say?

His mind heard her answering song as clearly as if it trembled against his flat, round tympanic membrane. "We still have our other children."

Yes. Their other children. . . .

Silently, he padded over to the facing rows of sleepers.

Side by side they slept, even as the Chosen did, separated by rank and species, even as the Chosen were. He peered into the first tank, at the handsome, still form folded there.

Despite the Chosen's careful tending of their ecosystems and vital resources, breeding inevitably meant children. To control the population, the Government had decreed over a hundred years ago that the first two surviving children of every female were her own, and were Chosen. But every child after that would be born in the Government's hospitals, and immediately taken so that the forebrain could be chemically stunted. These retarded, androgynous children were called "Industrious," and were wards of the State, though the Chosen could take them home if they wished.

Atle had never sired children with any female but his wife, though he could have had his pick. Four children had been enough for them—two Chosen, now dead, and two Industrious, who lay here on the *Flood*, opposite their parents.

Embracing the tank of his last living son, the dull-witted, gentle Arvis, he sang bitterly. This child had his father's wrestler's physique, but not his heart or cleverness, nor could his temper be roused enough to make his poison patches sweat. But he was a tireless and willing worker, and his parents took pride in his simple accomplishments.

His daughter, Sine, lay beside her brother. They were forever children, these two, if hardworking.

Atle pulled himself together. He was still the First. Stepping away from the tanks, he returned, aged and heavy-footed, to the patiently waiting computer.

"I am grateful for my Government's sympathy," he sang halfheartedly, the notes sticking in his throat pouch.

"You were not roused for that," the computer intoned.

*Of course not,* Atle realized dazedly. "Well, what then? Have we lost more probes?" They did not have many left.

*All for nothing, this insane search for a new Home.*

In spite of all their planning, their nurturing of their beloved planet, they were still overrunning their Home, their solar system, their space stations and free-space colonies.

That was why Atle, his children, and the *Deluge*'s First had been sent on this hopeless, futile mission—to find a new Home. Only the State's most popular heroes could fill the public with enough hope to convince them to pay the enormous expense.

Each ship, the Government had promised, would find a planet as rich as their own, planets with their own native peoples to conquer. Atle had once shared this hope, dreaming of the day the Industrious could be phased out. He believed the deliberate stunting of their children was eroding his people's spirit, their virtues, their heart—the genius that had made them conquerors in the old days. But the truth was they had no evidence that there were any other beings—never mind intelligent ones—in all the universe but them.

"You were roused, Glorious First," the computer announced, "because one probe has found a planet of promise."

Atle refused to rejoice. There had been too much lost already. "How much promise?" he sang desultorily.

Information began marching down the console's tank, then the tank's fluid shifted beside the column of information, coalescing into an image of a solar system.

*So many planets!* he thought, as they slid by the robot.

A red dwarf sun sat like an angry god on the system's outermost fringes, and the probe narrowly escaped being bombarded by its powerful X-rays. Planetoids whizzed past, radiated to a cinder as they spun in the shadow of the violent dwarf. A ringed gas giant swam into view, was analyzed, then ignored. Then another gas giant—the largest the computer had ever encountered—loomed ahead, monstrous and threatening with its squadron of captured moons, many of which were planets themselves, but none suitable.

More lifeless worlds followed until finally, closer to the heart of this system—a bright yellow dwarf sun—Atle saw it.

Data marched beneath its image as fleecy clouds drifted across the surface of the beautiful, blue-green orb. The air was good, the water real, pure water! Three lustrous moons circled its girth, pulling at its tides. The gravity was acceptable, if light. Scattered continents and islands teemed with plant life, surrounded by living seas. Animals moved everywhere, flying, swimming, running across land split by twisting rivers, land sodden with ponds and marshes.

Atle had never permitted himself to believe another planet like Home existed, yet here it was, spinning silently, waiting for him. A planet full of life. Complicated, organic life.

"The probe," he demanded, "has it landed safely?"

"It has, Glorious First."

"Give me the rest of the information, the pictures. . . ." Everything. He wanted to see everything.

"There is one concern," the computer interrupted.

"What is that?" he sang flatly, not wanting to be pulled from the sight of the place he'd already thought of as New Home, the place where the Chosen could breed freely again.

The picture in the tank shifted, pulling back through the planet's atmosphere, back into orbit, until it focused on an object glimmering above the cloud-filled sphere. The computer drew a circle around the spark, then enlarged it.

"An artificial satellite orbits this planet, First."

Atle touched the pads of his fingers to his chest, feeling his three-chambered heart tremble. What mad flurry of computations had this new sight inspired in the computer?

"Just one?" he asked. The tiny space station looked almost silly alone in the vastness of space.

"Just this one. There are fourteen small satellites scattered through the orbital plane that appear to be scientific monitoring devices. The probe easily evaded them."

"Where are the ships to protect this station?"

"Only one ship sits in its bays. The station's orbit is maintained automatically. There are no inhabitants, other than plants."

Plants. They could be used for oxygen, for food. It had to be a dream to find not just a suitable planet but a race of space-faring plant eaters waiting for him.

"But . . . where are the owners?" Atle wondered aloud.

"I cannot answer. If the owners are planetside, there are too many life-forms to identify them without further data."

Too many life-forms. That was a problem he would enjoy solving. His heart filled with sorrow and joy.

"We have the planet's coordinates?" he asked.

"Yes, Glorious First, and our course is already adjusted."

"Good. Speed us on our way."

"One more item, First. This message is being broadcast from the space station." The computer emitted bizarre alien sounds.

Wincing, he deliberately dulled his sensitive hearing until the sound was barely discernible. "What is it, a warning?"

"Unknown. It is repeated in different tones and patterns that might indicate a variety of languages."

*A variety. . . .* "Speculate on the message."

"It appears to be a greeting."

If he still believed in the ancient water gods he would throw a feast in their honor. "Delightful. We accept their greeting. And their world. How soon before we arrive?"

"Less than one month, Glorious First."

"I'll return to my tank. Adjust the calendars and clocks to the solar time of this new system, so we can adjust to our New Home. And . . . when we enter the system . . . wake me alone. I'll decide when to warm the others. Understood?"

There was a slight pause as the computer digested this override of normal procedure. But Atle had his reasons.

His Second-in-Conquest was Dacris, a green and yellow Troubadour who'd been picked for this mission against his will. Atle would have to be sure of the situation with this new planet before he spoke to his Second. And he needed some time alone with his wife.

The First climbed into his tank, feeling the warm fluid moisten his gleaming red and blue skin. It was a garden, this new world, a garden that, had things been different, he might have had grandchildren in . . . free grandchildren . . . Chosen grandchildren. Atle mourned silently for those grandchildren that would never be.

As the fluid cooled, the First's hindbrain pulled his limbs into their estivating position. As he drifted into sleep, he wondered again about a race of beings so confident they could place one small, unarmed station over a world and consider it theirs.

The *Flood* knew nothing of its Captain's concerns. It could not understand the desperation of its sleepers, their terrible need for a new Home. It only knew that its job was to find a planet and colonize it. But Atle knew, as did all those who had come on this mission, voluntarily or not.

While he slept, his ship would activate its complex chemical arsenal—toxins, drugs, neurotransmitters, hormones, and other biochemicals, many originally distilled from the One-Touch's own poison. By the time the First awoke, the vessel would be ready to begin colonization—and if that required conquest, the

*Flood* would have new programs in place and be prepared to handle that, too. Soon, the Chosen would own that planet, its station, the beings who built it, and all their children for future generations.

It mattered little to Atle whether the small station had weapons or not. The *Flood* had weapons, and in its belly slept an army to use them.

# CHAPTER I

## ♦

# The Interrelator

Ptesa' Wakandagi sat cross-legged in the Scott Hedford Memorial Shelter waiting impatiently for her call. The tall Native American was the Cooperative League of Systems' Interrelator for the wilderness planet Trinity.

A year and a half ago, Tesa had been sent from the Academy at StarBridge to help establish a First Contact with the planet's avian people, the Grus. Since then, she had lived with the White Wind people—as the Grus called themselves—as family to their leader, Taller, his mate, Weaver, and their son, Lightning. Tesa—whose light hazel, almost yellow eyes had earned her the Grus name-sign "Good Eyes"—had established peace between the Grus and their historic enemies, the predatory Hunters.

The young woman rubbed the bridge of her hawklike nose as she stared at the hologram field that read "Please Hold." Fiddling irritably with the gleaming white feathers covering her woven Grus shirt, she wondered if Bruce could tell her what was happening with her call. He'd gone up to Trinity's single space station, the *Singing Crane*, to do some routine maintenance.

Or so he said. While Tesa would've spent every minute of her life outside, Bruce Carpenter—meteorologist and xenoichthyologist by training, and a hardware handyman by hobby—missed the space station's elaborate equipment. Well, in a few months they'd get a whole new crew and then he could have fun training them. But now, the few Terrans were needed planetside.

Tesa fidgeted. Waiting only accented the tiredness that hung on her like a shroud. The last few weeks she'd slept poorly. She didn't want to think about the cause of her fitful nights . . . her nightmares. Tesa respected dreams. Her religion told her they could bring important messages. But lately, her nightly fantasies were formless, leaving her with nothing but a sense of dread. She'd wake shivering, the images scattering like feather-weed seeds in the wind, until Weaver would surround her with a wing, lulling her back to sleep.

She should discuss her dreams with Old Bear, her grandfather, but she didn't want to worry him.

Shrugging her troublesome thoughts away, Tesa tapped a code into her small wrist voder and the image of a lanky man with thinning gray hair coalesced on the screen.

"So, where's Rob, Bruce?" she asked, her hands shaping the question in Grus Sign Language.

"Just hold your. . . ." he signed clumsily, then paused.

Tesa smiled, realizing the middle-aged weatherman had just discovered there was no Grus sign for "horses."

"Be patient," he responded instead. "I've refocused one of the receivers. It's coming in now; your channel open?"

She nodded, a lock of her long, wavy, dark hair falling forward. "I've *been* ready!" she complained, her light eyes flashing as the hologram finally coalesced before her.

The tiny image of Bruce waved frantically to call her attention back. "You've got him now, darlin'!"

Nodding, she watched the hologram firm up. It always took her a few moments to get used to the holo's realism.

"Hello, at last, Tesa!" Dr. Robert Gable, the director of StarBridge, signed. His hand motions were slow, but she always appreciated his effort. The slightly built psychologist's dark hair curled in disarray. "I just saw your two recruits off."

"So they're on their way?" she asked.

Rob nodded, his expression rueful. "I really appreciate your taking this project on. . . . It won't be any picnic."

Tesa smiled. "Ambassador Dhurrrkk' " talked me into it."

"I'm not surprised. At least you'll enjoy seeing Jib again." Rewi "Jib" Parker, a nineteen-year-old Maori, had been Tesa's roommate and surrogate brother at StarBridge. "But as for the Simiu, K'heera," Rob spelled the name in American Sign Language, "she's only doing this because of honor."

"Is she at least . . . cooperative?"

"Anything less would be dishonorable. But her heart isn't in it. Her family is making her do this to recoup some of the prestige the Harkk'etts have lost since the *Désirée* incident."

The four-footed, baboonlike aliens the Terrans had dubbed "Simiu" had a culture dominated by a rigid, intricate honor code that had complicated a needless tragedy, marring the early, tenuous relations between the two races. Ten years after that botched First Contact, many Simiu still held the humans responsible, but others placed the blame on the Harkk'ett clan alone. The loss of honor had devastated the prestigious family.

"Dhurrrkk' assured me," Rob continued, "that the Harkk'ett matriarchs are eager to make whatever amends they can tolerate to regain some of their lost status. They *picked* K'heera—we didn't get to choose her. She might be StarBridge material in a couple of years, but right now?" He shook his head.

"She's not totally xenophobic, I hope?" Tesa asked.

"No, no!" he assured her. "Doctor Blanket feels she has good potential, but it's buried under resentment and family shame."

The young woman peered at Rob wryly. "And Jib? Don't tell me he's StarBridge's answer to this diplomatic crisis?"

"Honestly," Rob signed, smiling, "we didn't just pick him because of your past friendship. I'm sending Jib partly because he's so easygoing—I thought he might be able to soften K'heera's edges—and partly . . . because I wanted him to be forced to use his language skills again."

She detected something in his expression. "*Forced*? Jib? The galaxy's hyper-communicator? What are you talking about?"

"There's a slight problem." Rob was trying to be reassuring, which only had the opposite affect. "Jib's developed TSS."

*Telepathic Sensitivity Syndrome,* Tesa thought. A catch-all term for a condition that couldn't be easily diagnosed.

Telepathy was not common among humans, but some descendants of the failed first Martian Colony carried it. Nontelepaths could usually be trained to communicate with telepaths, but for people with TSS, telepathic reception had a different effect—it stimulated their brain's pleasure center. With repeated exposure, TSS victims grew addicted to it.

"How bad is it?" Tesa asked.

"Very minor," Rob insisted. "After you left, his next roommate was telepathic, and they grew close. Then, he was assigned to work with the Shadgui."

The Shadgui were actually two species, symbionts who could not be separated; they were a peaceful, telepathic race.

"The onset was so subtle, I never noticed it, but Doctor Blanket did. Jib's . . . still in denial. As long as he stayed here with telepaths all around him, there was no chance he'd recover."

Tesa hesitated. "You think he *can* recover?"

Rob shrugged. "Who knows? There haven't been enough cases to define the disease, symptoms, treatments . . . if there are any, besides avoiding contact. Even if he can't be cured, it might not hurt his career . . . if he stays away from telepaths. I decided a trip to Trinity was just what this doctor should order."

"Well, he won't find any telepaths here," Tesa agreed, "unless you're sending some out with the new crew."

"Nope," Rob signed, "not a one."

"Jib doesn't resent coming, does he?"

The psychologist shook his head. "He was pleased to help with this Simiu problem. His only regret is leaving his roommate, Anzia. He thinks he's in love with her. But don't worry about it. Jib couldn't be in a safer environment than Trinity, with you there. Oh, I almost forgot! There's one other thing you should know about K'heera. She's a techno-type."

The Indian woman's eyes widened. "Isn't that a little unusual for a Simiu female?"

"Very. You know how rigid they are about sexual role-playing. Females are supposed to lead the world, not putter around with circuits and chips and tools."

Tesa grew thoughtful. "That might be a way to get closer to her . . . encourage her to follow her own interests. . . ."

"I fully expect you to take this information and run with it," Rob admitted. "Who knows? Maybe she'll end up as Bruce's assistant. . . ." He trailed off at Tesa's skeptical expression.

Bruce still blamed the Harkk'ett clan for the deaths of his friends, Scott Hedford and Peter Woedrango.

"This is shaping up to be one of those dreaded 'learning experiences' you always warned us about," Tesa told him.

Gable grinned and nodded. "Probably. So, how is everyone?"

"Well, Dr. Li Szu-yi went up to the *Crane* with Bruce to restock her medical supplies. Meg's out with Old Bear, Lightning, and our cohort, collecting plants. Grandma Lewis is under the weeping tree with her 'sewing circle.' A dozen of the flock's best weavers are teaching her Grus techniques, in exchange for her demonstrating classic Navaho weaving to them."

The psychologist stared pointedly at her. "And how have you been occupying your long boring days?"

"Me? Bored?" She grinned shamelessly. "Only when I've got to fill things out in triplicate. Don't tell me you haven't been reading all those reports you're always asking for!"

He nodded, amused. "Oh, I read them. They make it sound like you haven't had a minute to be bored . . . or lonely."

"Is it time for my psych checkup already?" she quipped.

"That wasn't a frivolous question. You've got an intense job, surrounded only by elderly relatives, an aged biologist, a doctor who will never win any awards for warmth, a cantankerous middle-aged weatherman, and aliens with whom you are not biologically compatible. I'd say you're in a good position for feeling pretty isolated, if not downright lonely. And if you don't mind my saying so—you're looking a little tired."

Tesa shrugged, but it bothered her that he could see her fatigue in a hologram transmitted across the galaxy. "Believe me, Rob, I have all the companionship anyone could want."

"Well, I was just wondering how you were getting on . . . since Thom Albaugh left."

She recalled the young wildlife agent and their brief relationship fondly. "Sure, I miss Thom. I haven't heard from him . . . have you?" Thom had left to follow an investigation, warning her that she might not hear from him for years.

"Well," Rob signed cryptically, "he's left Hurrreeah. . . ."

Tesa didn't find the psychologist's words very comforting. "Rob, has Thom gone undercover into Sorrow Sector?"

The psychologist looked her squarely in the eyes. "I'm afraid so. That isn't what I wanted to talk about . . . I'm sorry."

She held up a hand. "Thom has to follow his own path, just like I had to follow mine. I'm just lucky that mine led me to the best job on all the Known Worlds. I'm really happy, Rob."

He watched her with an odd expression, as if trying to see what was really going on in her heart. "I want to know if you continue to have trouble sleeping. Will you tell me?"

She hesitated. She'd never been a very good liar. "I will. Honest. Now, what's the latest update on the new crew?"

He smiled, letting her close the subject. "Well, we've got the go-ahead to expand the station, and we've finalized most of the crew selections." He tapped a sequence on his desk, and images of strangers coalesced in the hologram beside him. "Meg will be happy to know we got her that ethnobotanist. . . ."

But later, when the conversation finally ended, Tesa watched Rob dissolve with an odd sensation, as though their talk had introduced something that would have been better left unspoken.

A chill breeze blew multicolored leaves around Taller's feet as he watched Good Eyes step out of the humans' shelter. She gazed around the high bluff that overlooked his territory as though she couldn't remember what all these various people—human, White Wind, and Hunter—could be doing here. Most of them were simply waiting for her.

The avian leader swiveled his long head to peer one-eyed at the solitary Hunter that had just dropped from her perch on the highest limb of the dead tree that clung to the edge of the bluff. The huge predator sailed effortlessly toward Taller's son, Lightning, and their small cohort, who'd just returned from a foraging trip. Taller still marveled at how devoted Thunder was to both Good Eyes and his son, as if they were her true parents.

He turned back to his human friend, wondering about her odd expression. The seventy-year-old avian approached this alien he considered his partner, and, lowering his head, draped a massive white wing around her, pulling her close in a Grus familial embrace. His iridescent wings ended in striking black primaries, two of which were actually long, jointed fingers, part of a nearly palmless hand with a short black thumb. The rest of his body was as white as his wings, except for the elegant black facial markings that framed his face, neck, and black bill. Taller peered at Good Eyes with both of his round, golden eyes, as his red crown—a patch of bare, warty skin on top of his head that colored and stretched with his moods—shrank to show his concern.

He inhaled her scent and blinked, realizing for the first time that she no longer smelled like a fur-bearer, like the other humans did. She smelled like a real Person now, she smelled like him. He wondered why he hadn't noticed that before.

The human shivered, so he pulled her closer. Moving his other wing so that he could sign behind the screen of his embrace, he asked, "Did the See-Through Man give you bad news?"

Taller had faced the eerie holographic transmission only once, but it had been too disturbing an experience for him to repeat. He had announced, as regally as he could, that Good Eyes would forever after handle such discussions for him. To the nontechnological beings, the person in the holographic field seemed like a spirit. Good Eyes seemed pleased to spare him that discomfort. She said that was part of her job.

"No, not bad news. . . ." she began.

"Has he heard something about Relaxed?" That was the name Taller had given the blond human called Thom.

She stared at him. "I . . . I don't think we'll see him again."

Taller kept the woman under his wing. "Our people say that the best cure for a lost lover is a new one," he confided.

She smiled at his frankness and nodded toward the few humans living on the World. "Oh? Who did you have in mind?"

Startled, he pulled his wings in, fluffing his feathers out, then shaking them into place. Truly, there were no prospective suitors in that group. "Matchmaking is best done by females," he reminded her. "We'll discuss this with Weaver."

"Private conference?" First-One-There asked, approaching. Her human name was Margaritka Tretiak, but names like that were meaningless to the White Wind people. The gray-haired woman was Taller's age, with sparkling blue eyes, a wiry build, and an attitude that dared you to call her "spry." First-One had had something done to her ears so her hearing could be turned "on" or "off" by small gold balls on her lobes. Taller eyed them covetously. Anything that shiny had to be delicious.

"Rob say when his kids are coming?" First-One asked.

"They left today," the younger woman replied, "so we have two months to get a project lined up."

"Will the new *Crane* crew be sent soon?"

His partner nodded. "In a few weeks. And they're definitely going to enlarge the station."

Suddenly, Good Eyes' paternal grandfather stepped out from around Taller. "Better put a limit on it," he advised the avian. The wizened old man stood as tall and straight as Good Eyes, in a sleek-fitting jumpsuit. Those un-Worldly clothes contrasted oddly with his short, silver braids tied with woven-grass thongs and studded with brightly colored shells. The old human had a weathered face that spoke of years of outside living. "If you don't, this place will get just like Grand Luna Station."

His long name was Grandpa Laughing Bear Bigbee, but Taller simply called him Old Bear, once he had learned that a bear was an animal like their ferocious Tree Ripper. Old Bear had received Taller's permission for an indefinite stay on the World. The avian had been happy to grant his request, and that of Good Eyes' maternal grandmother, Nadine Lewis, whom the people called "Teacher." Good Eyes needed her natural family with her. Taller wanted the World to be her home. He wanted her to stay—forever, if possible.

Old Bear now worked as First-One's assistant, and the two enjoyed each other's company. On Earth, the old man had had great powers. He'd been a contrary—what the Lakota Sioux called a *heyoka*—a person who'd been touched by the Thunder Beings and ever after had to do things the opposite from what others expected. Knowing this, Taller was not surprised when Old Bear appointed himself ombudsman for the World, freely advising Taller on the ways of humans. The avian respected the elder Sioux, weighing carefully whatever the old man told him.

"Is Grand Luna Station a terrible place?" Taller asked.

"Just crowded," Good Eyes interrupted.

She, too, had been touched as her grandfather had, and it had been her actions as a contrary that had enabled her to bring about peace between the White Wind people and the Hunters. For Taller,

that was proof enough of magical power. The Hunters had preyed
on his people for all the years they had existed. Good Eyes had
to be a visionary being to change that.

Good Eyes had warned Taller that her grandfather didn't want
to share the World with other humans. She said his knowledge
of human history made him too pessimistic about their motives.

"Remember, Taller," Good Eyes signed, "the new people will
stay on the station. They'll *never* come here without your approval, just as we agreed."

That agreement was all part of the many CLS "rules" Good
Eyes kept telling him about, rules that were supposed to ensure
the World's independence and safety. But Taller was not as
concerned about the new humans as Old Bear wanted him to
be. He trusted his partner to have his best interests at heart.
And he wanted her to stay, not just because she helped him in
his interactions with beings he couldn't always understand—but
because he loved her. For her to be happy, she would someday
have to mate. She couldn't do that if there were no new humans
on the World.

The avian watched Good Eyes coolly with just one eye, remembering their previous discussion. "I think we need at least a *few*
more humans here," he decided.

Suddenly First-One glanced at her wrist where a small red light
flashed on her translation device. "It's Bruce."

Taller recognized the human name-sign for the man they called
"The Fisher." The Fisher was known for his endless questions
about fish, where they lived, what their lives were like. He was
good at predicting the weather, too, but not as good as Taller's
neighbor, Cloud.

First-One stared at the small wrist screen, signed a few responses,
then turned back to the others. "Well, Bruce has a project for our
StarBridge pair! The satellites have reported something splashing
into the sea near the southern coast. He's guessing it's a meteor.
It survived entry, so he'd like to collect it after they arrive. He
says that it's a real vacation spot, Tesa—tropical beaches, warm
blue water, the works."

"Should be interesting," she agreed.

As the humans talked, Thunder, Lightning, the two-year-old
Flies-Too-Fast, and the rest of their cohort approached, all signing
rapidly. Taller marveled at the youngsters' ease in the raptor's
company; it was as if she'd hatched next door to them. Still,
the old leader kept one cautious eye on the avian. Her eyes had
recently turned red, which only added to her fierce appearance,

even though her feathers remained a dull bronze. It would be years before her head and tail molted out to a brilliant gold.

Lightning had changed, too, in these last few months. There were still some cinnamon-colored feathers on the top ridge of his wings, on his head, and halfway down his neck, but the rest of him gleamed white. His crown peeked through pinkly as the short brown head feathers molted out. His facial markings were still undefined, muddy streaks, but his bill had darkened, and he had his black fingers and primaries. Standing beside the pure white, strongly marked Flies-Too-Fast, the difference in their ages was apparent, but in another six months, Lightning would be identical to his friend and his father—except that Lightning was just a bit taller, as a new leader would have to be.

Flies-Too-Fast was the oldest of the group, and Lightning somewhere in the middle, so the other six ranged in color from the pure white Hurricane to the cinnamon and white Frost Moon. They were so young none of them had even found their voices. Their calls were irritating to humans, but not dangerous.

Taller realized he'd missed part of the discussion about the meteor. "I saw that star fall weeks ago," he told the humans. They watched him curiously. "I thought one of your satellites had failed. Where is it?"

"South," First-One signed. "A week's flight for you. Have you ever been there?"

"Where there's no winter?" Taller asked, concerned. "No, but our cousins the Gray Winds live there."

First-One cleared a spot in the russet and blue vegetation and drew an image of a fat, broad peninsula.

"Yes," he admitted. "That's the way it's been described."

She added a circle for forest, and lines of savannah and marsh. Then she cut in a wide, twisted river that slashed through the land from east to west, but did not cut through to the west coast. "Do you know anything about this river?"

Taller blinked, his feathers standing straight out, then settling down with agonizing slowness. His crown flared red, spreading in alarm. Good Eyes' expression changed subtly with his signals. "Why do you want to know about that River?"

"The Fisher wants to go there, to look for that fallen star, the meteor," First-One explained.

Why anyone would want to find a submerged star Taller could not begin to guess. And to search *this* River!

"What is it, Taller?" Good Eyes asked. "What's wrong?"

"That is the River of Fear. It flows through the Land of Confusion."

The humans glanced at one another.

"How did these places earn those names?" Good Eyes asked.

All Taller knew were stories passed on from people he trusted. "The River is prime territory, riven with deep channels and shallow sandbars. A safe place to feed, to nest, yet no one goes there. None of the Gray Winds will even *land* there. Hunters don't breed there, though the trees are tall and strong, and could hold a big nest. Around the River, there are many large, dangerous animals, yet even the largest, the Quakers, won't drink or wallow there."

The sign for the huge, mammothlike creatures mimicked the quaking of the ground, the vibrations made when the elephantine herd beasts thundered over the land.

"Why not?" Good Eyes asked.

"That River holds the Spirits that never reach the Suns, keeping them in misery and loneliness. In vengeance, the Spirits reach for the living. Their singing sends terrible dreams. They can make you forget how to fly, forget to eat. They pull the Hunters out of the sky. No one lives there. Only the dead travel that River."

Taller watched the humans, knowing his speech couldn't mean to them what it meant to his own people. The humans were a people who had to see everything for themselves.

"You still want to go there?" He already knew their answer.

As usual, even the elders left the talking to Good Eyes. "If you forbid us, we'll respect your wishes," she assured him.

"It's not for me to restrict your flight," he answered.

"It'll be a short trip," she signed, trying to reassure him. "I'll go with the Fisher, and the students coming from my old school. The River Spirits will see we're not-of-the-World. When they discover we can't hear their song, they'll leave us alone."

That might be true for the other humans; they were not of the World. But Good Eyes was different. The River Spirits would recognize her as a real Person. He couldn't risk that. "If you go," he finally signed, "the White Wind people will go with you."

"Thank you," Good Eyes replied, her expression easing. She turned to the cohort, who'd been watching the exchange with mixed reactions. "If you all came with us, Lightning could introduce us to the Gray Winds that live nearby. And we could make some diplomatic contacts among Thunder's people on the way." She stared at the young avians. "Unless you'd rather not . . . ."

Taller watched the youngsters crowd together to lend one another courage. They stretched their necks tall and flared their crowns. Not go? Where on the World would Good Eyes go that they wouldn't follow? His story would frighten them, but their devotion to her, and the respect they would earn for even attempting the trip, would be worth any danger.

"Would this be like a flyaway for the newcomers?" Lightning asked, referring to the Wind people's coming-of-age journey.

"A little bit," Good Eyes signed. "You know, we might find a way to appease the River Spirits, find some way to keep them from confusing us. And our machines might help."

Taller considered that. The thought of his youngest son, his partner, and his flock's finest juveniles braving those capricious, jealous Spirits didn't please him. But there had been a time when he would've never believed the Hunters would leave his people in peace. If anyone could pacify these singing River Spirits, it would be a contrary like Good Eyes. That thought should have reassured him but he found little comfort in it.

# CHAPTER 2
## ◆
# K'heera

"In *Grus*, please," the brown-skinned man signed.

"I *said*," the Simiu repeated manually, "I'd rather study than waste time at a . . ." she groped for the sign, "celebration."

*She still won't make eye contact,* Jib thought tiredly. "It's traditional to have a Captain's Night when the ship leaves port. We have a month to study before hibernation."

Rewi Parker, the lean, cream-colored Maori from New Zealand, whose love of sailing had earned him the nickname Jib, squatted on a cushion in quarters that were too warm and humid for him. The gravity, set at Simiu norm, made his lithe body feel heavy and old. The lazy ringlets of his shoulder-length black hair were shiny from sweat. As his large, expressive brown eyes saw his partner's small violet ones look away, he wondered how he was ever going to bridge the gap between them—a gap far greater than that separating two species and two cultures.

"A month!" the Simiu signed, snorting derisively.

Her fur was the color of dull flame, marked with a darker

brindle pattern. K'heera's short mane made her seem oddly femi-
nine, as the shining fur peaked in a crest over her long, sloping
forehead. Her long muzzle hid impressive teeth, which, along with
powerful, six-fingered hands, made efficient weapons.

Direct eye contact was one way the Simiu hurled honor-
challenges; however, sign language required strong eye contact.
Jib had reminded K'heera of this many times. Maybe she just
couldn't stand having eye contact with him.

"We're going to Trinity to *learn*," he reminded her, "not to
save the World. Let's study for a while, *then* go to the party."

"That's reasonable," K'heera admitted grudgingly, lapsing into
Simiu. "Let's discuss my notes first."

"Certainly," Jib growled back.

"I have studied the recent history of Trinity. But I fail to
understand why the Honored Interrelator didn't have her deafness
cured, once the conflict there was over."

Jib hesitated. "Tesa, and many other deaf humans, view their
deafness as cultural, not physical. But, frankly, as a hearing
human, I'm not sure I can explain it very well . . . ."

K'heera seemed unconvinced, then glanced at her computer
screen. "Perhaps you can explain this better. When the privateers
were attacking the Aquila nest—why did the Honored Interrelator
flee? The texts speak of this as though it were an act of great
honor, yet to me it seems sheer cowardice."

"Tesa wasn't running away to save her own skin," Jib reminded
her. "She had to protect Lightning and Thunder, also. They were
all in danger of being killed because they'd witnessed the attack
of the privateers, from a spacecraft fully armed . . . ."

"With *weapons*." K'heera's lip curled. The use of artificial
weapons violated the Simiu's worst taboo.

"That's right," Jib responded unflinchingly.

"And the Honored Interrelator later stole weapons, made her
own weapons, and *used* them."

"You cannot judge other cultures by your standards," Jib
reminded her patiently, his throat raw with the effort. "Humans
have always used weapons, just as Simiu have always fought in
the Arena. We must each respect our different values."

"Weapons are forbidden by the CLS," K'heera said, ignoring
him, "but the Interrelator *stole* them from the privateers . . . ."

"Weapons that had been *purchased* with *Simiu* funds!" Jib
interrupted sharply, then instantly regretted his outburst.

K'heera's short crest bristled. Her violet eyes met his squarely.
"*My* family's funds, you mean."

Jib forced himself to drop his eyes. "Forgive me. I never meant to insult you."

There was an uncomfortable pause and finally K'heera averted her own eyes, her crest drooping. "You spoke the truth, after I goaded you. It was dishonorable of me. The apology is mine."

"Let's forget it," Jib said, good-naturedly. "That's what I've been trying to tell you. Too much studying makes people cranky. Besides, I'm hungry. Let's go to Captain's Night now and study later. The food will be terrific." He stood up, reaching for his black StarBridge jacket.

"I bow to your greater experience," the Simiu agreed. The young human handed her a halterlike vest. Black like his jacket, it gave K'heera pockets for her computer pens and voders. The StarBridge logo—two colorful planets joined by a rainbow bridge set against a background of stars—was emblazoned across the back.

K'heera donned it, then padded on all fours to her doorway. Her bold, jaunty stride, and the way she held her short, top-knotted tail told Jib she'd forgotten the incident.

At least she'd stopped sulking. Maybe he could accomplish something with her, after all. It was the only reason he'd left StarBridge, the one thing that could make him leave Anzia. Dr. Gable could talk all he wanted about TSS, but Jib didn't believe in that. He had a knack for telepathic reception, that's all. A real talent. A talent he missed exercising. Being dependent on clumsy verbal languages was a strain after the free flow of ideas he'd experienced with Anzi and the Shadgui.

But he hadn't seen Tesa in almost two years. She *had* saved a world—Jib couldn't have her think he didn't have enough ability to improve relations with one irritable Simiu.

K'heera strode along jauntily beside Jib through the ship's corridors, the leathery palms of her hands and feet slap-slapping against the deck quickly, efficiently, the plume of her tail swaying in perfect rhythm with her strong, sleek hips. Her brisk pace belied her inner turmoil as she scolded herself for her poor behavior. Lately, she was always irascible, unreasonable, aching to humiliate these awkward, two-legged beings.

Especially this one. But all he ever did was endure her rudeness. *Anything to insult me,* she thought bitterly. *Captain's Night! The only reason humans have these gatherings is to find sexual partners. He'll be hunting for a female from the moment we get there. It's disgusting.* With an effort, she squelched her anger. *You're being unfair.*

Whatever was happening to her, none of it was Jib's fault. What he had said was true. Simiu money—her own family's—had purchased *weapons,* weapons that had killed innocent humans and Trinity's own people. It made her sick. How could she face those beautiful avians when her own hands were coated with their blood? How could Ambassador Dhurrrkk' think that this foolish "assignment" could do anything to erase such dishonor?

Her own great-uncle-cousin twice removed, Kkrraahhkk', whom she'd once loved and admired, had masterminded the entire thing. He would spend the rest of his miserable life as a criminal, hiding in Sorrow Sector, with *humans* hunting him.

Because of him, K'heera was forced to be what the humans called a "sacrificial lamb." No one had cared about the disruption of her own plans and ambitions—in fact, her family had happily shuffled her off Hurrreeah.

She had been too involved, they thought, with the students from the public technical school. Her mating prospects were dismal. She'd been grateful to leave before her first estrus.

"Here we are," Jib announced, ushering her into the lavish salon. Wonderful smells wafted from mounds of artistically arranged food. This ship, the S.V. *Norton,* was a human vessel, but all the tables holding traditional Simiu fare *and* human fruits and vegetable dishes were low enough for the quadrupeds. The courtesy both irritated and flattered her. Meats and the artificial protein concentrate Mizari consumed were on higher tables at the other end of the room.

"This is much more elaborate than I expected," K'heera said, surprised. She'd never seen such a banquet—but then, Harkk'etts were never invited to such high-ranking functions.

"Many people will be going into hibernation in the morning," Jib explained. "Captain's Night is their last opportunity for a good meal. Say . . . did you notice that group?"

He nodded toward five mature Simiu males with elaborately styled manes and tails. K'heera certainly *had* noticed them and now could scarcely pull her eyes away. "They're the drum dancers who performed at StarBridge before we left," Jib told her, "the Hurrraahhhkk'aa Troupe. Maybe we'll get to meet them."

K'heera's crest flattened anxiously. "Aren't you going to the protein table?" she asked when Jib began filling his plate.

"I can eat that fare anytime," he told her. "What I'd really like is for you to tell me about these Simiu dishes."

*Now he's patronizing me,* K'heera decided. *With all our stu-*

*dents on StarBridge, he wants me to believe he's never been exposed to our cuisine.* She pointed at something colorful. "You might like that," she said casually. "We call it Pp'hhh'tttkkk. It's a delicacy made from a spice bush in our southern hemisphere." *And it has enough acetic acid to burn the cilia off your simple tongue.* Even as he put some on his plate, she knew he wouldn't touch it. She indicated three other dishes that he could eat, and as she expected, he sampled those first.

"Simiu cuisine is known through the galaxy," a voice hissed in Mizari. A young, serpentlike alien sidled up to them, a halo of tentacles waving around the being's head like a nimbus cloud.

"Unfortunately, my people cannot eat it," the Mizari female continued amiably, "but we enjoy it vicariously by reading their recipes. I am Rassizza. I saw your StarBridge uniforms and knew you would speak my language."

Jib greeted the tall, limbless alien with the humans' version of the Mizari meeting gesture, tenting his hands over his head, then bowing low from the waist. "Greetings, Rassizza," the human said, smoothly slipping into Mizari.

K'heera used her own people's honor greeting, touching her eyelids, muzzle, and chest, then holding her hand out, her fingers curled inward. The being bowed graciously to them.

"It's too bad you can't enjoy Simiu food," Jib said, "I developed a taste for it at StarBridge, but cafeteria food may be the only cultural constant throughout the Known Worlds. Simiu students would talk wistfully about food from home that wasn't served there. I couldn't wait for this buffet."

*Oh, no,* K'heera groaned inwardly. *He really doesn't know those dishes! I can't let him taste that Pp'hhh'tttkkk!* But how could she stop him without revealing her attempted sabotage? Her eyes widened as Jib's fork hovered over the sinister morsel.

"I must confess," the Mizari said, distracting Jib from his plate, "I had an ulterior motive in speaking to you both. My voder is malfunctioning." The device appeared suddenly from the nest of prehensile tendrils surrounding the Mizari's head. "Without my voder I will be helpless. I thought you"—she nodded at Jib— "might introduce me to the Captain, and ask if her engineer could look at it."

"Why, certainly," Jib agreed amiably. "I'd be happy to."

"Actually," K'heera interrupted in halting Mizari, "I might be able to fix it."

The serpentlike lidless eyes held no expression, but K'heera imagined that she was shocked. Simiu females were not supposed to be mechanically adept; it was beneath them. "I would be honored," the Mizari said graciously.

K'heera put down her plate, picked up the small translator, and for a moment completely forgot about Jib's food or the opinions of others. Opening the device's casing, she peered at the interior. Pulling a few diagnostic tools from her StarBridge halter, she popped a small, high-powered magnifier, resembling a jeweler's loupe, into one eye.

"I'm at a total loss when it comes to electronics and circuitry," Jib admitted casually. "I envy your ability."

"Aren't you afraid of getting shocked?" the Mizari asked.

"This voder's power pack is well protected," K'heera explained, warming to her subject. "And here's your problem—there's a bad cell." She rummaged around in a pocket. "I may have a spare that will fit." Pulling out a packet of random-sized cells, she sorted through them, then installed the new one, finishing the work with a confidence she rarely enjoyed anymore.

"You've got real talent there, K'heera," Jib said quietly. Casually, he picked up his plate and speared the Pp'hhh'tttkkk.

K'heera flushed with confusion as she handed the now-functional voder back to the Mizari. Whether she warned him or let him experience the pain, her dishonor would be the same.

"Tell me I did not see what I just saw!" barked a deep Simiu voice, startling Jib so much he almost dropped the fork.

*Can things really get worse?* K'heera wondered. The handsomest male from the dancing troupe swaggered up to her—*her*—his glistening, luxurious mane swinging with the force of his graceful step, the rest of his companions close behind. K'heera glanced around, desperately wanting to slip away.

The male's face held amused shock. "Did I really see this lovely young female *repair* a voder?"

"You most certainly did," hissed the Mizari, admiringly. The dance troupe all wore voder earcuffs just like K'heera's, so they'd understood the serpent being. K'heera lowered her gaze.

"And what if she did?" asked Jib in excellent Simiu.

*Yes,* she realized, *things certainly can get worse.*

The Simiu's laughing bark felt like teeth fastening around her heart. "Any simpleminded boy can play with voders. A female's work is *world* matters, galactic concerns."

"In a world as wide and diverse as Hurrreeah," Jib said quietly, "there must be room for a female to work mechanically and a male to be a leader—if that's where their talents lie."

The five males laughed uproariously as K'heera cringed.

"You humans certainly have interesting ideas," the handsome male proclaimed. "But we already know where our females' talents lie." He turned the full force of his charm onto K'heera, moving so she couldn't miss the vivid honor scar that ran from ear to cheek. "We will be going into hibernation in the morning, young beauty, but tonight we're setting up the drums. Come dance with us! We have not had a female dancer since my sister went to the university. But, fortunately, you are no sister of mine!"

The males all laughed riotously at this, while Jib seemed confused. K'heera blushed again. He'd just asked her, none too subtly, that if she was nearing estrus to consider him a potential mate. No doubt they'd been drinking fermented beverages. If he remembered it in the morning, he'd be embarrassed. But dancers were like that.

K'heera squatted onto her haunches, her face burning. "No, no, I don't dance, I wouldn't know . . ."

"Look!" one of the others exclaimed. He was smaller than the leader, but still a striking male, who wore his mane trimmed in such a way that it displayed a missing ear. "She's got more tools stuffed in that vest than the ship's engineer."

"Surely, Ahrakk'," the handsome leader rumbled, "she's just holding them for her brother. Isn't that right, young beauty?" He loomed even closer.

K'heera wanted to shrink into the luxurious carpet.

"Honorable Dancers," Jib said softly, trying to turn their attention to him. "Perhaps if you started your performance . . ."

Suddenly Ahrakk' squinted at the fork Jib was using to punctuate his words. "Human, you've been at StarBridge too long if you think you can eat a whole bite of Pp'hhh'tttkkk. That stuff will burn a hole straight down that upright body of yours and sear its way right through the deck plates!" The group found this funnier than anything they had said before.

As casually as she could, K'heera glanced at Jib's face. He masked his surprise and anger, but not completely. She'd never make him understand now; there was no use in even trying.

"Is everything all right?" an evenly modulated female voice asked in English. K'heera's earcuff translator easily kept up with the language change as she peered up into the face of the S.V. *Norton*'s Captain, Jane Stepp.

She was not as tall as Jib, and seemed about twice his age, though K'heera wasn't sure. Her curled black hair framed an attractive face and clear blue eyes. She was built sturdily, and seemed capable and efficient.

"Things could not be better, Honored Captain Stepp," the dance troupe leader assured the American woman. "In all my years of touring, never have I known a finer Captain's Night! Your invitation to dance will make it perfect. We are privileged to entertain such notable—and fortunate—passengers."

"Thank you, Honored Dancer Kh'arhh'tk," the Captain replied.

"This is pretty special, ma'am," Jib said in English. His voice was cool as he ignored the Pp'hhh'tttkkk incident. "I've never been at a Captain's Night with live entertainment."

She grinned amiably. "This is a special trip for me and my crew, so we're going whole hog. It's our last journey on the *Norton*. After this run we're taking command of a brand-new vessel, a ship that will be servicing Trinity alone. There's her image." She waved at a three-dimensional hologram rotating in the center of the room. "The *Brolga*. Her maiden voyage will carry enough staff and supplies to enlarge Trinity's space station."

"Congratulations, Captain!" Jib said.

She bowed, clearly pleased. "I've been traveling to Trinity since it was found. Getting the *Brolga* is icing on the cake."

"May it bring you much honor," Kh'arhh'tk said graciously, then laced his fingers together and curved his arms over his head in an elegant version of the rarely used Simiu "honor bow."

K'heera was startled by their gesture. She'd never seen a Simiu use it before . . . but then, what Harkk'ett would?

"For you," Kh'arhh'tk told the Captain, "we'll dance the Warrior's Welcome"—he waved at K'heera—"with a guest star!"

"Oh?" said the Captain. "And this is . . . ?"

"Our native sister," barked the leader. "In another year she'll be ready for the tremendous responsibilities she and her sisters share. What more reason to dance?" Kh'arhh'tk turned to K'heera suddenly. "Little sister, what is your name? You must be properly introduced to the Honored Captain."

*They have no idea who I am!* K'heera thought, panicking.

The Captain peered at her as though trying to remember. Jib had turned away. But then, what could he possibly do?

"Immature females," Kh'arhh'tk proclaimed, "are so shy." Boldly, he encircled her arm with his. "Your name, sister?"

"K'heera . . ." she whispered, her throat tightening. Honor demanded she give her full identity. "Of the family Harkk'ett."

The dancers froze in recognition, sobering instantly. The handsome Kh'arhh'tk jerked his arm away. "*Harkk'ett?* That explains your other perversions. How *dare* you dishonor me? Honor obliged that you reveal yourself immediately! You are not worthy of a challenge." As one, the group spun and jogged away.

K'heera glanced at the Mizari's tentacles spinning and waving; she was clearly disturbed. However, she was unprepared for the disapproval etched on the face of Captain Stepp.

"Why is a *Harkk'ett* going to Trinity?" the Captain demanded.

"StarBridge business," Jib said curtly.

"But why a *Harkk'ett*?"

K'heera was humiliated; the Captain spoke of her as though she weren't even there.

"She is Ambassador Dhurrrkk's choice," Jib said simply.

"I feel proprietary about Trinity," the Captain said, annoyed. "The last thing I want to do is . . ." she cast around for the right expression, "deliver a serpent into the garden."

K'heera was baffled by the reference, and knew she'd have to look it up, only to be infuriated when she learned its meaning.

"That's not fair, Captain," Jib protested. K'heera couldn't bear to listen to him defend her anymore, especially since he was doing it so halfheartedly. "You can't hold an innocent person responsible for the actions of their elders."

The Captain took a deep breath and looked away. When she met his eyes again she seemed calmer. "You have to realize . . . I knew the people who died on Trinity. They were friends of mine."

K'heera couldn't tolerate this human female's official kindness. At least her own people treated her like the outcast she was right from the start. "Honored Captain," she growled, waiting until the female lifted her wrist voder where she could hear it easily, "you will not have to suffer my presence. I believe it will serve everyone if I stay in my cabin hereafter."

"For the whole trip?" Jib seemed astonished. "It'll feel like a prison after a few days!"

K'heera wanted to stuff his mouth full of Pp'hhh'tttkkk, anything, just so he'd shut up. "It is my preference."

The Captain bowed slightly to her. "Perhaps that'll be for the best. I promise you'll lack for nothing."

The Captain had accepted her offer with humiliating readiness, but K'heera would not rescind it. Public humiliation was part of life as a Harkk'ett.

"As I said earlier," the Simiu told Jib, "I should've stayed in my quarters. I will go there now, and remain." He seemed stricken, but did not attempt to stop her. Mortified, furious, and totally miserable, K'heera forced her crest and tail to stand tall as she strode from the room.

# CHAPTER 3

## ♦

# Jib

"You promised Tesa!" Meg insisted. The gray-haired biologist turned to the fiftyish man sitting beside her. "So bury that resentment before we pick those kids up, Bruce."

Easing the shuttle *Patuxent* into the empty bay of the *Singing Crane*, she closed the lock. The second shuttle, the *Baraboo*, was parked beside it.

The weatherman sighed as he shut down all systems. "Just tell me how baby-sitting a Simiu kid is supposed to 'make reparations' for what happened here?" He unsnapped his harness and stood, shrugging his dark jumpsuit into place. Seeing Meg's exasperated expression, he held up a hand. "I've never broken a promise to Tesa yet. I'll be Mr. Charming!"

"To think I've lived long enough to see that!" Meg grumbled.

"They'll be docking soon. Think I'll spend the time . . ."

"Checking out the equipment," Meg finished for him. "Going to scan for that sunken meteor again?"

"May as well, since we'll be diving for it next week. Lot of big life-forms nearby. They might've moved it, who knows?"

An hour later, when the S.V. *Norton* finally mated airlocks, Bruce joined the older woman beside the sealed doors. "How's this face, old girl?" he asked in a low voice.

She glanced sideways at him. He appeared pleasantly neutral, and had even freshened his appearance. "Don't call me 'old girl'!" she growled, making him grin.

The locks finished cycling, then opened. First through was Steve Manohar, the cargo master, who handed Meg a computerized bill. "Well, we've got more than supplies for you today," the portly young man told them matter-of-factly. "But the cargo's ready. Okay if we bring it in?"

"Sure, Steve," Meg said. "Have the recruits been up long?"

"Oh, yeah. We woke 'em yesterday."

Bruce and Meg exchanged a look. "I'm . . . surprised they're not here," she remarked. "Everything okay?"

The attendant dropped his eyes to his lading list as two others pulled a-grav sleds loaded with containers into the *Crane*. "Far as I know," he said noncommittally.

Bruce leaned forward conspiratorially. "What happened? The Simiu challenge everyone on two legs?"

Steve glanced up, then shrugged. "All I know is she hasn't been out of her quarters since the first night. Sign here, Meg."

The Russian woman felt a knot of worry coil in her chest as she pressed her thumb to the bill. Why hadn't Captain Stepp come down to say hello? Then she caught sight of a tall, dark head bobbing toward them down the *Norton*'s corridor.

"Here they come," Steve said pleasantly.

Meg finally spotted the Simiu marching beside the young man as the two StarBridge students drew near. "Sorry we're late, mum," Jib said in heavily accented English.

"No problem," Meg reassured him. To the Simiu, she made the traditional greeting. Then, in barely acceptable Simiu, she growled, "We are honored to greet you, K'heera of the Harkk'ett. I am Margaritka Tretiak, and this is Dr. Bruce Carpenter."

Bruce carefully imitated the greeting. Tesa had helped them work out the wording, since no honor could be given to K'heera herself because of her family's lost status.

The four-legged alien never met Meg's or Bruce's eyes, but returned their gestures. "I am privileged," she replied.

*So far, so good!* thought Meg. She turned to the New Zealander, shaking his hand heartily. "Tesa's said so much about you, I really don't feel the need for introductions."

"'Ope she didn't say too much. I don't want to have to live anything down!"

*Thank God we'll be signing on Trinity,* Meg thought, *I can barely understand a word he's saying!* It occurred to her they were probably sharing that thought, since Bruce always insisted her own Slavic accent bordered on parody.

Bruce shook the young man's hand. Meg could see the Maori's open smile softening him already.

"Do either of you need to stop for anything—bathroom, snack, change of clothes?" Meg asked, knowing the Simiu's voder would translate. One sentence in Simiu was all she could handle.

Jib glanced at K'heera, who said something to him. "K'heera wants to know," he finally said, "when we'll meet the Grus."

*Just like Tesa,* Meg thought suddenly. Would Bruce remember that? She smiled. "About two thirds of the way down."

The Simiu looked up at her, plainly startled, then her violet eyes hooded over with some dark emotion.

*          *          *

Tesa held up the last tule mat so Weaver could attach it to the shelter's framework with her fingers and bill. Her grandmother, Nadine Lewis, attached the other end. In a few minutes it was secure and the three stepped away from the wall of the small A-framed structure to admire their work.

"Oh, it's perfect, Weaver!" Tesa signed to the avian.

"I'm glad you like it," the Grus replied. "These story-walls are so different from ours it's hard for me to judge."

The White Wind people wove images into their shelter walls primarily in the ultraviolet range, so that much of it was invisible to humans. Tesa's shelter was a smaller version of Taller and Weaver's, built beside theirs on the same platform. But these walls showed stories any Terran could see—artistic renditions of her own adventures.

"The colors Teacher used are very striking," Weaver agreed.

Tesa hugged her grandmother. "I loved the way you wove my quilt's pattern into the walls. Your design is great!"

"Only young bones like yours could sleep here night after night, *takoja*," Nadine signed with a wry expression.

Weaver's head swiveled just as Tesa felt the vibration that meant the flock was calling. Her grandmother touched the nullifiers in her ears as powerful sound waves washed over them.

"It's the shuttle!" Tesa realized excitedly. "If I don't hurry, I'll miss my place in line!"

"Be careful!" her grandmother ordered, as the Interrelator grabbed her parked sled and dashed outside. Tesa slapped the controls, and the machine leaped into the air, even as she pulled herself across it on her stomach. Taller, who'd been fishing in the marsh, lifted from the water to quickly overtake her.

*Where's Lightning?* she wondered, glancing around. The cinnamon-colored head pulled up on her right with Thunder flying near, pumping her huge wings to keep up. The raptor never could maintain her interest in proper formation and usually just floated somewhere around the periphery of the escort. The other Grus had long ago learned to ignore her.

Flies-Too-Fast moved ahead of Tesa, behind Taller. The big, bold male, Hurricane, mirrored him on the right. She glanced behind and saw Snowberry's gleaming crown jockeying around near the young female Winter Bloom as they got into their positions. In the rear, the tiny None-So-Pretty, the gray-tailed Scorched, and the young male Frost Moon took their places. Before long, a tightly organized vee was winging ever upward.

The wind whipped through Tesa's hair and the feathers on her woven shirt. The rapid one-two, one-two beat of powerful Grus wings made her want to go faster, higher, until the air was too thin to breathe and the cold cut through her clothes.

Soon, the escort surrounded the *Patuxent*, spiraling around the descending ship. Bruce and Meg waved to them from the cockpit, as Tesa searched the windows, finally glimpsing a shock of black curls, then a flame-colored crest.

The flight was over too quickly. Soon, the *Patuxent* soft-landed on the bluff's pad as the escort backwinged onto the ground, blowing leaves and debris everywhere. Szu-yi and Old Bear emerged from the Hedford Shelter, the elder Lakota holding his perpetual coffee cup in hand. Szu-yi, more accustomed to working with Simiu than any of them, had dressed as though she were about to greet an ambassador. Tesa parked her sled.

"You're always so exhilarated after one of those flights," Szu-yi signed to her in passable Grus. "Ready for our guests?"

"Ready or not," Tesa signed, smiling, "here they come."

The *Patuxent*'s lock unsealed, and Meg exited. Jib was out next, and when he saw Tesa he grinned. Forgetting her planned speeches, she bounded over, throwing her arms around him.

"You're almost as tall as I am!" Tesa signed when they'd released each other.

"I'd thought you'd shrunk!" Jib replied. The two dark heads moved together and performed the *hongi*, the traditional Maori nose rub greeting, then they hugged again fiercely.

Someone tugged Tesa's shirt, and she turned to see Meg.

"We might need you to run interference," Meg signed.

"What do you mean?"

"K'heera doesn't want to come off the ship," the older woman explained. "She says she's sick . . . but I think she's afraid of them." She moved her head toward the waiting Grus.

Tesa turned to the ship. "Actually, there's someone better suited to that job than me. . . ."

K'heera had known fear before, but she'd never had to suffer it alone. For the first time in her life, there was no strong family member to console her or give her words of courage.

*Any honorable person would welcome this test,* she thought, looking onto a world in which she was the only one of her kind.

She told herself it was the change in gravity that overwhelmed her, but as her stomach rolled and twisted, she realized this was only part of the problem. The months she'd spent dread-ing this moment had infused her with horror. Even her odor had changed—she stank of fear. As K'heera gaped at the huge, white-feathered aliens her family had so violated, she could not force herself to step onto the soil of their world.

When K'heera remained perched at the lock's threshold fighting vertigo, the human called "Bruce" turned to her.

"You okay?" he signed.

The Simiu glanced at him nervously, knowing he disliked her. It was etched around his eyes, though he tried to hide it. She'd seen similar expressions on her own relatives whenever they were forced to interact with humans. Why was he pretending to care?

He extended a hand toward her. "You'll feel better once you walk around in the fresh air."

His gray alien eyes seemed to bore into K'heera. *He knows I'm afraid! It makes him feel superior; that's why he's acting the uncle to me.* She moved her hand in a Grus refusal.

"Have it your way," he signed, his expression stiff.

*You only draw attention to yourself,* K'heera castigated herself. *Step outside!* Slowly, the Simiu placed one palm on the ramp, then another, finally drawing her rear legs after her.

A female human approached. "I am Dr. Li Szu-yi. If you are suffering from nausea, dizziness, or other symptoms of low-gee illness, I can help."

"Yes, please," K'heera responded, hoping she might yet screen her fear from these humans.

The slight Asian woman rummaged around in her medical kit, then pressed a small patch against K'heera's inner forearm.

The Simiu could feel the drug's effect almost immediately. Her stomach settled down, her light-headedness faded, and she relaxed. She waved a sincere thank you at the doctor. *Too bad there is no medication for cowardice,* she thought.

Glancing past the doctor, K'heera's eyes took in the expansive bluff lush with rich vegetation in a riot of colors, colors that tickled her eyes and filled her with a sudden surge of optimism—until she glanced again at the flock of Grus, unabashedly straining their necks to get a good look at her.

The Honored Interrelator held court among them, standing with her back to K'heera, signing to the giant avians.

K'heera could not read the Grus' expressionless faces, but she was sure they must want to avenge their dead. That was why they'd flown up to the shuttle, to see the creature that had so unjustly and shamefully caused the slaughter of hundreds of their innocent people. She shivered uncontrollably.

She wanted to race away, and ached for the loving touch of her mother, or to bury her face in the mane of her beloved uncle.

The Interrelator and the flock moved as if they were one organism, as they surrounded Jib. His eyes widened, but he signed the appropriate greetings. K'heera felt depressed again.

Suddenly the tallest avian stretched, and his head spun on his supple neck as his piercing golden eyes captured Jib's. The human stood, his own dark eyes never flinching from "the look." K'heera could tell that Jib had quickly passed, that the Grus believed he was an honest, honorable person. What would happen when they sought what was honest and honorable in her?

The flock kept stealing peeks at K'heera, sometimes with one eye, sometimes with two—one Grus even dropped his head to peer through the others' legs to see better. Then, as she considered retreating back into the shuttle, one of them approached. This avian was also tall and stately, but his head and neck were a lovely brownish-red that gradually faded into white.

The avian stood at the foot of the ramp, holding his neck in a tight S curve, which made him seem smaller. "Good Eyes says your world is heavier than ours." He paused, tilting his head. "Is it hard to fly there?"

K'heera felt dizzy. What kind of question was that for the daughter of murderers?

"Forgive me," the Grus signed, dipping his head even lower. "This is my first introduction. I'm Lightning, son of Taller of the White Wind people. I welcome you to the World, and invite you to meet my father."

*Why, he's just a child,* K'heera realized. A child with responsibilities, even as she had. His guilelessness had thrown a blanket over her fear, smothering it. "It is an honor to be presented to your father," she signed slowly, then carefully walked down the ramp to join him. The doctor walked behind them, with Meg and Bruce following at a discreet distance.

"You have lovely eyes!" Lightning signed casually. "They're the color of a summer sunrise."

Before K'heera could respond to the unexpected compliment, she found herself staring at a thicket of thin, black legs. Lightning addressed the tallest of the flock. "Taller, greet our new friend— we can call her 'Sunrise.' "

The young Simiu was startled. Had he really used the informal sign for friend? And to be given a name that alluded to the Sun Family was . . . well, it was an *honor*! She glanced at the Interrelator, but her face was as unreadable as the avians.

"And this," Lightning signed to K'heera, "is Taller, tallest of the White Wind people in these parts."

Before K'heera could return a respectful greeting, Taller dropped his long neck, fixing her with a round-eyed stare. Burning with shame, she turned away. Without moving his huge body, Taller's face was before hers again, holding her eyes with his commanding gaze, his deadly bill inches from her muzzle.

K'heera felt as though she were being challenged, and her crest rose for a second, then collapsed. She dropped her eyes, and Taller's crown stretched and grew redder.

"I am sorry that your visit to the World has been so upsetting," the leader signed.

His concern was more than she could bear. "I . . . am a-shamed . . ." she signed awkwardly, "of the pain my family has caused you. I am . . . sick with sorrow and guilt for your loss."

Taller's crown dulled. "No child bears the burden of a parent's crime. *You've* caused no pain, young one. Look at me." He held her violet eyes with his steely gaze. His forgiveness was too shameful. It would've been easier to confront his hatred. After a moment, she had to turn away again.

"To see so much sorrow in young eyes hurts me," Taller signed. "Lightning is right, you need a new name. 'Sunrise' it is. Welcome to the World, welcome to you and Good Eyes' young brother, Jib. We are pleased to greet you."

With that, he threw back his head and called, and all his people called with him. Even through her sound nullifiers, the power of their call sent vibrations ripping through K'heera's body, raising her fur and her crest.

An old man she hadn't seen before suddenly appeared beside her, as though he'd always been there. As casually as one of her uncles, he squatted down, offering her some bright orange leaves. "These will help your . . . bad feelings."

The doctor seemed puzzled. "I've already given her . . ."

The old man waved a hand. "She needs a little help from the World. Go on, try it."

K'heera glanced suspiciously at the leaves, but then the old man stuck out his tongue and showed that he was eating one. Tentatively, she took a leaf and chewed it. Sweetness and a refreshing sharp flavor flooded her mouth and sinuses. The Simiu felt color rise to her face; her crest lifted.

The old man winked at her and smiled.

"The fishing is different down south," Thunder signed ear-ly next morning as Tesa packed her sled. The raptor perched

on the highest object lashed to the hovering machine, climb-
ing ever upward as her human friend attached more bundles.
"The fish are much bigger, and some of them fight back! Sometimes . . ." the Hunter glanced around as if to make sure no one
else could see her signs, "sometimes . . . they win. My mother told
me so."

"Your mother would know," Tesa agreed. Rain, Thunder's
mother, had gone south to find a mate. "I hear the water's warm
there, too."

"Yes, and clear," Thunder replied.

Tesa could tell that beneath the avian's casual conversation was
an underlying worry. "You don't have to go."

"But then you'd have only the White Winds to guard you!"
Thunder seemed shocked. "I *have* to go." She ruffled her feathers,
dust and fluff exploding around her. "Besides, I don't believe a
spirit can pull a Hunter out of the sky."

"Neither do I." Tesa swallowed a smile as she pulled her star
quilt high up on her shoulders. Father Sun was coming up first
these days, but even so, the temperature was dropping. She took
her Clovis-point spear, feathers from Earth and Trinity dangling
from its shaft, and wedged it securely onto the sled.

"You're not taking that?" Jib signed to her from his own sled.
The two of them had gotten up early to pack, enjoy the sunrise,
and share a few moments alone.

"I'm not leaving without it!" Tesa insisted. "We're not on
Disney Planet. This has saved my life on two occasions."

Jib turned away. "If K'heera sees that, she'll have a *fit.*"

Tesa stared at the young man. "Then, she'll have one. This
spear is the only weapon we have, except for the repulsors we're
allowed to use to ward off predators. And those are just scare
tactics. She must really be getting to you."

"You haven't been walking in my moccasins, *tuahine,*" Jib
signed, calling her "sister" in Maori. He told her briefly about
the incident with the spicy Simiu food, which had led to K'heera's
humiliation by the drum dancers. "I felt so *bad* for her, she had to
see the pity in my eyes. She must hate me."

Tesa nodded. "No one said this would be easy. First thing *you*
should do is stop feeling sorry for her . . . and yourself."

He turned to her, surprised.

"You didn't come here to save the World," she reminded
him.

"Funny—that's what I said to K'heera before all hell broke
loose at Captain's Night." He leaned against Tesa's floating sled,

his expression sober. "I'm beginning to think I shouldn't have been so quick to agree to this assignment."

She met his eyes. "What's that supposed to mean?"

Jib shrugged. "This last year, Tesa, I've been working with telepaths, with Shadgui. Now, language, spoken or signed, seems so restrictive. *Those* are the people I should be working with. I'm not going to be much help to K'heera . . . or you."

"Well, you definitely won't with *that* attitude," Tesa agreed. "You sure . . . there aren't other reasons you're having regrets?"

He seemed a little embarrassed. "Well . . . sure . . . I miss my *tahu,* my girlfriend, An'zia. You'd really like her, Tesa."

The young woman finally got tired of evading the issue. "Jib, I talked to Rob."

He stiffened instantly. "He . . . he *told* you? He had no right to do that!"

"I thought I was your *tuahine,* your sister," she reminded him. "I thought there were no secrets between us."

His hands hung in the air, then he sagged. "Of course you're my sister. There aren't even any tests for TSS, so how can they be sure I have it? It's just a title they've made up, the disease of the year." He peered at her intently. "They tried to tell me I don't really love Anzia. They're telling me it's this *TSS,* not my own honest emotions. Do you have any idea how that made *her* feel? We've been separated for months now. If my feelings for her were only from TSS, wouldn't they have faded by now? Well, they haven't! I feel the same way about her today as the day I left. Tesa, they're wrong about this."

The anguish on his face spoke volumes of what he'd been through. Could he be right, and Rob wrong?

"I write Anzi every night," Jib told her, more calmly. "I know I won't be able to send these letters till the next ship comes, but when I can, they'll be there to prove my feelings, even though we're apart."

"She loves you?" Tesa asked.

"She says so. When we're together . . . it's . . . like we think with one brain. We know what the other's going to say before we say it. I don't mean to rant on, but I really miss her. And TSS has nothing to do with that."

"I believe you," Tesa assured him, meaning it. She felt a pang of jealousy at him for having someone to share that with.

A hand fell on her shoulder, and she turned to find Old Bear. "Grandfather! I should've known you'd be up early. Everyone else still sleeping?"

"Yeah. I left the coffee on for them." He smiled enigmatically as he offered them orange leaves.

They each took one; Jib eyed his warily as Tesa popped hers casually in her mouth. It was one of the Grus' favorite herbs and they used it for many things, including scenting their feathers and cloaks. The plant was called "blood-of-the-World" because it grew everywhere. Its bright blue berries poked out of the light snow they had here in winter, but its leaves were especially good in the fall, when they were in full color. Its minty sweetness made her hungry.

"I had a dream last night," Old Bear signed casually, glancing quickly at Jib.

Tesa stopped chewing, feeling the hair on the back of her neck rise. Her grandfather's dreams weren't something to ignore— and she'd had a beauty of her own last night. There'd been terrible images of a river running thick with blood and she'd jerked awake, gasping. She wondered, not for the first time, if she should tell him. "What was it about?"

"Your trip." He stared out over the bluff as if recalling the images and framing their story. She realized then that he didn't want to speak in front of Jib, someone he barely knew.

Tesa noticed that Thunder had stopped preening and watched the old man intently. Jib glanced between her grandfather and herself, looking a bit skeptical and uncomfortable.

Finally, Old Bear spoke. "I dreamed . . . there were spirits in the sea. I couldn't see them because the water was all churned up, but they were big."

"And fierce?" Thunder asked, stretching her neck.

The old man laughed and shook his head. "No, not fierce. Not these spirits." He stared at his granddaughter. "I dreamed the sea spirits would touch *you*, Good Eyes. I dreamed you would *hear* them." He grinned at her.

Tesa smiled back. "Very interesting. Anything else?"

He sighed, his smile fading. "No . . . just . . . be careful, honey. I worry about you."

Thunder drew herself up tall, a behavior she'd picked up from the Grus. "Don't worry. I'll be there to protect her."

The old man nodded, and touched the raptor reverently. He was proud that one of Tesa's companions was a living Thunderbird.

There was something about the dream he wasn't telling her, Tesa knew. She knew also that there was no point in trying to drag it out of him, so instead she hugged him, kissing his cheek. "I'm *always* careful!" That made both of them laugh.

"By the way," asked Jib, gingerly chewing his leaf, "what's in these things anyway?"

"Some complex sugars," Old Bear signed, "vitamins, calcium, oils. At least, that's what Meg tells me."

"That's all?" Jib seemed surprised, obviously remembering K'heera's almost miraculous recovery after eating one.

"Not quite," replied the old man. "It also carries the blood of the World. That's powerful medicine, son."


Old Bear sat on the edge of the bluff, watching the mismatched group fly south. The rattling vibrations of powerful Grus voices washed over him as the flock called good wishes to their friends.

Meg joined him on the bluff, resting her shoulder against his. Such a fine woman, this blue-eyed Russian. Intelligent, curious, funny, and so attractive. He'd be a lucky man if she fell in love with him.

The dark shadow of his dream passed behind his eyes again, and he wondered again if he should've told Tesa all of it. No, he'd done the right thing. The part he'd told her had been the first part of the dream, the good part. If he'd told her the rest, she would never have left him.

He *had* dreamed that Tesa had heard the song of a sea spirit. He had no idea what that meant, if anything, but that wasn't what concerned him. No, that part made him glad, because it meant that she would not be here when . . .

He didn't want to remember, didn't want to see the terrible vision, but it was in his mind's eye and he couldn't shed it. There had been a shadow on the moon, on Father Moon, like blood, and it had grown, rich and red, mottled with bright blue arterial blood. The blood had dripped onto Trinity, spattering and spreading. It had covered the bluff. And he, Meg, Grandma Lewis, and Szu-yi were swallowed by it, completely devoured.

Slipping an arm around Meg, Old Bear watched their friends fly south and prayed that his dream was nothing more than the wicked workings of a tired mind.


"Thank you, Arvis," Atle sang as his son finished oiling his skin. "That was very relaxing." He held out his arm to be helped into his garment. "I don't get to relax much, anymore."

The amiable servant blinked his appreciation as he tugged at his father's sheer, one-piece outfit. It was tailored perfectly for the First, designed not only to help retain warmth and humidity, but to keep the poison patches open and visible, and to match, exactly, the wearer's mottled skin coloring.

Atle had had clothes designed for his Industrious children, but they never looked right. Where Atle's clothes complemented his wrestler's physique, Arvis's always made him seem oversized and lumpy and the dull color of his impotent patches made him appear ill. His sister, Sine, didn't wear hers much better.

The First had been much younger than Arvis was now when he'd earned his name, given him by his powerful mentor. He had earned it wrestling males twice his size and winning. In those days he'd loved to fight more than anything—but then he'd met Dunn.

"How's your mother?" Atle asked. "I haven't seen her since this morning."

The boy looked downcast. "No matter what we say to cheer her up, sir, she's still sad."

Atle's throat quivered as he patted his son consolingly. "Well, you keep trying. You and your sister are all she's got."

"Yes, sir," the servant sang, pleased.

"Tell your mother I'll have dinner with her this evening. After the staff meeting. Will you remember?"

"I'll remember, sir."

The First left his personal bath, taking an a-grav transport to the conference hall. While traveling through the ship's corridors, he scanned the computer's latest updates.

The *Flood* had parked herself behind the largest moon of this world and had sent her last two robots onto its surface. For the past month, as this planet measured time, they'd observed the comings and goings of the tiny space station and its planet.

Their discoveries excited his staff; morale soared. Then, halfway through the month, the ship had detected a new player entering the theater. A moderately sized spaceship had headed for the station as casually as an egg delivery service. A small shuttle had taken off from the ground camp and been swallowed by the station just before the newcomer had docked with it. A short time passed, then the shuttle had returned to the planet as the spaceship disengaged from the lock.

Atle stopped his flyer near the conference hall. Inside was the Council, the collected leaders of the different groups that represented a cross section of their society. As he entered, all music hushed. Everyone squatting around the low, circular table lifted to their feet. The First motioned them back down. "Who wishes to speak?"

"I do," sang Dacris, Second-in-Conquest. "These beings have a stardrive far superior to our own!"

"You think so?"

"I do. That ship traveled quickly. It wasn't a sleeper like the *Flood*."

"I agree," Atle admitted, looking around the table. "We could make good use of such an efficient stardrive." He sang this softly, this massive understatement.

"Then we'll pursue the ship before it leaves the solar system," the Second asked eagerly, "before it engages its drive?"

"No."

Dacris' throat quivered with surprise. Around the long table other eyes glanced back and forth. The Troubadour was well liked among the scientists.

"You disagree?" Atle asked.

"Respectfully, First, I do."

"What would you do?" Atle asked, honestly curious.

"Overtake the ship." The Second's mottling glowed with the passion of his convictions. "Capture it. Commandeer its passengers and crew. Discover its secrets."

"Who agrees with this?" asked the First quietly.

"We do," sang Gillat, a Flat-Spine, indicating the scientists at her end of the table. The mathematicians and physicists were hungry to get their fingers on a new spacedrive.

"What about you?" Atle asked Rand of the Hooded, squatting at the other end of the table.

This race consisted mostly of bio-scientists. There was grumbling, but finally the big green and brown pharmacist stood.

"We disagree," Rand grunted. "We're simply not ready." The pharmacist's wide mouth opened spasmodically, as though he were tasting something. "We need biological representatives. If we had even a *few* of the aliens, we could refine the drugs needed to control them. Then, there would be no risk of needless bloodshed and waste."

Papu of the Chorus stood. She was a powerful political figure as the senior member of a group that contained mostly accountants, bureaucrats, and political scientists. The Chorus always agreed among themselves, making them a formidable force. She was small and dull green, so she always had to stretch to be sure she could be seen. "The pharmacists are right. We *must* know more about beings who make 'routine stopovers' between the stars before we act. If their stardrive is more powerful than ours, then their weapons must be also."

Dacris swelled impatiently. "I respectfully remind Papu that your people were conquered centuries ago by just such an attitude. You feared the expense of war, but not of committees. You'd be in meetings still if we had not overpowered you."

"It's true, Dacris," she responded acidly, "we were conquered centuries ago. But we have been Chosen for over two hundred years. And it was because of our committees that the Chosen were finally able to conquer the last ethnic holdouts, the Cliff-Dwellers and the Armored, and bring peace to our Home. A peace we have enjoyed for one hundred years. I submit, Glorious First, that people who have not conquered a nation in one hundred years need to practice a little caution."

Dacris turned to his First. "If these aliens are warlike conquerors, then where are the cities they could surely build, where are their armies? Why isn't the space around this world filled with stations, crowded with ships going back and forth reaping resources? Where are the armies to protect this planet?"

"Those are good questions," Atle agreed, "and the answers are near, in that space station, just waiting for us to translate them. We've already translated the station's original message; we can use that to unlock their secrets—and make them ours."

Atle saw Dacris unsuccessfully mask his resentment. "Second, do you disagree with this decision?"

The Troubadour hesitated. One by one, the other staff members squatted down, leaving only the Troubadour and the First standing. The Second's skin blushed vividly.

Atle's own colors flared in response to the challenge. His poison patches flared yellow, then began to sweat.

The sight of the weeping poison brought fear to the table as the others stared straight ahead, motionless, dulling their color. But Dacris' look was one of stark terror—a look Atle had seen before. *He's wrestled a One-Touch,* he realized. It was hard to win a match when you could only concentrate on warding off the arms of your opponent. With immediate treatment a victim could survive, but recovery involved weeks of pain and paralysis.

"I follow your command, Glorious First," the Troubadour sang softly as he squatted on his heels.

"Then ready a transport and a crew of technicians," Atle ordered Dacris. "*You* will board the station—but prevent it from sending an alarm. Staff it around the clock. Papu, assemble translators, historians, and technicians for Dacris. Rand, you and your best pharmacists and biochemists will go also. We must understand these beings' biology if we hope to control them. The three of you will be personally responsible for that."

Rand and Papu blinked acknowledgment. Dacris sat immobile.

"Sooner or later," Atle sang, "the ship that left will return. And you, Dacris, will be waiting. You must be prepared to take it, and everyone aboard. Then you, your staff, and a skeleton crew of the aliens will take the ship Home. When that alien ship comes back, Dacris, will you be ready?"

The Troubadour faced his First, his color brightening. "Yes, First. Thank you, First." It was an important task. But was it enough to assuage the Second's boundless ambition?

"I'll need a crew myself," Atle continued. He turned to the far end of the table where the lower-classed Armored and Cliff-Dwellers sat. "Tipes, Bufo, I want soldiers and strongarms, your best, fully equipped. Rand, I'll want a small medical crew. And a zoologist. Dacris, I'll need a ground surveillance specialist. We'll surprise the station's ground camp and take them."

He paced around the table to face the Red-Legs, who were mostly technicians. "You, Ensa, will organize our first settlement, somewhere near where the probe landed. Once we capture the beings at the camp, we'll join you at the settlement and conduct research there. Your people should continue to awaken the staff and families, Chosen and Industrious, and send them planetside until we are at full capacity. Third-in-Conquest Amaset will be running the ship, and will coordinate transports."

Atle would be more comfortable once their resources were land-bound. It was a big planet; there they could spread out. Here they were one large, easy target.

He turned to face the table. "We don't know how long it will take us to learn how to control these beings. We will have only a finite number of them to work on, and a finite amount of time before the spaceship returns. But we have never been a people to abide waste or squander resources. To lose the potential of any of these intelligent beings would be terrible indeed. Go slowly. Go carefully. And remember." He paused for effect. "I will not hesitate to punish the careless—or to reward the careful."

Atle finally squatted down at the head of the table and took the vessel of water left there for him. These meetings always left him dry. Patting the fluid over his skin, he touched a pad on the console embedded at the head of the table. Despite his song, he didn't believe any of them could appreciate how much work they had to do. They weren't One-Touch, they didn't have the need for conquest written in their genes—a need that had been unfulfilled for over one hundred years. He needed to inspire them to embrace their huge task.

Touching the console, he called up the alien recording just recently translated. "Before you begin your work there is something I want you to hear. It is a message from the people we are about to meet." The hushed room filled with the strange sounds of the recording, followed by the translation.

"Welcome," the aliens sang in a flat monotone, "to the World known as Trinity. This World is the home of intelligent beings like yourself. Please respect their sovereign dominion. Do not land without authorization. The Cooperative League of Systems of the Fifteen Known Worlds greets you and invites you to communicate with us. Welcome."

*The Cooperative League of Systems of the Fifteen Known Worlds,* Atle thought. Fifteen Known Worlds. Facing the Council, the First slowly blinked his enormous eyes, watching as his subordinates heard the incredible words of the alien message. One by one the Council reacted, their throats quivering with musical laughter, until the ridiculous message was drowned out. As his staff roared with mirth at a people who so foolishly invited their own enslavement, he thought again, *Fifteen Known Worlds.*

Yes, there was *much* work to do.

# CHAPTER 4
## ◆
# Florida

Tesa stood motionless in the crystalline waters of the River of Fear, her leister poised as a large, sleek fish approached, his scales undulating pink, blue, silver. Feathers dangling from her shirt waved enticingly in the waist-deep water. Tesa's dark knuckles paled and the long muscles in her arms tensed as she gripped the three-pronged spear that once had been used by Northwest Coast Indians. The fish swam nearer, curiosity pushing him closer. Tesa swallowed, already tasting him stuffed with wild grain and a local peppery herb.

The back of her neck prickled, but she ignored it. Since they'd landed at the river early this morning she'd been hyper-alert.

She'd had a terrible dream last night about a ravenous water spirit but couldn't talk about it. She was worried that if she did, the cohort might start molting from the jitters, Thunder would get more foolhardy, she'd get another lecture from Bruce about primal belief systems while Jib wore his don't-tell-me-*you're*-going-native look—and K'heera would lose what little trust she might still have in Tesa's judgment.

And they'd only been in the Land of Confusion for forty-two Terran hours—a day and a half, Trinity time.

The cohort watched her nervously from the shore, crowded together for comfort, their heads swiveling in every direction. Since they'd entered this territory, the World felt strange, as if everything were canted off-center.

No animals or birds lived near the river, and the unnatural silence rattled the young Grus. Since silence didn't affect Tesa, they turned to her for security. Her willingness to enter the dreaded river both impressed and frightened them.

If she couldn't get them past their fears they'd never get enough to eat, and with their high metabolism, they'd soon be unable to fend for themselves.

It had taken a week to arrive at this short, broad southern penin- sula Bruce insisted on calling "Florida." His meteor had splashed into the nearby sea, close to the mouth of this wide river. As Taller had predicted, they were far enough from any Gray Wind people that nullifiers could be left handily slung around necks, rather than worn. The immature calls of the cohort, according to Bruce, were irritating, but not dangerous. He was enjoying the novelty of being able to hear on Trinity.

Once they'd set up camp, Jib and Bruce had taken the *Demoi- selle,* their small multi-use vehicle, and gone underwater exploring. Following the deep channels and crevasses the river's odd tides had carved would eventually lead them to the sea. She expected them back around dusk and by then they'd be starving.

A flash of goose bumps ran up Tesa's spine, but she repressed the urge to check behind her. The edgy cohort wasn't her only problem. From the shore, a pair of shocking purple eyes bore into her. K'heera had developed a "look" of her own.

Suddenly there was a flash of silver as the fish darted forward, grabbing a feather. Tesa drove the leister down, but her preoc- cupation made her strike late and the shiny tail sailed through the prongs. She thrust the weapon again, but the fish was gone, swimming away, trophy feather dangling from his mouth.

A shadow of massive wings passed by as Thunder swooped

low over the turquoise water. Her spread feet slapped the surface, snatching the escaping piscine. Huge wings struggled for lift as the heavy, thrashing burden twisted in her deadly talons.

Tesa splashed her way onto the beach, the cohort jogging behind, just as Thunder circled the camp and released her prey. He landed flopping on the bright white sand, and Tesa dispatched him promptly with her stone knife, as she offered a prayer of gratitude to his people for his sacrifice. The cohort, as if one organism, lowered their heads to examine the dying fish.

"There's plenty to eat in the water," Tesa reassured them. "The fingerlings nearly plucked my shirt bare, and there are big, fat river worms on the bottom. I saw a soft-shelled side-walker that was *three* times the size of the ones back home!" That made every crown in the crowd blush and spread.

When Thunder landed and folded her wings, the others stared admiringly at her. "I flew the whole width of that river," she signed haughtily, "and all *I* saw was *food*!"

The Grus glanced at one another, but finally Lightning raised his head. "I'm hungry!" he announced, appearing as unconcerned as Thunder. Regally, he entered the water until it was up to his thighs. Within seconds, his head dived under the waves and he came up with a fish so large he could barely swallow it. Flies-Too-Fast was soon beside him, with the others close behind.

Tesa smiled and went back to cleaning the fish. Thunder leaned over the corpse, peering at the creature hungrily. "You caught him," Tesa signed. "Do you want him?"

"We both caught him," Thunder retorted. "Your attack slowed him down. I would like the head, please . . . and . . . the liver?"

"Fine," Tesa assured her, removing the head deftly and eviscerating the fish. "If you don't want these entrails . . ."

"Oh, I'll eat those," Thunder assured her, "and the fins!"

Methodically, Tesa scaled the body. As she carried it back to the surf to wash it, she finally spotted K'heera in a tall patch of dune grass. The Simiu's violet eyes were politely cast aside, yet Tesa knew she'd been glaring in stern disapproval. That's the way it had been ever since their first meal together.

"Animal protein?" K'heera had signed, shocked when the cohort had offered bivalves to the humans. "It is fine for the White Wind people to eat their traditional foods," she'd lectured the humans, "but you are only visitors here. You have written, Honored Interrelator, that many of Trinity's beings communicate. How can you know which animals have a burgeoning intelligence, and which do not? How can you risk it?"

The Grus had been totally nonplussed by her reaction, while Thunder felt this was the first truly humorous thing an alien had ever said. But Tesa couldn't shrug K'heera's concerns off so easily. As Interrelator, she wasn't here just to speak for the Grus and safeguard their culture, but as a voice for all the intelligent beings on Trinity. But while CLS rules regarding her role might seem clear to a Planetary Council light-years away, on the World things were not always so easy to define.

She'd already reduced her own reliance on Trinity's animal food drastically, and at her urging, the other scientists had done the same. Bruce had assured Tesa that most of the fish on Trinity had only rudimentary brains, and bivalves had no brains at all. Even so, whenever Tesa added animal protein to their diet, K'heera would be nearby, silently protesting the murder of Trinity's creatures. It was getting to Tesa.

*Only because you're afraid she's right!* she told herself, washing the fish, then wrapping it in long, bright red leaves.

She stared across the river at Lightning and Flies-Too-Fast. They'd grown bold and had flown to the shallow sandbar in the middle of the river's wide expanse. Comfortable now that they'd eaten, they stopped to bathe and preen. The rest of the cohort had spread apart, some still eating, others just loafing.

She wished that she were here alone with them; nothing would feel like *work* the way this did now. But then, everything would be easier if Jib and K'heera enjoyed camping at all. K'heera and he shared that in common, at least.

Shelter construction and food foraging were nothing but drudgery to the two students. Jib only wanted to talk about Anzia and record letters for her, while K'heera couldn't find enough time to groom, as though one had to look perfect in the middle of nowhere. The grooming, Tesa knew, was partly for reassurance. The Simiu had to be sorely missing her own people.

She watched K'heera gather reeds for her bed. Like Jib, the flame-furred being had been outfitted with modern camping equipment, including a-grav sleep pads. But after Tesa had constructed her own shelter from natural materials, the Simiu had eschewed such modern trappings. It would have been dishonorable for K'heera to be more comfortable than a human.

*Life's too short,* Tesa thought, *for all this Sturm und Drang.* She wished that her grandfather were here. He'd been a sacred clown for so long, he'd make this somber creature laugh—and laughter was the most powerful medicine. *Well, if he were here,*

*he'd only be disappointed that I haven't heard any sea spirits.*
She smiled. Wouldn't her cohort *love* that!

She tucked the leaf-wrapped fish into a mesh bag and walked
over to K'heera, now carefully keeping her eyes downcast.

"Would you like to go foraging?" she asked. It made her
uncomfortable signing to someone who wouldn't look at her.
She never knew if K'heera was paying attention or not. "The
cohort's finished eating. We could all go." Tesa didn't like to
admit it, but she felt more secure when the group stayed together.

The Simiu moved a hand noncommittally. "I can go when
you're serving supper." Tesa would prefer that K'heera gather
her food early so they could all eat together, but whenever she
suggested that, K'heera demurred.

"Jib and Bruce might not be back till after dark," Tesa signed.
"I wouldn't be comfortable with you foraging after sunset." With
a Simiu, things had to be worded so carefully. If she flatly refused
to let K'heera go, she would dishonor her.

"Lightning has shown me a patch of bitterberries nearby. He
and I can gather them and still be within the camp light."

*But far enough away not to share our conversation,* Tesa
thought. Of course, Simiu did not use meals to socialize.

"Can I help you with those reeds?" Tesa asked.

"Thank you, Honored Interrelator, they're no trouble."

*I'll bet,* the woman thought, and returned to where Thunder
was finishing the last of her fish.

"You always wear that same expression whenever you talk to
Sunrise," Thunder signed, then wiped her bloodied beak on a
driftwood log. "Why is that, Good Eyes?"

"I'm just disappointed," the human explained. "I want her to
like us, but I'm not making much progress."

Thunder seemed unconcerned. "That one is as solitary as a
Hunter, even though she eats no animals. It's her nature."

"That's not true," Tesa signed. "Her people live more commu-
nally than the White Winds. For her to remain so far from others
must be a painful, lonely thing."

"You must be wrong about that, Good Eyes," the raptor signed.

"Can you *believe* these coral reefs?" Jib couldn't hide his awe
as Bruce piloted them through the calm ocean waters.

The older man whistled through his teeth as he stared through
the wide portals. "And those colors! The primary hues are elec-
tric, and the pastels more subtle than any I've ever seen. Like

nothing on Earth, that's for sure. Of course, I never got to New Zealand. . . ."

Jib shook his head, smiling. "Not even there, mate."

Growing up in the Land of the Long White Cloud meant never being too far from water, and Jib had mastered the waves in every vessel he could. His great-grandmother, Nui Tapuna, the family's lone traditionalist, said that he'd always be *waimarie,* lucky, with water, that his good fortune was kept inside an ancient greenstone tiki she'd given him at birth.

After a week mucking around in the bush it was a treat to be in this smart little ship hovering over a coral reef that no human had ever seen. "This *is* ever something. You're filming?"

Bruce nodded. "That, and mapping. We've got to come back with *some* hard data or Tesa will accuse us of pleasure cruising."

"Bruce, look!" Jib pointed straight ahead.

A massive school of fish suddenly poured out of a hole in the reef like a thousand clowns from a tiny aircar. Each one was about the size of Jib's hand, and each identical in shape with its neighbor, but no two held the same color pattern. Jib blinked hard, the vivid colors hurting his eyes. Each fish had its own pattern of stripes, spots, or mottling. He realized dazedly that the patterns *moved,* undulating and pulsing across their flat bodies, even when the fish were motionless. The flashing patterns were so disturbing, he had to glance away.

"Incredible," Bruce breathed. "This is a whole new phenomenon in natural camouflage! We've gotta see these guys closer." He leaned over and shut off the Automatic Protection System, and in seconds the entire ship was enveloped by the school. "Tesa would love this!"

Jib nodded. The fish floated right against the portals, touching the clear barriers with their mouths and their fins, undulating their colors so brightly it reflected on the walls of the small vessel like strobe lights.

Time passed quickly, so after a while, Jib glanced at the chrono. Humans had divided Trinity's long day into twenty-eight and a half Terran hours. It was now just past twenty hundred, which made it near dusk at this time of year. A hunger pang reminded Jib of one forgotten priority—dinner. Watching Bruce manipulate the controls, he asked, "We headed back?"

The weatherman nodded.

The fish followed the ship right into the river, along a deep crevasse. Bruce had no trouble navigating by instruments. "They'll return to the sea when the fresh water bothers them," the weatherman said. "We're gettin' really good film."

Jib could include a clip in the letter he'd record tonight for Anzi, and wondered—if she were here—if she'd be able to read anything mentally from such simple animals.

Then, without warning, the Maori was struck by a powerful wave of vertigo. He lurched forward, nauseated and unbalanced.

"Jib, what's the matter?" Bruce asked, grabbing his arm, steadying him. "You all right, son?"

He thought at first it was a reaction from the flashing fish, some obscure epilepsy. Dimly, he realized he was distracting Bruce from the instruments. Jib broke out in a cold sweat, suddenly terrified, convinced they were headed for disaster. Outside, the fish swam lazily and unconcerned, kissing the portals, bumping gently along the hull. Blinking, he tried to speak, but couldn't. He saw the APS registering something large, something close, but its force-field had been turned off. Time crawled, but the chrono only registered fractions of a second.

In his mind, Jib saw his imminent death, no, something worse than death. He felt a wave of fear like nothing he'd ever known. They were being pursued by something so primitive, so terrifying, it had no name, no shape. He could only think of it as the Mate Kai, the Great Hunger. He had to tell Bruce, make him turn the APS back on. His mouth gaped helplessly.

"Hang on, buddy," Bruce said, his face full of concern. "We'll be at camp in no time." Then he turned back to the instruments and saw the rapidly changing readings. "Oh, *shit!*"

Bruce reacted quickly. They were still in the crevasse, high walls on each side, surrounded by fish. Alarms sounded wildly as the instruments went crazy. The computers displayed a form, something as big as the *Demoiselle*, coming up fast beneath them. Bruce glanced at the school. If he turned on the APS now, they'd be stunned, maybe die. Jib knew the scientist in him would balk at that. He hesitated less than a second.

Something hit them like an underwater bomb.

The *Demoiselle* spun like a toy—but worse than that for Jib was his inner terror. He could *see* endless rows of teeth swallowing the ship, *feel* the heat of a watery breath. They were being consumed alive, devoured, but still there would be Hunger. He clutched his tiki as the thing struck again.

"Dammit!" Bruce shouted, fighting the bucking ship.

The ship shuddered, then suddenly Jib gasped, forgetting all about the Mate Kai. Pain bloomed in his back. There was one last tumble, and a sickening crunch as the left wing hit something hard and unyielding. Abruptly the fear and pain left Jib as he sagged back in his seat, weak and exhausted. Slowly, Bruce righted the *Demoiselle*.

"Whatever hit us shoved us into the wall of the crevasse," Bruce said. "The wing's ruined, but we're watertight."

The ship broke the surface suddenly, startling the cohort, making them leap into flight, bleating their harsh alarm calls. On the shore, Tesa and Thunder turned to watch.

Jib never thought he'd be so happy to see land. Descended from computer specialists, he was no traditionalist and had little interest in his people's "old ways." But right now Jib was questioning all his modern pragmatism right down to his soul. As the *Demoiselle* limped to shore, he found himself clutching his tiki so hard its twisted image imprinted his pale palm. Its luck had stayed with him all the way to another planet—it was the only explanation he had for why he and Bruce were alive.

The ship's tripod feet settled in the sand, and Tesa and K'heera ran toward it, as Thunder flew over, landing lightly on the battered wing. The Grus clustered nearby, their huge, round eyes staring. Moist, balmy air gushed in as Bruce opened his door. The meteorologist was talking nonstop, but Jib understood nothing. All he could do was remember the terrible Hunger and the monstrous gray shadow that tumbled the ship like a toy.

". . . My fault . . . ." Jib suddenly realized Bruce was saying. "Szu-yi'll shoot me if she finds out. It's all my fault. Damn, what a mess! We're lucky to be alive, that's all. I should've never turned off the APS. I'm really sorry, son . . . son? Jib? You okay? You're not hurt, are you?"

Jib came out of his trance at the mention of his name, and not a moment too soon. K'heera had just pulled up beside him and in a rare show of concern was about to open his door. *Can't let her see me like this,* he thought, ungluing his hand from his pendant. *She'll never have an ounce of respect for me if she sees this look on my face.* He almost started giggling. *But, K'heera, will you respect me in the morning?* He gave himself a mental shake, then clambered out of the ship, forcing his weak-kneed legs to stand steady. *Do Simiu feel fear during near-fatal accidents? Do they see their life flash before them?* Jib's own short one had gone by so fast he wanted to ask for a replay.

"Are you hurt?" the Simiu asked, for once, in English. She blinked slowly, examining him as though for injuries.

"I'm okay," he assured her. "It was a close call."

"It's very honorable," she said, "to suffer such an accident and remain calm." Suddenly the wind shifted and her sensitive nose twitched. Before Jib could admit to an honest terror, she smelled it on him. Her crest lifted, and she turned away.

Giving up, Jib went to the bow as Bruce explained things.

"I'm totally responsible," he told Tesa, finishing the story. "By the time we came out of the tumble, the *creature*, and the school, were gone." He ran a hand through his thinning gray hair. "Really, the wing looks worse than it is. I mean, it was damned scary being spun around like a tub toy, but she held up! She can still dive, we'll just have to go slow. And she can a-grav around like a sled, but we're not flying anywhere."

His face was drawn. "You know, Tesa, Rob Gable once sent us copies of his antique films and one of them was this real silly thing about a shark. When we watched it, I thought, How could anyone have been scared by something so phony-looking? But when that thing came up under us just now . . . that film was all I could think of. Frankly, when it happened, I was scared shitless."

Jib glanced at K'heera, seeing her shock as she reacted to Bruce's admission. *Maybe that's an advantage of age,* Jib thought. *Maybe you stop caring about what other people think of you.* He looked again at Bruce, and realized the older man had already shaken off the effects of the accident. Why couldn't he?

Tesa peered at the young Maori. "You okay?"

He nodded, then signed it for the cohorts who were staring in wide-eyed amazement. He knew what they were thinking. "It was just an animal," he told them. "It was big . . . and solid, but just another animal. Taller told us there were big animals here."

"Good Eyes' Brother Jib," Lightning signed formally, "you don't look like someone who's only seen an *animal*."

"You've lost your *color*," Scorched signed.

He swallowed and took a deep breath. "It . . . was a surprise."

The White Winds only glanced at one another and huddled closer together, their crowns shrunken and dulled.

The Maori jumped when Thunder threw her head back and gave her raucous, high-pitched call. "*I* caught food in that river!" she signed with a flourish. "*I* didn't see any big animals."

"Even if it *was* a River Spirit," Flies-Too-Fast decided, naming the enemy, "the Fisher and Good Eyes' Brother Jib are alive. Their machine protected them. That's good to know."

The heavy-bodied Hurricane stared suspiciously at Jib with one eye. "You *are* all right, aren't you?"

The young man suddenly felt overwhelmed; he shuddered and had to suppress the urge to weep. He lied when he signed, "Yeah,

I'm okay. I'm fine." He wanted to say, *I still have my soul,* but couldn't make his hands form the signs.

"That's the only thing that matters," Tesa assured them, interrupting the cohort's questioning. "Ships can be repaired."

"Maybe," Bruce signed, "but this thing's our *ambulance.* Let's call Meg. She can go to the *Crane* and make us spare parts. Meanwhile, we'll fix what we can. K'heera?" He turned to the young Simiu. "Will you help me? I could use your dexterity."

The Simiu's small crest rose to its full height. "I am honored to be of assistance."

Jib could tell she really meant that, but Bruce only smiled crookedly. "Yeah, okay, let's get started. Jib, you call Meg. And uh . . . listen . . . underplay it, will you?"

"Let's get out of their way," Tesa signed to him. "Come to my shelter. You look like you could use a drink."

He nodded, following her. The cohort trailed them so closely, they nearly stepped on him, but Thunder stayed behind to watch the mechanics. Inside Tesa's small wickiup, Jib took a container from her and swigged its liquid back, his hands trembling. Swallowing hard, he grimaced. "This is *water.*"

"Of course, it's water," she signed. "Jib, what happened down there? You looked like you'd seen death . . . or worse."

He wanted to tell her about his premonition, about the Mate Kai, the surprise of the goliath shadow beneath them, the feeling of helplessness as the *Demoiselle* tumbled head over heels—but as he moved his hands the memory of that raw terror just drained away. Suddenly . . . the whole thing didn't seem so bad. The print of the tiki on his palm itched and distracted him.

"Jib, talk!" Tesa demanded, waving her hands at his face.

He shrugged. "I *was* bloody well rattled, but I guess I'm over it. Bruce told you everything. I just overreacted."

She seemed unconvinced, but didn't push him. "Look, I'm sorry about all this, Jib."

"Sorry for what? You couldn't . . ."

"I'm sorry you're stuck in the wilderness when it's not what you or K'heera enjoy. Sometimes it's hard for me to remember that not everyone finds digging their own privy hole fun. And *this* place is enough to give anyone the willies. After we pull that meteor up, I'll get Bruce to take you both to the *Crane.* We've got plenty to do there, and I think you'll be happier."

He grinned unabashedly. "Fair dinkum? That'd be bloody fine! Hey, I'd better call Meg. Sooner we get the *Demie* back in shape, sooner I can catch that R and R." He tapped a sequence on his voder, then waited for a response. There was a long pause. Finally, the screen said, "No satellite available."

"Here, mate, look at this." He showed it to Tesa.

"It must be there." She checked the schedule. "Try again."

Jib shook his head. "Same thing. No satellite available."

"It must've failed. The next one comes around in four hours, at twenty-four twenty-two. We'll get through then, but we'd better tell Bruce about this one now. When we do reach Meg, he'll probably want her to go get the dead satellite before she goes to the *Crane*. They can repair it before she brings us those parts. Good thing we found out before we needed it for something really important."

K'heera pulled off a cluster of turquoise berries and popped them into her mouth, savoring the bitter taste. Four White Winds moved edgily around her, alternately eating and guarding. No one had gone fishing since the accident with the *Demoiselle*. But they could talk of nothing else.

"You saw the way he looked," Frost Moon signed knowingly, his cinnamon feathers turned gold by the distant firelight. "The River Spirits *touched* him. He *heard* their song."

Politely, no one pointed out that this voice of authority on River Spirits was the youngest member of the group.

"If he'd been of the World, like Good Eyes, would he have gone to them?" the gray-tailed Scorched asked. She kept watching for predators and so far hadn't eaten a thing.

"Of course," Frost Moon signed. "He'd have *lost his soul*."

"But he didn't," Winter Bloom reminded them, calmly eating. She stopped to quickly preen a misplaced feather. "The machine saved them. We'll all be safe with the humans."

"The Fisher says it was just an animal," Lightning reminded them, "and *I* believe him."

The White Winds turned at the same time to observe the open fire, the rest of the cohort, and the humans. K'heera could see it in their body language, the way they slowly lifted and settled their feathers. They didn't trust the humans the same way Lightning did. They hadn't been raised with them.

"That was interesting how you and the Fisher fixed that machine," Lightning signed to K'heera, in a plain attempt to change the subject. "Did you learn to do that on your World?"

"Yes," K'heera signed, offering some fat berries to Scorched. It distracted her and she ate them quickly. "Would you like to learn mechanical work, Lightning? You're well equipped for it."

The tall young Grus stopped eating and stared with one eye.

"I was joking, honored friend," K'heera told him, her eyes twinkling. "But it's customary among my people to share knowledge. It's one of the ways we make honor-bonds."

"Is that why the Fisher asked you to work with him?"

K'heera turned to Bruce, sitting nearest the small fire. She could smell the fish steaming in its peppery leaves. It was a terrible thing to do to those delicious leaves.

"He knows nothing of honor-bonds," she signed. "He needed my help. Our double-thumbed hands are more efficient. That's why he allowed me to do most of the work." It had been the first enjoyable thing she'd done since she'd gotten here.

"I see," signed Lightning, in a way that said the opposite.

"You don't agree?" she asked.

"I've watched the Fisher repair much more complicated machines without any help at all," Scorched signed.

"Do you remember when he dismantled most of the shuttle just to find a small problem?" Winter Bloom added. "Then he put it all back together again. He said it was *fun*! But he fixed it."

Lightning made no comment, just watched her reactions. K'heera stopped eating and sat on her haunches. Could Bruce have asked her to do something he could have done faster himself . . . because he *wanted* to share his knowledge with her? No male on K'heera's world would have been so self-effacing unless . . . he was an uncle . . . . K'heera's crest rose, bristling.

"Sunrise," Lightning asked, "have we offended you?"

"No, honored friend," she reassured the avian. She was not offended, just confused. Everything she'd experienced here was the exact opposite of what she'd been raised to believe. Her own personal guilt plainly did not matter to these avians. The Honored Interrelator maintained her own beliefs, and would not apologize or lie about them, nor did she resent K'heera for the arguments she raised. And now Bruce, this man she knew was as prejudiced as her own family, had again acted as an uncle to her.

"You have only said the truth," K'heera told Lightning. She glanced at the humans. Tesa, Bruce, Flies-Too-Fast, and Hurricane were signing animatedly. Jib sat by himself, staring out over the dark waters with an odd expression.

He and K'heera were supposed to be working together, yet since they'd left StarBridge they'd drawn even further apart. K'heera knew she was largely responsible for that. She'd been judging Jib by a standard that even a Simiu elder couldn't uphold.

*This is our pair project*, she thought, *we're supposed to be a team. Tomorrow I'll . . .* What? Be nicer? Treat him as an equal? Part of her was convinced she could only lose more honor befriending such a being. But another part of her now doubted that wisdom. Tomorrow, she decided, tomorrow she'd begin again.

"I don't see it," Szu-yi said, scanning the *Patuxent*'s instrument panels. "It's just not out here."

"*Chort!*" Meg swore. "How could a satellite just *disappear*? If it had been hit, there'd be *debris!*"

Szu-yi shrugged. "These things happen. We'll pick up another one and set it out when we leave the *Crane*."

"Your sense of practicality must come from your medical background. This kind of mystery makes me crazy."

Szu-yi's normally bland expression brightened. "As soon as you stop looking for it, the answer will appear."

"I suppose," Meg grumbled. "Nothing I like better than getting frantic calls at bedtime and having to make a midnight repair run! We should charge triple time!" She took the shuttle out of its low orbit, piloting it toward the space station.

Szu-yi felt odd going there. When she'd first come to Trinity, the station had been her natural environment. The planet was too dangerous, she felt, too raw. And she'd feared the Grus. But that was before. She belonged on Trinity now, and felt at peace there. Going to the *Crane* now was like visiting an old neighborhood—one without many good memories.

The airlock opened as invitingly as a giant's mouth, swallowing the shuttle. The lock closed behind them, then cycled the air back in. "It'll take us three hours to produce those parts and ready a new satellite," Meg said. "What do you think?"

"I think the Grus named you well, Speedy. Make it five. We'd be wiser to sleep, then do our work in the morning. Bruce and Tesa aren't expecting us before noon." Leaving the ship, they walked through the large bay to the airlock. When the door lifted with a sigh, Szu-yi sniffed. "Something must be wrong with the ventilation. What *is* that smell?"

"Smells like a swamp," Meg said. "Let's check hydroponics."

As the two women stepped into the hallway, Szu-yi turned to Meg, but the words she was forming never had a chance to emerge. Instead, she saw her friend enveloped by unrecognizable forms, even as she felt herself seized. The swampy odor grew overpowering, choking her. The hallway disappeared in a crush of bodies. Meg shouted, cursing luridly in Russian. Szu-yi struggled blindly, instinctively, futilely. Within moments, both women were buried beneath a wild mélange of brilliantly colored clothes and helmets.

# CHAPTER 5
◆
# The Anurans

*We're being mugged,* Szu-yi thought crazily as she was half dragged, half carried through the halls.

She choked and the gloved hand wrapped around her throat eased its grip. The beings—whoever or whatever they were—wore sophisticated, tight-fitting garments with small, clear helmets like contamination gear.

Their gloves were translucent, and tightly fitting. The skin she could see was smooth, completely hairless, and moist. Wiry strong arms held her torso, supporting her weight.

They varied in height, from slightly more than a meter to nearly two, bipedal, with two arms. Their extreme differences in heights and body types—some long and slender, others short and round—made her wonder if they might be different species.

Their wide, expressionless faces had large round eyes sitting atop a broad head, with flat, round tympanic membranes serving for ears. Szu-yi couldn't see any teeth, just wide mouths and rigid lips spread across their faces. The lips led directly to a soft, billowing throat, covered by translucent skin. There was no chin, no forehead, just a bony ridge. Two tiny nares pressed flat against the skin between the huge eyes and wide mouth, with no nose to shape the face.

*Anurans?* Szu-yi wondered. If they were, theirs would be the first known planet where amphibians were the dominant life-form. But this was hardly the way a First Contact was supposed to go.

Szu-yi couldn't see Meg, but she could tell by the woman's broken, gasping voice that she was struggling wildly. *"Sukin-sin!"* Meg yelled in Russian.

*"Don't fight!"* Szu-yi called out. "Save your strength."

The strange thrumming noise she'd been hearing had to be their speech, a bizarre but lovely cacophony of tones made deep in their throats, which never emerged from their mouths at all. *There must be some way to speak to them, to make a peaceful contact.* But beings interested in peaceful contact didn't sneak aboard your space station and pounce on you like street thugs.

They wrestled Szu-yi around a corner and forced her onto one of her own surgical tables. Quickly and efficiently, they disrobed her, examining each item of clothing with clinical interest, totally apathetic to her humiliation. As warm, moist air hit her unprotected skin, she became absurdly grateful that these aliens needed more warmth and humidity than humans.

Once she was nude, the aliens stretched her limbs onto the table's extensions, her arms out at right angles from her torso, her legs spread shoulder width. Using surgical restraints, they strapped her arms, legs, abdomen, and forehead down tight.

Her calm demeanor began dissolving into terror.

Suddenly a piercing alien scream cut through the air. A loud scuffle ensued and everyone surrounding Szu-yi disappeared. Straining to turn her head, she watched a tall, brown alien double over, shrieking. Its helmet had been torn off, and it was clutching one eye. The entire complement of beings converged on Meg's table. Through the frantic melee she caught a glimpse of weathered, tanned skin as the older woman fought, pulling at containment suits, punching flexible helmets.

"Oh, Meg, don't!" Szu-yi yelled as the biologist fought like a panther. The fear of witnessing Meg's death and then being left totally alone in this nightmare completely panicked her. "MEG!" she screamed.

Finally, everything stilled. When the beings drifted away, Szu-yi could see that Meg had been restrained. She seemed pale, but her thin chest lifted regularly, and her blue eyes glowered.

"Are you all right?" Szu-yi called, broken-voiced. "*Meg?*"

"I'm fine," the biologist answered weakly. "Just tired."

Szu-yi wanted to weep in relief but controlled herself. If she slipped, she'd slide into hysteria. She distracted herself by looking around her once-familiar workplace.

Everything was up and running, every screen filled with information. So many of their instruments had been brought here, the infirmary looked like an insane computer fun house.

Then she spotted the missing satellite, perched in a sink, its compartments violated, its boards removed. She tried not to view it as a grisly prediction of her own fate.

Around her, the aliens calmly went about their business. Some—

technicians?—acted disturbingly familiar with the station's equipment. Szu-yi tried not to think of the wealth of data here—information on the Known Worlds, the Cooperative League of Systems . . . the history and location of Earth. . . .

The alien Meg had struck was being tended while others hovered nearby with equipment. One held a Terran scanner, and seemed to be synchronizing it with the alien equipment. Finally, they all conversed excitedly, even the one who'd been struck. His eye was closed, but only by a lower lid since they had no upper one. He gestured, pointing to their scanners.

The brown alien with the injured eye spoke to a tall green and gold standing in the background. That one sang back in a rich bass voice, its clear notes ringing through the room, claiming everyone's attention. *The leader?* Szu-yi wondered.

All the aliens removed their contamination suits, excitedly chattering among themselves, revealing startling colors and close-fitting clothing that matched their myriad patterns.

*Wonderful,* Szu-yi thought gloomily. *We're no danger to them.* No doubt they had already tested the *Crane*'s air and water, and perhaps even the blood and tissue samples kept on board. But they must've still had doubts. Meg's lucky punch had forced them to confront the issue.

Szu-yi glanced at the assorted beings as they returned to their duties. *Males and females,* she decided, recognizing what had to be secondary sexual characteristics.

Another tech guided an a-grav cabinet between Meg and Szu-yi's couches. On it lay Terran medical equipment, and a variety of the drugs and chemicals Szu-yi frequently used. She recognized the distinctively packaged psychotherapeutics. Beside them sat alien vials, with their own designs and inscriptions. Szu-yi moistened her dry mouth.

Suddenly the green and gold leader loomed over her, blocking her view, pulling her attention to his face. *His?* thought Szu-yi, but instinctively knew she was correct.

He leaned closer, and Szu-yi pressed against the table, wanting to sink into it, away from those terrible, marbled eyes. Clenching her teeth, she stifled a moan. His shape had nothing to do with her feelings. It was the way she was forced to view him—as a frightened lab animal must have faced human scientists hundreds of years ago. Of all the myriad beings she'd ever encountered, this was the only true *alien* she'd ever met.

He held up a cobbled-together computer device and touched a small membrane on it. It emitted sound, and Szu-yi recognized the recording that the *Crane* broadcast out into space, giving its greeting first in Mizari, then Simiu, on and on through the languages of all the Known Worlds, then finally in English. The leader touched Szu-yi's arm and pointed to his device.

She flinched from the clammy touch, then realized he was trying to communicate with her. *He heard me speaking English*, she thought. *Does he want me to acknowledge I can speak that language?* Her mouth was so dry, she had to lick her lips to speak. "Yes, that's English. I speak English."

The alien moved over to Meg. The feisty biologist kept a wary eye on him, but remained silent. When he pointed to the device and tapped her, she spat back a torrent of angry Russian.

He returned to Szu-yi. Touching another pad, he sang. The machine bleated in stiff and halting English, "I am Second-in-Conquest Dacris, Commander of this station. Tell us your name."

Szu-yi's eyes widened. That was a functioning translator!

"Don't tell them anything!" Meg shouted defiantly.

"Who are you?" Szu-yi asked. "Why are you treating us like this? We are intelligent, peaceful beings, emissaries of our people. Free us, so we may talk like equal beings."

Everyone in the room was paying rapt attention, waiting for the machine to sing its equally halting song. A soft trilling circled the room, going from creature to creature.

The leader replied as the machine translated his words. "We are the Chosen and we have no interest in war. We *want* you to speak for your people. But we are *not* equals. We are the Chosen. You are not. We will learn about you. You will help."

"Only if you release us," Szu-yi answered.

Suddenly one of the alien technicians sang out. Dacris snapped off the translator and went over to that one's console, but Szu-yi couldn't see past them. The two conferred, then moved away from the computer. On the screen was her own face and data. Beside it a translator was turning the information into music. Her curriculum vitae was oddly melodious in their language.

"You are a physician?" the leader asked.

She hesitated, finally answering, "Yes."

He barked short flat notes and technicians quickly removed Szu-yi's restraints. With a gesture that was almost gallant, one of the techs extended his hand to help her off the table. She took it gingerly, easing herself onto her feet.

"Thank you," she responded automatically, and rubbed her wrists, her skin lifting into goose bumps. Slowly she moved over to Meg's couch and touched the older woman's forehead. "It's going to be okay," she murmured as her fingers traveled to

Meg's throat. The strong pulse and steady respiration reassured her that Meg was physically fine, and the anger flaring in her eyes spoke well of her mental state.

"Sure it is," Meg grumbled.

*They must have some kind of bizarre professional classism,* Szu-yi decided. *Maybe that's what they mean by the "chosen."* Standing on her own two feet, she felt her confidence return. "My friend is an important biologist, a *doctor* in that science. Release her, give us our clothing, then we'll talk, as equals."

Another ripple of sound spread among the aliens.

"We *have* biologists," Dacris replied. "That one has another purpose. Even as you do. I repeat, you're not the Chosen."

"I'll do nothing as long as we are held against our will," Szu-yi said stiffly. "This violates the most basic rights of any intelligent creature. . . ."

The strange sound rounded the room again as all the beings made it. With a sickening feeling, Szu-yi finally realized it had to be their laughter. Dacris did not laugh; however, his color grew more brilliant.

"You are a physician," he sang. He gestured at the green and brown alien that was still tending the one Meg had struck. "This is Tato, *our* physician." He indicated the alien with the swollen eye. "And this is Rand, our chief pharmacist. Together, you will discover how many of our drugs can be safely adapted to your physiology. We will use this one"—he indicated Meg—"to test these drugs. That is your purpose here. Understand?"

Szu-yi felt the shreds of her confidence dribble away. "That's . . . immoral . . . illegal . . . . I *won't* help you!"

"You will," the leader sang succinctly. "Tato, begin the study. We have wasted too much time already."

"You don't need to use her," Szu-yi explained urgently. "We have computer models, tissue samples, even nonsentient genetic reconstructions. They're safer, more reliable. . . ."

"We will use the prime subject," Dacris insisted.

"She's an old woman!" Szu-yi blurted. "She can't take it! Use me instead, I'm much younger, I could tolerate . . ."

"We are aware of this one's age," the leader sang. "We are also aware that by your own standards she is in excellent health. We will take precautions, but she *is* the subject. We will use *you* after the pilot studies are completed."

"I won't help you!" Szu-yi screamed in frustration. Suddenly the leader stared past her and Szu-yi collapsed, struck down by an enormous blow. She writhed as pain engulfed her.

As the sensation gradually dimmed, Dacris' song picked up in intensity and even the translation conveyed his heightened emotion. "Understand this. Centuries before we learned to refine drugs to ensure obedience, we knew the mind's tolerances and the body's limitations. This was the first information we took from your medical library. Drugs are more efficient, but we have other, older methods. Touch her again."

Pain seared through her, and Szu-yi arched in agony. She tried to crawl away, even as she heard him sing the tone she quickly learned meant "Again. Again. Again . . ." over and over.

The next time it stopped, she curled into a fetal position and wept unashamed. A moist hand tangled in her hair and jerked her head up. Dacris was inches from her face, pulling her hair with his own hand. "We are the Chosen. You are the Conquered. You *belong* to us, now, and for the rest of your life. You will work, live, and procreate for our benefit alone. Your aged and your young will die to feed us. Accept it and survive."

Szu-yi's eyes roved the room, silently pleading for help, but no one moved.

"Explain this to your people as we collect them," Dacris sang. "Only your eloquence can spare them this lesson. Learn it for them. Persuade them." He released her hair and her head thudded against the deck plates.

With a sickening terror, she realized it was about to start again and tried to scrabble out of reach. It hit her harder this time and she slammed against the floor as her limbs gave out. Finally, the only thing in her universe was an all-encompassing agony and the futility of her echoing screams.

Eventually, it stopped. There was blood in her mouth, and her tongue was swollen and sore. She focused on a small technician with shockingly bright red legs and a green torso who crouched behind her, holding an innocent-looking rod about two decimeters long. Had that small thing . . . ?

The technician watched Tato and Dacris argue. Dimly, Szu-yi understood that the physician had ended the punishment against Dacris' wishes. The sadistic bastard was enjoying himself so much he might've killed her.

When the argument ended, Dacris approached her, his colors burning her eyes. She flung herself away from him, but was grabbed by technicians. Someone collected the tears falling down her face as another tech reached into her mouth, sampling the blood and saliva welling there. Dacris loomed closer, and Szu-yi recoiled into the techs' embrace.

"We are the Chosen," he sang. "You are not. Do you understand?"

Her mouth opened but only a breathless gasp emerged.

"REPEAT IT!" he boomed in her face, the tinny sound of the translator making a mockery of his powerful voice.

"You . . . you are the Chosen . . ." she whispered. "I am not. . . ."

"Good," he purred, his colors dimming. "We understand each other. Begin the study." He turned to the physician. "You worry needlessly, Tato. She's fine, but keep the rod near. The lesson is new. She may forget."

Dacris stood where he could view Meg's table, yet not interfere with the work. The technicians eased away from Szu-yi slowly, as though they feared she would fall without support.

The alien doctor approached. "*Are* you well?"

Szu-yi searched the strange eyes. Amazingly, she began to feel better, and understood that whatever the rod had done had affected her mind alone. As the pain receded, she knew she had no bruises, no broken limbs. Just the memory, and fear, of pain.

"Yes," she said simply, "I'm all right."

"We'll use minimal doses," the doctor sang. "We wish to cause no lasting harm. The subject has too much value to waste."

Szu-yi realized the doctor was trying to console her.

Meg stared at her worriedly. "Are you okay?"

Szu-yi nodded.

"Well, I will be, too, *golubchik*," she reassured her.

The Asian woman's eyes welled up, and tears fell down her face, splashing onto her thin breasts. As quickly as they fell, they were collected by dispassionate hands. The alien doctor pressed a diagnostic scanner into Szu-yi's hand and signaled to her technician. An alien hypo hissed against Meg's flank. Szu-yi blinked and forced herself to stare at the scanner.

Jib awoke, sweating, gasping like a fish out of water. Throwing back the thin thermal sheet, he peered around the tent, blinking slowly in the darkness. According to the chrono it was oh five hundred, not even dawn. Bruce was across from him, huddled on his floating pad, sleeping soundly.

The young Maori had had a terrible dream, a real horror show, filled with gray, faceless monsters with giant maws and thousands of teeth. He shivered. Tesa had been swallowed . . . no . . . not her . . . the grandfather? The memories skittered away. Never mind. It was only a dream.

He rubbed his face and rolled over, sticking to the sheet, his body slick with sweat. He took a deep breath and shut his eyes, making himself relax. He'd think about Anzi, that'd help him have better dreams. He hadn't written about the accident—no need to worry her about it after the fact—but he also hadn't included any footage of the fish in his last letter. Truth was, he didn't want to look at them again, at those moving colors. He swallowed, wishing she were with him.

If Anzi were here, she could change these bad dreams with a thought, put herself in them, and make them funny. He pictured her so clearly, her round, pleasant face so different from his, her red-gold hair. . . .

Then Jib heard it, a soft, high-pitched melodious sound, like a sorrowful keening. He sat up, blinking. *That* was what had roused him, that moaning, pitiful sound. He glanced at Bruce— still sleeping. Leaving the mat, he slid on his cutoffs. The song pulled him out of the tent, toward the beach.

Barefoot, he left the shelter, staring out at the night. There were insects everywhere, clouds of them, from beautiful, giant moth-type things as big as a flying fox, to annoying specks like sand flies that whined by your ears. The lush growth of the nearby forest and its arching fern trees stood like black giants swaying gently in the evening's breeze.

Three Moons hung over the inky water—the fat, full Father Moon, the Mother Moon at three-quarters, and the tiny Child Moon that was only the slimmest crescent. The celestial family hovered over the gently lapping river, casting bright, fragmented reflections along its broken width. The Moons provided a surprising amount of light—so much that Jib could see his shadow on the bright sand.

He searched the river—the river that had almost killed him, and now sang to him as though to apologize. The tide had been higher earlier but, even now, the water covered the sandbars. He shivered in the warmth, rubbing his arms.

The music lingered, tantalizing him with its symphony of sorrow, but it was so faint, he could barely make it out. He felt a sudden chill and looked around dazedly.

He was *in* the river. The water lapped lazily against his thighs. He felt disoriented, and couldn't remember leaving the tent. He turned, but couldn't see the camp. He'd come down the shoreline, his footprints were outlined darkly in the moonlight. He was standing . . . right where the *Demie* . . . Someone touched his right shoulder and he jumped. It was Bruce.

"Didn't you hear me?" the older man asked worriedly. "I've been calling you. Were you sleepwalking?"

Jib had heard nothing but the song. He searched for the notes, found them, and felt oddly reassured. "Can you hear it?"

"I heard something, like music," Bruce agreed. "Woke me up." He glanced back up the beach and Jib followed his eyes. K'heera was on the shoreline, closer to their camp. She peered about as if confused. "Funny," Bruce said, "you'd've thought with her hearing, she'd have been the first one out here." Then Bruce turned and his eyes widened, as he turned toward the mouth of the river. Jib followed his gaze.

The whole cohort was out on the sandbar, dancing, he thought. He squinted: no, not dancing. They were darting, splashing, their wings outstretched, their heads jerking up and down. They were moving so fast he couldn't tell one from the other at this distance. He heard a scream, and was startled to find Thunder circling the group low, shrieking.

"What the hell . . ." Bruce murmured, watching the scene. "*That* girl doesn't fly at night 'less she *has* to!"

Bruce moved toward them and Jib followed. The water around the Grus was past their hocks, and it slowed them down. Wings bumped into wings, and there was a sudden break in the circle. That's when they saw Tesa, in water up to her chest.

Jib could barely believe it. She'd swum out there in the dark? Alone? No wonder the avians were frantic. The Grus surrounded her, blocking her as though afraid to let her go forward. But she ignored them, pushing her way roughly past them, searching, seeming almost frantic. She turned her head in one direction and then another as though . . .

"Look at her," Bruce whispered, grasping Jib's shoulder.

Tesa faced left and moved forward, then turned right and went that way. But she wasn't watching where she was going . . . no, Jib realized, that wasn't it at all.

"She's *listening!*" Bruce whispered. "She *hears* it!"

# CHAPTER 6

## ♦

# The Singers

"Come on," said Jib, then dived into the water, kicking hard. After a long swim, he finally stumbled onto the sandbar, then waded toward Tesa. She kept forging ahead, despite the efforts of the Grus. The water fell away as the sandbar rose, until it lapped about her calves.

"The River Spirits are calling Good Eyes!" Lightning signed as Jib pushed his way past him. "They'll take her with them if we can't stop her!"

Distractedly, Jib remembered the avians' concerns and their deep-seated religious beliefs. He couldn't imagine the courage it had taken for them to follow Tesa out here.

"You are not-of-the-World," None-So-Pretty reminded him. "The River Spirits won't be able to harm you!"

The young Maori was no longer so sure of that. "Tesa!" he called, rushing to catch up with her. "TESA!"

"She can't hear you," Flies-Too-Fast reminded the young man. "She only *hears* their song."

*She hears something*, Jib realized, but when he touched Tesa's shoulder, she spun, surprised to see him.

"Hurry," she signed, "we've got to help. . . ." She turned as a high, clear note ripped through the air. Looking out over the dark water she tried to go around Jib, but the Grus surrounded her again with a barrier of wings. Jib grabbed her arm just as Bruce caught up to them. K'heera hovered nearby on an a-grav sled. They both appeared as confused as he felt.

"Tesa," Jib signed, "can you *hear* that singing?"

"Of course not!" she signed impatiently. "I'm Deaf!"

Jib, Bruce, and K'heera all exchanged glances. The Maori thought if either of them said one word about Spirits . . .

The Interrelator shook her head. "That's not sound—it's telepathy!"

*Telepathy?*

"Doesn't it all make sense?" Tesa signed, her hands moving

so fast he could barely make out what she was saying. "All the legends about the Spirits, how they've affected the behavior of the local animals . . . ? Something out here is telepathic . . . and now it's hurt. I woke up from a horrible dream, in pain, terrified of drowning. Then I felt . . . I *heard* the music . . . it's in trouble."

"The Gray Winds say that's how the River Spirits lure their victims," Lightning warned, "by singing their saddest songs. They want you, Good Eyes! Please, leave with us!"

"Someone's in danger, but it's the singer of that song, not us," Tesa insisted.

Jib nodded, thinking back to the accident and how it had affected him. Now that he was open to it, it felt right. The River Spirit . . . the Singer . . . whatever or whoever originated that song, was crying for help. He opened his mind, wanting to receive the message, the way Doctor Blanket and the Shadgui had taught him. But this was so different . . . there was none of the friendly familiarity he'd had with those beings, and it was certainly nothing like what he'd shared with Anzi. But the sadness that filled him, the heartbreaking music . . . The Singer . . . it . . . no, *he* . . . was trapped, hurt . . . frightened. The alien emotions conveyed in the song washed over him.

"Don't be afraid," Tesa signed to the cohort, but she was too distracted to be very convincing. She continued wading along the sandbar, while the others tried to hold her back. Thunder wheeled overhead, screaming in frustration.

Suddenly a spout of water geysered through the air, startling them. Tesa broke into a jog, the others chasing her.

Lightning and Flies-Too-Fast took to wing, coming down in front of her, frantic with concern. "Good Eyes, wait!" Lightning begged. "We can't let you go to the River Spirit's embrace. . . ."

"No time!" she answered, impatiently darting around them.

Jib agreed. Now that he'd stopped thinking of the song as something he could really hear, its sorrow and desperation touched him even more. He mentally searched for the notes, using them to trace the mind behind them.

Tesa stared so intently at the sounding spot that she discovered the being by tripping over him, falling facefirst into the shallow water. The feathered hands of a half-dozen Grus lifted her so quickly, she seemed to have levitated. "I'm okay," she signed rapidly. "Everyone watch your step!"

Another blast of water fountained so close to them, they all jumped, even K'heera. A huge, submerged, spade-shaped fluke rose from the dark waves and slapped the water, causing most of the cohort to leap into the air. Lightning and Flies-Too-Fast grabbed Tesa roughly and, fanning their powerful wings, started towing her backward. She fought, yanking away from them.

Then K'heera flooded the area with light from her sled. Hundreds of indistinct water creatures scurried from the blast of unexpected brightness. There, lying helpless in the shallow water, lay the massive bulk of the only creature Jib had seen on Trinity that wasn't brightly colored.

"My god," Bruce whispered, "that's the thing we hit!"

As the searchlight outlined the large oblong creature, Jib was overwhelmed with by the same powerful vertigo he'd felt on the *Demoiselle*. He swayed, ready to pitch forward.

Hurricane was suddenly beside him. "But . . . you are not-of-the-World!" the big avian protested as he steadied the young man.

*That's why I was so scared on the Demie,* Jib thought dizzily. *I wasn't dealing with my fear . . . I was receiving his!* He felt immediate empathy for the now-helpless being.

Tesa, seemingly unaffected, sloshed her way toward the head of the creature as Bruce hurried to her side.

*Is he wounded? Will he die because we hit him?* Jib wondered, concentrating on the powerful, raw emotions swamping his mind. He'd thought he was used to telepathic thought, but this wasn't anything like what he'd experienced at StarBridge. There were no words or pictures attached to these chaotic messages, no way to organize the tornado of feelings.

As the group drew closer to the creature, Jib felt . . . no, *heard* the song change somewhere inside his mind. Before, it was mostly sadness, but now there was real terror, more intense than when the ship had struck him. For all this animal knew, the aliens surrounding him were voracious predators ready to feast. For a flickering moment, Jib saw again the terrible vision of the Mate Kai, and then it was gone.

Jib pulled away from Hurricane and walked alongside the six-meter, oblong-shaped animal that resembled an odd cross between a walrus and a whale. Besides the powerful, spade-shaped fluke, his only other appendages were two flat flippers that ended in stumpier fingers. The barrel-like shoulders, round with fleshy folds, nearly hid the neckless, oblong head.

Moving closer, the young man stared at the dark bruises on the drab gray back that marked the being's contact with the

*Demoiselle*. Gouges in the sand testified to his futile attempts to rock off the entrapping sandbar.

"See, it's just an animal," Tesa signed to the cohort as they clustered around the creature. "It's not a spirit at all, just a helpless, frightened animal."

A terrible scream rent the air and before Tesa could stop her, Thunder attempted to attack the wounded back that lay inches below the water. Instantly, a blast of mental energy struck Jib like a hammer between the eyes. He fell, but Hurricane and Winter Bloom caught him. Thunder, however, was not so lucky. She shrieked and wobbled, then plummeted helplessly into the river.

"Oh, *shit!*" Jib heard Tesa yell.

"I've got her!" Bruce yelled back, forgetting in his excitement that Tesa couldn't hear him.

Jib shook his head, trying to clear it, then saw Tesa and Bruce lifting a dazed and saturated Thunder onto the back of K'heera's sled. The Maori groaned and clutched his head.

The Grus had seen enough, and started forcibly pulling Jib away. No one had to tell them that this animal wasn't helpless. Lightning, Flies-Too-Fast, and the rest of the cohort enveloped Tesa and attempted to lift her out of the water, blaring out alarm calls. The frightening cacophony was terrible and Jib would've given anything for his sound nullifiers.

"Stop it!" Tesa demanded, pulling out of her friends' hands. "We're just scaring him! He needs help." Suddenly her eyes met Jib's and it was as if someone pulled her plug. He didn't need telepathy to realize she'd just recalled Rob Gable's warnings. "Oh, Jib! You . . . shouldn't even *be* here! Are you all right?" .

He wanted to reassure her, tell her he was fine, but that last transmission had rattled him. He felt like all the blood had left his brain, leaving him giddy and high. He wished he could focus better. Tesa's expression was strained.

"I'm okay," he finally managed. "Look . . . why don't I try to make contact, try to cut through his fear, so we can help him. We can't stay out here all night fightin' this bloke. He outweighs all of us!"

Tesa set her jaw. She clearly wanted to say no, wanted to send him . . . where? Back to StarBridge? Confused feelings raced across her face, as he damned Rob Gable for telling her about that TSS crock.

"Tesa . . . let me try. It's the only thing that makes sense." Without waiting for her answer, he moved to the being's head.

"Is that wise?" K'heera suddenly barked in Simiu. He turned

toward her, surprised, while Bruce and Tesa glanced at their voders. "Are you sure its thoughts are honest? Couldn't the Grus' concern be sound? It could be a trap to lure you closer."

Jib would've been touched by K'heera's concern if he hadn't known how most Simiu felt about telepathy. They viewed it with a deep suspicion, disagreeing with the generally held notion that telepathic beings were inherently more honest than nontelepaths.

"I'm willing to take the risk," Jib decided.

As he edged closer, the creature lifted his muzzle and sounded, gulping air, spraying water all over him. His watery breath smelled like hay and crushed flowers and reminded the New Zealander, oddly, of a lamb's breath. Circular nostrils sitting atop a rounded, fleshy, bewhiskered muzzle opened wide to admit air, then closed tightly as the head sank beneath the waves. Two tiny, dark eyes were the only bright feature in that dour face. Pendulous, prehensile lips completed his odd, homely look. Not only did this creature lack color, he was burdened with being the only thing Jib had seen on Trinity that wasn't beautiful.

Wanting to reassure the being, Jib projected comforting images. Knowing nothing about his biology, he pictured the only thing he thought the animal might crave. He envisioned the huge creature swimming free through the river, then, impulsively, pictured himself swimming alongside.

So, you're the taniwha, the big water monster, eh, mate? he thought, kneeling down and gently slipping his hands under the massive head. He lent it enough support so that the nostrils were lifted above the waterline, and the creature could breathe without effort. The skin was surprisingly smooth and sleek.

The animal suddenly stopped struggling and gazed at Jib. As the young man continued the visualization, the mournful background "music" stopped. Jib smiled, thinking he was finally getting through to his new friend. "E hoa, what's your name?"

Without warning, a mental surge invaded Jib's mind, shoving into it clumsily, causing the low throb of his headache to flare into blinding pain. The mental contact was forced, heavy, too powerful for the human's limited receptive abilities. Jib grunted, his head snapping back as if struck, as he desperately tried to cope with the torrent of information.

Suddenly he knew everything and everyone, the entire herd that the taniwha called family, they who sang, the Singers. He sampled the smells and the tastes of the River, the sweetness of its food, the richness of his mother's milk, the safety of his father's protection, the happiness of his life. So simple and good was that life that Jib absorbed those memories, making them his own. What more did anyone need but the buoyancy and warmth of the great River? Jib felt euphoric, intoxicated. He groaned softly. Then, as suddenly as it started, the contact ended.

His headache was gone. Blinking, he glanced around dazedly, finally focusing on the tiny, sad eyes staring at him from just beneath the water's surface.

Tesa and Bruce were beside him, surrounded by a curtain of white feathers. "What happened?" Tesa asked worriedly. "The music stopped suddenly, and you acted like you'd been gut-punched. Are you okay?"

He wanted to nod, but thought better of it. "Give us a minute, mate," he signed. Jib could *hear* the mental tones that stood for the being's name, but there was no translation. That was all right— Taniwha couldn't understand Jib's name either. The young man peered at the bulky animal differently now, completely forgetting his immediate reaction to the homely features and the colorless hide. He knew now this was a complex, beautiful being, a member of a race so unusual, Jib still didn't know if they were animals or intelligent people.

"He's just a baby," Jib signed to the others. "He's no older than Lightning, and only about half-grown." Every member of the cohort expanded their already brilliant crowns.

"*Half*-grown!" Bruce protested. "Is he *talking* to you?"

"I can't call it language," Jib signed.

"Is he intelligent?" Tesa asked.

"I don't know," Jib answered honestly. "It might take a trained telepath to determine that."

"We should err on the side of caution," Bruce signed, and Tesa turned to the meteorologist warily. "We need to document this," he continued. "It *could* be another intelligent species!"

The Indian woman stared at the weatherman as though amazed that he would come to that conclusion. "Actually, I hadn't thought that far ahead." Then she looked back at Jib. He could see her reluctance to have him deliberately continue his contact with the creature. "I think . . . we need to solve this being's *problem*, and worry about everything else, later. Do you know what's wrong with him, Jib? Why he's even here?"

He nodded, pulling up the memories as though they were his own. "Yeah, *he's* what we ran into before bouncing off the crevasse. Banged up his shoulders. He'd snuck away from his herd, so after he was hurt . . . he wouldn't call his *mum* . . . afraid she'd be cheesed off!" Jib grinned at that. "He decided to rest in the shallows till he felt better, but waited too long and got hung up on this sandbar when the tide went out. So, now he's hurt, hungry, and scared . . ." he squinted, not wanting to recall this particular memory, "afraid that he'll fall prey to . . . the Mate Kai . . . some animal? He thinks of it as the Great Hunger. When we showed up, he thought he was about to die." Jib turned, saw something, and pointed. In the deepest channel of the River they could see two sounding spouts. "That's them! His parents!"

"Why can't we *hear* them?" Tesa asked.

"They're adults and have more control over their minds. Probably the same reason the Gray Winds only *hear* the Singers when they try to take up residence here. Projecting their thoughts to protect their territory is their only defense." Jib ran a hand over the water creature. The wet, sleek skin felt smooth and taut. "He'll die when the tide goes completely out. His own weight will suffocate him." Even now, Jib's chest tightened every time the creature gulped for air.

"We can handle that," Bruce announced. "K'heera, go back to camp, please, and take the a-grav units off the other two sleds, *and* the *Demoiselle*. They'll lift him off the bar."

"Bring us the medi-kit, too, please," Tesa asked. "He looks mammalian. We may be able to repair some of that tissue damage."

Without a word, K'heera returned to the camp, Thunder still clinging, wet and miserable, to the front of her sled, her wings outstretched as if she were some bizarre figurehead.

The cohort milled nervously around until Tesa convinced them that they should fish for breakfast, that when this was over the humans would very much need whatever food they could provide. The responsibility helped them focus on something besides their own fears and they prowled the sandbar for fish or bivalves.

It was almost dawn before the humans successfully attached the a-gravs. Tesa had activated three small cell regenerators over the sensitive wounds on the calf's back and had helped give the youngster a fair amount of pain relief.

The tide had dropped so low the Singer no longer had to lift his head to breathe, but every inhalation was now an effort. Jib's chest felt as though someone had enclosed his lungs in a vise. His limbs moved as if he were on Jupiter, not Trinity. He struggled to ease the fear radiating from Taniwha's mind as he pulled his arm out of a narrow tunnel he'd dug under the being.

"Mine's in place," he signed, gasping. "We almost ready?"

Bruce nodded, watching K'heera calibrate her voder. Her sled sat in the water, its own a-grav removed, and she worked in the water uncomplaining. Jib was impressed—he knew her people hated getting wet.

"It's time," Bruce signed. "K'heera, wait for our signal."

The older man positioned himself behind Jib and across from Tesa as they prepared to guide the large animal across the sandbar. The Grus watched, fascinated, as the humans used their machines to aid the "River Spirit." Bruce nodded at the Simiu.

Slowly the Simiu ordered the a-gravs to lift. The Singer's great tail swung up, hitting the water hard.

"Jib," Tesa signed, "calm him down!"

The young man projected images of the two of them swimming free, without a care, and finally, the creature stilled.

"Okay, everybody," Bruce signaled, "let's push." K'heera came up behind Tesa to place her palms against the alien's bulk. Gently the four moved the huge body across the wide sandbar to the River's deepest channel. Lightning and Flies-Too-Fast followed, overseeing.

Jib and Taniwha wheezed synchronously as the lack of water compounded the animal's great weight, further straining his lungs. *Just another minute*, Jib *told* him, frustrated at being unable to visualize that brief passage of time. Suddenly Jib fell, and the water closed over his head. He'd been concentrating so intently, he'd stepped right off the sandbar.

His hand slid over the bruised shoulder, and down the flat flipper. Stubby fingers wiggled against his own, then grabbed his hand. Even when his head bobbed back into the air again, the Singer clung to him, though the young man couldn't tell if that was to help him or calm the Singer's own fears. "I'm okay," Jib signaled to the others.

The huge creature settled slowly into the water as K'heera manipulated the a-gravs. Breathing easier now, Jib dived under the submerged animal and pulled the four a-gravs off his chest.

*You're free*, Jib thought, gulping air into his own tortured lungs. He was busy visualizing Taniwha swimming to safety when he was startled by two spouts of water sounding almost beside him. Instinctively, Jib backed away at the sight of the massive parent Singers. How long had they been hovering there?

The youngster released Jib's hand and darted away, nearly bowling him over with the powerful fluke. He was surprisingly graceful in his own element. Jib watched the youngster nuzzling his parents, touching them, even as the parents patted and snuffled the calf in return. Then, human hands touched him.

"You'd better get out of there, son," Bruce said, leaning over the shelf. "They might view you as a threat."

Nodding reluctantly, Jib hoisted himself back onto the sandbar. Tesa, Bruce, and even K'heera seemed inordinately pleased at the happy outcome, and the cohort, including Thunder, appeared more relaxed as they witnessed something they had no trouble understanding—the love of parents for their child.

Suddenly Taniwha left his parents and approached the sandbar, just barely lifting his head above the water. He eyed Jib squarely as he sent him back his own image—greatly enhanced. In the young Singer's mind, the two of them swam free and unfettered through the warm, sweet womb of the River.

Every hair lifted on Jib's body, and he shuddered, the odd euphoria nearly overwhelming him. Swallowing, he focused on the marble-bright eyes of his new friend, Taniwha of the Singers. "Yes," the Maori whispered softly, and before anyone could stop him, he plunged into the water just as Father Sun kissed the sky.

"Jib," shouted Bruce, "come back!"

The young man sank beneath the waves, the sound of human voices distant and muffled, of no concern. His arms and mind reached out for the huge creature as the young Singer spun in the water, suddenly as graceful and lithe as an eel.

Taniwha pressed stubby fingers against Jib's chest as a new picture formed in the human's mind. The image was clear and he realized he'd adjusted to this very different telepathy. *Yes,* he thought, knowing Taniwha, too, was learning to understand him. The calf turned so that Jib could straddle his broad back. Grabbing hold of the two flukes, Jib clung tight as the powerful swimmer sped through the water, his huge parents flanking him.

Jib's head broke the surface and he gulped air greedily as they sounded. Off in the distance, he could hear the oddly melodious warble of Tesa's voice, the voice she only used on the rarest of occasions, angrily calling his name. But the joyous music in his head quickly drowned her out as dawn broke over Trinity, and the Singers carried him west, through the warm waters of their River of Life.

# CHAPTER 7

♦

# The Probe

"Damn it!" Tesa shouted as she watched the Singers ferry Jib away. There was no music now; the big mammals were directing all their attention to the one person she wished they'd never met. To compound things, every one of their sleds was down, since they'd dismantled them to aid the calf. She had to restrain herself from diving in after the retreating figures. Instead, she begged the cohort, "Follow him before we lose them!"

The avians hesitated long enough for her to realize what she was asking. She could see it in their bodies, their crowns, their faces. The River Spirits had claimed her brother, and now she would risk *them* as well. Then, as one, they turned their heads. Thunder, still perched on K'heera's sled, had thrown her head back in her own cry. The rising suns glistened off her freshly dried bronze feathers.

"We can't just let the River Spirits take Good Eyes' brother!" the raptor signed, then launched herself after them. The Grus all glanced at one another, their fears battling their reluctance to be shown up by a Hunter.

"Flies-Too-Fast, Hurricane, and I will follow," Lightning decided. "We'll call so that you can guide Good Eyes when her machines can fly again." Without another moment's pause, the three oldest Grus ran across the sandbar and lifted into the air.

When Tesa turned back to Bruce and K'heera, she could see them working feverishly to get K'heera's sled back on line. Within seconds it lifted, dripping, from the mud. Without thinking, Tesa moved to mount it, but Bruce stopped her.

"Whoa, there, friend," he signed. "You're not goin' on this wild critter chase alone."

She started to argue, but he interrupted her.

"We're goin' back to camp," he insisted. "K'heera and I can get the *Demoiselle* in the air just as quick as we did this sled. I'll grab a few things and we'll *all* go."

He was just following regulations, she knew. Szu-yi had really tightened them, following the lone expedition last year that had resulted in the appearance of Tesa's death. Frustrated, the woman peered over her shoulder at the receding flyers.

Bruce had to touch her to get her attention. "I can't believe the Singers will hurt him, Tesa."

She met his eyes, remembering all at once that she was the only one who knew about the possibility of Jib's having TSS. Finally, she signed, "We don't know that. They didn't have much trouble dropping Thunder, did they? Let's *hurry!*"

It seemed like hours before they were finally in the *Demoiselle* and airborne. The Suns were bright now as two humans and a Simiu traveled west along the River, farther inland. The remaining five cohort members surrounded Tesa on her sled, as if protecting her, but all they managed to do was limit her visibility. She could feel their calls as they responded to the faint sounds of their friends, who were now miles away.

Finally, she could see Thunder wheeling above the River, the Grus circling in a wider arc below her. The Singers had stopped, gathering with others of their kind in a wide bend where orange-leafed water plants bloomed thickly. Even from the air, Tesa was impressed by the size of the great herd as they grazed among the lovely purple flowers. In the midst of the huge gray creatures Tesa spied Jib's bobbing head.

She pointed him out to Bruce and K'heera, signaled for her cohort to stay behind, then dropped out of formation. She took a deep breath, forcing herself to be calm, and projected mental images of the same kind of parental concern for Jib she'd received from the young Singer's parents. She couldn't afford to have them affect her judgment while she flew.

Hovering low over the herd, she was startled by their numbers, as she watched them watching her. Jib never even noticed her. He was treading water, turning this way and that, touching the massive beings and being touched by them in return, grinning rapturously. She might as well have been invisible.

Tesa opened her mind as Doctor Blanket had taught her, and the music came to her again, only now it was lighthearted tunes ringing with gladness and curiosity. The herd was fascinated by Jib, the novelty of communicating with a noncompetitive, nonpredatory creature completely charming them. Each of the large beasts impatiently waited his or her turn to touch Jib's mind, to have a chance to say "hello" to the unusual stranger.

Tesa's heart sank. If Jib *did* have TSS, this was like dropping an alcoholic into a wine vat.

She brought the sled up beside him slowly, just inches above the water. She'd seen how frantic the calf could get when startled, and didn't want to risk having Jib crushed in a panic.

Finally, she caught his attention.

"Tesa!" he cried aloud, grinning like a fool. "*E hoa*! Come on in, the water's fine! I'll introduce you!"

*He can't even remember to sign to me*, she thought. The water *was* warm, but it wasn't body temperature. Jib's lips were blue. She glanced up, saw the *Demoiselle* hovering nearby. Ever the scientist, Bruce was filming their interaction with the herd. K'heera gazed around, amazed.

Tesa leaned over the edge of her sled. "Jib, come on. You've been in the water too long. You'll get hypothermia if you don't come out now." He hesitated, his expression confused. She realized he was having trouble with the concept, probably because the Singers couldn't understand it. Her jaw clenched. "You'll get sick if you don't come out, Jib. You need some warm food and time to dry off. You can go back in later. Come on!" She offered him her hand, and finally, he took it.

Once he was beside her on the sled, she slapped on the forcefield to ensure that he couldn't leave. She signaled to Bruce, and they gained altitude until they'd rejoined the cohort. Then they turned east, back to their camp. The whole time, Jib leaned over the side, waving at the Singers, completely ignoring her.

Some of the Singers followed them for a while but, reluctant to leave their food, eventually returned to the herd. Jib visibly deflated as the distance between them grew.

When they landed on the white sand beach by their camp, Tesa handed Jib the blanket she'd brought. He wrapped it around his shivering shoulders with casual disinterest, even as the long, curling tendrils of his hair dripped over it. Tesa's eyes flared with frustration and anger, though she couldn't say exactly who or what she was angry at. "Are you all right?"

He nodded quickly, looking out over the River, watching for Singers. She stood stock-still in front of him, waiting for him to really *see* her, remember she was there. Finally, his expression cleared. He blinked, meeting her eyes.

"I didn't mean to frighten you," he signed, at last, "but if I said I was sorry, it'd be a bloody lie and you'd know it. Being pulled through the water by that young pup, communicating with him and his people . . . this has been the most incredible thing I've ever experienced. I'm hardly sorry."

Tesa did not respond. Thunder's shadow crisscrossed over her, and Jib looked up, hearing her cries. His eyes returned to the River more slowly this time.

"To them, that's the River of Life," he signed. "This time of year, the sea starts to grow cold. The River stays warm, feeds them, nurtures their children. It's their River."

Bruce came up behind him, carrying out dry clothes. "Better put these on, son," he signed. "They've got warmers in them. You're pretty blue."

Jib nodded gratefully and began stripping the wet clothes off from under his blanket, and redonning the dry ones. The warmers would engage immediately on contact with his chilled skin. Glancing around, Tesa realized that K'heera was still sitting in the *Demoiselle* where Bruce had parked it near the shelters. The Simiu was not watching them, as though completely disinterested in anything the humans might be doing.

The cohort suddenly parachuted to a landing around Tesa, blowing sand against her legs. She could feel no vibrations and realized they'd curtailed their normally raucous landing in deference to the serious talk she was having with Jib. As soon as they were on the ground, the Aquila joined them. The young avians stared at Jib until finally Lightning stepped forward.

"Good Eyes' Brother Jib, you are the only being on the World that has ever willingly swum with the River Spirits! Do you still have your soul?"

Looking into Jib's eyes, Tesa wondered about that herself.

"Yes, Lightning," Jib signed respectfully. "My soul's completely intact. These Singers aren't Spirits; they're just people who sing mind-to-mind. They mean no one harm. They only want to protect their River, even as you protect your own territories. They protect it differently, that's all. You don't have to fear them, just respect their River."

The avians stared at one another, their crowns shrunken and dulled. They didn't know what to think about that.

Tesa wanted to discuss the effect the massive onslaught of raw telepathy might have had on Jib, but felt constrained by her audience. If he did have TSS, it was no one else's business. She would save that talk for later; however, his behavior was another matter. "Well, Jib, you *did* frighten me! We know *nothing* about these creatures. They could be carnivores. . . ."

"Oh, no," Jib assured her. "They're harmless. They're veg . . . herbivores." He glanced around to see if K'heera might be watching. Simiu didn't appreciate the human tendency to equate vegetarianism with a pacifistic nature.

"Did *they* tell you that?" Bruce asked.

He fugued out for a moment, unsure. "I . . . just *know* it now."

Tesa nodded, unable to suppress the need to vent her anger. "*Know* this. That was a damned foolish stunt. You're in the wilderness. Just because this species isn't predatory doesn't mean there isn't a nearby predator capable of killing them."

"I thought it was our *job* to foster new contacts on Trinity," he argued.

"He's got a point there, Tesa," Bruce signed. "You've taken plenty of risks yourself when you thought it would pay off."

She shot the weatherman a venomous look.

Jib scowled, as though trying to recall something. "Still, you've got a point, mate. I felt something in my mind . . . just before we hit Taniwha, the calf, when Bruce and I were in the *Demie*. Something the Singers are terrified of . . . I can only call it the Mate Kai . . . the Great Hunger." He turned to his audience, as though framing what to tell them. "I can't really see a clear picture of it, just that it's huge—bigger than them, with lots of teeth. An eating machine more primitive than a shark."

The Grus watched him curiously, their crowns brightening.

"Perhaps," Frost Moon suggested, "*that* creature is the *evil* River Spirit, and *these* beings are kindly Spirit Singers?"

Jib turned to Tesa for help, but she let him see he was willing on his own. "I can't answer that. I can't *see* this thing clearly enough to know much about it. It was a big fear in Taniwha's mind, but far less distinct to his parents. They consider these waters totally safe . . . or *did* until we bumped into their baby. The predators live in the sea and occasionally follow them into the River, but . . . not recently." He glanced at Tesa wryly. "I'll try to find out more in my next contact. . . ."

"*Next* contact?" she signed. "What next contact?" TSS or not, she couldn't run the risk. "Meg will be here soon. . . ."

Jib looked like he'd been slapped. "You're still sending me up to the *Crane*?" He held up his hands, then signed quickly, making sure K'heera couldn't observe him. "I know I was eager to go before, but things have changed. I need to stay and make more contacts with the Singers. I'll be cautious, I promise."

Tesa suddenly found it hard to be objective. This was the kind of thing every StarBridge student dreamed of, to make a First Contact—get to know the people, find out who they were, learn their culture, their language. She remembered the moment Thunder's mother first spoke to her—she'd felt the same euphoria . . . and that had nothing to do with TSS! Yet, she was responsible for

Jib's well-being. She had to be cautious. "I know how you feel, but . . . this isn't why you were sent here."

Jib's heavily lashed eyes darkened. "I know, but . . ."

"You're supposed to be doing a pair project," Tesa reminded him. She felt self-conscious having this conversation with everyone hovering around them, but Jib needed to learn this now. The others politely turned their attention elsewhere. "You've stopped working with K'heera. The two of you are now pursuing *different* interests. Is that what you want?"

Jib pondered that for a while. Finally, he signed, "Yes."

Tesa's eyes opened in surprise.

"I think this whole plan of Rob Gable's and Ambassador Dhurrrkk's was a mistake from the beginning," Jib declared. "She didn't want to come, she has no interest in us. . . ."

"*You* were supposed to be the counterbalance to K'heera's lacks, but you gave up on her," Tesa reminded him. "It may have been a mistake to send you both here, but I'm not ready to admit that yet. If the Singers are intelligent, it'll be wonderful, Jib, but they'll always be here. K'heera needs to have contact with humans *now*, and you've been letting Bruce do your job." She glared at the weatherman, daring him to interfere, but he had wisely turned his attention to his shoes.

"And my going to the *Crane* will be the answer?" Jib asked.

"Only in part. You have to work *with* K'heera. You have to make a contact with *her*. *You* have to make this assignment a success." Tesa recognized his expression—it was the one he made whenever she prodded him to do things he didn't want to, but knew he should.

After a tense moment, he nodded abruptly. "Right. I'll give it a fair go." Then he turned toward the River.

None-So-Pretty stepped up to him, openly curious. "Can you really talk mind-to-mind with the Spirit Singers?" The others seemed just as interested in his answer.

"Not really," Jib admitted. "We'll need to bring in a true telepath for that. But I can *hear* them, and communicate a little. It's sort of like trading *feelings* more than talking."

Flies-Too-Fast peered at Jib with one eye. "Can you *hear* spirits behind those feelings?"

Tesa knew that Jib would have normally been amused by such a suggestion. While he respected the Grus' beliefs, he had no primal faith of his own. But the look in the avian's eye, and the way he phrased the question, made Jib hesitate. Tesa had recognized an almost spiritual feeling when that alien mind touched hers. For

Jib, that would be something he couldn't analyze or explain away.
It would be a new experience for him.

She saw him touch the tiki hanging around his neck. "Maybe . . ." he signed, "but if so, they're friendly spirits."

K'heera ran her fingers over the *Demoiselle*'s control panel,
enjoying the feel of the well-designed board against her leathery
palms. Its design was a variation on a classic Simiu one. It never
bothered humans to use the best of other cultures for their own
benefit. Her own people were often held back by a stubborn
chauvinism, insisting on using only their own products.

Bruce had told her that he still hoped to go after the meteor
later today. He asked her if she'd accompany him on the dive,
and she agreed. Bruce wanted to be sure K'heera still felt she had
some purpose on Trinity.

The young Simiu stared out over the wide river. As much as she
tried not to think of it, and as much as Bruce tried to distract her
with talk of work, she couldn't deny the fact that the humans had
made yet another First Contact right in front of her. What would
her family say? Especially when they discovered—and K'heera
had no doubt that they would—that she'd nearly slept through the
whole thing. She'd tried to ignore the tenuous mental song that
finally woke her. But only the Grus seemed to understand the
natural aversion she felt to receiving that song. To have someone
else's thoughts in your head was as unnatural as seeing someone
else wearing your face, K'heera thought.

She glanced sideways at Jib, sitting at the river's edge. His
glassy-eyed rapturous look made her flesh crawl.

She had thought that "tomorrow"—now, today—she would
begin making amends to Jib . . . try to get closer to him. Seeing
how easily he had responded to the Singers shattered that hope. It
did something else, too—it made her understand why her people
would always have problems with First Contacts, and why they
frequently had problems dealing with the CLS.

Her people just weren't adaptable enough, they were too ethno-
centric. The humans were so malleable, so eager to contact other
races. Her people had always viewed it as a worthwhile task, but
they didn't have that eagerness to accept an alien as a friend, as
an equal, the way so many humans did. Ambassador Dhurrrkk'
did, but he was different from anyone in her family.

K'heera felt despondent. She tried to look forward to diving
after the meteor, but basically once you'd captured one chunk of
space rock, you'd captured them all.

She thought of Ambassador Dhurrrkk' again, and his high hopes for her. He'd spent a lot of time with her, flattering her, acting the uncle, trying to open her mind to opportunities this task might supposedly give her.

He had helped discover the planet Avernus and its race of intelligent fungi. Avernus was so small, and Trinity so big . . .

Big enough for the Grus, the Aquila, and now the Singers. K'heera followed Jib's gaze over the water, wondering what the chances were that there might be another intelligent race somewhere on this planet that *she* might contact? *Slim to none*—as the humans would say. But it would take nothing less than a First Contact to help the Harkk'etts. Without that, K'heera would return to Hurrreeah with even greater dishonor than when she left. The hopelessness of it was as suffocating as water rushing over her head.

Tesa sat cross-legged in the shade of her lean-to, her woven feather shirt in her lap. Holding a comb that Taller had made for her, she used it with a dressing made from the hearts of reeds to preen the shirt's feathers. Four of her cohort—Frost Moon, None-So-Pretty, Snowberry, and Lightning—lay sleeping, tightly bunched around her, their legs folded under them, their necks intertwined. Two had their heads hidden in her lap under her shirt. Outside the shelter, Thunder perched on the roof, while the rest of the cohort preened, except for Hurricane and Flies-Too-Fast, whose turn it was to guard.

Lunch had been hard-shelled fruits that fell from nearby trees, and a crunchy seaweed that Jib said was one of the Singers' favorites. It *was* tasty, and for once did not cause any recriminations from the Simiu.

The Simiu. Tesa stopped her preening, and stared out over the River. It was sixteen-twenty. Bruce and K'heera had been gone about six hours. She was glad Bruce had taken K'heera to go after the meteor—the tension level had dropped dramatically as soon as they had clambered into the small vessel.

She didn't know what to think about Bruce. She'd been surprised when he'd easily accepted the possibility of the Singers' intelligence. He'd been really solicitous of K'heera, too. It seemed as if he'd really pushed his prejudices aside.

Peripherally, she realized the avians that had been preening stopped when she did, gazing where she gazed. Smiling, she went back to her shirt. It made them uneasy when the *Demoiselle* went below.

Her eyes moved to the River's edge. Jib lay wrapped in his blanket in a sandy, sunny spot, catching up on some of the sleep he'd lost last night. This would be a good time to have a private talk with him, before the *Demoiselle* returned.

She folded the shirt Weaver had made for her, put it in a mesh bag, and hung it from the ceiling. All she really needed to wear in the warm tropical sun was her aged, cut-down StarBridge jumpsuit. It was barely more than a camisole now, and even the indestructible logo of the rainbow bridge spanning planets that sat over the breast pocket was cracked and faded. Gently, Tesa extricated herself from the mass of warm feathers and left the shelter, signaling to the others to stay behind. The spot left vacant by her absence filled in quickly, and only Lightning watched her approach the sleeping Jib.

The young man blinked as her shadow crossed his face, then glanced around disoriented, finally turning toward the River. As soon as he did, water spouts sounded in the deepest channel . . . ten . . . twenty—Tesa lost count. Opening her mind, she felt their music wash over her. It was different from last night, more like conversation. Or maybe she was more accustomed to it.

*Where are we going? Are you hungry? This plant is sweet.* It wasn't that simple, but it resembled that kind of exchange.

Jib turned to her, that other-worldly expression on his face. "Can you *hear* them?"

Tesa nodded. It was a special, intimate contact, and she regretted deeply that she had to ask him to give it up.

"I *heard* them even in my sleep," he signed. "It was hard to rest . . . but . . . still, very enjoyable. Like someone putting dreams right into your head."

"Jib. . . ." Her signs forced his attention back to her. "We've got to talk. . . ."

His face was innocent of expression, as if he couldn't imagine what she wanted.

"I want to be honest with you," she told him. "I want to be sure you know why I'm sending you to the *Singing Crane*."

His expression darkened. "We've already had this talk. . . ."

"Not completely. I didn't want . . . to discuss this in front of Bruce. I'm worried about you . . . about . . . your health."

Now he only seemed confused.

"Your *mental* health."

"Oh, come on . . . not *that* again. . . ." His expression changed. As if something had just occurred to him, he asked, "You're not planning on keeping me there for our whole stay, are you?"

She'd hoped he wouldn't ask her that question.

"Tesa, you've got to give me a fair go! It's *my* contact!"

"I know. And I know how disappointed you must feel. But before I can let you continue communicating with the Singers, Jib, I've got to talk to Rob."

"You *know* what he'll say!"

"No, I don't," she insisted. "You said yourself that telepathy with these creatures was different from anything you've experienced. I agree with that. There may be no effect on a TSS-sensitive individual . . . or the effect may be worse. I can't use you as a guinea pig to test that out. What kind of a . . . *friend* would I be if I did?"

He seemed crushed, and Tesa was surprised at how little he could hide it. After mulling things for a few moments, he signed, "Right, then, I'll oblige you, mate . . . on one condition."

She peered at him warily, agreeing to nothing.

"Ask Rob to send Anzia to 'talk' to the Singers. She's got a natural rapport with nonverbal beings, she's a *real* telepath, and she loves the water! If she were here, at least I'd get to *see* and talk to her through hologram . . . and I could work with the Singers through her. I could stay on the *Crane* and handle documentation, stuff like that. At least I wouldn't be out of the loop. Then, if I could get someone to clear me of this bogus health problem, I could go right back to work. If *you* ask for it, Tesa, they'll give it to you. Come on!"

She thought of herself being pulled away from Taller, Weaver, and Lightning, thought of never flying with the cohort again. She nodded. "Okay, Jib. It's a fair trade. I'll push for it. *If* you'll fulfill your obligations with K'heera."

He nodded agreeably this time. "I promise. Still, it's hard for me to believe any effort of mine will change her much."

"Keep that attitude, and you're bound to fail," Tesa admonished him.

Jib turned his head abruptly, and stood, pointing. Tesa noticed the avians all respond to his alertness as, in the midst of the herd of beings, the *Demoiselle* slowly broke the surface.

K'heera piloted it to the beach, setting it on the sand. In front of the small ship, grapplers held something in a safety container, but the transparent receptacle was full of lemon-yellow seaweed and water, making it impossible to see the prize.

Bruce was the first to open his door. He nearly leaped from the small ship, shouting and signing, "Wait'll you see it!"

"What happened?" Tesa asked. "What did you find?"

Bruce pointed at K'heera. "She saw it before I did. Tell 'em, l'il darlin'."

K'heera's vivid purple eyes glanced at Bruce quizzically when he mouthed that strange endearment. "Well . . ." she signed hesitantly, "it *was* quite a surprise. You see, it's not a meteor at all . . . it's an alien probe."

The words struck Tesa like a blow. Like an ominous flashback, Old Bear's face floated before her, his hands saying, "There was blood in the water, and something un-Worldly. . . ." Was that from one of her vague, formless dreams?

"Whose probe?" she finally asked. The cohort slowly gathered around her. She felt the distinctive texture of the Aquila's feathers brush her thigh, even as Lightning's neck rested against her shoulder. They'd read her body language; they knew something was wrong.

"That's just it!" Bruce signed delightedly. "We don't know! Some unknown race sent an exploratory probe out like we used to in the twentieth century. Once we get this baby to the *Singing Crane*, we can figure out how old it is, maybe trace its origin."

"Its shape and style is similar to some of the early probes my people sent out," K'heera signed. "If there are other similarities, then the satellite may have its own power source, its own internal computer and library."

Even Jib grew interested. "D'you think we might figure out what sector it's from? Could it . . . lead us to *another* Contact?"

"Now, that's getting ahead of ourselves," Bruce told him. "But many of Earth's old probes actually had solar system maps on them in case intelligent people found them. There could be something similar on this, or maybe in its programming. It'll sure keep us busy for a while. It's some discovery."

Tesa should've felt as excited as Jib, Bruce, and K'heera, but she didn't. Instead, she was overwhelmed with dread. With all the celestial orbs in this solar system, why had that thing come to Trinity? Something about the probe and her ugly, formless dreams made her shiver with a dark premonition.

"Let's look at the container's diagnostics," Bruce signed. He and K'heera removed the bulky container from the ship's grapples and hoisted it to a flat spot. Bruce touched the control panel on the front of the clear container and watched its scrolling information. "Well, it's not emitting radiation," he read, "so we can drain the seawater."

He tapped a sequence on the panel, and the sandy water leached away onto the beach. Bright orange algae and yellow seaweed slowly sank to the bottom of the container, except for one long strand that draped itself decorously around the probe.

"The two months it's been underwater have given it a beard," Bruce signed as the multicolored organisms on the surface of the object began to sag without their watery support. "There are still clean places, though. See those hieroglyphics?"

Tesa saw some unusual writing embossed on the artificial surface. The probe itself was not much bigger than a soccer ball, and most of it was smooth. Growing increasingly uncomfortable, she glanced away, only to realize that she was surrounded by avians, who were peering at the thing uneasily. She knew she should reassure them . . . but couldn't find the signs.

"I can't wait to get inside it," Bruce added. "Haven't you heard from Meg yet, Tesa?" The weatherman's question pulled the young woman away from her thoughts.

*Typical*, Tesa thought. He hadn't noticed the biologist's absence before, but *now* it was an emergency. "She didn't think she could get here before fourteen hundred, and it's only two hours past that. You know she always underestimates how long a task takes. Manufacturing new parts takes time, and who knows what the story is on that silent satellite?"

Bruce waved an impatient hand. "We've got a real find here, and we're stuck staring at it. She can forget the parts if they're not ready, and just pick us up!" Lifting his voder, he tapped in a sequence. "Oh, for cryin' . . . Look at this!"

Tesa glanced at her own device.

"The personnel you have called are not available at this time," the *Crane*'s computer reported. "Please leave a message."

"They must be asleep!" Bruce signed irritably. "It'd be just like Meg to work all night, then spend the day in the sack."

"So, just override the 'don't disturb' and have the computer wake them," Jib suggested. Tesa smiled. It was everyone's favorite trick on StarBridge.

Bruce nodded, tapping in a sequence. Then he tapped in another. And another.

The original computer message was still on screen. Tesa stared at the small voder, feeling oddly light-headed.

"Meg's gotten too damned good with the *Crane* computer," Bruce decided. "But I'll be leaving one *cranky* message!"

"No!" Tesa signed impulsively, before the weatherman could log it in. "Don't, Bruce. Just end transmission."

He regarded her oddly, as did Jib and K'heera. "Why not?"

*Yeah*, she asked herself, *why not*?

Suddenly Lightning interrupted. "Don't send the message, Fisher, please. Good Eyes has a good reason for asking, even if *she* doesn't know what it is."

Flies-Too-Fast ceremoniously lowered his head in agreement, and the rest of the cohort followed. Tesa faced them gratefully. They were Trinity's own people; their request couldn't be easily ignored.

"Sure thing," the weatherman agreed amiably, but his eyes held disappointment. "But Meg and Szu-yi better get here soon!"

Tesa touched Lightning and Thunder absently as Bruce and K'heera stared at the alien probe and Jib turned his own gaze toward the sprays of the splashing, playful Singers. Unable to understand her own seemingly irrational fears, she focused instead on Meg's and Szu-yi's imminent arrival. When they took the strange probe off Trinity, maybe her concerns would go with it. That was something to look forward to.

# CHAPTER 8

◆

# Lene

The Suns' light dimmed as it slanted through the tule mat walls of Taller's A-framed shelter. The avian leader ran his feathered fingers over an ancient, preserved buffalo skin as Old Bear sat beside him, interpreting its faded pictographs. At the same time, Weaver's calendar cloak was spread across Teacher's lap while she translated the symbols she'd made in its weave. Teacher held an "ultraviolet lamp" over the picture that signified the Year the Humans Came, recording the revealed image on her small wrist voder. The four elders often shared cultural exchanges in the late afternoon and Taller always looked forward to that.

But finally, Teacher stood, stretching and rubbing her back. "Forgive me, my friends, I've got to move around a little."

"Then, let's step outside and enjoy the passing of the Suns," Weaver suggested.

Old Bear smiled, then nodded politely to Teacher, holding the entrance open for her. She accepted his assistance graciously, without ever meeting his eyes. Of all the humans Taller had met, he found the genteel formality of these two the most charming. They were always unfailingly polite with one another, calling each other by their most honorific, formal names—"Mister Bigbee" and "Missus Lewis." It had something to do with cultural taboos and relationships, since Old Bear was Good Eyes' paternal grandfather, and Teacher her maternal grandmother.

The foursome stepped onto the nest shelter's platform to watch Father and Mother Sun drop toward the horizon. The Child Sun appeared at night now, enjoying its independence from its parents, just like Good Eyes and Lightning.

Taller realized that the humans' eyes were glistening as they gazed at the sunset. Old Bear had once said he'd thought the past could never be recovered, but that being on the World made him question that. Taller was proud the humans loved his World.

As the Suns slipped below the horizon, Teacher glanced at her voder. "I'm surprised we haven't heard anything from Meg and Szu-yi. They were supposed to call when they left the space station for Florida."

Old Bear agreed. "It's close to twenty hundred—almost twenty-four hours since they left here. Call them."

Teacher tapped her device and waited.

Just then, a distant alarm call split the still air, making the two avians lift their heads. Fall brought predators, and this call came from the edge of the marsh, near the base of the bluff. Another group picked up the cry, passing it on.

A young cohort burst from the reeds and circled in the air, calling loudly, nearly panicked. Taller's feathers lifted, his crown expanding. The alarm spread, coming now from a thickly occupied area just beyond the bluff. A mass of Blue Cloud people rose into the sky, turning, somersaulting, circling. Short vees of waterfowl joined them, squawking rudely.

Old Bear touched Taller; when the avian turned he saw the human holding "binoculars." The human male pointed at the bluff that held the humans' shelter. Taller followed his gaze.

Something was walking along the bluff, something on two legs—but not human. This creature's skin and clothing was brightly colored in blue and red, and its head was oddly shaped. Taller bristled, his feathers standing out. No one had asked him to permit visitors. From what strange world had these emerged? "Who are those beings?" he demanded.

"I don't know, my friend," Old Bear answered simply, holding Taller's gaze. "They're not members of the CLS. . . ."

Taller's crown flared even more. "I thought everyone who traveled among the stars belonged to that flock."

"So far, all the star-traveling beings that have been discovered *do* belong. These must come from a place the CLS has never been." Old Bear stared at the bluff, troubled.

"This is still the World of the White Wind people," Taller signed. "I'll greet these visitors, and ask their business."

Suddenly Teacher barred Taller's way. "Wait! I'm getting an odd message when I call the space station. If those beings were there last night, when Meg and Szu-yi arrived . . ."

It had never occurred to Taller that his friends could be in danger in their sky shelter. "Are these creatures predators?"

"I don't know," signed Teacher, "but . . . I can't reach Meg or Szu-yi. If these beings wanted peaceful relations, they'd have contacted us from their ship. To just *land* here is aggressive. This must have something to do with Meg and Szu-yi's silence."

"I agree," Old Bear signed, looking through his binoculars. "They look like they're searching for something."

Taller gazed again at the strange beings converging on the far bluff, just as three yearlings parachuted to a landing right on his platform. Their rude arrival was so shocking, he stretched his neck to attack.

"Forgive us, Taller," the oldest signed, as they all lowered their heads appeasingly, "but something terrible is happening!"

"Tell me," the avian leader ordered, relaxing his posture.

"Strangers are in the marsh! The Blue Cloud people warned us as they crept up on the bluff. When they found the humans' shelter empty, they invaded our marsh."

The youngster's feathers fluffed out, even as his two companions stood nervously staring at the bluff. "We spoke to them, but they tried to capture us with weapons. We got away, sounding the alarm. Then they continued through the marsh until they came to Snowberry's parents' shelter."

"They have an egg ready to hatch!" Weaver signed.

"Not anymore," the youngster signed. "Snowberry's father, Cloud, stood his ground, calling a challenge. We all thought his great voice would make them collapse but nothing happened. They pointed their weapons. He fell, and they took his body away."

"They killed him?" Taller asked.

"His eyes were open, but he was limp and helpless. They took Small Shell, Cloud's mate, as she sat on the nest, then gathered up their egg. At the next shelter, the pair fought while their flightless chick ran, but they captured all of them anyway. They're also taking Blue Cloud people, and other marsh-dwellers. What can we do, Taller?"

The leader observed the small figures on the bluff. What did they want with his people, the marsh animals, and the humans?

Abruptly he ushered everyone inside his shelter. He turned to Teacher. "Can you contact Good Eyes?"

"I'm afraid to," she signed. "It could alert those aliens to her presence. They could trace the signal."

Taller peered out his doorway as Old Bear signed to him, "If you're thinking of fighting these beings here, I'd advise against it. We don't know anything about them, we can't communicate with them, and they're obviously prepared to use force against us. That gives them a big advantage."

The old avian listened to the alarm calls ringing his territory and made a decision. "The flock will have to leave," he told the youngsters. "Everyone, young and old. We'll find Good Eyes. She'll know what to do."

"Once we find her," Teacher agreed, "we might be able to safely get word to the Cooperative League of Systems."

"Will *they* wage war on these invaders?" Taller asked.

The two humans seemed unsure. "In honesty, Taller," Old Bear signed, "I don't know what they'll do. I can't even tell you how long they'll take to get here."

"Then we can't depend on them to deal with these new beings. We'll have to do it ourselves. We'll take the flock south, gathering our people as we go. The Travelers will spread word of the trouble that's come to the World." The leader thought of something else. "You and Teacher have only one flying device. Will that be enough?"

"It'll have to be," Teacher signed. "However, our things are all on the bluff. We have no blankets, no extra clothes."

"You will have all the cloaks you need," Taller assured her. He turned to the yearlings. "Go to every corner of the territory, every nest shelter. Tell the people we're leaving, *now*. Tell them to gather their cloaks, to wrap their eggs and carry them in mesh bags, to do the same with their youngest hatchlings. We're going south."

"But what of older, flightless chicks?" the youngster asked.

The question tore Taller's heart. "Tell their parents to hide with them in the forests. They can travel on foot to Blackfeather's river until their chicks can fly. Hurry. Let me hear your call ringing through the marsh. If all the people lift their voices, that great sound might conquer these beings."

Weaver was already gathering up her cloaks as Teacher helped tie them in thick rolls.

"We'll leave from the rear of the nest shelter," Taller told Old Bear, "and fly low until we are far from the marsh. Then we can spiral up for altitude. We can't risk them seeing you."

"Taller," Old Bear signed, "you're taking a terrible risk flying with us. Teacher and I could surrender. . . ."

Taller gave Old Bear "the look." The human returned it unflinchingly. "You are part of our family through the blood of your granddaughter. Are you ready to leave?"

Old Bear smiled. "Yes, old friend. I'm ready."

Weaver carefully removed a tule mat from the back of the nest shelter, opening it, while Taller went outside to retrieve the diamond-shaped flying sled. Flaring his wings, he blocked the device as he clumsily hauled it inside the slitted doorway, using hands that had never been designed for heavy lifting.

"I've got it," Old Bear signed, taking it from him and turning it on. The predominantly white sled had black tips that imitated Grus wingtip markings. Covered with hatching cloaks, the humans would be hard to spot from the air, once surrounded by the flock. Old Bear led the now-hovering sled over to Teacher, then helped her load the cloaks onto it. Old Bear rolled his buffalo skin, covering it with a cloak. Weaver took two cloaks and helped the humans fasten them on like robes, to help disguise them, as well as keep them warm during the flight. Within minutes, they were ready to step out the new back door.

Taller regarded his nest shelter with one golden eye. It held the best weavings he and Weaver had ever done. If there was to be another egg, he'd hoped Weaver would lay it here. . . .

The crystal wind chimes given to them by the people of Earth spun and rang delicately from the breeze gusting in through the new doorway. The old avian felt a fierce resentment at being forced to leave this special home.

Turning, he stepped onto the back of his platform. The humans were already on their sled, sitting tight, back to front. To have to travel so intimately would be a strain on them. More importantly, they'd have trouble reaching altitude that way.

The sky filled with Taller's people as they left their homes in family groups of twos and threes, and the larger vees of young cohorts. The humans touched their ears, wincing from the intense sound, but the wonderful noise filled Taller up, made him younger, stronger. He threw back his head, called to his people, and his mate joined him. They were not leaving forever!

The Wind people would defeat these invaders, with their elaborate machines and their ability to live without air. They would defeat them and send them back to their airlessness. All the World's people would rise up until the skies were black with them, and drive these creatures away. Taller made this promise to the Suns, his people, and his World, then launched himself off the platform. Spreading his great wings, he headed south.

First-in-Conquest Atle ran a hand over the rough-hewn wood of the plaque mounted beside the door of the primitive alien shelter. His translator told him the plaque was a memorial. An interesting death ritual, he thought, something the cultural anthropologists would enjoy investigating when there was time.

He watched the mass of huge avians flying south. They had moved too quickly here, but these creatures were a dominant species and not hard to find. The waves of sound they emitted washed over Atle, but he simply lowered his hearing when the volume became uncomfortable.

Entering the alien building, he wandered around, examining the interior. He was pleased that they'd captured so many specimens to study, not only the huge avians, but smaller birds, water-dwellers, and insects. The insects looked promising, considering how many there were.

However, he'd been bitterly disappointed that none of the space-faring humans had been here. According to Dacris, the records said there were five more humans and a Simiu still on the planet's surface. Well, his team would stay here a few days anyway and learn what they could. Maybe they could add to the data the Troubadour was sending them.

Atle examined work areas sectioned off by movable walls and furniture; there was clutter everywhere. It was a strange way to do research. He wondered if the varied arrangements of things was aesthetic. Except for this building, the humans didn't show much artistic ability, seeming to prefer things that were as blandly monochrome as they were.

Drin, the doctor Atle had put in charge of this expedition, stepped out from behind his sterile field. One of the Hooded, Drin was brown like Rand, but also had the searing orange head coloring more typical of his people. The doctor signaled to Atle to don protective garb and join him.

"See this, Glorious First," Drin bade eagerly as Atle adjusted the form-fitting gloves, filmy coverall, and mask. On a portable table lay one of the immense, white avians. It seemed smaller now, with its legs folded and its neck coiled back on itself. The eyes were open, an inner eyelid half covering the golden orb, and they slowly tracked his entrance.

The doctor stretched out one of the huge wings, spreading the flight feathers apart. "These three are fingers, just as the Second said. And their nests are lined with this." He gently returned the wing to its folded position, and turned to another table, taking a heaped mass of whiteness from it. Shaking it out, he revealed a rectangular, feathered cloth. "The Troubadour tells us this is woven, so these creatures are capable of work."

"They're also capable of flight," Atle sang. "Yet, if you damaged their wings, you would also limit their ability to work."

"You can cauterize the feather growth cells," the doctor assured him. "They'll never grow back, and the avian will be flightless forever."

Atle's color brightened. "Could they be trained to do something besides this weaving?"

"They have potential," the doctor assured him. "The question is, can they be conquered? The records say they are primitive hunter-gatherers who fight for territory. The medical logs indicate we might be able to refine a few drugs for them, but their high metabolism could make them hard to maintain as docile workers. It might not be worth the expense."

*When our ancestors conquered races*, Atle thought, *they had no accountants. Now everything must be cost-effective.* But he also knew how difficult hunter-gatherers could be to conquer. "What about protein production?"

"Come see this." The doctor led the First to another table, and handed him a hollow, oblong object.

"Egg-layers?" the First sang, examining the mottled shell.

The doctor waved a hand at a specimen container. In the clear preservative floated a round, rich, yellow yolk and a spidery map of blood vessels. Floating against the yolk was a small embryo. "I've analyzed the muscle tissue of this embryo and its parent. Perfectly edible. Potentially, we could collect semen from worker males and inseminate worker females while artificially increasing egg production."

*Yes*, thought Atle, *that might work.* They already did that with the Industrious, using hormones to force increased egg production from mentally stunted Swimmers, their most prolific egglayers. Incubating those fertile eggs made embryos rich in protein. "You've done this work quickly. You'll be commended."

"In fairness, Glorious First," the doctor trilled, "my work was greatly assisted by the staff on the space station."

"Yes," Atle agreed. "Second-in-Conquest Dacris may earn a promotion for their work." Atle would like that. It would get Dacris out from under his command.

Drin made no comment, but Atle's keen eyes didn't miss the subtle dimming of his color.

"Of course," the First continued, "the Troubadour's specimens walked right into his arms. We've had to search for ours, and all the humans are gone." There was no mistaking the dulling of the doctor's skin now, as his eyes fixed on the table.

"Doctor, has the Troubadour damaged his specimens?"

"Oh, no, Glorious First, I was assured during my last communication that both were still strong and alive."

"Yet, there is something you know that you are not telling your First. Are you confused in your loyalties?" Atle flared his poison patches.

"No, no, Glorious First, my loyalties are true!" The doctor shrank, squatting before the First.

"Stand up, Drin," Atle sang. "Don't fear me."

"It isn't you I fear, Glorious First," the doctor sang quaveringly.

Atle was not surprised. Dacris had the professionals cowed, hiding his inability to lead behind harsh, even cruel discipline. "I'll protect you. Do you trust me?"

"Absolutely," sang the physician clearly.

"Then tell me what you know. Is the Troubadour punishing his crew without cause? Working them too hard?"

The doctor's throat fluttered. "No, First. It . . . it's the specimens . . . the humans. Of course, he's had to force their cooperation, but Dr. Tato says he uses pain too freely. She fears the human doctor may become psychotic. He won't feed her, give her water or clothing, or let her sleep. When she refused to reveal information about these avians, Tato said Dacris gave both humans the rod until the old one fainted. Then the alien doctor *did* reveal the information."

Drin faced Atle squarely. "The humans *are* alive . . . but to inflict so much pain as well as withhold *water* and sleep is in violation of all our laws governing the care of the Industrious. The Second says those laws were never intended to protect the Conquered, that our ancestors used these same techniques."

"That's true," Atle sang neutrally.

"Perhaps," the doctor agreed, "but the suggestions of Dr. Tato and Rand have been completely ignored. They fear that the specimens will die, and that they'll be blamed."

Atle's patches flared, even though he struggled to appear calm. "I wondered how Dacris had gotten so much information so quickly. Thank you for telling me this, Doctor. I'll go to the station. The medical records will reveal the truth, and you and the others will be safe. I'll bring the subjects planetside and put them under your care. Then we'll go south and establish our colony while waiting for that alien ship to return."

The doctor peered gratefully at the First. "I should have realized you would know what to do."

Atle blinked acknowledgment of the doctor's song and left the sterile area. There was so much to do, yet now he'd have to leave and tend to this foolishness. Unfortunately, the Troubadour's behavior was all too common among higher officials. It was just another sign of the deterioration of their people.

Leaving the shelter, Atle signaled to a technician to prepare his transport. Looking up into the sky, he realized that all the avians had left. The silence was eerie.

It didn't matter. They could not, after all, leave the planet. They would still be here when Atle wanted them.

Atle glanced at the time as he entered the small, spare chambers of his personal quarters, and was shocked to see how late it was. It was halfway through this planet's night, a quarter span till dawn. He ached for his pool, but it would be hours before he could join his wife, Dunn, there. This room was designed to give him a place to plan strategy; there were few pleasantries in it—a small table, a water dispenser, some body oil, a computer. Even the colors of the room were muted, as if the designers wanted nothing to distract him from his work.

At least he was back on the *Flood* following a trying time on the space station. He wished for one of Arvis' massages, but his son, along with his wife and daughter, had long since retired.

His door sang a greeting and he invited the caller in automatically. Atle was not surprised to see the doctors, Tato and Drin. Tato squatted before him before he could stop her.

"Glorious First," Tato sang, "I, and my entire staff, wish to thank you. Your fairness will never be forgotten."

"Stand," he told her. "Will the two humans recover?"

"Oh, yes," she reassured him. "They're sleeping now, and Drin and I have ordered fluids for them and extra protein."

"Good. I'll want to talk to them later. They'll be invaluable in helping us understand more about their people, and the politics behind their Cooperative League." Without that knowledge, and the secret of their stardrive, Atle could not hope to advance beyond capturing this lone planet.

When the First had seen the condition of the humans, he'd furiously reprimanded the Troubadour The Second had openly defied him, singing of the old Conquerors' rights as though they had thousands of humans to squander. It irritated the leader to even recall it. The First had left Dacris with enough soldiers to capture the alien ship when it returned, then removed the professionals. He looked forward to having Dacris capture the alien ship. He'd dispatch him back Home with his prize and be rid of him.

Atle wondered whether the two human females knew when the ship would return. Dacris had not learned that.

"Be sure you document the humans' care," he told Tato. "And let me know when I may speak to them."

The two doctors agreed, thanked him again, and left. As they exited, Jebe, one of his One-Touch aides, entered.

"Glorious First," the youth reported, "we've heard from the new colony at . . ." he blinked slowly, as though thinking, "a third of a quarter . . . that is . . . a few moments ago. . . . They want to know when you'll be arriving."

"Yes, Jebe, thank you. The days are much longer here than home, aren't they?"

"Yes, First. And with the reverse rotation . . . keeping track of the time is hard!"

"I imagine we'll have to develop a new system. Perhaps we'll adopt the humans' clock. They seem to have made the switch easily enough. Do you know if any of the other humans have tried to communicate with either their camp or the space station?"

"There was one attempt to call the space station as we were refining our programs, so the call could not be traced. Then another call came to the station . . . from the marsh. It, too, was very brief, and we weren't able to verify its exact location."

Atle thought about that. "If humans were with the avians in the marsh, they could've seen us and fled with the flock."

The aide went to Atle's computer and called up a screen. "That might explain these readings," the aide sang.

Atle turned his attention to the shifting tank. They'd started tracking the huge flock as soon as it had left. His computer showed the avians had settled for the night at a staging ground south of the humans' camp. Their numbers had grown even in the short time that they'd traveled. This could be a natural migratory cycle . . . but Atle doubted that. The humans insisted the great avians were intelligent—even their equals. What kind of a people gave away their superiority so easily?

"Here, First, see this," Jebe sang.

Atle scanned the computer's information. At the center of the flock was an anti-gravity device. He picked it out easily, then watched its signal blink off as it was shut down for the night. Well, that accounted for at least one more alien.

"Interesting, Jebe. Keep a close eye on this. We don't know where they're going . . . or why. If we wait, they might lead us to the rest of the humans."

Jebe changed the tank's image, calling up a representation of the area Atle called New Home. It was warm and humid year round, the perfect climate for raising One-Touch children.

"Beside that reading," Jebe sang, "we've also found this." He showed Atle a tiny spot of extreme heat close to a wide, southern river, near where it fed into the sea, very close to where the probe had landed. "It appears to be intermittent combustion, maybe a small localized fire. It comes and goes."

Atle focused on the data. Their colony was located on that same river, only much farther west. Already, several transports of his people had landed, and were setting up self-contained buildings. Their first city would be there.

"More humans?" the First wondered aloud. Could they need fire for warmth in such a warm place?

If humans were there, the Chosen colony was far enough away that it was unlikely they would stumble across the new city. He thought of the four-legged alien the humans called "Simiu." *That* was the one he really wanted. According to the records, the strength of that one being matched several of the humans. What kind of work could you get from such a creature?

"Keep track of that fire," he told Jebe. "And scan for electronics, a-gravs, radios, anything. That'll be all, Jebe."

"Yes, Glorious First," the aide sang, and left the quarters.

Atle's door had barely closed before it sang another greeting. Trying to remember who else he had to see, the First admitted his caller.

"Glorious First," sang a matronly female, entering hurriedly and squatting on the floor, "forgive our untimely intrusion."

"The First always has time for his own," Atle sang wearily. He sighed, making no attempt to disguise his irritation, hoping it would hurry the female along.

As he eyed the biochemist, he realized that was unlikely. A One-Touch, Anchie was married to a male beneath her station, a lowly geologist with little interest in **achieving** rank. It was not the first time she'd visited him with **some desperate** suggestion she hoped would get her husband a **promotion**. Usually, all she accomplished was a jump in rank herself.

"Stand up, Anchie, and tell your First how he can help you."

"Not me, Glorious First," she sang, rising to her feet. "I would never bother you just for myself."

*Of course not,* Atle thought, increasingly irritated.

"It's for my daughter, Lene, that I come," she sang, and, lifting a hand, signaled to someone outside the doorway.

Anchie's daughter stepped into the room, boldly staring the First in the eye. The youngster was the most beautiful female Atle could ever remember seeing. Could a dolt such as Anchie's mate, Valli, really produce such magnificent offspring?

"I can see by your color that you find my daughter pleasant to look upon," Anchie sang in the humblest of tones.

"Any male would," responded the First in a voice that was clearly not his best. Pulling his gaze from Lene, the leader collected himself, then trained his coolest stare on the mother.

Suddenly she motioned to her daughter, who turned her back to the First, then removed her pattern-matching garment.

Atle's colors flared. "Put that garment back on! Anchie, you go too far!" Both females squatted subserviently, but neither made any attempt to drape Lene's elegant, slim back.

What if Atle's wife should enter? What would she think? "Anchie, you know what my marriage vows mean to me! How *dare* you try to . . . to *sell* me the rights to mate with your daughter for rank advancement? I won't tolerate . . ."

"Forgive the poor impression a desperate mother has made on her First," sang Anchie coolly. Atle's shoulder patches sweated. "The First has misinterpreted my intention. The fault is mine."

Atle wanted to throttle her. She knew that exposing her daughter in this compromising way could force him to bestow a special favor. Had anyone seen them enter his room? "Speak your piece," he growled, "but only *after* you cover that child."

Anchie did as she was told while Lene remained respectfully motionless. "I never intended that the First think I showed him my daughter's beauty for *his* interest."

Atle was tired of the semantic game. "What other reason could you have had?"

"My daughter's father is low-ranked, as you know. I worry about her future. Parents once arranged marriages for their children to improve their rank. Now, for the first time in centuries we have a people to conquer. Many of the old ways could be renewed." Her song was well practiced, Atle realized. This was something she'd been planning for a long time. "Here on this new world *you* are the law, Glorious First. The old traditions are yours to claim, if you choose."

"*If* I choose," he agreed. "Go on."

"I've come to arrange a marriage, Glorious First. My daughter respectfully requests to marry your son."

Atle felt weary to his bones. Anchie must be rubbing on too much euphoria drug these days. "In the first place, my son *was* married, and in the second, he is *dead*."

"Not *that* son," Anchie sang in a near whisper. "Lene wishes to marry . . . your . . . *other* son."

Atle blinked at the female stupidly. His *other* son? Slowly, her meaning grew clear. His other son. His Industrious son. "Do you know what you are saying?"

"Yes, Glorious First . . ." Anchie began.

"Shut up!" he ordered, and she dropped to the floor. "Lene, look at me." The young female obliged, turning the power of her blue and red marbled eyes on him. "Whose idea is this?"

"Mine, Glorious First," she insisted. "Because of Father's lack of ambition, I will suffer a poor marriage. My children, grand-children, and great-grandchildren will spend their lives struggling out of that low rank. Meanwhile, my First has only two Industri-ous children to comfort him on this new world, a world where he is the law. Your only grandchildren are back Home, on a planet you may never see again. *I* can give you grandchildren here, on *this* world, my First. Grandchildren who will *never* be Industrious. All the grandchildren I can bear!"

*Oh, she is her mother's daughter,* thought Atle. "Lene, my son is Industrious, he is older than you, and has never mated."

"The doctors have hormones . . ."

"Yes, they can bring him into breeding condition . . . but he's a *child,* he'd have no idea what was happening to him. Also, he's strong, he could *hurt* you in his clumsy ignorance. . . ."

"I'm not afraid," she sang haughtily.

Atle sighed. Her eagerness made his flesh crawl. "And what kind of a father could he be, what kind of a husband?"

"A faithful one," she answered. "No matter how scarred or broad my back becomes, it'll mean nothing to him. Who could want more than a high-ranking mate who's both faithful *and* kind? Everyone knows how gentle he is, how affectionate. He will be a companion to his children, never tiring of their games."

"They would outgrow him!"

"But they will never outgrow the rank his birthright will give them. They *will* respect him, be sure of that!"

They were mad with ambition, these two—true One-Touch.

"Glorious First," the daughter sang, "don't you think I could make your son happy?"

Atle turned the full force of his imperious stare on her. "Frankly, no. I think you would use him—and *abuse* him—as a menial servant when he's not needed as a sperm bank. I believe the first time he surrounded you with his clumsy grip, and you were trapped in his uncontrollable, hormone-induced amplexus, you might well learn to hate him. It's what any young female would feel. Even the Industrious egg-layers are mated with experienced Chosen males so they won't be frightened."

Lene returned the First's stare. "Please! The state uses Chosen males to save the money it would cost in the lost labor of Industrious males. And the Chosen *pay* to be hormonally treated so they can fertilize the Industrious egg-layers. It gives them the pleasure of a breeding that doesn't include their wives."

Anchie hissed at Lene. This time she had gone too far.

But Atle wouldn't punish her for honesty. "Lene, I will give you a chance to convince me. *If* you can convince my son."

The young female watched him warily.

"Befriend him. Spend time with him. Learn who he is. *Seduce* him. Make him *love* you as he loves his mother and sister. If I see that he is happy with you, that he wants you, I will consider it. But if I agree to this . . . marriage, you must live with *my* family. My wife will attend your breedings, not your mother. You will live under Dunn's watchful eye." Atle's gaze held hers. "And if my son *ever* seems unhappy . . . if he suffers one moment of cruelty at your hands . . . you will spend the rest of your breedings in the grip of an Armored. Is that understood?"

Anchie sprang to her feet. "No, Glorious First, not that!" That hybrid breeding would destroy Lene's already low rank.

"It's all right, Mother," Lene replied calmly, never taking her eyes off the First. "I agree. Glorious First, I look forward to the day when I hand you your *sixth* Chosen grandchild."

# CHAPTER 9

◆

# The Land of Confusion

Old Bear wiggled the sound nullifiers sitting uncomfortably in his ears. He yearned to take them out, even for a moment, and hear something, anything, but that wasn't possible. The huge flock of Grus surrounding him on this wide coastal swamp was never silent, with their ear-shattering guard calls, alarm calls, and the sporadic location calls of parents or mates who'd lost sight of each other. Nearly three hundred avians were busy feeding in the brackish water, tidal pools, and on the burnished gold seed heads of the waist-high grass as Father Sun brought in the dawn. When they left, the place would be stripped.

Yesterday, they'd flown until nearly midnight, then settled for the night. Already, new flocks were joining Taller, swelling his flock's numbers, building an air force of winged people.

In a short while, they'd be airborne again, and not land until nightfall. It would take longer for a big flock to reach the southern peninsula, Old Bear knew, especially when that flock had to hide its slowest, most vulnerable members in the midst of the long, trailing vees that darkened the sky.

His fears for Meg and Szu-yi never left his mind, but he had more immediate concerns now. He glanced at Mrs. Lewis. She'd been a schoolteacher, preserving and passing on her people's culture to modern children. She hadn't spent much time actually living off the land, as he'd done. The hours in the air, the nights spent on cold, damp ground, were slowly crippling her, even though she tried not to show it. Loves-the-Wind, the healer from Taller's flock, had given the old woman some special seeds to eat and an aromatic ointment that had helped for a while. Old Bear shrugged his own stiff shoulder. It might not be so bad if they could only make a fire.

"Why would the Grus need fire, Mr. Bigbee?" Mrs. Lewis had warned, and she'd been right. They couldn't endanger the very people who were trying to safeguard them.

Old Bear had a sudden strong memory of his last dream and shuddered. He should've told Tesa, shared it with her before she left. He could've examined it closer, taken a sweat bath, prayed more. . . . He should've done the exact opposite of what he had. . . . He stopped his mind from running in circles.

The most important thing was to get a message to the CLS, and warn the *Brolga* away, but he didn't know if that was possible without help from the space station. The *Brolga* would be here in three weeks. Old Bear shook his head. His dreams had shown him blood dripping from the Moons, covering Trinity, but now he feared that that blood might engulf all the Known Worlds.

He turned as a shadow crossed him.

"Tired, friend?" Taller asked kindly.

"You know," the human signed, "I thought when I came to the World I would end my days in peace and contentment."

Taller's crown stretched. "And is that what you *wanted*?"

Old Bear smiled. "I thought so at the time."

Taller watched the hordes of his people foraging for breakfast. "I thought the same when your granddaughter came to the World. Perhaps we will get what we want, sooner or later."

Old Bear nodded, thinking, *later, I'm afraid. Much later.*

"You didn't sleep well last night," Lightning signed, his small, dull crown speaking eloquently of his concern. When Tesa didn't answer, he commented, "You were having bad dreams. I tried to ease you out of it like Weaver does, but I couldn't."

She wanted to reassure him, tell him that he'd helped, but she couldn't lie to him. She'd dreamed about her grandparents, about a river running red with blood, and awakened nervous and irritable, thinking about Old Bear, as if he'd sent her the dream. That's why she was here in her lean-to now, in the middle of the day, trying to catch a nap, but that eluded her, too. Only Lightning and Flies-Too-Fast were with her; the rest of the cohort milled restlessly around the beach. She couldn't see Thunder. She changed the subject. "Why don't you fish?"

"The River's too noisy," Lightning explained.

"Too noisy for what?" She didn't feel alert enough to be sensitive to the difficult nuances of being hearing.

"For anything," Flies-Too-Fast explained crankily. "The Spirit Singers keep swimming through the River, telling each other about the alien who *hears* their song. They sang the night away, and most of the day. No wonder you had nightmares." He fluffed up his feathers disgustedly. "They're scaring the fish."

Reminded of the strange creatures they'd discovered only yesterday morning, Tesa opened her mind. She could still *hear* them in the back of her mind. Squinting, she saw Jib on a sled hovering over the sandbar, communing with the curious herd. She gnawed her lower lip. She wanted to remove him from the area, get him out of here. But when would *that* be? She checked her chrono. Fourteen twenty-five—noon on Trinity. Noon. And still no word from Meg and Szu-yi.

She took a deep breath, aware that her two avian friends could read her every emotion. Near the parked *Demoiselle,* Bruce and K'heera fiddled with the alien satellite, still in its safety container. She rose and left the lean-to, the Grus close behind.

Bruce was using the container's internal systems to give the satellite a rudimentary cleaning. K'heera sat nearby, watching, appearing disinterested. She could see Bruce signing to the young Simiu, trying to include her, but she remained aloof. Tesa was surprised how much of the surface Bruce had revealed. Odd-shaped hieroglyphics and impressed designs made artistic, marbled patterns in the metal. It was beautiful, she thought, but that didn't assuage the vague sense of dread she felt whenever she looked at it. *You sure picked the right part of Trinity to splash down in,* she thought at the alien sphere.

The weatherman acknowledged her presence, but there was no welcoming smile on his face.

"Have you called the *Crane* lately?" she asked, trying to make her signs casual.

He nodded.

K'heera watched their exchange. Tesa realized everyone was now watching them—the scattered cohort; Thunder, who was in a nearby tree; and even Jib, though he couldn't follow their signs at that distance. He adjusted the sled and flew in and joined them. Using the flyer as a convenient chair, he dangled his legs over the side to watch their conversation.

"Same message?" Tesa asked.

Bruce nodded again.

Her throat tightened. "Did *you* send a message?"

He faced her. "No. I told you I wouldn't, and I didn't."

Tesa eyed him anxiously. "What's wrong? Why are you . . . ?"

"I called your grandparents, thinking they might know what was going on at the station. I got the same message."

There shouldn't be any message from the camp's computer, Tesa knew. Those computers were always open to relay communications, especially when anyone was away from camp—that was

SOP. The "do not disturb" was as wrong as cheese-scented plastic on a rodent trap. "Did . . . did you leave a message there?"

"No, ma'am." Bruce's eyes grew soft.

She wanted to say something but found she couldn't.

"Now, there could be a perfectly logical reason for these wonky messages," he suggested.

"Two *identical* messages?"

"The failed satellite," he said, "like all the others, is linked directly into the AI. Like I told you months ago, we're way behind on our maintenance program. If the robot brain started deteriorating, it could've infected the AI, spreading it like a cancer. When Meg and Szu-yi went up there they might've found major problems waiting for them. We've got the diagnostics and the equipment to solve it, but it takes time, and in the meantime they'd be out of touch. Neither Meg nor Szu-yi are that adept at working with the AI. They could be stuck up there for a week without help. Your grandparents might've been trying to reach *us* for the last forty-two hours."

*If you believe that,* Tesa wondered, *why are you so edgy?*

"Let me send a message," Bruce insisted gently. "Forcing the computers to accept information might help the AI reprogram itself, at least enough to handle a simple communication."

"*If* that's the problem," Tesa replied, shaking her head. "If Meg found that much trouble on the *Crane,* don't you think she'd just come down here to get you?"

"You're talkin' about *Meg,*" he reminded her wryly. "She'd have to be really stumped to come after me first. She'd keep insisting they could fix everything in 'just another hour.' "

*Yes,* Tesa had to admit, *that's what Meg would do.*

"If we send a repetitive signal," Jib interjected, "the computer would receive it. Meg might be able to respond."

K'heera remained silent. Tesa resented the Simiu's lack of participation, but she couldn't force her to give an opinion.

"That kind of interaction," Tesa signed to Jib, "could pinpoint our location. . . ."

"Why worry about that?" Jib asked.

Tesa stood, hands poised hesitantly.

"Are you worried that someone from Sorrow Sector, someone involved with the privateers, has come back to Trinity?" Bruce asked. "How could they? We eliminated or captured the human crew. Any collaborators left in Sorrow are busy staying one step-ahead of the investigators. . . ." Bruce suddenly caught sight of K'heera's change of expression and frowned self-consciously.

"Besides, this is a mighty long way to come for revenge."

Tesa started to say something, then paused as Jib signaled for her to look at K'heera.

The Simiu's mouth moved in the unique way that indicated she was speaking her own language. It was impossible to lip-read with its guttural throat sounds, which K'heera had to know. She was deliberately forcing Tesa to communicate through her voder, or use Jib as a translator. It was a subtle way of making the Indian feel less than capable when she already felt helpless. The Sioux woman controlled her temper with an effort.

"Repeat that in sign," Tesa demanded in the short, choppy motions Grus parents used with misbehaving children.

K'heera did not miss the significance of the reprimand, and her eyes widened. She barked a response.

"I said in *sign*," Tesa repeated. "And *look* at me when you're signing!"

There was an uncomfortable pause, then finally K'heera signed reluctantly, "Are you insinuating that my family is somehow responsible for the problems we are experiencing here?"

"Not at all," Tesa insisted. "You're being oversensitive."

"Then what *are* you implying?" K'heera demanded.

"No one meant to insult you or your family," Bruce assured her. "We were talking about the past. It wasn't personal."

The young female wasn't mollified. "You hide your true feelings by saying Trinity is too far to go for revenge. But honor knows no limits. And Simiu honor is *always* personal!"

"Which is why you're here today," he reminded her irritably, "*supposedly* learning how to counterbalance that overblown honor code so you can learn to *cooperate* with other beings!"

"And this is something I'm supposed to learn from *humans*?" she demanded furiously. "A people who nearly wiped out their own kind because of their insane love for *weapons*?"

"A people," Bruce fired back, "who've learned to control their baser natures. A people who've made one successful First Contact, and now possibly a second. Your beloved honor code prevented your people from doing that sixteen years ago, and will hold you back until you learn to compromise."

"I've heard enough, human!" K'heera's mane bristled.

"Stop!" Tesa moved between them, hands up, forcing them to pause. She couldn't believe how quickly things had deteriorated between them, and worse, she felt responsible. "We're *all* overreacting! We're just . . . tense . . . because we don't know what's going on. Let's calm down."

K'heera's crest flattened slightly as she turned to Tesa. "You accuse me of being oversensitive—a common racial slur made by humans against my people—but you never answered my question. Do you think my family is involved in our problems?"

"Now, K'heera," Bruce signed slowly, his jaw clenched, "it never occurred to *anyone* here to think your family could have anything to do with our current situation. . . ."

"Do not patronize me, human!" she signed angrily. "I am not a child for you to guide. Examine your prejudices and say there is no truth in what I've said. Tell me, *Honored* Interrelator, that you do not fear an attack from the renegade Harkk'ett clan."

Tesa lifted her hands to try to explain her concerns, but K'heera had already risen off her haunches and trotted away without a backward glance. Jib started to stand.

"Let her go, son," Bruce signed. "She won't listen, not while she's angry. I guess some of the things we said, the way we said them . . . it would have to look that way to her."

*Even Bruce thinks that's what I meant,* Tesa realized. Or was the sin in what she couldn't say? And why wouldn't she say it? Because she'd allowed K'heera's attitudes about honor and decorum to infect her own feelings about her instincts. She didn't want to appear foolish in front of the Simiu—of losing honor in her eyes. But, she'd done that anyway. As if a *heyoka* could've done anything else!

Old Bear's dream warning, the mental intrusions of the Spirit Singers, and the sudden appearance of the alien probe had her instincts thrumming like a plucked string. She'd felt the same way last year when she'd taken young Thunder and Lightning and fled to an ancient caldera. That was what she wanted to do now. Take her friends, her children. Run. Hide.

"You're probably right," Jib signed to Bruce. "I've never seen her this pissed off. I'll talk to her after she walks off her mad. Still, there's our main problem. . . . If we're not going to try to break through the programming, what else *can* we do?"

The two men gazed at Tesa.

"We can wait," she signed, taking a deep breath and rubbing her forehead. "If this is a computer glitch, as you suspect, waiting will do no harm. If the problem's more serious . . ."

"Such as?" Jib asked pointedly. Tesa could tell he was tired of her evasions.

She stared him in the eye. "Such as . . . Columbus. Such as Captain James Cook." Tesa pointed toward the alien probe sitting benignly captive in its container. "You're assuming that thing was

sent from its builders' homeworld. It could've been sent from an
exploratory ship just as easily."

"Possible," Bruce admitted, "but a long shot."

"You're being too complacent," Tesa insisted. "Up till now, the
CLS has been in the enviable position of discovering new species
under peaceful conditions. Because the Mizari are such an old
race, they've been able to refine First Contacts into a science.
But Trinity's off the beaten path, in a part of the Orion Arm the
Mizari know little about. As you yourself once said, Bruce, this
place is a colonist's dream."

She turned to Jib. "Our people were nearly destroyed by invaders who changed our worlds forever. Can't you even *imagine* that
the beings who launched that probe might be a threat? Or has
StarBridge made you think that every First Contact is automatically a peaceful dialog between equals?" Having verbalized her
worst fears, Tesa felt oddly relieved.

Jib glanced at Bruce as the older man signed, "You've got to
admit, the specter of alien invaders is pretty unlikely. . . ."

"Because it's never happened before?" Tesa asked.

"Considering all the years the Mizari have been in space, that's
not a bad reason," Jib agreed.

Tesa clenched her jaw. "Okay, fine. It's unlikely. So *where* are
Meg and Szu-yi? *Where* are my grandparents?"

"I might be able to find that out," Bruce insisted, annoyed, "if
you'd let me send—"

"No!" Tesa signed. "No messages. No invitations to orbiting
aliens, come and get us, here we are! What's more, we're shutting
down our equipment." She indicated the ship, the sleds, the stove.
"*Everything* off. No a-gravs. And no fires."

"Oh, come on, Tesa," Jib complained.

"If we don't keep trying to reach someone," Bruce insisted,
"we'll never make contact."

"Meg and Szu-yi can contact us when they land here. When
they give us a nice, logical explanation for those computer messages, then I'll admit I was acting foolish and you can all enjoy a
good laugh at my expense. *But* . . . if Meg and Szu-yi aren't here
in two days, we're moving camp. Jib, when you talk to K'heera,
make sure she knows. Tell her, *no* arguments. Besides . . . we've
got other ways to send a message."

She turned to Flies-Too-Fast, who was standing beside her. "I
want you to fly home. Speak to any Wind people you meet on
the way, or any Travelers. Ask them if they've seen or heard
of anything unusual, anything un-Worldly. Halfway home, you'll

start seeing Blue Cloud people. If anyone knows anything, they will. Ask the Travelers and the Wind people to bring the news to Lightning, so we can learn it."

"I understand," Flies-Too-Fast agreed. "Alone, I can fly home in as little as four days."

"It'll be a *week* before we learn anything!" Bruce protested.

She ignored him, focusing on Flies-Too-Fast. "Time to live up to your name, friend. If we're not here when you return, find the branch of this River that we followed down from the north. We'll be near the shore. And remember, whatever happens, *be careful.* I'm depending on you to learn what we need to know."

"I'll find you, Good Eyes," the youngster assured her. "Be careful yourself." The huge avian ran, opened mammoth wings, and, pumping hard, lifted into the sky.

K'heera watched the misty spouts of spray marking the passage of the Spirit Singers. Whatever the humans had discussed after she'd left them angered the Terrans. The tension among them was palpable, and K'heera basked in secret delight over it—a most dishonorable emotion.

Jib had returned to the River, standing in chest-high water, communing with his Singers while Bruce fiddled desultorily with the *Demoiselle.* The Interrelator had gone back to her shelter, studiously preening one of the cloaks she slept on, while her cohort stood grouped about her, engaged in the same activity. All except for Flies-Too-Fast, who had left hours ago. K'heera didn't know why, nor did she care.

*Her* people were oversensitive, but humans were worthy of a Simiu's friendship? This must be another incomprehensible human joke. Bruce's acting the uncle to her had been mere patronizing. Jib had made a polite attempt to engage her in conversation after her argument with the Interrelator, but he had no real interest in her. A telepathic *animal* held more fascination for him.

K'heera wondered how it was possible to be on such an open world and yet feel so claustrophobic.

All this agonizing only compounded her isolation. It was dishonorable to wallow in self-pity, or delight in others' disagreements. She had to find something to distract her.

On a clump of coarse, bright red grass rested the container holding the alien probe. It still sat near the *Demoiselle,* but Bruce was so engrossed in the internal workings of the ship, he wouldn't notice her. Besides, she'd watched him clean the device and was familiar with most of the simple functions the container could perform. Patting the pockets of her tool-laden vest, K'heera approached it.

She examined the hieroglyphics closely and asked the container's computer if they appeared to form the kind of pattern that would indicate a map. Frankly, K'heera thought maps were unlikely. Of all the Known Worlds, humans had been the only beings so naive as to put clear directions to their homeworld on satellites destined to rove aimlessly through space.

The computer couldn't find a map, but it did identify a raised design that might indicate a panel. What she really wanted to know was whether there was an inner power source. She thought they might be able to tap into it to help solve their communications problem. Bruce had even agreed with her about that . . . but first she needed more information about the exterior. Power cells could be dangerous.

Impulsively, she asked it to identify the alloys making up the probe's shell, as she'd seen Bruce do earlier. The scanner hadn't been able to identify the casing, but K'heera thought she could boost it by adding a different power cell. Once they knew more about the shell, they could learn more about any possible control panels, or even think about removing the casing. She'd suggested upgrading the computer, but Bruce pointed out that Meg was due imminently, and the *Crane* had much better equipment. How many hours ago was that?

Opening the tiny computer, she sorted through her extra cells, finding the one she wanted. Clipping it into an empty slot, K'heera closed the computer and asked it to scan again. New information scrolled across the screen. She drew closer.

Then, without warning, the small probe sprang to life. Bright rays flashed out of nearly invisible seams, stretching impossibly far, brilliant even in the strong daylight. One of them hit Thunder, sleepily perched in a nearby tree, and she squawked and leaped into the air. Terrified, K'heera scrambled away while the alien machine continued its bizarre light show.

Bruce darted around the ship and stared at the probe. He lunged for the container, slapping the controls, shutting the computer off. Instantly, the rays disappeared, and the probe resumed its harmless appearance.

K'heera's heart slammed, her face burning. Jib ran up from the beach, dripping water. At the same time, the Interrelator, who had bolted out of her shelter, skidded to a stop. All around them, airborne Grus landed with a flurry of nervous calling. Sand blew everywhere. Overhead, Thunder wheeled, still shrieking. K'heera approached the container cautiously.

"What happened?" Bruce demanded. All eyes were on her.

"I . . . I don't really know . . ." she answered.

"The container's scanner was on," Bruce continued. "And it'd been *boosted*. Did you do that?"

*And who else would have?* she thought. "Yes." She forced herself to sign evenly. "I wanted to analyze the casing. I thought it would be a good way to pass the time."

"I told you not to do that!"

"You said we should not bother because we would soon be on the *Crane* where there was superior equipment."

"Well"—Bruce paused—"that's true. I should've been more specific. I didn't want the scanner boosted because sometimes a scanning device can alert certain satellites—like spy satellites—that they're being read. There have even been some satellites made to fire on anything probing them. On the *Crane* we can contain it, so even if it did that we wouldn't be in danger. I should've explained my reasons more clearly."

*Weapons, again,* K'heera thought disgustedly. *They think other beings are all like them. What perverted creatures could be so insane as to put weapons in a probe?*

"What *did* it do?" Jib asked.

Bruce examined the container's diagnostic analysis. "Looks like the boosted scanner triggered it, turned it on. I guess the rays are part of its workings."

"So this thing just told its owners everything about us?" the Interrelator asked, alarmed.

"I don't think so," Bruce reassured her. "It was just on for a second. It barely had time to store that information."

"I don't want *anything* electronic used, I thought I made that clear!" Now she was addressing them all. K'heera could tell she was furious, which only baffled the Simiu more.

It was Jib's turn to look embarrassed. "Sorry, Tesa. We talked . . . but I'm afraid . . . it slipped my mind." The Interrelator shot Jib an irritated glance.

*You mean you were too eager to return to the Singers to remember,* the Simiu thought.

"Forgive me, K'heera," the Interrelator signed. "We won't be using any modern equipment near the camp until we know more about what's happening with our main computers. If we aren't joined by Meg and Szu-yi in the next two days, we'll reevaluate. I should've told you myself. It was my oversight."

*It must madden them to keep apologizing to me,* the Simiu thought. Then she realized she'd just been cut off from doing anything interesting. The next two days would creep along with painful slowness. What had she ever done to deserve this? She felt the very presence of these humans suffocating her.

Suddenly her stomach growled. "Honored Interrelator, since there is little else for me to do, may I go foraging?"

Tesa nodded. "Of course. The Grus will go with you."

She was about to suggest that was not necessary, but the look on the woman's face was not indulgent. "Very well," she agreed with forced good cheer.


"But why is she carrying that?" None-So-Pretty asked Lightning, stretching her head to see around him.

As Lightning watched the Simiu, Sunrise, lumbering ahead of the group, walking along on three legs, he wondered that same thing. They'd been traveling along an animal path through very dense forest for a long time now, but the alien continued to pass shrub after shrub of rich fruit. Twice he'd asked her why she felt it necessary to carry the clumsy flyer but she had rudely refused to answer him. Her bringing the sled disturbed him.

"Good Eyes doesn't want these un-Worldly devices used," Scorched reminded him, as if she needed to.

Sunrise seemed to be in compliance, Lightning rationalized, since she had not turned it on. Instead, she'd strapped it to her back and trudged along, holding it in place with one hand.

"Obviously," Frost Moon announced, "she carries it in the hopes it will protect her from the Spirit Singers' songs."

Lightning began to wonder how sensible it had been for him to bring the youngest cohort members with him. He'd wanted Hurricane, Snowberry, and Winter Bloom to stay behind with Good Eyes, just in case anything happened. He trusted his human friend's instincts. They'd saved his life more than once.

"If she's carrying it for protection," None-So-Pretty pointedly asked Frost Moon, "then why did she sneak it out from behind her shelter, when she'd gone for her mesh bags?"

Scorched agreed with the little female. "She was hiding it from Good Eyes. And she won't answer Lightning's questions. It's plain enough to me."

"What is?" Frost Moon and None-So-Pretty asked at the same time. Scorched just blinked at them, suddenly confused herself. They all turned to Lightning for clarification. But he already knew that understanding un-Worldly creatures was something that he had yet to master.

Finally, the Simiu stopped, unstrapped the flyer from her back, and took a few moments to groom her matted crest. Lightning could see nothing available for the alien to eat.

"This isn't a very good place," he told her. "We should go back to where we passed the sweet briar bushes."

"You go back," she suggested. "I'm going west." She finished her grooming, leaned over the flyer, and turned it on. It lifted eerily into the air, hovering there. The three young cohort members watched Lightning, waiting to see what he'd do.

"Good Eyes does not want that on," he reminded her gently.

"The Interrelator said she does not want any equipment operating *near the camp.*"

*Yes, that was what Good Eyes had signed, but . . .* He took another tactic. "Why do you need the sled?"

Sunrise turned her vivid purple eyes on the young avians. "I *need* to *fly.* Surely you can understand that, my friend. I feel surrounded. I need to be alone."

Lightning understood that need well enough, yet . . . "Good Eyes would not want you to fly far."

"We will all be together," Sunrise insisted.

"This forest is too dense for us to fly through," he told her, though he had the feeling she already knew that. "I suggest you turn the flyer off and . . ."

"What are you, the Interrelator's pet?" Sunrise demanded angrily, "or are you an independent thinking person? Must you do *everything* she tells you?"

Lightning stood tall, glancing back at his cohort, aware that things had taken a turn he didn't understand. "I'm Good Eyes' friend. She's more than friend, she's been a parent to me. She teaches me about un-Worldly things I must understand to lead my people someday."

Behind him, he saw None-So-Pretty sign, "What's a *pet*?"

Before Frost Moon could offer an explanation, Sunrise responded angrily. "How can you stand to be so beholden to her? She is perverse! Refusing to have her handicap corrected. And she is without honor. In the face of the enemy, she *fled* and hid. Is this what she teaches you, how to be dishonorable?"

Lightning's feathers stood out slowly and he drew himself up to his full height, even as the youngsters around him drew back.

"Do *not* insult Good Eyes again!" he ordered the Simiu, his eyes blazing. The patch where his crown would soon be stretched and the short feathers covering it stood up. "Good Eyes' decision to take us away led to the greatest compromise my people have ever known. She has more than your tiny *honor*, Sunrise, she has the power to forge alliances between the people and creatures we once called Death. You will *not* speak badly of her again."

K'heera's crest lifted. He knew her people were easily goaded into bodily combat, but he did not fear that. Simiu were not the only ones who could defend themselves.

Suddenly Sunrise leaped upon the flyer and turned it west. "I will *gladly* never speak of that human again. I only wish that I might never have to see her again, either." Touching the controls, the Simiu sped away along the winding animal trail.

Lightning watched her leave, his heart sickened. He was supposed to stay with her! He should have anticipated that her bizarre behavior might lead to something like this. What would he tell Good Eyes?

"What will you tell Good Eyes now?" Frost Moon signed worriedly, as if he could read his mind like a Spirit Singer.

"He will tell her the truth," None-So-Pretty announced. "The Simiu has gone crazy from staying in the Land of Confusion. Good Eyes will not be surprised."

Lightning peered up through the canopy with one eye, searching the trees' upper reaches. Spying Thunder, he bleated an alarm call, and in answer the raptor launched herself from the high perch. Flying in the dense canopy would be hard for her as well, but she could climb out of the forest and hover above the highest trees much more easily than Lightning could. From that lofty elevation she would be able to follow the Simiu's progress. At least one of them would still be with Sunrise.

"It'll be dark soon," Scorched announced to the group, as if none of them could tell the time in the dense wood.

"Go back to the camp," Lightning told the youngsters. None-So-Pretty hesitated for a moment, as if she would argue, but he towered over her, and she lowered her head. "Tell Good Eyes what happened. Tell her . . . that I'll stay in the forest until Sunrise returns, and bring her out myself. Tell her not to worry."

The cohort hesitated only a moment before obeying, stepping smartly down the path. Since the Simiu would no doubt return along this same route, Lightning went down the path, looking for the sweet briar. He might as well eat while he was waiting for her to come back. But as he pondered what he'd have to say to Good Eyes if Sunrise took too long to return, he found his appetite waning.

# CHAPTER 10

♦

# The River of Fear

Arvis blinked slowly, trying hard to understand what his mother was telling him.

So much had changed since they'd found this new planet. He, his mother, and his sister had been sent to live here without his father, and that upset Arvis. Who was taking care of his father, cleaning his clothes, giving him his massage? And they were living in a house that was barely a shell. His old house had been huge with lots of pretty things in it, but this small one only had bare floors and empty walls. At least the back wall was transparent, like their old house, and he could see the beautiful scenery of the marsh they were calling "New Home."

But now . . . that female was here again, the one named . . . ?

"Lene," his mother sang softly. "Remember Lene?"

"I remember," he answered, looking at the floor. He always remembered *her*, it was her name he had trouble recalling.

"She wants to take you swimming. Would you like that?"

Arvis' mind swirled in confusion. He loved swimming, but except for his mother, he'd never swum with a Chosen female. Something about it made him uneasy. Lene made him uneasy.

"Are you afraid of the river?" his mother asked.

"Oh, no. I'm not afraid . . . of the river. . . ."

His mother looked at him oddly. "Are you afraid of Lene?"

"No. She's very nice." He remembered the food she'd brought yesterday when they'd first met—eggs marinated in sweet broth. His favorite. But she'd insisted on serving him herself, and that had made him so nervous he'd only eaten a few.

"Arvis," his mother asked, "do you like Lene?"

The question took him by surprise and he blushed deeply. "Oh, yes. She's . . . she's . . . beautiful!" Her beauty was the only thing he could think of when he was with her.

"But is she *always* nice to you, even when I'm not there?"

Arvis wasn't sure what to say. He could tell there was something about Lene his mother didn't like. Did she want him to dislike Lene, too? He didn't know if he could do that. But he had to tell his mother the truth. "She's always nice, but she . . . makes me feel . . . funny inside."

His mother relaxed. "Well, lovely females make most males feel funny inside." She patted him lovingly. "Have fun, then."

"By ourselves?" he asked, blushing harder.

"Lene won't let anything happen to you, of that, I'm sure!"

"But I haven't finished my work. I still have to . . ."

"You can do that later, Arvis. Lene's waiting." His mother gently ushered him from the tiny servants' quarters onto the outside porch where Lene stood, looking out across the lush, beautiful marsh.

His new house was built right over the river that cut through the grasses in a meandering green ribbon of water, contrasting sharply with the russet hue of the grass itself. Clumps of taller golden reeds dotted the river's edge. Massive, dark forests ringed the river and their settlement, but the wide shoreline, the "floodplain" his mother called it, was open, and the short bluish ground covers were soft under his feet.

"Good evening, dear Arvis," Lene sang in a voice so musical that Arvis could barely stand to hear it curl around his name.

"Where will you be going, Lene?" his mother asked bluntly.

"There's a secluded place I've found on the riverbank. There don't seem to be any animals, and it's not far, but it's private. Arvis gets nervous when too many people are around."

He certainly did. Any Chosen could make demands of him once he was away from his parents, and some were mean. Sometimes they said awful things to Lene, and Arvis hated that.

His mother seemed to understand. "Once our pool's installed you won't need to use the river, Lene. You and Arvis can spend time together in the privacy of our home."

"I'll look forward to that," Lene agreed, "but to be somewhere where no one else has been has its own attraction."

Arvis noticed his mother's eyes soften, then. "That's true. I still haven't adjusted to being on a *new* world. For you young people, it must be quite an adventure. Have fun swimming."

As his mother went back inside their small prefab home, Arvis was surprised by Lene's hand on his arm. She was always touching him, and he was always being surprised by it.

"Come on, Arvis, I've found the most beautiful place." She tugged him gently and he walked beside her, down the short walkway onto the soil of the new world. He looked back longingly at his house. The colorful house sat up on short stilts, with its self-contained solar-powered energy units cleverly disguised. Dozens of these small buildings had sprung up like rampant plant growth along this stretch of the river. His mother said that in a few months they would have a city here.

Of course, it was nothing like the cities he was used to, any more than their new house was like their old. That one had been huge, perched on tall, thick stilts. Its numerous slat walks, designed to cause minimal impact on the delicate marshes, stretched out in all directions over the vast expanse that was the First's own property, given to him for his glorious service. Arvis had been told about the honor that came with that house over and over again, but he didn't regret leaving it behind. After all, the new, small one had much less to clean.

Lene led him onto a beaten trail that entered the forest where the dense growth came right up to the river's edge. "It's our own private beach, my love," Lene whispered. It made him nervous when she sang that way.

After walking for a long time, the path suddenly ended as the wide river meandered into a bend. The water had carved a small, gentle pool against the shore. Arvis blinked. As Lene had said, it was beautiful. The water was clear and inviting, and the current not very strong. He started to tell Lene how nice he thought it was, then realized what she was doing.

She had taken off her garment, and wore nothing underneath. Her back was to him, her lovely slim back, and all he could do was stare helplessly. Something told him this wasn't a good idea, that he should leave, but she was so beautiful, he couldn't move or speak. His chest hurt so much, he could barely breathe.

"What's wrong, Arvis?" she sang sweetly, looking over her shoulder at him.

"You're not wearing anything." He answered so softly, he wondered if she'd even heard him.

"Of course not! We're going swimming in our own private part of the river. Why would I want to wear anything?"

The question baffled him. "I'm wearing something! I always wear something to swim in. My mother reminded me to put it on under my garment. Didn't your mother remind you?"

Lene turned and approached him, putting her hands on the fastenings of his over-garment, the one that matched his skin pattern. "Arvis, haven't you ever seen your parents swim?"

"Of course, when they swim with me and my sister."

Now Lene seemed confused. "I thought all the Industrious assisted their Chosen during breeding. . . . It's true, then, what they say about your father, that he refused to go through any more cycles, because he doesn't want to make more Industrious."

Arvis had no idea what she was talking about. "When my parents swim with us, we *all* wear something. You should, too!"

She gently aided him out of his clothes, eyeing the suit beneath it. "That's a nice suit, but when . . . people who like each other in a special way . . . go swimming in a private place . . . things are different then. You *do* like me, don't you, Arvis?"

Arvis felt his vocal cords freeze up as he tried to fathom what Lene was talking about. How many ways could you like someone, and what way was special? The way he liked his father? Or did she mean the way she made him feel when she came close like this? Arvis wasn't even sure he even *liked* this feeling, he'd never had it before. It hurt deep inside, and now, looking at Lene's beautiful body, her lovely skin, it hurt terribly. He wondered if this was what his mother meant when she asked if Lene was nice to him. The whole thing scared him.

"You're shaking," Lene sang. "Here, squat down in the water. I've got something to help you relax."

Used to the commands of the Chosen, Arvis did as he was told, and sat in the pool, wishing someone would explain to him why Lene did such strange things. Her long fingers rubbed something oily into his skin and he twitched.

"What's that?" he asked. He shouldn't ask questions of the Chosen, but his parents had always indulged his curiosity.

"It's a special oil my mother made," Lene sang. "It'll make you feel good!"

Arvis doubted that. He never really felt good until Lene left him alone. Then he would remember all the things she'd said and done, filter them through his limited intelligence, and alter them so he could understand them. *Then* he'd feel good. His skin felt warm where she rubbed the oil, and to his surprise, his muscles relaxed. Lene began to remove his swimsuit. Realizing he could not refuse her, Arvis squeezed his eyes shut as she undressed him, while stroking more oil onto his back and tail.

"It's going to rain soon, dear Arvis," Lene sang, almost to herself, he thought. "I can smell it, I can feel it. You've got to be ready for the rain, my sweet, because it's going to change your life. And mine. Most importantly, dear Arvis, it's going to change mine." She pulled him deeper into the warm pool, and as the soothing wetness surrounded them, he opened his eyes and watched as she rubbed the strange oil over his skin.

*      *      *

K'heera couldn't believe how exhilarating it felt to fly through the forest, free for the first time since she'd landed on this lonely world. She traveled west, just for the joy of flying, of being alone. If she couldn't enjoy the company of her own people, the least she could do was have a few hours without being forced to endure *humans*.

As the distance grew between herself and the camp, she began to feel bad about the harsh words she'd exchanged with Lightning. She'd have to apologize to him. His loyalty to the Interrelator was an honorable thing. But she was so tired of everything, so sick of this place . . . she supposed she'd have to apologize to everyone when she finally returned.

Well, she could put that off. She'd been pushing the sled fast, so she could still go a little farther before she'd have to return. The sled could find its way back in total darkness.

K'heera slowed the flyer and stepped off it, telling it to follow her. Here, the river lapped right up to the forest itself. She followed the beaten path, looking for an opening to the river's edge so she could get a drink. Then she heard it.

She stopped, standing perfectly still. There it was again. Over the constant hum of insects, something was splashing nearby. Splashing, and . . . trilling some odd song. But nothing like the mental music of the Singers.

Silently K'heera advanced, following the noise. She didn't expect to find any animals in the Land of Confusion. What creature had been courageous enough to brave the mind tricks of the River Spirits? The trilling and playful splashing continued. She heard two distinct voices, one high and tremulous, the other lower. She hunkered down beside the brush that edged a tiny clearing bordering the river's edge.

Two brilliantly colored creatures were submerged in shallow water, playing, swimming, splashing—and communicating. K'heera thought they might be male and female, perhaps a pair performing a pre-mating ritual. She slowed her breathing. She'd never seen anything like them in anything she'd studied, but Trinity was crawling with so many species of animals, it would be years before they could all be documented. These two had such a small brain casing, they might not be susceptible to the Singers' telepathy. If she couldn't make a First Contact, it would still be enjoyable to give these creatures their scientific name. It would be a small honor, but a Harkk'ett could not be fussy.

Suddenly one of the creatures stood, revealing its form. K'heera was stunned to realize it was bipedal, with four-fingered hands and opposing thumbs. The being, whose hairless skin was colored a stunning red and blue, sang something to its partner, but the submerged being seemed strangely unresponsive. The one standing, the smaller, sleeker of the two—the female?—stepped onto the shore and picked up something from the ground.

K'heera stared. The being held a small container. As soon as she lifted it, the Simiu could tell it had been manufactured of some natural substance, perhaps wood. It was simply but elegantly designed.

Scooping something from it, the creature playfully splashed back into the water after her companion. She rubbed her hands along her partner, singing all the while. The male must have found the experience pleasurable because he just lay in the water passively while the other one massaged him.

*A bipedal creature, with hands, who can communicate vocally, make containers, and perhaps even medicinal ointments?*

How many measurably intelligent beings could one planet evolve? Could K'heera's flight have helped her stumble upon the one thing that might pull her family from their shameful caste?

She had to communicate with them, she *had* to. K'heera watched with a suddenly inexhaustible patience as the two beings played. Finally, the female stood in the shallow water. Slowly, the Simiu parted the vegetation, allowing the two to see her.

Both creatures were plainly startled by her presence. Calmly, K'heera stepped from behind the vegetation and sat facing them. Then she made the Simiu greeting sign, extending her hand in the gesture of welcome, peace, and honor. She did it again, then waited for them to make the next move.

Lene's first thought when she heard the rustle of the brush was that Arvis' mother had come spying on them. Her hindbrain tried to force her into panicked flight, because the stodgy matriarch would be furious if she found them both nude, with the scent of male mating hormone rich on Arvis' skin.

Arvis became frightened, too, and crouched behind her, hiding there as if her small body could somehow protect his huge frame. But when the brush parted, out stepped . . . an animal? No, Lene realized, not an animal. No animal wore clothing, and this beast had a garment slung over its back and shoulders. There was artwork on the garment, and things bulged from its pockets.

This had to be one of the *humans* they'd been hearing so much about. Even now, the Glorious First pursued them in his private transport. Lene hadn't seen one yet, but she hadn't realized they had so much hair. Also, they were supposed to walk on two feet, like the Chosen, yet this one clearly walked on all fours.

Well, those details hardly mattered. This human had to be unaware of the capture of its fellows on their space station, since it was plainly eager to communicate. There were only a few humans widely scattered on this planet, and she'd heard they were here for scientific study and peaceful interactions with native species. Lene paused. Could this human think *they* were natives? That would explain its willingness to interact. And wasn't that the whole purpose of the League these beings belonged to?

Lene considered her actions carefully. If she handled this right, she might be able to capture this human. What would the First think of that? He had a small army and still hadn't captured one personally. The Second, Dacris, had had his humans just placidly walk into his trap. This would take cunning.

The creature made a gesture toward them, and when they didn't respond, repeated it more slowly. Lene lifted her head. It could be a greeting. Slowly, she repeated the gesture. The tiny, monochrome eyes of the alien widened.

Arvis watched Lene carefully, then clumsily repeated the gesture. The alien then tapped itself and made a terrible sound, nearly panicking Arvis completely. Lene held his arm firmly.

"It's all right," she reassured him. "This human is trying to tell us its name. Don't be afraid."

"This is a human?" Arvis asked.

"Yes," Lene sang.

He stared at the alien for a long moment. "What's a human?"

She sighed, trying not to think of the years ahead, the endless, childlike questions, that slack, expressionless face, or the passionless, clumsy touch of this idiot her father's stupidity had forced her to marry. To marry him was bad enough, but to have to woo this creature . . . ?

Lene turned to the alien, and pointed to herself and sang her name. Then she turned to Arvis and did the same.

"Why did you tell it *my* name?" Arvis asked fearfully.

"We have to make friends with it," Lene explained. "You have to help me." Arvis was good at making friends among the Industrious. That tendency was the remnants of the strong political personality the First's family all had. She hated thinking about the potential that had been lost when Arvis had been stunted. But then, if he hadn't been stunted, he would have been too highly ranked to marry her.

Lene stepped out of the water, urging Arvis to join her. Cautiously they moved closer to the alien. Lene squatted on her haunches, much as the alien did. Arvis sat also, but first he moved a bit closer to the alien. He pointed to it and sang, "Human. You are a human?"

The alien must've thought he was trying to say its name, because it repeated that terrible sound again. Lene wondered how they were ever going to use these people as workers, when communication between them was clearly impossible. Suddenly the alien held up its hands. Slowly, deliberately, it gestured, then made the sound for its name again, then pointed to itself. Lene was confused. The alien gestured again.

Arvis chirped cheerfully, imitating the gesture. The alien made a different hand motion, then pointed to them. Arvis repeated that gesture as well. The Industrious were all very imitative, and the First's son was more intelligent than some.

The alien made a third gesture, and Arvis copied that as well. Surprised, Lene realized the alien could use its *hands* to make a language of gestures. What a clever creature! No wonder the Glorious First was so excited about their potential.

Arvis and the human were happily building a small repertoire of gestures. Very appropriate, since it was destined to spend the rest of its days communicating with the Industrious. As the two proceeded with their language interchange, Lene considered how she might lure the human back to the settlement. It would have to be overpowered and drugged, but the only thing Lene had with her was the male mating hormone.

That oil was Lene's gift to Arvis. Rubbing that hormone on the lower back and tail had begun an unstoppable process that would culminate during the next long rain. Then, whether Arvis' mother liked it or not, Lene would bear the First's grandchild.

Lene knew that if the rains came before Arvis was truly in love with her, his mother would demand they wait until the next season. And what if Arvis could never transfer his emotional attachment from his parents to her?

She had no intentions of waiting for future rains or the fickleness of an Industrious' emotions. She had been waiting her whole life for the rank she should have been born into. When the rains came, whether Arvis loved her or not, he'd *have* to breed.

Distractedly, Lene glanced around for the oil container. For her, that was more valuable than even this human. It wasn't where she'd left it. Arvis and the alien were still happily gesturing to one another; in fact, the First's Industrious son seemed completely smitten with his new language skills. Then Lene looked again. Her round eyes opened wide.

Arvis was holding the oil container so the alien could see it. The human sniffed it, then, before Lene could move, Arvis smeared some on the alien's bare palm, singing that the oil would make the human feel good.

*Oh, no!* Lene thought, fighting panic. What effect could that hormone have on an alien physiology? The human must've had a similar concern, because it jerked its hand back and rubbed it on the ground to remove the oil. Arvis acted confused. The hormone must've begun stinging because the alien shook the affected hand wildly and, darting to the river's edge, plunged its arm under the water, scrubbing its hands.

*Water will make it worse!* Lene thought. The human didn't have the moist, glandular skin she had, but she couldn't risk the chance that water might speed the absorption of the hormone into its blood, as it did on her people. Impulsively, she leaped at the alien, grabbing its arm, pulling it out of the water.

The alien shrugged her off with surprising ease and washed frantically, in obvious pain. Desperately, Lene tackled the creature, wrapping her long limbs around it. If she could only immobilize it with a wrestling hold!

Suddenly Arvis screeched, "NO! Don't hurt the human! Don't hurt!" and flung himself at her. The three of them tumbled into the river in a jumble of fur, skin, arms, and legs. Completely terrified, the human fought against the pain in its hand, their combined arms, and the pull of the river.

"Stop, Arvis!" Lene sang in her most commanding voice. To her amazement, Arvis defied her, grasping the human and pulling it out of Lene's grip. "Arvis, watch your patch!" she shrilled.

The warning came too late as the dull yellow tissue on Arvis' right arm brushed the human lightly.

*The Industrious' poison is too weak,* Lene thought desperately. *The water would've washed his small toxin residue away. The male hormone couldn't have strengthened it so soon. . . .*

The human stiffened, a soft moan of pain escaping its clenched jaws. Then it fell like a stone under the water.

Arvis stared at the limp form as Lene thrashed toward it and grabbed a handful of its hair, yanking its head out of the river. "Help me!" she demanded and the frightened Arvis assisted her as they wrestled the creature onto dry land.

"Did . . . I kill . . . ?" Arvis' song dissolved into whimpers.

"Did you kill the human?" Lene asked him viciously. "Yes, you did! You didn't listen to me, and look what happened."

"But you tried to hurt the human," Arvis argued back. "I only tried to make it feel *good*!"

Lene started to explain about the hormone, then realized how useless that would be. Instead, she went on the defensive. "Who are you to *disobey* me? I am *Chosen* and you are *not*! Do you know what can happen to a disobedient Industrious servant?"

Arvis' big eyes became huge. "No. . . ."

*No, you wouldn't,* Lene realized, *the son of the Glorious First has never tasted the rod in the hands of a good punisher, or had a day's hunger, or been sold to a pharmacist and forced into maximum toxin production. You have no idea. . . .*

The spark of defiance Arvis had displayed dissolved, and the childlike servant began trilling in terror.

Lene took a deep breath to regain her decorum. These damned, stupid Industrious could make you enjoy hurting them. Then she heard a strange whistling sound.

She stared down at the prostrate human, who was dripping water onto her feet. Slowly, the alien's breath whistled into its lungs. With agonizing deliberation, the air whistled back out again.

Arvis was looking at the human, also. "Oh, good," he sang pathetically. "You're *not* dead. I didn't kill you."

But the laborious breathing was the only positive sign the human could give them. Its eyes, opened wide, did not blink as they had when it communicated with them, and its limbs were held out rigidly. Perhaps the doctors could save it.

"You *disobeyed* me, Arvis," Lene sang softly. His fearful expression was now tinged with confusion. "I'm *supposed* to punish you, you know that, don't you? But I'm sure you didn't mean it. You'll never do it again, will you?"

"Never!" Arvis sang in a soft whisper.

"Do you know *why* I won't punish you for your disobedience?"

"No." Arvis seemed baffled.

"Because that's not the way you treat people you *love*. And I love you, Arvis, *don't* I?"

The servant didn't answer, just stared, confused.

"I love you very much," Lene insisted, her tone soothing. "I could never hurt you, dear." She let him think about that. Then she asked softly, "Do you love me?"

Arvis closed his eyes, obviously at a loss as to what to say. Even someone as simple as Arvis understood the significance of the word "love." He loved his parents; he'd learned the power of that word from them. Their love protected him.

"If you didn't love me, Arvis, I would be so sad. . . . I don't know what I'd do. Do you love me?"

He blinked. "You'll never tell . . . about my disobeying?"

"I couldn't . . . if you loved me . . . ?"

Finally, he sang, "Yes, Lene, I love you."

"You've made me so happy, Arvis," she sang sweetly. "Now, get dressed. We've got to get this human to the doctors, to see if they can counteract *your* toxins." He flinched at the reminder, but docilely began pulling his clothes on. "And one more thing, my love." She considered how to phrase this next command. It couldn't be a suggestion, because then he might not do it, yet she didn't dare demand it too blatantly. "Please tell your mother, Arvis, about your love for me."

"She won't like that," he sang bluntly.

"Oh, she will, my dear, you'll see," Lene assured him. And once the old matriarch heard that song from her son's own throat, she'd be helpless to stop the marriage. The First's wife would never deny Arvis the joy of a wife, the pleasure of a breeding cycle. Lene suppressed a shudder at that eventuality, as she leaned down to lift the heavy, water-soaked human.

Every breath that K'heera pulled into her paralyzed, pain-wracked body was liquid fire, but it was one more breath away from death. And when she'd first felt the poison course through her blood, she knew death would be her next experience. The ointment the alien had slapped into her palm had burned without leaving a mark, but that had been nothing compared to what had happened when the spot of yellow on his arm had touched her.

She'd felt as though she'd wrapped her hands around a voder's power pack, and then there'd been a brief respite as she'd lapsed into unconsciousness. When she came to on the dry riverbank, both aliens were conversing animatedly.

K'heera sensed when they realized she was still alive. Their conversation changed, and suddenly they pulled garments out from under a shrub and donned them quickly. The Simiu wanted to moan in dismay. The clothing had to have been manufactured. These were *not* a primal people.

The aliens clumsily carried her down the trail, heading farther west. This caused K'heera more agony, but breathing took up so much concentration, she could not waste the energy to even sigh in pain. After a moment, the female realized K'heera's faithful sled was following her, as she'd programmed it to do before their disastrous encounter. Within seconds of their discovering the anti-gravity device, they'd placed the Simiu on it, and using it as a stretcher, guided the sled through the forest.

K'heera barely had time to dwell on their casual acceptance of such advanced technology when they pushed through the trees and into a wide riverside clearing.

Her breathing turned into ragged gasps. Prefabricated buildings dotted the clearing, with what the humans would call catwalks connecting them. A-grav devices, different from hers, but with the same function, were common. Dozens of aliens wandered everywhere, some having different body styles or coloring. Even in pain and confusion, K'heera knew a new colony when she saw one. She thought of the silent satellite and Meg's and Szu-yi's absence, and the Interrelator's nervous concerns. Then she thought of the probe—the probe that had worked like one of the feather lures the Interrelator used to catch her fish.

The female alien bleated loudly as she pushed the sled toward the colony, and other beings raced over to them. They surrounded K'heera, singing rapidly and producing technical equipment. They attached things to her, prodded and poked her. The two aliens that had captured her (that was the only way she could think of it now, as being captured) disappeared in the crowd. Someone slapped a patch on her flank, and her stiffened body relaxed. Another patch was stuck on, and she felt her lungs expand more evenly. Finally, she could blink her dry, painful eyes.

K'heera began to think she might actually live. Was that good news? She waited for a drug that would free her from the frightening paralysis, but that didn't happen.

The crowd (a medical team?) acted more casual now, examining her curiously. One of them peered in her eyes, another pried open her jaws. Then one of them searched through her sodden crest and found the sound nullifiers tangled in her fur. The alien ripped the nullifiers free and showed them to the others.

The medical team walked K'heera's sled toward one of the buildings. Distantly, in the background, she thought she heard the distant calls of Grus in flight. Her heart lifted—was it the cohort? It had to be. They'd followed her, they would see her, they would tell the others! The sound tickled her ears like a promise. The aliens drew near one of their buildings, and K'heera panicked as she realized they would probably have her inside before the cohort ever had a chance to see her. *Wait! Wait!* she begged them in her mind. *They have to see me!*

The calls grew louder, more irritating, and K'heera struggled to identify individual voices. She thought she could hear Hurricane, who had the deepest, loudest voice . . . but he hadn't been with them. . . . To her relief, the medical crew slowed down as they, too, heard the avians. They conversed, looking for the birds, oblivious to K'heera's helplessness.

A wave of painful sound rippled through K'heera as the Grus flew even closer, eating up the distance with their enormous wings. Only then did she realize the approaching avians couldn't be the cohort. *It has to be Gray Winds traveling over the river,* she thought with a sickening rush. That was why they always kept the nullifiers around their necks, because of the Gray Winds. Whenever they crossed the river, they called frantically, frightened that River Spirits would pluck them from the sky. Where were her nullifiers?

Two of the crew were discussing the little instruments, disassembling them, laying the parts near her head on the sled.

*No!* thought K'heera. *No! I need them!* She projected the thought wildly, screaming it in her mind. Didn't *they* need protection from the sound of the Grus?

*Their buildings must be soundproofed,* she thought. But they were moving toward the shelter so slowly! The cascading sound was so loud now it rocked her spine, and made her ears ache. *HURRY!* K'heera's mind shrieked at the aliens. *GET ME INDOORS! PLEASE, PLEASE HURRY!*

They were only steps away from the building's entrance when the family group flew over, calling loudly, crossing the river as quickly as possible. The sound waves ripped through K'heera in an explosion of pain. Her eardrums and the capillaries lining her ear canals burst under the barrage of sound. But only her mind screamed. Her helpless body never moved.

The medical team, unaffected by the onslaught of sound, stopped to watch the avians' flight. They didn't notice the blood trickling from K'heera's ears and nose.

As she struggled with her inner agony, K'heera realized that she was deaf, as deaf as the Honored Interrelator herself. This, then, was an appropriate punishment for a dishonorable person, to be as afflicted as the person she'd unfairly criticized. What an appropriate First Contact for the dishonored Harkk'ett clan.

As the medical team finally led K'heera's sled into their building, she took one last glimpse at the World. For just a second, she thought she saw a lone, immature Aquila in one of the tall trees.

But this time she didn't hope that it might be Thunder. She'd learned her lesson.

Then K'heera was swallowed by the alien building and could see nothing but bustling aliens, bright lights, and what had to be a fully equipped hospital.

*Or,* she thought fearfully, as they lifted her off the sled and onto a platform, strapping her limbs in place, *could it be . . . a lab?*

# CHAPTER 11
♦
# Looking for K'heera

Father Sun had set and the dim light of dusk waned as Tesa stared into the forest, waiting for Lightning. No matter how foolish K'heera might be, Tesa knew she could trust the Grus youngster. He knew he had to return to camp before dark. She folded her arms and shifted her weight, her eyes boring into the darkening woods, as if wishing would bring them out. Behind her, the entire cohort clustered together, shifting from foot to foot.

A hand touched her shoulder. "None-So-Pretty was right," Bruce signed, coming around to face her. "Her sled's gone. I should've looked earlier. I feel really responsible."

"Stop blaming yourself," Tesa ordered angrily. "K'heera knows better than to take off on some wild excursion."

"Tesa," Bruce signed patiently, "she's done what any kid would do. She's gone off to show us she doesn't need us."

"She's a Simiu *female,*" Tesa signed angrily. "They're trained from infancy to accept more responsibility. . . ."

Bruce's mouth turned up. "Why, Tesa, that's sexist! I'm surprised at you. She'll come back when she's good and ready."

Tesa nearly exploded. "Suppose she can't! She's in an unexplored wilderness, Bruce, not a manicured Simiu courtyard!"

He patted her arm. "You're worried about Lightning."

Angrily, she blinked tears away. "I told him to stay with her! No matter what she does, he'll do what *I* asked!"

He paused, finally signing, "We could call K'heera on the voders . . . or go out on our sleds. . . ."

Tesa chewed her lip. "No. We'll wait." And she and her cohort watched the forest as shadows swallowed the undergrowth.

Jib needed to come out of the water; his feet were almost numb. Taniwha, however, couldn't understand how such warm water could make Jib so cold. The calf bumped him, enticing him to swim some more.

To the herd, the World consisted of warm water, easy travel, and good food. Through them, Jib had seen their River, traveled their ocean, tasted a hundred water plants, and drunk the rich, cream-laden milk of Taniwha's mother. He'd wallowed in so many mental flavors, he had to be reminded to eat real food. The herd's songs washed over his mind like a gentle, seductive touch.

Communicating with the Singers was nothing like talking to the Shadgui. Those telepathic people could speak and had been in touch with verbal-based languages for generations. Doctor Blanket could think in language as well, since seloz had learned that skill from Mahree Burroughs and the young Simiu, Dhurrrkk'.

But the Singers were different. To Jib, much of their mental music was still nothing more than a flood of chaotic but pleasurable emotions. Day and night they flooded his mind, making him drunk on their mental caress. There were times when he knew he was falling into a dangerous telepathic euphoria, but he couldn't stop. Rob and Doctor Blanket had warned him, but he hadn't believed them . . . and now he couldn't make himself care.

Dazedly, he realized it was nearly dark and waded away from them reluctantly. His time sense was gone, since time meant nothing to the Singers. They dozed fitfully if at all, and their wakefulness disrupted his sleep.

"I was just coming to get you," Bruce drawled softly from the edge of the beach.

Confused, the Maori forgot for a second how to speak. He began sloshing his way toward the weatherman.

"You all right, son?" the older man asked. "Your feet look like blue prunes."

Jib blinked, then scanned for Tesa, finally realizing something at the camp wasn't right. "Where is everybody?"

Bruce sighed. "Looks like K'heera took off on her sled, against orders. Lightning's with her, wherever they are."

He hadn't even thought of K'heera for hours, he realized guiltily. "So, we're going out to search for them now?"

"Tesa doesn't want to use sleds," Bruce answered slowly.

Bruce's words startled the younger man into anger. "She's watched too many of Dr. Gable's old movies; she's seeing *Invaders From Mars* everywhere! We should search, *now!*"

The weatherman raised his hands placatingly. "Tesa understands the danger K'heera might be in. But she's concerned about that probe, and it's been my experience that her instincts are not to be ignored. I'm willing to wait."

*Things would've gone differently here if I'd done my job!* Jib thought. "Does Tesa know where they might've gone?"

"They followed the animal path west, along the river. Why?"

Jib turned toward the beach. "The Singers could 'listen' for them. They're planning to go in that direction, anyway."

Bruce seemed interested. "Lightning will probably sleep near the River. They should be able to find him. Ask them."

The young Maori thought of Taniwha as he watched water spouts circle near the shore. Picturing the River as it wound its long way westward, he then pictured K'heera and Lightning, concentrating on his concern for their safety.

Soon the herd's silent songs permeated his mind, and he felt their sympathy. Their music changed, the tones rearranged, as they picked up his cadence of concern . . . and his guilt. Fascinated, he realized they were altering their music to reflect his thoughts. The new song sounded eerie and beautifully haunting. Suddenly the water spouts turned west.

"They *heard* you," Bruce said. "They're going!"

The music soared through Jib, captivating him, making him ignore what Bruce was saying until finally, the lilting melody diminished. Slowly, Taniwha's tenuous mental touch dissipated as the calf became entranced with the journey. Jib felt hollow as the contact ended and the wonderful music faded away. He almost regretted asking for their help. *You should be thrilled*, he scolded himself, *now, you can get a good night's sleep!*

"This'll make Tesa feel better," Bruce said.

Jib watched the Singers swim away, wishing he were with them.

Taniwha swam hard beside his mother, pumping his fluke furiously to keep up with the herd. They'd been traveling for a long time, and it was dark now, but the youngster was still exhilarated. Where were they headed? When would they get there? Would there be anything good to eat?

His mother absorbed the barrage of questions, but like mothers everywhere, only countered with her own. Are you tired? Cold?

Can you see? Are you hungry? The last question stilled his thoughts, and he nuzzled against her side.

She lifted her right flipper, giving him access to the small nipple beneath it. While he nursed, the warm, sweet milk coursing down his throat, his mother propelled them onward.

Spontaneous adventures were a delight to the eternally hungry, curious creatures, but to touch an unusual mind was a thrill. Their new friend had sung a song that was not-of-the-World, but yet they'd understood it. The un-Worldly friend sang poorly, but he and his people had helped one of their calves, and that favor must be repaid. So the herd swam west, searching for a missing White Wind, a solitary Hunter, and a furred, four-legged being. What an adventure!

Of course, the River of Life was hardly new. They'd lived in it for generations, swimming to the sea when summer came and the ocean warmed, then returning in the winter when the ocean chilled again.

The summer had just ended and it had been a good season; the seaweed had been lush, and not once had they been preyed upon by the Great Hunger. It had been years since that monster had savaged them, so long ago that none of the herd had ever seen it— but its memory lived among them. Every summer they ventured out to the sea cautiously, the fear as sharp as yesterday, and rejoiced when the season passed and none had died to feed it.

It had been the violent assaults of those predators countless generations ago that had forced the Singers to expand their minds. Even though their fear of the vanished terror was still keen, they'd allowed the method of its defeat their powerful mental abilities—to fall into disuse. Now, they only needed to keep the Wind people from building their shelters, confuse the Hunters and large reptiles that might attack a newborn calf, and keep the massive Quakers out of their River. If they could only learn to baffle the weather, they would not have a care in the World.

The gentle touch of stubby fingers along Taniwha's back made him look up as his father swam over them. Mother waved a flipper and the male gestured lazily back at her.

The youngster suddenly felt his mother cast her mind, touch a stranger's, then retreat. She'd spied the lone White Wind, perched on one long leg on the River's bank, head tucked, sleeping. Even in his sleep, the herd could sense the troubled thoughts of the young avian. He'd lost his friend, the Simiu.

The herd swam on. Taniwha thought about sending a picture of the sleeping White Wind to Jib. How funny they looked, the calf thought, with their weed-thin legs and feathered bodies standing up in the air. But Jib was asleep, too. Land beings craved sleep, Mother had explained, because they had to endure their terrible weight without the benefit of water to buoy them up. It exhausted them so much they had to sleep the night through, and could actually die if they didn't get enough of the deathlike torpor, she'd told him. Remembering that, Taniwha decided to wait until they'd found the Hunter and the Simiu.

The herd pushed on through the dark night waters as the Moons climbed high, two of them full, and the smallest half-dark. In the Moons' cycle of the Parents and Their Calf, the calf was now half-grown, just like Taniwha. When the smallest Moon grew full it would pull away from its parents, just as he would in another year. Over the Moons shone the Calf star, and the four orbs dappled the water silver.

Eventually, the herd came to a wide bend where there was a broad open beach and an adjoining marsh. The herd had not been here since spring, and weren't prepared for the surprising changes they saw. Strange, unnatural objects perched up high on odd-looking legs had grown out of the River mud, some of them growing over the River itself. The Singers swam closer, having never seen anything like this on the World before.

Taniwha's father sniffed the air, tasting the new scents floating there. When an upright, two-legged being emerged from one of the things and began observing them, the herd realized the objects had to be some kind of shelter. This must be another settlement of un-Worldly beings, Father decided, like Jib's, and the herd agreed. Creatures on brightly lit flying things, not unlike the one Jib had used, roamed the beaches, marsh, and River even at this late hour. Several of the beings flew lower, as though to greet the herd, so the Singers threw water into the air as a welcoming gesture.

Soon, there were more hovering aliens than the herd could count. Father wondered why Jib's group was so small and this one so vast, but Taniwha didn't know. He'd never seen anything in Jib's mind that had indicated this group even existed.

The aliens warbled and pointed at the Singers, their sounds different from those made by Jib and his friends. But Mother explained that creatures that vocalized depended on air to carry their messages, and air distorted sound.

Suddenly a being leaned over its flyer, waving a multicolored device. Taniwha wanted to touch the un-Worldly being's mind, so Mother joined him to soften the connection and probe unobtrusively. But this being was nothing like Jib, whose thoughts were warm and always curious. This being's mind was fragmented, its thoughts cold and calculating, as if its brain held nothing but appetite and need. Mother grew perplexed and probed further, following the trail of neurons. Bored, Taniwha cast about for a mind that he might understand.

Finally, he found someone he knew. It was an avian, dozing fitfully in the highest tree. He stroked the mind the way Mother had taught him, cautiously, so as not to wake the creature.

It was the missing Hunter, he realized delightedly. Could the Simiu be near? Even in sleep, the Hunter's mind was filled with concern for that four-legged alien. Taniwha began searching for K'heera. Finally, he located her un-Worldly mind song deep inside one of the odd shelters.

Thinking she, too, must be asleep, he moved cautiously around the outskirts of her thoughts. Curious as to what the inside of the shelter was like, Taniwha searched for the Simiu's vision center. It didn't occur to him that K'heera might sleep with her eyes closed, as he did. Finding the proper pathways, he peered through her opened eyes. Small, cool suns blazed brightly, while vividly colored beings scurried around. There were two aliens nearby, but like the creatures around him, their minds were too fragmented for him to understand.

Taniwha wanted to know why K'heera was here when Jib was back at the other camp, worried about her. He wondered, too, why she was not resisting his mind-touch, as she'd done before. The Simiu disliked the Singer's music, and Taniwha had found it difficult to sing with her. Her lack of response now could only be due to her sleeping. He considered leaving. Having found her should be enough, but he knew Jib would want to know more.

The calf searched through her eyes again, so he could show Jib later. Everything was bright, the strange creatures bustling around busily, tending alien machines, and . . . Taniwha stopped, sensing wrongness. Something . . . was happening . . . . The aliens . . . were *doing* things to K'heera. Something was happening to her teeth and to her fur. Another creature was doing something to an arm . . . . Taniwha was baffled. Just then an alien dripped a liquid into K'heera's open eyes. It stung furiously.

Confused, the calf cautiously ventured into the Simiu's consciousness, prepared to leap out as soon as he sensed her rejection. But instead of a harmless, random sleep pattern like Jib's, he found himself plunging into an abyss of pain and terror, a sickening morass of helplessness and agony. Instantly, Taniwha understood everything that had happened and was happening to

K'heera. She was *not* asleep—she was paralyzed, but totally conscious and aware. Terrified, the calf absorbed her meeting with these aliens, her poisoning and capture, and the cruel treatment she'd suffered for hours now.

Taniwha understood the significance of their experiments because K'heera understood them. They were pulling blood from her body, while pumping a variety of substances into her to discover her reactions to them. The things she'd been through had exhausted her, yet her captors cared nothing for her need for sleep or respite from pain. Instead, they patiently analyzed her endurance. Anytime she lapsed into sleep, a device strapped to her forehead delivered an excruciating shock. Falling asleep had become so painful that K'heera now feared it with hysterical terror. The substances the aliens inflicted on her were sometimes painful, occasionally pleasant, and often mind-numbing, a thing she'd once feared. Now, though, she longed for the mind-numbing drug, even pleaded for it in her mind. If they'd only give it to her again, she'd be . . . so grateful.

While the experiments continued, her captors efficiently depilated her fur, leaving all her skin glistening and bare. But worse than that was what was happening to her mouth.

Her large canine teeth, the fangs her people bared in honorable challenge, were being ground down to short, harmless, squared-off stumps. The Simiu had been given nothing to dull the pain, and the huge nerves in her canines screamed. K'heera could glimpse monitors she thought were measuring her brain activity, and helplessly watched them register every new sensation.

The Simiu's mind sang a song of terror unlike anything Taniwha had ever known. Suddenly a new substance coursed through her, dulling her sleep-fogged mind, and she dozed involuntarily. The device strapped to her head shocked her unmercifully—and the sensation flooded Taniwha's mind as well. The calf sang out from the pain, and K'heera *heard* him. Instead of the rage and rejection he'd expected, the Simiu's consciousness grabbed at him with an insane urgency.

*HELP! SAVE ME! THEY'RE KILLING ME, OH, PLEASE, DON'T LEAVE ME HERE, DON'T LEAVE. . . .*

Taniwha was so shaken by the frightening onslaught, he forgot to come up for air. Then Father was under him, pushing him up until his nostrils broke the surface and opened automatically. Coming back to himself, to his own body floating pain-free in sweet, warm water, Taniwha realized the entire herd had *heard* K'heera's frantic pleas as they flowed through him. The herd grew frightened. What kind of beings could so blandly torture another creature? None, since the Great Hunger.

Taniwha reached for his parents, but their thoughts were not reassuring. Mother could not sing to these aliens, so she decided they were insane, it was the only explanation for their split minds and their sickening cruelty. She urged the herd to leave, to return to the sea.

Father agreed. As the herd's senior bull, he swam near the rear and pushed the herd eastward, urging them to swim swiftly, to ignore their hunger, their exhaustion. As unified as schooled fish, the Singers turned toward the sea.

The aliens followed, whistling their bizarre songs. They flew ahead of the herd, lining up across a narrow place in the River. Suddenly a jolt of white power erupted from the flyers, striking the water like lightning, making it boil. Painful shivers trembled through the Singers. Another jolt fell and another, until they became a curtain of energy and pain. The bolts solidified underwater, meshing together like plant roots, weaving tighter and tighter. Water flowed through the web of power, but the openings in the shining mesh began to shrink.

A young bull near Taniwha panicked, imagining the Great Hunger, seeing its terrible face, its bloody, tearing teeth. He turned from the power web, away from the sea, and everyone near followed, his panic overwhelming Father's calm urgency. Taniwha felt the power of his parents' mind guiding him, urging him toward the web, but a crush of massive bodies twisting and turning suddenly surrounded him. He was pushed back, away from the sea, away from his mother, and found himself swimming west with the others. The herd's cohesiveness evaporated as the fear of the Great Hunger engulfed mind after mind.

Then the calf *heard* his father sing reassuringly. There was no Great Hunger. There were only these aliens and their un-Worldly things. The old male ordered the herd to find openings through the shrinking web and swim through. His song was strong, but the younger males were afraid to pass through the tightening mesh.

Then his mother touched Taniwha's mind, and he realized she was on the other side of the web. She'd been pushed through when they'd been separated, and now she called for him frantically, urging him to come to her so they could swim to the sea.

The calf hesitated. His father was on this side with him, his mother on the other. When he finally surged toward the grid, there were so many squeezing through the tightening mesh, he was pushed aside. The web's power stunned whoever swam through it, and every painful shock caused more panic in the herd.

When the last portal became too small for even the youngest calf, Taniwha and his father were only two of many trapped on the wrong side of the web. Father ordered those who had escaped to swim for the sea.

Still, they paused. All of them had loved ones behind the web. The old male's mind was strong, though, and he projected confidence that they would defeat these aliens as they had once conquered the Great Hunger. As the free Singers moved away from the web, they maintained contact with their friends, ready to lend their power to destroy this alien force.

Taniwha's father appeared beside him and together, they swam westward, away from the web, only to face another grid pinning them into a small section of the River. After a few moments, they realized that the grids were moving, corraling the herd into a smaller area. Taniwha felt his father reach deep into his own mind and call up power his people hadn't used for generations. The entire herd linked with him.

Taniwha listened as his father reached for the mind of the nearest alien and probed, searching its brain for its knowledge, its motives. His son and the combined herdmind followed him, even as aliens surrounded them, heedless of their mental assault. Father sang as hard as he could, using the fear Taniwha had taken from K'heera as a weapon. The creature shook its head slightly, then ignored the onslaught of the powerful telepath. Leaning over its sled, the alien touched Father with a small device.

A terrible fire coursed through the great bull's body; as his flippers went limp, his body grew rigid. At the same time, the aliens struck another male, then a female. The helplessness coursing through the afflicted ones shattered the Singers' tenuous unity. They panicked, swimming wildly around and around the shrinking corral, pulling Taniwha helplessly along.

A few elders stayed with the paralyzed ones, pushing them up to the air so they wouldn't drown. The rest of the herd surged wildly between the two power grids, their massive bodies slamming against the alien lightning webs, shocking themselves again and again. Taniwha *heard* his mother fighting to get in, to come to the aid of her calf and her mate.

Even in his helplessness, Father tried to calm the herd, but it was too late. When the aliens attached devices to the three Singers and lifted them out of the water, even as Taniwha had once been lifted off the sandbar, the captive herd felt their friends' raw fear. The helpless Singers were beached in low water, where the World's terrible gravity crushed them.

An alien tended each of the helpless creatures, struggling to keep their massive heads in the air, even as Jib had once helped Taniwha. But the one handling Father was careless and allowed the old bull to inhale water. Taniwha and his mother both agonized as his father coughed painfully. Aliens swarmed out of their shelters and surrounded the beached Singers, chittering excitedly and waving alien devices.

Mother tried to force Taniwha to find an opening in the grid, in spite of the herd's confusion and the fear she felt for her mate. But the mesh was too small, and Taniwha too afraid. Desperately, he cast his mind. Despite the agony he knew she'd still be in, he touched K'heera again.

The Simiu was just as he'd left her, only the dental work and depilation were completed. A new shift of aliens had come in and she thought they were reviewing the analysis of the previous group. Since the grinding had stopped, she'd grown indifferent. She'd convinced herself she didn't need sleep, that Simiu were strong enough to remain awake indefinitely. The loss of her fur made her cold even in the warm, humid environment, but she welcomed that, since it helped her stay awake.

Even though Taniwha was young, he recognized the song of madness. The calf entered her brain rudely, wanting her to know he was there. He demanded answers. K'heera was not of the World, surely she understood these evil beings. What were they doing here? What were they doing to his people, to his father? K'heera tried to shut her mind down, not wanting to cope with anyone else's pain, but the youngster would not be shut out. He showed her what was happening on the beach.

Slowly, she responded. *The aliens are studying your people,* she thought at him. *Why. I don't know. I don't know what they want, I'm a prisoner, just like them. Save yourselves. There's nothing you can do for them. . . .*

Taniwha made K'heera see through his father's eyes as groups of aliens guided huge vats over to the Singers, vats that sloshed and dripped pungent liquids.

Together, they watched the aliens surround the female Singer. Her panic surged through the herd, even as Taniwha's father uselessly urged calm. The being holding her head suddenly pushed her snout underwater. Every Singer and K'heera experienced her desperate struggle for air, but eventually her nostrils opened convulsively and she inhaled. Her lungs pumped furiously, pushing water out, then sucking it back in again, her mind-thrashing panic driving the herd insane.

Finally it was over, and Taniwha's father watched as the aliens flayed the flesh from the dead female and threw it into the vats. Her blood poured into the River of Life, and its scent was more than the captive Singers could bear. The Great Hunger was truly among them—no longer content to hide in the ocean, it had invaded their beloved River to feast on them!

Hysterically, they battered the energy corral, burning themselves on the webs. Taniwha was caught in the throng, no longer able to see his father or *hear* his mother, as the Singers pushed against their prison with all their might. Finally, the aliens must have realized they would suicide on the grid. They dropped one of the webs, allowing the captive herd to flee westward up the River.

K'heera, carried along on the tide of panic, watched their flight. She knew it was useless, and her knowledge shocked Taniwha as he was swept away. *They can find your people whenever they want,* she told him bitterly. Just then, the aliens began drowning the other bull. The dying male's panic overpowered all other mental communication.

Taniwha felt his parents try once more to affect the mind of the alien holding his father's head. They used every bit of mental ability they could muster on the creature's intellect, but the alien ignored them. Its comrade handed it a chunk of hot, bloody flesh, cut from the not-quite-dead young bull even as their victim's mental death screams shook the herd to their core.

The alien holding Father took the steaming meat, and calmly popped it into its wide mouth. Only then did the herd realize that every alien on the beach was eating flesh cut from the bones of their friends. The atmosphere among the un-Worldly creatures was one of feasting and joy.

Taniwha *heard* K'heera as she thought wildly of the Captain's Night party she'd attended with Jib. The Simiu fought back nausea, but her stomach was so empty she had nothing to bring up.

Suddenly the happy crowd turned its attention to Father. The young calf tried to turn back, to somehow rescue his father, but his mother's sister suddenly appeared beneath him and physically stopped him. At that same moment the old bull's captor dropped Father's huge head under the waves and sat on it while licking gobbets of Singer meat off its fingers. Other aliens clambered onto Father's back, hacking at his tough, aged skin with sharp tools, ripping it away from the fat and muscle. The aliens scraped at the bull's rich fat stores, ignoring the blood and grease that covered them.

Still, Taniwha *heard* his father's song. The bull struggled futilely to keep the images of his death from his youngest child. Despite Father's efforts, Taniwha, his mother, and K'heera, too, witnessed the slow, painful death of the old male.

*Tell Jib!* K'heera begged Taniwha. *Tell Jib and the others, before they're captured, too.*

Suddenly Taniwha's aunt blocked him from responding to K'heera's plea. She could *hear* her sister wailing her widow's song as her mate died horribly to feed these aliens, this new Great Hunger. Their people were captured, betrayed, slaughtered. What difference was there between one un-Worldly being and another? There would be no contact ever, ever again.

*NO!* K'heera begged. *Please, listen to me, don't shut me . . .*

Taniwha's aunt blocked K'heera's desperate pleading as she pushed him westward, away from the alien village. The calf's mother, on the east side of the web, was pulled away from the grid and finally swam with the free herd toward the sea. All Taniwha could smell through the great River of Life was blood and fear and death. And through the herdmind, beneath the mourning wail of his people, all the young calf could *hear* was the dying song of his father.

# CHAPTER 12
## ◆
# The Invaders from Mars

Tesa swam through the River of Fear . . . no, the River of Life. Underwater, in the dark, her arms propelled her body through the murky depths. Was she searching for Jib? She couldn't remember.

Suddenly she thudded into something solid. She turned, only to bump into something else. Blocked, she swam to the surface.

Before a curtain of stars in the dark night sky the Child Sun hung above the Moons. Two full, one half—the Moons of the Fledgling's First Adventure. She started to smile, but ... the Moons weren't their usual ghostly white. They were ... red.

All three glowed that ominous shade as Father Moon oozed, then dripped blood that fell straight down from space to plop into the River as though the big satellite were nothing more than a floating balloon. Drip. Plop. Drip. Plop. Tesa watched crimson ripples slap against the obstacles clogging the River.

Brushing against the huge skeleton of a Singer, she suddenly realized the whole River was choked with those creatures' big white bones. Backing away, she collided with the stiff corpse of a White Wind, its elegant feathers waving limply on the current, pointing to others like it. Before she could move, the flaccid wing of a Hunter draped across her shoulder. Gasping, she floundered for the shore, pushing her way through the River of Death. A long, thin human corpse rolled up in her path. It was Meg. Beside the aged biologist floated Szu-yi. A short distance away bobbed Tesa's grandparents. Not far from them a lifeless Bruce rode the gentle waves, and next to him, floating facedown, was a tall, slim form with dark hair and a white feathered shirt.

Just then the water bubbled and churned. She glimpsed something big—*a fin? a snout?*—just before a massive, open maw ringed with scalpel-like teeth engulfed Bruce's body. Tesa screamed, her voice soundless, her lungs pushing air through her throat in panicky spasms as she splashed backward furiously.

But the water was still again with only a ripple and an open space where Bruce's body had once been. Then something smooth slid against her thigh, something strong and full of hunger.

Her feet touched ground—if it *was* ground they touched—and she struggled for land, pushing past bodies, stumbling over one last corpse, its ravaged brown face and sightless orbs staring sightlessly at the Moons. *Jib?* She pulled herself from the River and collapsed, her feathered shirt soaked red, coated—sticky with blood. But at least she was finally safe.

Then the Mate Kai shot up out of the River like a living mountain and came after her, its sleek skin marbled a searing red and blue, its wide mouth hanging open from the weight of its terrible teeth. She scrabbled backward, knowing it was too late, that she could never escape. The Mate Kai fell on her, grasping her shoulders roughly, and she swung out desperately.

It blocked her blows easily and shook her, then slapped her face gently. She blinked . . . and found herself warm, dry, in her own shelter. Bruce was holding her, trying to wake her, to pull her from the sickening dream. "Okay," she signed. "I'm okay!"

"You were yelling your head off," he signed worriedly.

She collapsed against his chest, incredibly relieved to feel the warmth of his body, his thumping heart. He hugged her, but after a moment she pulled back. "Did you dream last night?"

Bruce shrugged. "If I did, I can't remember."

"Is Jib awake?"

"Not yet. Father Sun's just now rising."

She was out of the shelter in a second, wearing nothing but her faded StarBridge sleep shirt. As she burst through her clustered cohort, they leaped into the air in surprise, leaving a rain of feather dust in their wake. When she finally ducked into Jib's tent, he was on his back, mouth agape, eyes half-opened and staring. When she then nudged him, he sat up quickly.

He cried out, wild-eyed, but Tesa couldn't read it.

Bruce, coming in behind Tesa, moved to the young man's side. "You're awake now, son, in camp in Florida. Everything's okay."

"No," the boy moaned, shaking his head.

"No," Tesa agreed. "Something terrible has happened."

He continued shaking his head, but remembered to sign. "It's fading, I can't remember. . . . The Singers . . . Taniwha . . . K'heera. . . ." He rubbed his face. "It's gone. Faded away. I hate bad dreams." His expression changed, as though he finally realized how odd it was for them to be there. "Did I yell loud enough for *you* to hear me?" he asked Tesa wryly.

She held his gaze with her own. "It was more than a dream."

The young Maori turned gray. "Yeah, it was a bloody *mess* of a dream, that's what. That's enough, isn't it?"

"Did you see the Moons bleed? Did you see the Mate Kai?"

Jib tensed and Bruce stepped between them, giving her a warning glance.

"Come on, Tesa," Jib complained, "you always look for answers in dreams. You stayed up till all hours waiting for your lambs to come home, and when they didn't you went to sleep full of worry and guilt. Did you think you *wouldn't* have bad dreams?"

He was fully awake now and Tesa could see that he didn't want to believe that their shared dream had any significance. Could he be right? After days of direct mental contact with the Singers, their minds could simply be reacting to that absence. Beside her, Bruce said nothing.

"Dreams don't give me answers," Tesa told Jib finally, "but sometimes they give me . . . suggestions that I'd be foolish to ignore. If you'd listen to your primal self . . ."

"My *primal* self only knows that it's hungry," Jib signed peevishly, "and that it didn't get enough sleep."

Before the Indian woman could counter his argument, a huge winged shadow passed over the tent. Looking out, Tesa saw Thunder's dark outline silhouetted against the bright sky. She darted outside as Lightning parachuted down. Seconds later, the Hunter dropped, her powerful wings blowing sand into small tornadoes. The cohort flew over to join them, heralding their friends' return with their raucous, juvenile calls.

"Thank the Suns you're here," Tesa signed, throwing her arms around Lightning, nearly knocking him off balance. He spread his wings to steady himself, then encircled her fondly. When the Hunter approached, Lightning surrounded her with his other wing and the three enjoyed a private moment together.

Bruce and Jib emerged from the tent. "Where's K'heera?" the young man asked.

Lightning ducked his head low. "It's all my fault," he began regretfully and explained the chain of events that led to K'heera's leaving him. "By the time I realized she wouldn't return, it was too dark to come back to camp."

"I followed her," Thunder continued the story, "along the River, until she stopped to eat. That was when she discovered the new creatures that are not-of-the-World."

Tesa watched the Aquila make her flat statement with a cold detachment, as though she'd been waiting to see those signs all along. But for the others, the news was shocking. The entire cohort, including Lightning, stood tall in surprise, their crowns shrinking up hard. Bruce and Jib framed quick questions, but Tesa held her hand up so Thunder could finish.

"The aliens attacked and overpowered K'heera, then placed her on her own sled and guided it inside a building. It was nearly dark then, so I had to wait until morning to return."

"A building?" Bruce asked quickly. "Were there others?"

"Yes. Many." Thunder quickly described a cluster of alien structures, and ongoing construction.

"Were these humans, Thunder?" the Interrelator asked.

"No, but they walk upright with two arms and legs."

"Heeyoons?" Tesa asked. The avians were familiar with the many races associated with the CLS.

"No. They didn't appear like any of the people you've shown me. Their skins were hairless but shining, as if moist, and very colorful. They reminded me of distant cousins of the circle-swimmers. Even the strange trilling notes they used for language seemed similar. And like the circle-swimmers, I thought . . ." she hesitated, as though embarrassed, "they looked delicious."

"Ever hear of beings like that?" Tesa asked the humans.

Bruce shook his head. "Sounds like they evolved from amphibians. They could be Anurans."

"The CLS hasn't met any beings like that," Jib insisted.

Tesa turned back to the Hunter. "Is it possible that these creatures were only helping K'heera? Maybe she was ill?"

The avian stared at Tesa full-faced. "They attacked and overpowered her. When they carried her into that shelter, she saw me. Her eyes said what her hands couldn't. She was in pain, and helpless. I am not mistaken about that."

Bruce turned to Jib and indicated the space probe. "Tesa's instincts were right. It *was* sent by the invaders from Mars."

"Now, wait a minute," Jib interrupted. "If we *have* stumbled onto another space-faring species, we can't assume the worst."

"Believe me," Tesa signed, "I wish this were nothing more than a StarBridge diplomacy exercise, but we sent two people to our space station two days ago and haven't heard from them since. These aliens have a *colony*—they could've been here for months . . . maybe . . ." a sudden flash of dream-memory danced behind her eyelids, " . . . maybe waiting behind the Moons. . . ."

"If they're antagonistic, then why didn't they capture the *Norton* when K'heera and I were dropped off?" Jib asked pointedly.

"I don't know," Tesa admitted.

"You can't just assume these people are *invaders*," the young man argued, "because of what happened to K'heera. And we don't know why we haven't heard from Meg and Szu-yi." He stared pointedly at Bruce. "And what's the difference between invaders and *colonizers*, anyway? We need more information."

"I don't know the difference between invaders and colonizers," Lightning admitted suddenly. "But I know what a predator is. Thunder, tell them about the Singers."

Tesa's stomach lurched at the same time Jib's expression went slack. "What about the Singers?" she asked.

"A pod of Singers swam up the River and discovered the alien settlement," the Hunter began. "Before the Singers could react, the aliens trapped them with power beams. Then they killed and ate them. One group managed to escape, but the others were only herded farther west up the River, cut off from the sea. They can be taken whenever the beings hunger for them."

The bleached skeletons from Tesa's dream swam before her eyes; she swayed dizzily. Lightning and Hurricane moved beside her instantly, supporting her with their bodies. She touched them, felt the cohort gather closer to give her strength and take some in return. She drew a shuddery breath.

Jib's face was ashen. He stared out over the deceptively calm River. "That's my dream. I remember now . . . I only wish I didn't. The Singers were . . . being killed . . . but the killers . . . weren't aliens . . . they were us. Me, Tesa, and Bruce. . . . But it can't really have happened . . . it was a dream!"

"It *happened*," Thunder told them, bristling her thick feathers. "The River turned red, and their mind screams nearly knocked me from my perch. Once"—she swiveled her head around, blinking nervously—"I thought I heard K'heera keening, begging me to go for help. It was a night to make me want to never hunt again . . . unless it's those un-Worldly aliens I hunt. . . ."

"They aren't out there . . ." Jib signed, staring across the River. "Not Taniwha, or his mother . . . or . . . any of the herd." He stared at Tesa and Bruce as though just realizing this. "I can't *hear* them at all. They're *gone*."

"Did the aliens have machines?" Tesa asked Thunder.

"They had flocks of small flyers like yours, and several bigger ships like the shuttles. They have weapons."

"Taniwha! Did he survive?" Jib moaned, sinking down onto the sand, "I *sent* him, I sent them all, to look for you."

None-So-Pretty approached the young man and draped a wing around him. "You couldn't know," she signed to the Maori.

"*They* think I did," Jib signed. "I saw it in my dream. They think we're all the same. They'll never trust us again. I can't explain . . . or say I'm sorry . . . or help them."

"We can't worry about this now," Tesa signed abruptly. Jib seemed shocked by her reaction, especially when Bruce agreed.

"She's right, son," the older man signed. "What's happened to the Singers is terrible, but it's only the beginning."

"They must have Meg and Szu-yi," Tesa decided. "And the space station . . . and the camp. . . . My grandparents."

"Our people would have fought them," Lightning suggested.

"That's true," Tesa agreed, feeling a moment of hope.

"Unfortunately," Thunder interrupted, "these aliens suffer no ill effects from the voices of the Wind people."

There was a long silence as the group thought about their friends and loved ones and their possible fates.

"We can't do this now," the Indian woman decided. "We can't sit around mourning. If those Anurans have the space station, it's only a matter of time before they translate everything in it—including all the information about the CLS. What they can do to Trinity is bad enough, but that information could help them overrun other planets, or even the League itself."

"I'll tell you something else," Bruce added. "They won't let the next ship that arrives get away."

The small party stared at him as the realization hit them.

"Bruce," Tesa asked, "that ship's bringing our new staff, who knows how many passengers, and a full ship's crew—not to mention all the hardware needed to enlarge the *Singing Crane*. How many days before the *Brolga* arrives?"

"Roughly, I'd say twenty. If we can't get a message to it before it enters our solar system, it'll be just a fly in a web."

"Then let's say fifteen," Tesa signed. "We've got fifteen days to find some way to send a message to the CLS, and stop the *Brolga* from entering this solar system."

"That's a pretty tall order," Bruce commented. "Our best equipment's on the *Crane*. All we've got is stuff to transmit to the station." His eyes strayed over to the probe.

"We've got to get out of here," Tesa decided. "At least we know where *they* are. We'll pack out on foot, and follow that branch of the River that goes north. We'll hide everything we leave behind. . . . Jib, are you paying attention?"

The young man turned, his youthful face suddenly aged. "On the *Norton* . . . K'heera was so worried about coming here. . . . I kept telling her . . . we wouldn't have to save the World. . . ."

It was almost dark when Taller's feet touched down on russet-colored meadow grass. The land here was, unlike his own, dry, peppered with water-filled potholes instead of marsh. It was Gray Wind terrain, inside the boundary of the Land of Confusion.

Weaver backwinged to a landing beside him. "It's too bad we can't finish this trip today," she signed.

The Grus leader glanced at the two elderly humans as they eased their sled to a halt. He and Weaver and a small escort flock of juveniles had left their people as they gathered in the north. The elder Grus had decided to move ahead because the trip was taking its toll on Teacher. Once they arrived at his partner's campsite, the old woman could be made more comfortable.

The avian leader stood tall as he examined his surroundings warily. Flying with the two humans sharing one sled meant the Grus could never gain much altitude. This was not a place where your eyes were enough. He would have liked to travel higher, to see farther, to search for . . .

He listened to the hums and chirps of insects, the distant calls of Gray Winds two days' flight away, the chatter of lesser avians. He strained to pick up any un-Worldly sound. There was nothing. Realizing the others had finished drinking from the pothole, Taller scooped water up with his bill, then tipped his head back to swallow. He did not want to think about the aliens and their invading ships, their terrifying weapons.

"It's warm here," Teacher signed to Weaver. "Dry, too."

Old Bear was watching the woman solicitously. "How are you feeling, Mrs. Lewis?" he asked politely.

"The same as you, Mr. Bigbee," she answered, smiling. "Tired. Creaky."

The old man laughed and started to reply when one of the youngsters bleated an alarm call, making the humans wince.

Taller turned as another White Wind bore down on them, startling the old leader. Could it be a messenger from the north? Had there been more trouble? The avian, a two-year-old, landed on the other side of the pothole and called a greeting.

The aged leader recognized the voice. "Flies-Too-Fast, is that you?" he signed as the young male approached, head lowered.

"Travelers told me you were near," the young male signed. "I was so sure they were wrong. What's happened?"

"Our territory has been overrun by un-Worldly aliens," the leader responded. "We had to escape."

Flies-Too-Fast stiffened. "Good Eyes was right." He faced the humans. "Where are the Healer and First-One-There?"

"Aren't they with Good Eyes?" Old Bear asked.

"No," the young White Wind signed. "We were hoping they were still at home." The two humans looked at each other, until Teacher shook her head and silently turned away.

"Tomorrow," Taller told Flies-Too-Fast, "you'll take us to Good Eyes."

"Of course. Have you seen any aliens since you left?"

"No . . . but I've been uneasy." The avian scanned their surroundings suspiciously. "It's a different wind that travels the World now. These beings have changed even the currents of the air. It's not our World any longer." He dropped his head suddenly, apologetic. "Forgive me. Let's eat, then sleep. We'll need to be fresh."

The small group said little as they foraged in the dusk. Taller watched the Child Sun hover near the Moons. It made him think of Lightning staying with the three humans.

Standing in the shallow pothole, Taller preened, yearning for sleep, suddenly conscious of the weight of his years. A breeze ruffled his tertial feathers, and he bent to smooth them.

Then his head snapped up. There was a wrongness in the air, something he could *feel*. He blared out an alarm call, then another, his powerful voice startling his small group.

Before his call died, an enormous flying thing, twice the size of the human's large shelter, crested the horizon, moving with a Night Flyer's eerie silence. Weaver sounded her own call, as the humans scrambled for their sled. The youngsters took to the air, Flies-Too-Fast in the lead. Recklessly, the two-year-old flew straight at the monster.

It was no accident that their enemy was bearing down on them now, Taller knew. They were too far from their people to secure any help. They were full of food and exhausted.

"Hurry!" he urged the humans.

Old Bear pulled Teacher onto the flyer, abandoning all their goods in their haste. Taller and Weaver took to the air, keeping the humans between them.

As they sped away, Flies-Too-Fast and the other juveniles mobbed the behemoth, harassing it the way the Blue Cloud people did predatory avians. But even as they circled the thing, Taller knew they were as helpless as the soft-winged night insects that beat themselves to death against the humans' artificial lights. He called to his mate to fly faster. Old Bear kept up as Teacher was forced to hug him tightly to stay on the speeding sled.

The invading ship ignored the escort flock, easily overtaking the humans. Hovering over them, the ship forced the sled and the White Winds to skim dangerously low to the ground. Suddenly an orifice on the belly of the ship opened over them like a gaping, ugly mouth. Weaver moved between the ship and the humans, as though to protect them with her own body.

Taller blared a warning, as a beam stabbed through the twilight, enveloping his mate and the humans. Before he could react, the outer edge of the beam knocked him aside, just as the others were pulled into the maw of the ship, Weaver's cry of fear ringing in Taller's ears. He regained his balance and swerved up to follow his mate, but the opening slammed shut behind the captives. The ship rose into the atmosphere and headed south as the White Winds flapped futilely to catch up.

As the ship dwindled to a tiny spot, the juvenile escort surrounded him, Flies-Too-Fast on his right, ready to follow Taller even in darkness. But finally, the ship disappeared and he realized how helpless they were. His body screamed with fatigue. He'd only die if he insisted on pursuing something he could neither catch nor conquer. He was as insignificant to that machine as the shimmerings were to him. Morosely, Taller stumbled to a landing, unable to muster the energy to even lift his head. How could he call, with no partner to answer his cry? What point could there be to a life without Weaver?

"We'll leave at dawn," Flies-Too-Fast signed quickly. "Good Eyes must know what's happened. Our only hope is . . ."

The condition of Taller's dull, shrunken crown stopped the youngster. "*Hope?*" the leader signed. "How can we escape that voracious thing? There's no hope for us, or the humans, either."

There was a long uncomfortable pause as the startled cohort stood, tense, while their leader yielded to sorrow and defeat. Flies-Too-Fast stepped between them and Taller, blocking the sight of his grief from the others. *He'll challenge me,* Taller thought, *and I'll surrender. He's young and full of courage. That's what my people need now.*

"Taller," the youngster signed nervously, lowering his head to match his leader's, "I grieve with you . . . but . . . Good Eyes, Lightning . . . all of us . . . need your leadership, your experience."

The elder stared at him incredulously. Most males his age would have used this opportunity to strike out for power without thinking twice. He lifted his head slightly.

Flies-Too-Fast kept signing. "From my first flight, I've wanted to fly at your side. I thought it would be years before I could work my way there. I ask for that privilege now."

The humble request touched Taller's heart, and he raised his head higher, forcing his crown to a strong crimson. "You've earned that right, Flies-Too-Fast. Tomorrow, you'll take your place on my right. . . ." *Where my mate once flew,* he thought.

"Until Weaver returns," Flies-Too-Fast signed hopefully.

Szu-yi slept fitfully on the floor of the dimly lit, tiny cubicle she shared with Meg. While the heat and humidity of the garishly painted, unfurnished cell and the unyielding floor did not lend itself to an easy rest, that wasn't what stopped her from sleeping soundly. The aliens had conditioned them against sleep to make them more pliant servants—one of their more effective training techniques. Szu-yi could no longer imagine herself refusing any of her captors' requests, no matter how traitorous or bizarre.

Szu-yi didn't mind the lack of sleep. She was relieved to be on the Glorious First's personal carrier, even if she was imprisoned behind a shimmering power field. Since coming into the First's care, she and Meg had been treated well. The food was too high in protein, but it came regularly. There was a warm pool to bathe in, and they'd been given clean clothes. And, occasionally, alien scientists came and discussed things with them.

Neither Meg nor Szu-yi attempted to keep anything from them. Szu-yi had helped develop a pharmacopoeia of behavior-altering drugs, and the aliens had all the information from the *Singing Crane*, so there was no point in secrecy. And Meg had learned what would happen to Szu-yi if she did not cooperate.

Inside, Szu-yi felt troubled. She shouldn't be so accepting, she should be doing . . . something . . . about their situation. . . . She . . . should . . . try to find a way to . . .

Fear suddenly washed over her in great waves. How many hours had Dacris brutalized her while a recording of her own voice whispering to an unconscious Meg repeated, at maximum volume, over and over . . .

"I PROMISE YOU, MEG, WE'LL FIND A WAY TO ESCAPE."

Or had it been days? There'd been no sleep, no food, just pain and sound and the anticipation of pain as the only reliable constants. Dr. Tato had protested, so the alien physician had been forced to monitor the "training" and keep Szu-yi pumped full of stimulants. Dacris wanted the human's awareness to be razor-sharp. He said it was necessary for the "conditioning" to "take." The brilliance of his color had seared her eyes.

The conditioning had certainly taken. She'd never forget that pain, and the betrayal of her own voice. She remembered, too, the drone of the translator as Dacris sang of the rights of the Chosen over the Conquered. The Chosen . . . a people who had elevated the ritualized destruction of their conquered victim's spirit to an art form.

She could still feel Dacris' moist, hot hands slapping her flesh, see the rod in his hands . . . . She shut her eyes tight.

But that was before their rescue. Before the Glorious First took them, and Dr. Tato, under his own care. There'd been no more pain, no punishment. A tear leaked from under her lids.

There was a sound in the hall outside their cell, and her eyes snapped open. She must not be found sleeping! She must be awake, alert, ready. Beside her, Meg tensed.

The power grid that kept them confined dissolved. Without a word, the two stood stiffly, nervously. Szu-yi began trembling. In spite of their recent benign treatment, she was terrified of unexpected visits. Her eyes widened as two green and gold aliens came into view. One of them had that familiar swagger . . . could Dacris be here, on Atle's ship? Was he coming to take them back?

She realized it was only two guards, and felt a second's relief before wondering what they wanted. Suddenly she saw two *humans* walking behind them, with two more guards in the rear.

"Oh, no," Meg gasped, "no!"

Szu-yi's heart swelled with joy at the sight of Tesa's grandparents. She should be distraught that they had been taken, too, but it was so *good* to see another human, she couldn't help herself. She forced the emotions down, afraid to let them show on her face.

"Oh, Meg, thank God you're alive," Old Bear said and embraced the biologist. The Russian woman returned his hug weakly. When he really examined her, his alarm was plain.

"Are you both all right?" Szu-yi asked finally.

"We were stunned during the capture," Nadine said softly, "but other than that. . . ."

There was a melodic trilling followed by the drone of a mechanical voice. "They are well," it said.

Szu-yi glanced past the guards. She knew that voice.

"Or so Dr. Tato assures me," the translator whined as the Glorious First stepped around his officers.

Stiffly, Szu-yi dropped into the respectful squat she'd been taught. "Glorious First, you honor us," she said automatically. Glancing up, she saw Nadine's and Old Bear's shocked expressions. Meg, as usual, only turned away.

"Stand, my friend," Atle sang, helping her to her feet. "I hoped you would be pleased to see your companions. We also captured an avian with them. A lucky accident, really."

Szu-yi's heart thudded. She knew the Chosen regarded the Grus as little more than food.

"They have Weaver," Old Bear said.

"This avian is someone you know?" Atle asked Szu-yi.

"Oh, yes, a dear friend," she told him. "Is she hurt?"

"She is unconscious, but she'll recover."

"Please," Szu-yi implored shamelessly, "don't harm her. She can stay with us here, she can . . . she can . . ." Her brain tried to stop her from saying too much, but her mouth was out of control. "She can be very useful to you. Her mate is leader of all the White Wind people. She's a fine crafts person, as well."

Szu-yi avoided the stunned expressions of her own people, staring instead at the luminous, multicolored eyes of the being who'd rescued her from unspeakable agony.

"That's good to know, my friend," Atle sang. "It would have been a shame to waste such an important animal. What would I do without you?" He turned to the other humans. "My doctor tells me you are all elders. You humans must be a powerful people to so readily send your aged into space. But your days as independent people are over. You now belong to the Chosen."

He stepped closer to Szu-yi, and she had to force herself to hold her ground. When he reached out to touch her shoulders, she flinched and trembled. "Your friend here understands what that means. She has had difficulty adjusting, but she *has* adjusted. It speaks well for your species. Listen to her. Do as she says. It will save you sorrow"—he squeezed her shoulders gently, comfortingly—"and it will save *her* pain. For if you do not cooperate, *you* will not be held responsible. *She* will. As your persuader, she will suffer for you. And she has already suffered so greatly, it would pain me to discipline her further."

Szu-yi wept tears of terror. "Please," she whispered, "Glorious First, please. . . ."

He watched her compassionately. "Teach them well, my friend. I would hate to have to witness your punishment."

*This'll hurt me worse than it'll hurt you,* she imagined him saying, and bit her cheek to keep from screaming.

"Bring them the avian," Atle ordered the guards. Without another word, the Chosen all left the cell.

"They've taken our nullifiers," Old Bear whispered.

"It doesn't matter," Nadine said as she gathered Szu-yi in her arms. "We'll be together. We'll find a way to . . ."

The Asian woman slapped her hand hard over Nadine's mouth. Her eyes were round and touched with madness.

# CHAPTER 13

♦

# Human History

"The Simiu's *smart,* too," Arvis sang. "She's already learned how to maintain the hatchery's water system."

Atle listened as his son massaged him, marveling at the youth's changed demeanor. In the short time they'd been separated, Arvis had *grown.* His body was more developed, his musculature more defined, and his poison patches glowed. More importantly, his son's growth was mental as well as physical.

"But I'm worried," Arvis continued. "She's not eating."

The youth was struggling to understand complex problems. Even now, during the massage, when he would've normally worked in silence to concentrate on his task, Arvis could not keep still. Capturing the Simiu had awakened his conqueror's heart. Atle's pride almost erased the pain of his other children's deaths.

"Her keepers have offered her eggs with half-grown embryos, insect larvae, and even marinated meat from the river animals," Arvis sang, "but she won't eat."

"What would you like to do about that?" Atle asked.

His son seemed confused, but finally said, "Couldn't she live with us? I could take care of her . . . and make her healthy. I wouldn't neglect my own tasks!"

Atle's skin glowed. His son was a Chosen, and craved his own captive, craved to be her master. "She is the only one of her kind here—that makes her terribly valuable."

The youngster said nothing, merely continued the massage.

"Perhaps . . . we could bring her here in the evenings," the First sang, "so you could train her. Later, when we take others, she could be yours."

"But," Arvis murmured, "the Industrious can't own anything."

"Yes, of course," Atle agreed. He'd have to do something about that. He would introduce a new law at the next Council meeting. . . . "We'll bring the Simiu here at night, nevertheless. She mustn't die. She'll be your responsibility."

Arvis flushed. "She'll eat for me, sir, and be well behaved, too. I think she likes me."

Atle sighed, pleased. All the young Chosen thought their servants "liked" them—if the servants were smart, they fostered that fantasy. Life was easier that way.

"And she's so *strong*," Arvis repeated, never pausing in his attentions. "As strong as three males . . . in breeding prime!"

Arvis' innocent enthusiasm brought the First up short, and he rolled up on one narrow hip, stopping the massage. "And what do you know of the strength of a male in breeding prime, son?"

To the First, breeding was a private, sacred thing. Unlike most servants, neither Arvis nor his sister had ever helped at a mating. How could his son have come by this knowledge?

Arvis blushed furiously.

"I'm not angry." Atle deliberately dampened his color. It was too soon for the Chosen to be breeding here. Something had to have happened in the hatchery . . . where the Simiu worked.

The Industrious servant was so nervous, his song became a whistle. "Lenc . . . uh, told me . . . not to tell. . . ."

Atle's hindbrain surged with emotion. When he'd returned to his family, Arvis had flooded him with questions about Lene. While many of them were the puzzlings of a child baffled by the politics of seduction, others showed a startling insight into the strange relationship he was developing with the female. But as to Lene's feelings—Atle could only guess.

"Lene is your special friend," Atle reassured his son, "and friends share many secrets, but I'm sure she never meant for you to keep this from your father."

"Yes, she did. 'Don't tell your parents,' she sang, 'especially not your father.' She said we would be mated soon, and that meant we would have special secrets."

*Good work, Lene,* Atle thought. He needed to get back to the topic. "How did you learn about males in breeding prime?"

"I asked Lene to take me to see the Simiu. I'd hurt her, you know. . . . Lene said she was better now and she could take me to the hatchery, where the Simiu was being trained."

"Did you see her being trained?"

Arvis blinked and thought hard. "Yes."

"In the hatchery?" Atle prompted gently.

"Yes, sir."

"Where?" The egg-producing plant was a complex factory.

"That day . . . she was working in the breeding pools. . . ."

"Lene took you to the pools?" Atle asked bluntly.

Arvis was so rattled his poison patches sweated. "She said you'd be mad."

The First struggled to control himself. *He's just a child!*

"She said you didn't want us to mate and have children."

"I want . . . I only want you to be happy. Do you want to mate and have children?"

His son's marbled eyes lit up. "Oh, yes. That'd be fun!"

"Arvis, what happened in the breeding pools?"

The youngster's throat pouch quivered. "Lene said that the Industrious females fell in love and wanted to lay eggs, so the Chosen males that loved them held them to fertilize their eggs. She says that'll happen to us when the rains come."

It was a clever deceit, the First thought. "Did the females look like they were in love?"

Arvis thought about that for a long time. "No. Everyone there acted like they'd gone crazy. The females were tired and dull and had to be restrained in their pools by harnesses. Their songs were sad. But the males were in love! They were handsome and strong, their colors bright and gleaming! But they were restrained, too, by attendants. That's how I found out about the Simiu's strength— she controlled the males by herself. I think the keepers were afraid of her, so they moved her out of there."

The Industrious females in the hatchery were the most mentally stunted of all workers, egg-layers genetically bred and hormonally induced to produce continually. Living egg factories with only the vestiges of a forebrain, they were forced to pump out eggs until their last follicle was exhausted. Their short lives were spent in a drug-induced torpor to combat their fear and resistance to the breeding males. Most died in their pools atop their last, huge egg mass, while some low-ranked Chosen male gripped them in a desperate, hormone-inspired breeding frenzy, fertilizing eggs that would be nurtured in special baths to speed their growth. The clear, gelatinous eggs filled with plump, living embryos were a prime food source for the Chosen.

"Lene said," Arvis continued, "that things would be different for us, that you and mother would help."

"Son," Atle asked hesitantly, "are you in love with Lene?"

"Uh . . . yes . . . I guess . . . I mean . . . I don't know! When I'm with her I feel . . . *terrible*! But when I'm not with her, I feel worse."

Atle had never heard a better description of that complex emotion.

Arvis stared at his father intently. "I want Lene to love *me*. I want to do . . . something *special* . . . to please her."

The First heard himself saying something similar, if more articulate, to his own father. To win a mate, really *win* her, you had to outshine your rivals. When Atle had fallen in love, he'd been a renowned wrestler. But Arvis had other talents. He was attentive and careful. And he made friends easily.

"If you have success with the Simiu," Atle suggested, "you will have done something none of the professional trainers were able to do. These aliens, the humans and the Simiu, are the first races we've conquered in many hundreds of years. Succeed with the Simiu, and Lene will be impressed."

Arvis took a deep breath. "I'll do a good job, sir."

Just then Atle's wife came into the room. "Your father has to get dressed," she told Arvis gently, then turned to the First. "Your Third is here with Rand, the pharmacist, to speak to you."

Atle slipped his garment on as Arvis left. "Send them in."

The Third, Amaset, a One-Touch, entered with the tall pharmacist behind him. The two squatted, then stood quickly.

"Glorious First," the Third sang, "we've translated much of the history of the humans from the space station's computer." He approached the small desk computer and dropped a sphere in its slot. "There are some things you should know."

"Go ahead," Atle sang.

The Third touched a membrane and the tiny tank lit up with interesting images of a planet with a sole moon. This was the original home of the humans; they called it . . . soil? No, Earth.

The images changed, showing Earth's natural habitats. "In the past," the Third sang, "this beautiful world, covered in marshes, wetlands, and seas, was devastated by its inhabitants. Its marshes were drained, wetlands filled, forests stripped, and countless species of animals, insects, and plants were consumed and exterminated. It's only been in the last few hundred years that they've controlled this wasteful destruction, and for much of the planet, change came too late."

The Third coded some new information into the machine. "That's strange enough, but their method of war is stranger yet. Most of their resources and sciences have, for hundreds of years, been devoted to developing advanced weaponry."

"We put a lot of energy into refining weapons," Atle sang.

"Yes," the Third agreed, "however, we waged war to overtake people. Our goals were, and are, to conquer others for the benefit of ourselves and our children, not to destroy nations wholesale.

These humans *slaughter* each other, males, females, even *children*, sometimes simply because they exist."

The screen showed the truth of the Third's words. Huge projectile weapons threw powerful missiles at distant targets. War fields were strewn with corpses, and containers rolling on parallel tracks were stacked with bodies.

"This group enslaved another," the Third continued, "but instead of training them for productive work which would enhance their economy, they wastefully starved and exterminated them because of cultural differences and the fear of hybridizing.

"But worse than all of that, Glorious First, is that during their wars, the land was *devastated*. They *defoliated* whole forests, poisoned rivers, and rendered the environment toxic. They even used weapons of *nuclear* power."

"That's ridiculous," Atle sang. "A weapon like that could destroy the entire ecology of a planet."

"These people threatened each other with just that scenario. At this time even *they* consider it miraculous that they didn't destroy their world then."

"How did they ever reach the stars?" Atle wondered.

"They did it to find new worlds to support their population, much as we've done. They show more responsibility now, but that's not important. Their stardrive . . ."

Atle watched the Third's color dull.

"If it's engaged too close to a sun, that sun will be *destroyed*. The humans are well aware of its potential. In their first meeting with the Simiu, there was some concern that some humans might do that to escape confinement."

What kind of people would destroy a solar system simply to be free? "But the crew of that ship would be destroyed as well!"

"Some of the humans' cultures consider suicide a glorious way to end their life," the Third explained.

"They're insane," Atle breathed. "They'll have to be carefully controlled."

"Anticipating your concern, I consulted with Rand."

The pharmacist stepped up. "Glorious First, you should know of . . . the limitations biochemical controls have on the humans."

"What limitations?" Atle asked.

"The humans have evolved from mammalian ancestors, and are much more primitive, biologically, than we are, who evolved from air-breathing water-dwellers. . . ."

"What of it?" Atle snapped.

"Their body chemistry keeps finding new ways to blunt the effect of our psychotropic drugs. We keep having to change the dosages. Sometimes, they have adverse reactions. We may have trouble controlling them with chemical restraints."

"Then we'll use the methods our ancestors used," Atle sang.

Rand and the Third exchanged concerned glances.

"Are you going to tell me that the techniques our ancestors used to successfully conquer an entire *planet* won't be good enough for these *humans*?"

"We would not be serving our First if we didn't point out the limitations," the Third reminded Atle. "The old methods require more controllers per capita and raise the costs. Also, those methods can cause certain personality types to rebel."

"So, it will not be as easy as we had hoped," the First agreed, "but things will be different when their children are born in our pools, and grow up under our rods. Thank you for this information. I'll study your presentation further."

The two squatted, then departed, leaving Atle watching grainy images of a mushroom cloud explosion. This was supposed to be the deciding factor in a huge and costly war that had ended countless lives and devastated entire portions of the planet. Atle watched it with a terrible fascination. These were the people his fortunes had sent him to conquer.


"I wish I had watched her do it," Bruce signed.

Tesa shook her head, exasperated, as they bent over the enigmatic space probe, an array of hand tools scattered around them. "Just all of a sudden, it came *on*."

"She enhanced the holding tank's diagnostic computer," Bruce explained, peering at that dismembered machine. "See, these are her cells. . . . Then she did something else. . . . Must've been magic. . . ." He went back to examining the satellite.

They hoped that if they could tap the probe's power source they could use it to boost the power of their ground-to-station equipment and send a warning to the *Brolga,* and possibly even the CLS. Bruce felt that if they could tap the power source, their communications would be strong, but primitive. He wasn't sure how they could keep the beam directed at the proper frequency either, but that worry was for the future.

Nearby, Jib sat, arms folded, watching the exchange.

Tesa gnawed her lip. "I know you want to use the diagnostics. . . ."

"You're damned right, I do," Bruce admitted. "K'heera found a way to tap into this thing's power source. I've got to retrace her path, and figure out what she did. . . ."

"But if you use the computer," Tesa reminded him, "that thing's owners could detect it and come down on us."

"Maybe," Bruce agreed, "but if I never use the computer, then I'll never figure out how to tap this thing's power source to send a call to the *Brolga* or the CLS. The Anurans will take the *Brolga*, and no one will miss her for weeks."

Tesa's head wanted to explode. They'd been over this again and again. The tension among them was palpable. They'd moved three times in the last four days, but none of them could shake the feeling that they were moments away from capture.

"Good Eyes," Lightning signed, "the Gray Winds have told me that the Anurans are leaving their colony in small groups and moving along the River."

"Probably exploring," Bruce decided. "Maybe sending out biologists, or other specialists, to see what's available."

"The Gray Winds say that the small groups move on flyers," Lightning told her, "and they carry lots of *things* with them. Mechanical things."

Tesa waited for him to make his point. Information from the Gray Winds regarding the activities of the Anurans was critical to their safety.

"We were all wondering," Thunder started signing, indicating herself and the cohort, "if these groups could somehow 'hear' your machinery, how they could tell it apart from their own."

"I'm afraid it's very easy," Tesa explained. "Not only do our peoples use different languages, the machines themselves have their own way of talking, and those ways are so different. . . ."

"Wait a minute, Tesa," Jib suddenly signed. He'd been depressed since the slaughter of the Singers, and had contributed so little to their conversations that Tesa and Bruce had grown accustomed to his silence. Now both of them watched him as he became suddenly animated. "There's something else to consider. You know at StarBridge, most of the telepaths are diurnal—they're awake and busy during the day. There's enough of them on the 'Bridge now that communications during daytime, especially with some of the poorer trained students, can be difficult. Because . . . there's so much of it going on . . . understand?"

Bruce's face lit up. "I see what you're saying. The Anurans are diurnal. They've got exploratory groups scouting around, sending reports. Communications are whizzing back and forth. . . . If we use our equipment during midday, the chances are there'll be so much communications chatter . . . our tiny emanations could just be white noise."

" '*Chances* are . . . ' " she repeated.

"That's right," Bruce admitted. "It's a chance. But I can't find my way into this thing on luck. I've got to have help. Electronic help."

"He's right," Jib prodded. "We'll have to take the chance."

The young woman squeezed her eyes shut, not wanting to see any more signs. Then she felt a wing on her arm. She opened her eyes to face Thunder.

"Let them use their machines, Good Eyes," Thunder suggested. "I'll ride the high thermals while they do and watch for the enemy. My brother and his cohort can hear my call and warn you if the enemy approaches."

"We'll set a time limit," Bruce added. "Fifteen-minute intervals, four times a day . . . well, maybe six. . . . Something like that. When we're done for the day, we'll move camp again."

They all watched her, waiting for her decision. She couldn't ask Bruce to perform miracles; she had to accept *some* risk. . . . "All right. But only after the Suns are all up."

"Great! I'll start right now."

"Come on," Tesa gestured to Jib as Thunder climbed into the sky. "Let's gather some lunch while he's working. We won't have time to do that if we have to leave in a hurry, and I want to keep watch for Flies-Too-Fast."

Jib nodded, but his despondency had returned.

As they collected nearby fruit, Tesa wished she could find the right thing to say to him about his sorrow. "Jib . . . I understand what you're going through. I felt that kind of helpless rage when I watched Thunder's father get killed, and when I learned about Black Feather's flock being slaughtered. It's painful, but you have to get over this. What happened to the Singers wasn't your fault. There was no way you could know."

"Tell *them* that," he signed simply, and turned away.

Tesa's hands hung suspended in air. She could think of nothing that would buffer the loss of the Singers' mental contact, or remove the brutal images of his dream. She wished she knew more about TSS, more about the withdrawal symptoms. She tried to think of something to distract him. "Look, I know we can't use the electronic equipment for this, but I always carry paper. It's a holdover from when I worked on Earth with hearing people and never knew when I'd hit a communications snag. You can have it. You can write Anzi *real* letters on it!"

He paused, thinking about that, then his face brightened. "Thanks, mate, that's right nice of you. I'll take you up on that. A bit of writing therapy, eh? Let's hope it works!"

Tesa nodded curtly and watched the sky, as Thunder's dark silhouette circled above them. She only wished she could indulge in her own therapy, to soar through the sky with Lightning, Thunder, and her cohort and leave her fear and anger behind. The nervous youngsters helped her gather fruit as each took their turn watching and listening for danger. How odd for them, she thought, to spend so much energy waiting for a predator when the land around them was devoid of animal life.

Taniwha swam through the shallows of the tributary, carefully touching the minds of the three humans without letting them *hear* him. He was convinced Jib could explain the evil aliens to him. He thought, too, that if Jib was hiding an equally evil nature, he should confront him—pull the evil from the corners of his mind into the light. But whenever he probed Jib's memories, like now, all he could find was agonizing guilt over the pain Taniwha's people had suffered.

He was confused. Jib had sent him to that place of blood and death, and the human felt those deaths were his doing . . . yet he enjoyed no satisfaction or gladness, only profound grief. Taniwha worried over this, wanting to understand.

Suddenly the shadow of his aunt passed over him, surprising the calf. Taniwha knew she'd be angry. As his nearest living relative, she was responsible for him now, nursing him and her own calf equally. She'd forbidden him to contact the humans, but the youngster knew the answers they needed lay with these beings. In his defense, Taniwha showed his aunt Jib's heartfelt mourning.

The female rolled in the water, looking at her sister's son. Taniwha was sure Jib's feelings touched her deeply, but when he tried to persuade her to let him contact the human openly, she wouldn't respond. Disappointed, the calf had no choice but to swim away with her to feed.

# CHAPTER 14

♦

# The Rains

"But it's been raining three days!" Lene complained as the steady downpour washed over her face and shoulders even as it dimpled the rising water. Her mother, Anchie, patted her consolingly as they strolled along the prefab walkways that crisscrossed the river, linking the colony's many buildings.

"Why did the rains have to come? We've only been on this miserable planet twenty-one of its days." Her song grew mocking. "But the First says there's no time to breed. We can breed the *next* time. The *next* time! I'm ready *now*!"

She'd never sung so honestly. She ached to shed her clothes and sing her passion while the sweet water flowed over her body. They'd been ordered to take hormone suppressants, but Lene had refused, hoping the rains would push Arvis into a breeding cycle.

But they'd heard nothing from his family. Soon, Lene's hindbrain would override her sense and she'd fall into the arms of any available male. Her mother didn't dare leave her alone.

"It's futile," Lene wailed. "He'll never breed!"

Anchie stared over Lene's shoulder, her eyes widening, then instantly the matron fell into a squat. Lene spun in surprise as the First appeared behind her, his colors blazing.

"No, dear Lene," he sang harshly, "your efforts were hardly *futile*." Before she could react, he grabbed her wrist roughly. "To give *my* son hormones . . . your plotting goes too far!" He yanked her rudely toward his home but she shrank back.

"Glorious First," Anchie cried, "please! She's a child!"

"No longer that," he replied, towing her forward.

The older female paddled after them, singing timorously, "I have a right to be there! As her mother I have a right!"

The First froze her with a stare. "Your conspiracy lost you your rights. Say good-bye to your daughter."

"What will happen to her in the pool?" the frantic mother shrilled. "He could drown her, or claw her to death! And if he's infertile . . . she will be *ruined*! Glorious First!"

"Mother, *stop it*!" Lene snapped, startling both adults. "Dunn will be there. I'll be fine." She fixed the First with a deliberate look. "And if Arvis is infertile . . . he will never be a citizen. That's what the Council decreed. So, the Industrious son of the First *will* be fertile. I can guarantee that, Mother."

"Lene!" the elder female hissed, shocked into paleness.

Atle glared. "You dare imply I would . . . ?"

"*I* know that you are too honest, Glorious First, to substitute another male to guarantee your son's status . . . even though there *is* another fertile male in your household—you. But the drugs my mother supplied me have insured Arvis' potency. I haven't plotted only for my own welfare!"

"Yes," Atle replied, somewhat subdued. "Of course. Go home, Anchie. Lene will be safe in our pool."

"As will the First's future *grandchild*," Lene reminded him.

Her mother winced as Atle's color flared anew. He marched them along the walkway leading to his home. "Be smug," he warned. "Be clever. Soon we'll see where that has gotten you." He drew up to his front door and stared down at her. "How much did you give him? The rains here are potent. . . . Arvis is . . ."

"He's *ready*?" she prompted hopefully.

Atle laughed. "Ready? My son is . . . as he would have been, had he been born Chosen . . . he's . . . magnificent."

Lene's colors brightened.

"But without the ability to control his strength. He does not have the conscience a breeding male needs. . . ."

"You're wrong," she argued. "Arvis has *all* the *conscience* any male needs." She did not need him filling her with fear before the most important moment in her life. Did he expect her to dissolve into one of those terrified, scrambling females that had to be held in place? She passed him, opening his door.

"He's in my pool," Atle told her, indicating the way. She walked through the compact rooms, passing Arvis' sister, who was dutifully filling lotion jars, oblivious to the drama taking place in her own home. Finally she entered the First's private chamber. She was surprised that it was as clean and spare as the group pools she shared, only smaller, and more intimate. She'd expected it to be opulent, but the brightly colored interior wasn't very different from what she was used to. The transparent walls and ceiling allowed natural light to flood the room. Sheets of rain drummed musically against the house, cascading over the room as if they were under a waterfall.

Next, she eyed the small, oblong pool itself. She stared, mesmerized at its beautiful, placid water, feeling its ancient call. Shuddering in desire, she imagined its liquid warmth surrounding her.

Atle hissed against her tympani, "See your *mate*."

The Industrious servant stood hunched near a rear wall, his mother nearly propping him up. Draped in an ill-fitting robe, he seemed miserably out of place. Shaking, he rocked back and forth, his voice a low, tuneless whine. Lene's heart sank.

"Are you ready?" the First asked roughly.

She'd imagined this moment a thousand times—the perfect political marriage. There would be a magnificent pool, richly garbed servants, all their parents proudly attending. And she'd envisioned *him* swathed in immaculate robes that would be dulled by his luminescent color. He would sing his need for her, his magnificent body filled with passion, yet still under his control. His embrace would be gentle, but powerful, and be impossible to resist. His expert technique would release her own passion as his legs stroked hers, freeing the egg within her.

Reality slapped her hard as Arvis spied her from across the room and lurched clumsily in her direction. His mother nearly lost her grip as he reached wildly, crying, "Lene! Lene!"

"No . . ." she gasped, stepping back, but the First held her still. Her fantasy burst like an oily bubble on a polluted pool.

"Into the water," Atle growled.

"I can't," she whispered. She ached to breed, but the shambling, stunted male before her filled her with fear and revulsion. "I can't . . . I won't!"

"You *will*!" Atle ordered, and shoved her toward the pool.

"Atle!" his wife shrilled from across the room. "She *must* be calm or we'll never be able to help them through this!"

Dunn's rational voice tempered the First. It helped Lene, too. This had been *her* idea. She pulled away from the First. "I'm all right!" She dropped her garment and Arvis glowed as he gazed at her. "He's still *your* son, my First. You've taught him to attend your every physical need. He hasn't forgotten all that now." Without a glance back, she entered the calm water.

As the First helped his wife get Arvis out of his robe, Lene realized what she'd said was true. In breeding condition, Arvis was the image of his father. His body was magnificent, but the confusion and pain on his face ended the similarity. For the first time Lene realized the tragedy of the First's loss.

Arvis and his parents entered the water. The Industrious youth lunged at her, his tail twitching so violently she feared he might release his seed too soon. "Lene! Lene!" he panted.

The membranes on her back were swollen, itching, ready to enfold a fertile egg. Her mother's warning echoed in her mind, but she shut the frightening images away.

Arvis surged forward and the First restrained him, but soon, Lene knew, she would have to control him. "Arvis, listen to me!"

The youth paused, staring as if he'd never get enough of her beauty. He'd be totally devoted, she realized, forever faithful. He would never shame her with trips to the hatchery, never breed young virgins when she grew old. "Arvis, do you love me?"

He blinked slowly. "Oh, yes. Yes, I really do!"

"If you love me, then won't you help me . . . like you help your father?" Both Atle and Dunn stared at her, confused.

"Yes, I'll help you," Arvis declared.

With a twinge of fear, she turned her back to him. "Then . . . give me a massage, dear Arvis. I'm . . . so tired . . . please?"

He groaned. "A . . . massage?"

"Yes . . . like you give your father?"

She could see him thinking furiously, but his tail slowed and he relaxed. "All right . . . a massage . . . ?"

"Yes, please. Your father says . . . you're so gentle. . . ."

She saw awareness growing in Atle's eyes. He nodded at Dunn and they released their hold. Instead of lunging wildly and grappling her frantically, the Industrious male, trained from infancy to serve others, gently massaged Lene's back. He sang softly as his desire raged within him, and Lene felt her body responding to his light but confident touch. Carefully, she reached behind and took his hands, pulling them around her.

He gasped and embraced her in the true amplexus, his grip powerful but controlled, his legs stroking hers, slowly, sensuously. "Oh, Lene, I'll love you forever," he sang shakily.

Lene settled back into her lover's embrace, her joy and happiness melting her smugness away.

"You mean . . . it's finally *ready*?" Jib asked incredulously.

Bruce made one final connection from the transmitter he'd removed from the *Demoiselle* to the alien satellite and stepped away from the hybrid device. "If K'heera had been here, we'd have been done days ago."

The tired weatherman had been trying to mate those two disparate parts for the two weeks they'd "been on the lam" as Bruce kept saying. His work had slowed to a crawl these last three days, once the rains started. The torrential downpours saturated everything, making food gathering difficult, and working on electronic equipment close to impossible.

Even though he'd helped, Jib didn't think he'd ever understand how Bruce had managed to isolate and extract the alien satellite's power source even as they kept breaking up and resettling camp. The tricky experiment had cost the old Yank two powerful shocks, and he still had some minor memory loss from the last one. Figuring out how to adapt the alien power cell for their equipment took a level of Rube Goldberg jury-rigging that was absolutely artistic. As Bruce kept telling them, this was definitely your one-chance opportunity.

In spite of their constant relocations, Flies-Too-Fast had caught up with them ten days ago. Since then, he and Taller and his flock, along with their cousins the Gray Winds, had scattered over the Land of Confusion, watching out for the invaders and acting as an early warning system for the three humans. The two men were wearing sound nullifiers all the time again.

Jib glanced out the door flap of their camouflaged shelter to Tesa and Taller as they stood in the rain. She'd been badly shaken by the story of her grandparents' and Weaver's capture. It'd changed her, he thought. *Still, she's taking her bad news a mite bit better than you, eh*? he chided himself.

He watched the falling rain, trying not to think of water, trying not to think of the River, *his* River, his people, the Singers, trapped there, waiting for death. But he was unable to stop the memories, or the repetitive nightmares of that horrible slaughter, and nothing could silence the songs of mourning drifting through his mind. Even as he longed for respite from the sorrowful music, he ached for more contact, his mind calling out, night and day. But there was no real contact, just those sad songs, like the distant weeping of lost souls.

Tesa entered the shelter abruptly, water streaming from her saturated feather shirt. The waterproofing on it had failed days ago, but it didn't seem to bother her. These days, little did. She pushed back her hood as Bruce signed, "Looks like we're in business." For once, she seemed surprised.

"Great!" she replied. "I'll tell Taller and the others. You can turn it on, then we'll get the hell out of here."

Bruce held up a hand to stop her. "Well . . . it's not that simple, darlin'. . . . There's still a few bugs in the system."

"We're running out of time!" she complained, more to herself than to them. "We've got to get this warning *out*!"

"We can do that. . . ." Bruce agreed slowly.

"*But* . . . ?" Tesa asked pointedly.

"The system's too cobbled-together. There's no way to stabilize the signal. If . . . I don't stay with it to keep it focused, it'll deteriorate in minutes and no one'll hear it."

None of them said anything for a moment, then Tesa exploded. "No, damn it, no! That's out of the question. Just . . . *no*!"

"There's no other way," Bruce explained.

"They'll follow the source of the signal," she fumed, her hands flying. "They'll *find* you! We'll turn this stupid piece of shit on and go! If it works, fine, and if it doesn't . . ."

"The Anurans take the *Brolga*," Bruce signed neutrally, "and the CLS never gets the signal."

Tesa seemed ready to scream.

"Why don't *I* stay?" Jib offered suddenly. They both seemed startled at his suggestion. "You two can survive out here much better than I can. If they take me, I can try to negotiate. . . ."

"*No one's* staying!" Tesa signed angrily. "And you can just get over your self-sacrificing guilt trip, it's not helping us."

Jib glanced away.

"How are we going to do it, Tesa?" Bruce signed, bringing them back to the subject. "How are we going to send the message and be sure someone gets it?"

"Can't you leave a large cohort around the shelter?" Jib suggested. "They'll call if the invaders come near. Even with nullifiers, Bruce'll feel it. It'll give him time to escape. . . ."

"We can't endanger them," Bruce signed before Tesa could respond. "Our job is to *protect* them."

"True," Tesa agreed, "but Bruce is not staying, either. . . ."

They argued for another hour before she gave in.

Finally, Jib and Tesa had nothing to do but pack. Jib couldn't believe they were really going to leave him here.

Only Bruce had fully accepted it. He seemed unnaturally calm, puttering with the satellite, getting everything just so.

Finally, they had all finished their preparations. Bruce tapped Tesa on the shoulder. Reluctantly she turned to him. "I'll give you three hours' head start before I crank this baby up," he signed. "Will that be enough time?"

She nodded and started to tell him where she would meet up with Taller, but he stopped her hands. "The less I know . . ." he began, then trailed off. Instead, he warned sternly, "Don't take any crazy risks. You can't help anyone if you get your fool head shot off."

"Look who's talking!" she signed angrily, her bottom lip quivering. Jib turned away, a hard knot tightening in his throat.

"Let's not do this to each other," Bruce signed slowly.

Tesa nodded. "Do you know about the Kiowa Dog Soldiers?" Bruce shook his head.

"The Kiowa also called them the Ten Bravest. They wore a long sash to war, and in the thick of battle . . . they'd anchor that sash to the ground with their lance. They'd stand in that spot and fight . . . to the death . . . or until another Dog freed them." She touched his cheek gently, then pulled her hand away. "If . . . *when* you see my grandparents, tell them . . . watch for Iktomi." She knew he'd understand her reference to the notorious Native American trickster.

The older man grabbed Tesa and hugged her tight, then she snatched up her pack and rushed out of the shelter. Bruce turned to Jib. "Don't let anything happen to her."

"Don't worry," he replied. "She'll be too busy keeping *me* alive to get in trouble."

Bruce smiled, and clapped him on the shoulder. Hoisting his pack, Jib stumbled out of the shelter. Tesa was rubbing her eyes when he got there.

"Lightning and Thunder have gone ahead," she told him brusquely. "They'll warn us if they see any danger. We'll be meeting up with Taller and the flock farther north. You ready?"

*I'm ready to go home, is what I'm bloody well ready for,* he thought, but he nodded anyway. Then suddenly he felt a *pull*. His head jerked in the direction of the River.

"What is it?" she asked, concerned.

He strained to feel it again . . . but it was gone. "For a moment, I thought I felt Taniwha . . . but it slipped away. . . ."

Tesa watched him worriedly. "Once we meet up with the flock we can try and free the trapped herd before . . ." She didn't finish the sentence.

*Before they're all killed,* Jib thought angrily, and glanced back at the shelter where Bruce sat.

"Jib," Tesa signed, "did you bring your letters, the paper ones?" She was plainly attempting to distract him from his morose thoughts, but all she'd done was confuse him.

"What letters?" he asked, looking at her blankly. *Paper letters? Written to whom?*

She stared at him oddly, her expression both disturbed and sad.

Abruptly she signed, "We've only got three hours." Bouncing her pack into a more comfortable position, she jogged off down a narrow animal path.

Jib followed, wondering how long he'd be able to keep up.

Javier First-Light-of-Day ran a brown, long-fingered hand over a model of the ship he was traveling on. The *Brolga* had been designed to resemble the great gray crane it was named for, but to Javier, it seemed more like a cubist's interpretation.

Two large, thick, triangular "wings" were attached by narrow pylons to a long, graceful center portion—the "body." On this, the ship's maiden voyage, the versatile wings—which could be detached—contained everything needed to expand Trinity's small space station and stock it. On this trip, personnel and crew were housed in the body, even the hibernators.

He imagined a small arrow and a "You are here" sign at the forward bow—the crane's head—where he currently stood. That was the observation lounge. Now that they were out of metaspace, there was actually something to see. The stars were magnificent, in more colors than he'd ever dreamed, and he reveled in the sight.

Javier returned the model to its mount. They were almost at Trinity. He tried to imagine how much work a wilderness world filled with an unspoiled native population offered to an ethnobotanist, but he couldn't. He was only in his thirties. A good scientist could make a world like this his life.

He ran a hand through his thick, wavy black hair, trying not to think about the new scattering of gray there, and in his moustache, too. That's all there had ever been for him—work.

A gentle touch at his elbow made him turn.

"Looks like you could use another trip to the hydroponics lab, Javier." The ship's Captain spoke clearly and he read her lips easily. "You look homesick."

He managed a token smile. It was impossible to feel homesick when you'd never felt at home.

Captain Jane Stepp was a small woman. At a hundred eighty-three centimeters, he topped her by a head. She smiled up at him and said, "I never really understood the term 'landlubber,' till I met you. The only time you ever appeared comfortable was when you helped us solve that germination problem in hydroponics."

"As I told you," he said, "this is my first trip into space. With a little luck, it'll be my last."

She wore a wry expression, and he was instantly sorry he'd

reminded her of that conversation. It had taken place as he'd worked on the germination trays. Somehow or other, he'd ended up alone with her, and soon realized that she was interested in him.

He shouldn't have been surprised—women liked strong, quiet men that were secure enough to let them be themselves. In spite of his rough, swarthy skin, and the jagged scar across his right cheekbone, he'd been told he was attractive. Stepp had complimented his "intense" black eyes, but he suspected she just wasn't used to lip-readers.

It had been difficult to turn her down. She was attractive and intelligent, and it had been a while since he'd been around women who were "available"—that is, not part of the community he was studying. But, he didn't belong here, on a ship, in space. And for something that intimate, he needed to feel comfortable, needed to have a sense of belonging.

*Which is a good excuse for the few failed relationships you've had,* he thought irritably.

He lacked a sense of community, of being a part of a whole. His father was Navaho, his mother Costa Rican—both professional people with few ties to their own cultures. He'd never really fit in with those groups, even when, as an adult, he'd gone to learn more about them.

And as a deaf child growing up in a hearing world, he'd always been on the outside. Neither of his parents signed, and with their constant moving, he'd never been exposed to other deaf people, or had a chance to become part of their community.

It was almost as if he'd spent his life "visiting"—working, learning, studying, looking for a place to fit in. Which was why he'd turned down Jane Stepp. It was nice that she wanted to share her "place"—but that was not enough anymore. He needed something more.

The Captain spoke again, but he missed it. She realized it, too, and pointed to his right ear, to the gold earring there. *Oh, yes*—he kept forgetting. He touched the earring, turning "on" his good ear.

"I said," she repeated, "that I hope you find what you're looking for on Trinity." Her blue eyes were kind, as though to tell him there were no hard feelings.

"I think working with the Grus will be enough," he told her.

He thought of the first time he'd gone to the Smithsonian to see their cloak on display there and remembered the marvelous patterns revealed only under ultraviolet light. Vividly, he recalled the loop of tape that showed the cloak's maker at her task, working so effortlessly at her art. Her name was Weaver, and she was . . . she was beautiful, the way the Navaho think of beauty. He'd fallen in love with her that day, with her people and her planet. From that time on, Javier knew he *had* to go to Trinity, to see it for himself. If he was destined to never belong anywhere, it may as well be where the world was new and full of beauty, where he could walk in beauty every day.

"It won't be long before we'll be docking," Captain Stepp said. "Everyone's pretty excited."

Yes, he could tell. The constant hum of activity and the background drone of voices had been so distracting, he'd kept his hearing off most of the time. As one of forty new people assigned to Trinity, he'd managed not to fit in with that group either. Oh, he'd made acquaintances, but while the other scientists and technicians clustered in groups, he'd found himself more comfortable on the periphery.

"And," the Captain continued, "if . . . you ever get tired of Trinity, the *Brolga* will be back. You won't be stranded."

He really smiled then. "I'll remember that."

Just then two members of the Hurrraahhhkkaa' Drum Dancers approached them. They all exchanged the traditional bow, then the leader, Kh'arhh'tk, said, "Honored Captain, my troupe is ready to perform for the Grus. We have three completely new routines for the occasion." The Simiu's earcuff voder translated easily.

"That'll be quite a cultural exchange," she agreed. "You know," she told Javier, "it's very unusual to transport the same passengers on such a circuitous route—first on the *Norton*, now on the *Brolga*—but by following our itinerary, Honored Kh'arhh'tk and his troupe have been able to bring a part of their culture to people who have very limited exposure to the Simiu."

"The CLS has given us much honor," the second dancer, Ahrakk', explained, "by promoting this goodwill tour. We hope to demonstrate that we are more complex than is often believed."

The Simiu were still smarting about their image since the trouble at Trinity, Javier knew. He had learned, too, about the incident on the *Norton* between these dancers and the young StarBridge student. While everyone that had talked to him of it seemed outraged that a Harkk'ett had been sent to Trinity, all Javier could feel was sympathy for the poor female.

"Well, after we leave Trinity, your next stop is Shassiszss," Stepp reminded them.

"Yes," Kk'arhh'tk agreed, "and after a short tour there, we will finally go home. We all miss our families. . . . I have a young niece who may not even remember me! As performers, we have enjoyed this opportunity . . . but we long to go home."

Javier wondered, not for the first time, what that must feel like. And he wondered, too, if that was an emotion the young outcast, K'heera, shared with the dancers.

"Captain?" a new voice interrupted the conversation.

Stepp turned, automatically reaching for the report that was being held out to her by Martin Brockman, her chief engineer. Brockman was as blond as Javier was brown, his crew cut a sharp contrast to Javier's longish style, and their chosen fields about as different—yet Brockman was the one person on this whole voyage that Javier had felt comfortable with.

The Captain scanned the computer board, placing her thumb on the signature block. "So, we're in hailing distance now?"

"Yes, ma'am," Brockman replied.

"What's this about communications problems?"

"We're getting a garbled, repetitive transmission. Might be an AI problem. We'll get them back on line."

She handed him back the board. "I'd better touch base with communications. Gentlemen, if you'll excuse me. . . ."

The group dispersed and Javier found himself alone, contemplating the stars.

Atle watched his son gently enclose Lene's fertilized egg into the freshly opened pouch on her back. In a few hours there would be no wound at all, merely a slight swelling that would grow into his grandchild. His Chosen grandchild. Arvis tenderly took Lene back into his arms and held her as carefully as his own mother often held him.

"Can you believe that is our son?" Dunn whispered. "It . . . almost makes up for . . ."

She didn't finish, but he knew what she meant. For the loss of their Chosen children. For the loss of their Home. For the stunting of Arvis and his sister. *Almost,* he thought bitterly. He gazed at his lovely wife. "They'll sleep now. We should go."

"Yes. I'll speak with Anchie, assure her all went well."

"That *could* wait," Atle grunted, then they both laughed.

But just as Dunn went to the door, its signal chimed. She opened it to reveal Leuth, Atle's Fourth-in-Conquest, a handsome One-Touch. The soldier stood at attention.

"What is it?" Atle asked. Dunn's color dulled in concern.

"The humans' ship, sir, is just outside the solar system."

"Excellent! Dacris is prepared! This has been a good day." Atle genuinely hoped for his Second's success. If he captured the ship, Dacris would be permitted to take it, and its human crew, back Home to a hero's welcome. And he'd finally be out of Atle's way.

"The Second is ready, but . . ." Leuth glanced at Dunn.

"Go ahead, Leuth. My wife has shared my service all these years." What wife of an officer did not?

The young Fourth blinked worriedly. "There's a transmission being beamed from this world . . . it's a warning, sir."

# CHAPTER 15
## ◆
# The *Brolga*

Captain Stepp took one last tour of her new ship before she docked with the *Singing Crane*. This maiden run had been remarkably free from glitches, and Jane already felt as if this cooperative, well-behaved vessel was "hers." Entering the spacious dining area, she nodded hello to the few passengers there. The ship's mess had tables seating four in a brightly lit area that could accommodate one hundred.

Several of the *Crane*'s new staff communicated animatedly in Grus Sign Language, the only one they had in common. Seeing her, one of them signed a greeting. She waved back.

Finally, she entered her bridge. Glancing at her command seat, she ran a hand over the still-immaculate console. Cradled in the belly of the ship's body, this bridge had a better layout than the *Norton*'s. All the consoles were placed against the walls under easy-to-see holo-displays. In the middle of the room, the large control center was manned by her red-haired navigator, Renata Taylor, and her copilot, Chris Bartus. Renata scooted her seat back and forth along its tracks, running her hands over the controls, while Chris stayed in place, checking their trajectory. They were almost ready to dock.

"Looks like everything's under control," Jane commented.

Moshe Rosten, the first mate, entered the bridge, gave Jane a nod, and went to his station. "I'm going to the airlock to greet Meg and Bruce," the Captain told the room.

"I'll holler if there's any problem," Renata responded.

"I'm sure you will," Stepp said dryly, exiting the bridge.

Jane looked forward to seeing Meg and Bruce again as she walked toward the ship's blunt, fan-shaped tail. She still felt bad about not greeting them the last time they were here . . . but she hadn't been ready to face that damned Harkk'ett again. . . . She wondered idly what repercussions there would be from bringing that particular Simiu here. Serious ones, she feared.

A cluster of passengers had gathered at the bulkhead nearest the airlock, eager to finally meet the scientists from Trinity. Excited chatter filled the area, and the flash of moving hands rippled through the crowd.

Martin Brockman stood beside the lock, repair kit in hand, as did Steve Manohar, the rotund, bearded cargo master. "I've got everything we need to fix their comm link, ma'am," Brockman said, patting the case.

"I'm sure they'll be happy to hear that, Martin." She glanced at Steve's manifest and raised her eyebrows. "How long do you think it'll take to unload all *that*?"

"We'll be lucky to get the *passengers* checked off today," he said, scrolling through the seemingly endless list. "We won't even start going through the hardware till tomorrow."

She nodded.

"There's something weird though, Captain," Martin added as an afterthought. "I've tried to talk to the *Crane* ship-to-ship for the last ten minutes, but no one's responded. They should be able to do that, even with serious equipment failure."

Stepp peered at him quizzically. That *was* odd.

The ship kissed the docking port. *Nice, Renata.* The grapples engaged, and they waited as air filled the vacuum of the lock. Finally, the outer door cycled open. When the green panel lights lit up, she punched in the command to open the inner door.

Smiling, she stepped back, facing the lock. As the door rose, a blast of warm, humid air swirled around her feet, making her frown. Jane took a step back, then smelled a foreign odor.

"Captain Stepp!" Renata's voice rang out sharply, distracting her. "Emergency transmission from Trinity—from *Bruce*!"

"That can't be," Steve said. "He's meeting us *here*."

"He says," Renata continued quickly, "that they're under *invasion* from some hostile force. Says they need help from the CLS. Captain? What should I do?"

The *Brolga*'s officers could just see the feet and legs of the figures behind the airlock door. The footwear and jumpsuits were the familiar garb of the *Crane* crew.

"Get a location on that transmission," the Captain ordered, as knees became visible. "Are you sure it's Bruce?"

"The message is on the right frequency, and he's using the correct priority code."

Stepp slapped the control panel, halting the now nearly open door. "Get out of here, you two!" she barked, just as one of the uniformed figures ducked under the descending door.

A green and gold, slash-mouthed alien wearing a Terran jumpsuit rushed her. Before she could react, Brockman threw the repair kit at it, then tackled two others who were scrambling under the door. Steve dropped his clipboard and shoved Stepp toward safety just as yet another alien grappled him from behind.

Taking advantage of the scant seconds the two men had bought her, the Captain spun, feeling like she was nailed to the floor.

"RUN!" she screamed at the stunned passengers as she raced for the bulkhead. If she could get through and seal it . . .

Some of the scientists bolted, while others stood, confused. Alien hands latched on to her and she fell, hitting a passenger, all of them landing in a heap on the floor. An alien had her around the knees, but she was through the bulkhead.

*"Hit the controls!"* she shrieked at a woman immobilized in fear beside the control panel. The passenger stared at the panel, then at the alien clawing its way up the Captain's body.

*"I SAID HIT THE GODDAMNED CONTROLS!"* Stepp bellowed, kicking the alien viciously in the gut. Flipping onto her stomach, she slammed her fist onto the passenger's soft-shoed foot. The woman yelped, then jabbed the button as if snapped out of a trance.

The being and Stepp played a grisly tug-of-war with her body as it tried to drag her back under the descending door. Jane felt herself losing ground in the battle, when suddenly the befuddled woman passenger kicked and chopped the alien expertly in the side, making it squeal. The door descended just as Jane pulled her foot free and the invader was forced to back away.

Stepp scurried away from the door on hands and knees, yelling at the intercom, "Taylor, the *Crane*'s been invaded! They've got Brockman and Manohar! Blow the damned airlock!"

"Blow the lock, Captain? That'll damage the station. . . ."

The bulkhead door rose half a meter, then stalled.

"They've got computer overrides, understand? All hands, arm

yourselves! Passengers, lock yourselves in your quarters! Taylor,
BLOW THAT DAMNED LOCK!" Jane suddenly realized the
aliens had managed to kill her intercom, that she was talking
to herself.. "Shit!" She bolted away from the traitorous bulkhead,
shoving the woman passenger ahead of her.

*How many weapons do we have?* she wondered as she moved
toward the bridge from the tail, sealing doors behind her. The
answer was hardly any. *Why hasn't Taylor blown that lock?*

The terrible sound of tearing metal reverberated through the
ship as Stepp fell to the floor, thrown by the force of her vessel
ripping itself away from the *Crane*'s dock. Jane bounced back to
her feet as damage alarms and human voices screamed in concert.
*Come on, Renata, get us the hell out of here!*

"Airlock Twelve has sustained serious damage," the safety
program intoned. "Repairs must be instituted immediately. Engi-
neering staff please respond. . . ."

The *Brolga* responded sluggishly. The ship's safety systems
would have to be manually overridden to permit the vessel to
take off now. Stepp raced for the bridge.

"We're moving away, ma'am," Renata said as soon as she
arrived. The woman's voice was edged with tension, but she'd
obviously already plotted their course. The copilot and first mate
were all business as they handled the controls of the ship, but
they were visibly shaken.

Stepp stared at the holos, fascinated by the garish damage
her ship had done to the *Singing Crane* as its gaping wound
spewed out equipment and bipedal bodies. She'd delivered the
materials to build the station when there'd been nothing here but
vacuum.

"Dear *God*," Moshe gasped, and everyone turned. His holo
showed a different angle of the same scene. Stepp squinted and
suddenly recognized the clothes, then the face, of one of the
rotating bodies. She felt her knees go weak as Steve Manohar
tumbled stiffly, over and over, his arms and legs outthrust. His
face was frozen in surprise, the half of it facing the sun seared
brown. Blood had spurted from his nose, eyes, mouth, and ears.
Some of it had crystallized against his flesh, but the droplets
facing Trinity's sun had burned black against his exposed skin.

"Captain!" Chris called out, and Jane pulled her eyes away to
see spacesuited figures propelling themselves out of the *Crane*,
toward the *Brolga*.

"Renata, override whatever you have to," Stepp snapped, fighting to keep her voice steady. "We've got to get out of this solar

system and into metaspace. Moshe, send an emergency S-O-S, and boost Bruce's signal. We've got to let someone know . . ."

"Captain," Chris said with unnatural calm, "ships are closing in off the starboard bow."

"What *ships*?" Stepp asked, astonished. Five space vessels emerged from behind the *Crane,* then moved to surround her vessel. They fanned out, approaching the *Brolga*'s many air-locks.

"Captain," Renata said, "the spacesuited aliens are working on our other locks. They must be trying to dock their ships."

"Moshe, keep those locks closed. Renata, whatever happens, keep transmitting that S-O-S."

"But where are you . . . ?" the navigator began.

"I've got to coordinate the crew," Stepp told them. She reached into a cabinet and pulled out handheld communicators. "Most of the passengers are wearing voders. We can communicate through them. Lock the doors behind me. If . . . we're boarded, hold them off the bridge for as long as our weapons hold out."

"That won't be very long, ma'am," the copilot pointed out quietly. "We've only got two repulser guns and a blaster."

Bruce made another minute adjustment in his jury-rigged comm unit. *Come on,* he thought desperately, *someone's got to hear this.* Would he ever know?

The worst thing was the terrible silence. There should be forest sounds outside the tiny shelter, the calls of animals, the snapping of dry twigs, but in the Land of Confusion there were no animals. There would be nothing to warn him when . . .

The signal drifted and he compensated. He'd been broadcasting for twenty-five minutes. How long would it take the *Brolga* to pick it up? She could still be in metaspace, and this device was not sophisticated enough to trigger her emergency beacon.

Bruce thought he heard something rustling through the under-growth, but forced himself to ignore it. It was the wind. Branches falling from trees. He imagined the Kiowa Dog Soldiers, pinned in place of their own free will, their defiance in the face of incredible odds, their courage . . .

The signal drifted again. He adjusted it, the eerie silence build-ing up. He ought to put his nullifiers on; he was used to that soundlessness. Sweat broke out on his upper lip. *Something* was nearby. He could feel its presence hovering around the shelter like an ominous spirit.

*Not yet,* he thought desperately, *please, not yet.*

\*    \*    \*

Javier read his voder in stunned disbelief. He'd entered his quarters just as his wrist voder flashed. They were under *attack*? He read the Captain's orders. Lock your rooms, stay out of the way, let the crew handle it.

The crew? A dozen against an invasion? He moved into the hallway to find a cluster of other passengers. Carlotta Estafan, the linguist, was speaking rapidly. He read a garbled account of how her slow reaction nearly cost the Captain her life. Abdul Kadir, the biochemist, tried to calm her, even as a steward urged them to return to their cabins. Javier turned on his hearing.

"We cannot stay in our rooms!" Kh'arhh'tk, the lead drum dancer, growled. "There is no honor in hiding like children."

"Please, you *must* follow the Captain's orders," the steward insisted. "Secure your quarters and wait for instructions."

"But those aliens are trying to board the ship!" someone in the back cried out.

"They will *not* be able to breach the locks," the steward assured her calmly. "Besides, none of you have any weapons or training for this kind of conflict."

"Are you so defenseless without *weapons,* human?" Kh'arhh'tk grumbled. "My people can fight with our hands alone!"

"He's right," Carlotta agreed, surprising everyone. Her voice was steadier. "The engineer and the cargo master defended the Captain with their bare hands. Then she did the same to save me and the ship. Can we do less? I've had survival training, and so have others here. And I'm a black belt in karate. I'm not going to sit in the belly of this ship and *wait* like a turkey for Thanksgiving!"

*That's why she's so embarrassed at freezing up,* Javier thought. *She'd never been tested before.*

As if his thoughts had caught her attention, she turned to him, her dark eyes bright. "Javier, you've worked with native people. Don't you know how to make weapons?"

"From *natural* materials," he reminded her. Everyone turned to him. He thought for a moment. "Well . . . there are transparent monofilaments in the blankets. They could be used for trip wires. Flexible cabling and small, heavy objects could be made into crude bolos." He thought of the funneling traps native people used to capture large game. Once a herd had been lured or driven, one by one, through the trap's small opening, it was hard for the group to escape. And the ship had detachable wings. . . .

"Abdul," he asked, "would the infirmary have the right chemicals to make incendiary devices . . . smoke bombs . . . ?"

The chemist grinned. "Don't tell me you've heard about my escapades in college!"

"You can't do that!" the steward protested. "The safeties will seal any room with smoke or fire in it. . . ." He trailed off suddenly, realizing that was what Javier had in mind.

"Call your Captain," Javier said. "We need to talk."

Dacris sat in the small Terran vessel the humans had given the untranslatable name *Patuxent,* watching the data flow over his tank, listening to the rapid-fire reports with utter dismay. How could his soldiers have failed to commandeer the lock? It was such a simple ploy! He watched the ravaged space station spin wildly, its devastated airlock gaping like a hungry mouth. Inside, his troops fought the alien machine, struggling to get it restabilized in its orbit. What would Atle do if he lost not only the ship but the station as well?

Well, it was *Atle* who had failed to pursue the humans still roaming the planet. If Dacris lost the ship, it would be Atle's fault. That warning message had come at the worst possible moment, and Dacris would lay that right at Atle's feet.

He watched the human ship he'd been charged with capturing creep away from the station. It was barely one-tenth the size of the *Flood*. Where was its speed? Whatever was slowing it to this crawl could only be temporary. He scanned the *Patuxent*'s instruments and the myriad translators working frantically to keep up with the barrage of information passing through them. As far as he could tell, his quarry only had minor damage, but since it was designed for transport, not for combat, its own safety programs were attempting to halt its progress until repairs could be affected. Its crew must be working frantically to override systems carefully designed to ensure their welfare in the inhospitable environment of space.

Still, he needed more information. If only the human computers had known more about his prey. There were no maps, no schematics, little information on its cargo, or its drive. He'd told himself the joy would be in the discovery, but now, he wondered if that joy would be his. He maneuvered the *Patuxent* around his prey, watching his soldiers futilely attacking its locks. They should've defeated its codes by now, they should be calling the ships to dock. Nothing was going as he'd planned. That was why he'd risked taking out this alien vessel. Its systems were compatible with the wounded transport. If his soldiers could not break into the larger ship's system, perhaps this vessel could hold the key to its companion's betrayal.

A change in the tank caught his eye. He saw a weakness there, in the large, triangular outriders. He followed the figures. Yes, they could get in there. Why didn't that please him? Because . . . instinct told him it was too far from the bridge. Those outriders were too exposed to shelter the command center. It had to be elsewhere. Safe. Protected. He didn't relish a long battle to find and capture it.

Two of the ships attached themselves, one to each triangular wing, but the locks hadn't opened yet. But his eyes rested on a small lock near the narrow head of the ship, even though the reports indicated their ships would not be able to break its code. He might waste valuable time here, and even if he could get in, he would still not know where the bridge was.

Dacris' throat pouch quivered and his tail lashed back and forth. His soldiers had special weapons filled with the chemical controls they needed to capture every human on this vessel, but it would do them no good if they couldn't get in. And in his heart he knew he alone would bear the blame if this ship were lost. His colors burned as he maneuvered the *Patuxent* to the head of the wounded transport, lining its lock up with its mate on the larger ship; all his hopes rested in the traitor's kiss of this commandeered shuttle.

"We've got to get out of here," Idoto Okigbo whispered to her companion. "They'll be through any minute!"

Abdul nodded hurriedly, punching the last few commands into his voder. The computer announced that the huge cargo lock at the wide end of the wing was about to be breached. He took one last glance at his contraption, and wished he could see the lock from here. However, twenty of them had just finished rearranging the cargo in this cavernous place to match Javier's diagram, and he could no longer see the lock.

The computer announced that the lock had been breached, that ". . . unauthorized personnel are about to enter the cargo bay." Abdul heard the lock cycle and the doors open.

"Come on!" Idoto hissed in his ear, tugging on his shirt. The dark woman's sculpted face was flushed, her eyes wide.

"Can you see them? Are they coming?"

The tall Nigerian grabbed the chemist by the collar, physically hauling him away from his trap.

"But suppose they *aren't* funneled to this one spot?" Abdul worried. "They aren't deer or fish, they're *intelligent*."

Idoto said nothing, just kept towing the balding chemist till they'd slipped behind the maze of crates and entered the pylon elevator. "It'll work, it'll work," she reassured him, once they were safely behind its doors.

They could hear feet, lots of feet, pounding on the floor, echoing wildly around the cargo. The elevator started to descend, bringing them back to the body of the ship.

They both turned to their voders, watched the scene the small sentry camera relayed back to them. Idoto shivered at the sight of the alien troops searching for them. The elevator descended placidly, as if they were in a department store, not a spaceship, fighting for their lives.

Soon, their screens were so filled with soldiers, they could see nothing else. "Now!" she said to Abdul. "Now! Now!"

He waited two more seconds, then punched the last command into his voder. Suddenly their voders went gray as thick, cloying smoke engulfed the camera. Alarms in the elevator clanged raucously and lights flashed.

"Attention!" the computer voice intoned. "Attention! There is a fire in B wing, cargo area sixteen. The wing is sealed; fire containment protocol is being enacted."

Abdul and Idoto grinned at each other and hugged, giddy with their success. Every lock and bulkhead in the entire wing would be impossible to raise now without special override codes punched in by the Captain herself. The elevator stopped, opening its doors into the body of the ship, near their quarters.

Abdul spoke into his voder. "B wing is secure, Captain Stepp. Tell the crew to detach." Now if only the team in A wing was as successful.

Javier and Carlotta tied another invisible trip wire across a wide space framed by a cluster of chairs in the observation lounge. The chairs were a decent anchor for the wires, and the other chairs would block the area so this would seem like the only logical path. He scanned the lounge, hardly believing he'd been killing time here just a few hours before.

He glanced at the nearby airlock, its framework, computer system, and controls all decorated to meld in with the lounge's decor. The innocuous-appearing airlock was now framed by the strategic placement of chairs. That lock had been the entrance through which Javier had first boarded this ship from the Terran space station that orbited Earth's moon. This lounge had been his introduction to the *Brolga*; it was where those destined to travel to Trinity had first been assembled for introductions and an orientation to the beginning of their new careers. And now, aliens in one of the *Singing Crane*'s own shuttlecraft were hovering outside it, working doggedly to breach it and invade the *Brolga*.

Noriko Imanaka sat beside the control panel with a full array of computer equipment, as the software specialist counteracted and overrode the electronic invasion from the other side of the lock. In the last few minutes her intent expression had turned positively grim. Javier nodded to Carlotta.

"Are they going to get in?" the linguist asked bluntly.

"Not if *I* can help it," the Asian woman grumbled.

Suddenly the lock's lights began flashing, warning that it was about to cycle. Noriko's fingers flew over her equipment, shutting the cycle down. How long could she keep that up?

"You can't stay here," he said softly. "Put in some codes and come with us."

Noriko shook her head. "You go on. I'll keep them out for as long as I can. I'll leave before they get in. Go ahead!"

He knew she was lying, and by the look on Carlotta's face, the linguist did, too. They'd done all they could here. Their poor traps were all set; Javier and Carlotta's job was finished.

Leaving Noriko in the lounge, they traveled through the halls, closing and locking every bulkhead, running more trip wires, some at ankle height, some at the knees, some at eye level. They attached them to anything they could find. If the invaders entered through the observation lounge lock, they'd have to go through the passenger decks and the dining room to find their way to the bridge.

Javier told himself they'd never get past Noriko as he and Carlotta opened every cabin door on all four decks, even ones that had never been occupied. Good soldiers would have to check and secure every room . . . and some of them held surprises.

Captain Stepp ordered Renata to detach A wing—the second one to go—then sagged against a hibernation unit, exhausted. She couldn't believe what her chrono told her—that it'd only been eighty minutes since they'd docked with the *Singing Crane*. At least they'd managed to disable most of the cumbersome safety programs; the *Brolga* was moving faster now. They were almost at the big moon, and still broadcasting their alarm—though Bruce's had stopped, she wasn't sure when.

The detached wings had large companies of soldiers trapped inside them, and that pleased her. But the *Patuxent* was attached to the *Brolga*'s body like an engorged tick, ready to send its virus into her vessel. Well, once they were past this moon they'd really pick up speed. She wondered how her uninvited guests would feel about an unprepared jump into metaspace. She pictured them all appearing in Mizari space, with ships full of League Irenics waiting for them.

Her voder flashed and she glimpsed Renata's latest message. The aliens had breached the observation lounge lock. They were in. Actually *in* her ship. Her beautiful, new ship. She blinked, shaking off the sick feeling inside her.

The hibernation area stood between the bridge and the tail, and the invaders were coming from the head. Even so, aliens traveling through the upper decks of the passenger cabins could go *over* the bridge and end up in the hibernation area. So, two of her crew, Brian, the hardware specialist, and Misha, a steward, had unlocked and darkened each and every one of the hundred empty hibernator units. Each unit had a cabinet beneath it, and each of those had been unlocked. And each one would have to be checked by an invader before it could be secured. Having finished, the three of them collapsed together behind one of the sleepers.

Misha handed Jane a makeshift bolo, but she waved it away. She'd never been much good at throwing. He'd secured a medical scalpel onto a sturdy plastic pipe, and Brian hefted a makeshift club. She found herself wishing that she and her crew knew Grus Sign Language, so they could communicate over their voders in silence, the way the passengers did.

They were sitting near an air vent, and suddenly a Simiu roar echoed out. "Oh, no," Stepp whispered. She should be with the passengers. How had she ended up here, behind the action?

Her voder flashed, seeming impossibly bright.

"Captain," Renata's voice said tiredly, "they're in the passengers' quarters. We're still not past the outer moon."

*Still within the solar system*, Jane realized. *We still can't go to stellar velocity.*

"Okay," said Stepp, trying to think of what else they could do. She felt incredibly helpless.

Suddenly the harsh mechanical sound of a crude, artificial translator voice blared from the ship-wide intercom. "Passengers and crew. Your ship has been conquered by the Chosen. Avoid injury. Surrender now. You will not be harmed."

The startling announcement lent an air of unreality to everything that had happened, as if those words were more powerful than invading ships, soldiers, or anything else.

Jane tried to get her voder to bring in an image from some of the safety cameras in the passengers' area, and finally found herself staring at a full-blown battle. A surge of soldiers charged a handful of passengers, then some of the aliens went down. The aliens charged over their fallen comrades, shooting at the passengers with some more odd weapon. Other aliens entered into individual cabins, only to have cabin doors slam shut behind them. Fire alarms sounded. There were screams, alien and human.

More troops came into view.

*Where are they all coming from?* she wondered frantically.

Just then, Stepp felt a hand on her shoulder and turned to face the deaf ethnobotanist. He'd startled Misha and Brian as well.

"The aliens are in the passengers' quarters," Javier told her.

"Yes, I know. How's it going?"

He paused for a moment. "We lost five people in A wing. They didn't get to the elevator in time. As the aliens go through the cabins, whoever's been captured has been *removed*."

"Killed?" she asked, but he only shrugged.

"We were badly outnumbered to start with," he said. "But soon, there'll be only a handful of us left. We need to talk about . . . what will happen if they take the bridge."

*If they take the bridge before we get into metaspace, we're finished,* Jane thought. This wasn't a battleship, it was a passenger and supply vessel, not as fancy as a cruise ship, but with more amenities than a tug. There was only *one* bridge, no real weapons, and—contrary to popular fiction—no auto-destruct sequence.

"You went to all the trouble to come out here to talk to me, so you must have a plan," Stepp said hopefully.

Javier gave her a half smile. "We've got maps of the service tubes. If they take the bridge, they'll probably call on you to surrender again. The rest of us can storm the bridge through the tubes *after* you give yourself up, while you're pretending to persuade us to submit." He watched her, waiting to see what she thought. "While we engage them, you can evacuate the air from the rest of the ship, killing the troops outside the bridge. Without their army, the few left on the bridge will have to yield."

Stepp watched him, her mind working furiously. Suppose the other passengers weren't dead? Suppose they were holding them in the observation lounge? She could scan the holos that showed the ship's interiors. If she didn't see any humans . . . it could work.

Stepp glanced at the men flanking her. "What do you think?"

"Giving up doesn't feel right to me," Misha said.

"I want to keep fighting," Brian agreed.

Stepp faced Javier. "Take these two with you, you'll need them. If the aliens ask me to surrender, I'll follow your script. You'll have to move quietly."

"We can be quiet, Captain." Javier reached over and shook her hand. "Good luck."

The two crewmen followed the ethnobotanist around a hibernator and disappeared.

The minute they were out of sight, the Captain regretted her decision. There had to be a better way, a plan that made more sense . . . but she'd been wracking her brain since this whole thing began and hadn't come up with anything better. There was nothing in her training that prepared her for this kind of emergency. She shook her head, trying not to second-guess her decision. Not fifteen minutes later, her voder flashed, grabbing her attention.

"Jane, they're outside the bridge," Renata said breathlessly, her composure fraying. "We're just about ready to come around the back of the moon . . . we should really be able to increase our speed then . . . ."

Chris called her, and the navigator turned her back to Jane, responding to her crew, trying to keep them together. She left her station, and Jane watched her lean over Moshe's console, and rapidly punch in some codes, while glancing at the doors.

*I should be there,* Jane thought guiltily, wanting to bolt from her hiding place.

"We're okay," Renata told the crew loudly, sounding as though she were trying to reassure herself, "we're okay!"

"No good!" Chris called out. "It's not working!"

Jane's stomach clutched as the sealed bridge doors lurched, then opened. She watched, mesmerized, as a dozen bodies poured through the doors. Renata worked mindlessly, as if there was still something she could do to keep them out. Chris leaped from his chair, grabbing the red-haired woman by the shoulders and yanking her away from the console. But it was useless; they were surrounded. Moshe sat at his station, wide-eyed, as the aliens loomed over him.

Stepp pressed her forehead against a hibernator, wishing she could just wake up.

"Captain Stepp," the mechanical translator voice rang out tonelessly over the ship's intercom, "your control place—your 'bridge'—has been secured. We wish to cause no harm. Please surrender and order your crew and passengers to do the same."

Jane shook her head, wondering how she should respond.

"Captain Stepp," the bodiless voice intoned, "we have your . . . navigator. She will persuade you."

*That'll be the day,* Stepp thought contemptuously. Renata and she had served together for years. She'd like to see anyone make that woman do something she didn't want to.

Renata yelled out, loud and clear, "Don't give up! Stand your ground!" Her admonition was abruptly cut off, and instantly replaced by a long, pain-wracked scream. Jane covered her ears, and turned to the voder, but she could only see the backs of aliens, everyone moving, scrambling.

Renata's screaming stopped, and Stepp could hear a sob, but then the navigator called out raggedly, "Don't give up, Jane!"

Then Taylor screamed again, and again, and yet again. Moments later, her shrieks were joined by a male, Moshe, Jane thought.

"No!" Jane yelled helplessly at the voder, forgetting the sounds were coming over the intercom, that no one was paying attention to their voders. "Stop it, damn it! Stop it!"

"Captain Stepp," the hated mechanical voice intoned, as if it had heard her, "listen to your staff." The screams stopped, but she could plainly hear muted sobbing in the background. "It is wasteful and unnecessary for you to make us abuse them in this way. You are in a damaged ship, with no hope of rescue. Meet with us, and negotiate instead."

"No," Renata whimpered in the background, "don't, Jane."

"You have five . . . minutes . . . to consider our offer," the mechanical voice intoned. "After that, your staff will persuade you again. They will continue to persuade you until you come forward. This persuasion causes no corporal damage and can be administered indefinitely."

*That's it,* the Captain thought bleakly. *I can't make them go through that.*

The short walk to her bridge seemed interminable. Once outside the bridge doors, she had to compose herself before facing the beings that had raped her ship, and captured and tortured her crew. Finally, she touched the controls, and the door slid smoothly up in its tracks.

That smell hit her again, the same odd odor she'd noticed when the airlock to the *Crane* had started to open. Her gorge rose, and she forced it down. She made herself face the nearest soldier. "I'm Captain Stepp," she said softly.

"No," moaned Renata through clenched teeth. Her face was red and blotchy, and she was restrained by two of them, as were

Moshe and Chris, but otherwise they all seemed unharmed.

"It's okay, Renata," Stepp murmured. She scanned her bridge, staring at the strange aliens who'd totally changed her life. "So, who's in charge?"

A rotund, green and gold being stepped forward and trilled oddly. "I am Dacris, Second-in-Conquest, and new Captain of this vessel," its translator rasped.

*Not yet, buddy,* Stepp thought angrily.

"Captain Stepp," Dacris said, "there are still passengers and crew unaccounted for. They must come forward or . . ."

"I know, I know," she said anxiously. "I was cut off from them, completely alone. They must be scattered all over the ship. Let me talk to them. They'll surrender, but it'll take time for them to get here."

Dacris stared at her with his bizarre, marbled eyes. "Tell them to hurry . . . or you will have to persuade them."

Renata paled as he said that and Jane felt a flush of goose bumps travel over her skin. She stepped over to the intercom. "Before I call them . . . please tell me . . . why have you done this? What do you want? We are only interested in peaceful interactions with other intelligent beings."

The alien moved close to her, and she had to force herself not to flinch. "Your people have caused the death of over twelve of my soldiers, while I took the space station and this vessel without a single death on your side. You talk of *peaceful* interactions? Your people aren't fit to live."

"Is that what's going to happen to us, now?" Stepp asked worriedly. "Will you kill us because we resisted you?"

"We are a civilized people," Dacris said. "We don't waste resources, and now, that's what you are. A resource, to be trained, cultivated, bred . . ." he ran a clammy digit over her face, "*consumed.* . . . Your offspring and their offspring will serve my house and my table. I'll look forward to that."

Jane took a deep breath and pulled her eyes away from him, trying not to think of the foolhardy group creeping through the service tubes. It had to work. It had to.

She turned to the intercom. "Attention . . . Attention . . . All passengers . . . All crew . . . This is Captain Stepp . . ." She swallowed. "I am asking you to give yourselves up. Come to the bridge, and give yourselves up. You won't be harmed. Just come to the bridge as soon as you can." She paused, then repeated it over and over, assuring the empty rooms and hallways that there was no choice, that it was time to give up.

Twice her voice cracked, while Renata's quiet sobs sounded as bitter background music to her speech. Dacris moved to the bridge doors, waiting for the first person to appear.

"Do you command so little loyalty," he asked Stepp, "that you can get no one to obey you?"

"I told you, they're scattered . . . it'll take a while."

"Hold her," Dacris commanded his troops casually. "Give her the rod. They'll move faster if she persuades them."

The nearest soldiers grabbed Jane's arms as a third pointed a short, black club at her.

Renata shrieked, "NO! DON'T DO IT! NO!" distracting everyone on the bridge.

At the same moment, the two service doors slid open, and four enraged Simiu leaped out, teeth bared, roaring their battle challenge. Behind them, humans poured through the doors armed with clubs, scalpels, garrotes, and chains.

Renata lurched, freeing herself from her distracted captors. Grabbing a keyboard, she wielded it like a bat, attacking the soldier nearest her, smashing its skull. Taking advantage of the sudden confusion, Stepp slammed her booted foot down on the instep of the alien holding her right arm. She felt delicate bones snap, and the being screamed and released her. Swinging her fist with all the power born of desperation, she plunged it into the huge eye of the guard holding her left.

Freed, Jane tackled the alien with the black rod. The device barely brushed her, but Stepp's heart jolted at the sudden, shocking pain. Shrieking, she scrabbled after the weapon before it could touch her again. The Captain and the alien struggled back and forth, but finally, she forced the rod against its wide, blunt tail, and its high-pitched scream echoed throughout the bridge. Jane yanked the rod out of its fist, and left the creature flopping in convulsions.

Swinging the thing like a gun at arm's length, she kept the aliens at bay as she edged her way to the control panel. Some of the troops brandished weapons at her, but none of them fired. She suspected the range was too close.

The bridge was in chaos, as aliens swarmed the battling humans. They piled onto the Simiu, who were viciously fighting for their lives. Alien blood shimmered everywhere—at least, Stepp hoped it was alien. It was thin, but still red. Trying to keep her attention focused on her job, she scanned the holos, searching for any humans that might still be collected somewhere in the ship. The cameras showed none.

The Captain's hands hovered over the panels, setting up to evacuate the air. She trembled inwardly, feeling this was wrong, all wrong. Who would she kill? How many? Jane thought of Dacris' boast that he'd conquered the station and her bridge without taking a single life. In her forty-three years, Stepp had never physically harmed a living soul.

Pushing all that away, Jane focused on the monitors. She could see no humans, just soldiers, alien soldiers, everywhere in her ship. *Where the hell were they all coming from?* Her fingers touched the panel.

Suddenly Dacris landed hard against her, shoving her away from the console as he wrestled frantically with Javier. Stepp swung the rod, hitting the alien in the back, again and again. Javier had their lone blaster and tried to aim it at Dacris, but Stepp was right behind the alien and he couldn't. Then the humans were grabbed by two other aliens who joined Dacris in wrestling the ethnobotanist for possession of the weapon. Jane shoved at them all, frantically trying to get back to her console. For a moment, she regained her place, and quickly searched the nearest holo.

They were on the other side of the outermost moon! She felt wildly elated, thinking she'd evacuate the air, kill the invaders; if they could hold the bridge for just a few more seconds, she'd rush the *Brolga* out of the solar system!

But as her fingers hovered again over the panel, she finally saw it. In a synchronous orbit behind the big Moon. The largest ship she had ever seen . . . bigger than any Mizari ship. It was hiding there, behind the Moon, disgorging shuttle after shuttle, all of them aiming straight at her vessel. That's where all the soldiers were coming from . . . those little shuttles. The troops must be packed in there like cattle. If Stepp evacuated the air, the next replacements would be wearing suits. She stood transfixed, despondent as a futile war raged around her. She had lost her ship.

Suddenly the blaster discharged, and over a chorus of shouts, Stepp smelled charred flesh and hair. An instant later, she was tackled to the ground by clammy hands and alien bodies, and the rod was wrestled away from her. The blaster whined again, and again, followed by human and Simiu screams.

Suddenly it was over and silence fell.

Immobilized on the floor, Jane could see nothing when the combat ended. There were grunts, whistles, and twitters from the aliens and the sound of a Simiu panting.

*We're finished,* she thought, *they'll kill us all.*

Moist hands grabbed her arms and hauled her to her feet. Fearfully, Jane watched Dacris' expressionless face. His emotion was all in his eyes and his skin, his colors blazing so brightly she had to squint. He pushed the cool snout of the blaster against her face, and his musical voice took on the unmistakable sound of hysteria.

Stepp waited for a translation, but it never came. Glancing at his arm, she realized he'd been shot. His skin was charred and blistered, and the translator was destroyed.

The alien was out of control with rage, but now Jane couldn't communicate with him. Whistling and shrieking, he waved his uninjured hand around at the carnage. Dead soldiers littered the deck, and others lay wounded or bleeding.

Then Stepp saw one of the drum dancers. It was the soloist, Ahrakk'. His body was blasted, charred; he lay lifeless on the deck. The sight of it shocked her; Jane was overwhelmed by her responsibility for his death. Remembering his beautiful performance, she swallowed a sob. The Captain tried to turn away, but Dacris forced her to see more. Two passengers lay facedown, plainly dead. Then a shock of red hair caught her eye.

"Renata!" Jane choked.

Her navigator lay sprawled, faceup, an expression of horror on her face. Realizing she was dead, too, Jane wept openly, no longer caring who heard her or what they thought. She gazed around for the survivors, but there were no other humans, no other Simiu. Somehow . . . they'd already been . . . removed. Alive? Dead? Would she ever know?

Dacris continued to harangue her in a language she could never understand. "I don't know what you're saying," she said through her tears, thinking it might bring him back to reality.

He immediately struck her across the face with the blaster. Jane's tooth shattered, and her mouth filled with blood. He raised the weapon again and she braced herself, thinking that he would probably pistol-whip her to death in his rage. She hoped, vainly, that would satisfy him, that he would let the others live.

Then, another song rang out through the bridge, and every soldier stopped. In spite of her pain, Jane turned toward the doors. There stood another invader, but this one seemed different. It wasn't just his color—he was red and blue, like some others— but the way he held himself. Stepp knew this had to be Dacris' commander. She knew, too, that he was furious.

The soldiers moved, making a path for him, then squatted on the floor. Dacris, however, did not squat. But he did stand stock-still, his eyes locked on the big red-and-blue. Calmly, the leader walked to where the dead lay. He stared at the bodies, at the carnage on the bridge, then at Stepp's ravaged face. Finally, he turned to Dacris.

He held out his hand and sang a few notes. For a moment, Dacris hesitated, but finally he placed the bloodied blaster in his leader's hand. Then Dacris left the bridge.

The leader turned to Stepp and she tried to stand up straight. As he sang, the translator on his wrist spoke for him. "I am Atle, the First-in-Conquest. I regret that you were injured. Your wounds will be attended to by a physician of your own species. I mourn with you for this terrible loss of life. We consider killing the most heinous waste, especially in warfare. Apparently, we may have to reconsider this attitude."

He paused, as though that last thought was the most repulsive he could imagine. "When you are feeling better, we will meet. There is much about your ship we need to know before we can take it back to our Home."

"And you think I'm going to tell you?" Stepp asked wearily, surprised that there was any defiance left in her.

"You will tell me," he said simply. "You can be persuaded."

Jane Stepp looked over the bodies of her friends and passengers, and thought bitterly that he was undoubtedly right.


"Tesa, don't do this," Jib begged.

The two humans stood on a dry, russet-colored plain north of the River of Fear as the evening breeze blew warm and humid around them. The rains had stopped, and the Wind people foraged, taking advantage of the swarming insects. The sight of more than a thousand Grus flocking together, eating and dancing, would've normally filled Tesa's heart with joy. She would've walked among them, caught insects for their young, maybe even danced.

But now she wondered if she'd ever dance on Trinity again. Around her Taller, Lightning, Flies-Too-Fast, and the rest of her cohort clustered like a squadron. Without a sled, she was landbound until this was over—if it was ever over.

Clutching her lance until her knuckles were pale, the Interrelator tried to subdue her anger. " 'Don't do this.' 'Wait.' That's all you can say, Jib? *Don't* save my *people*? *Wait* for their deaths? I can't do that! That's not why I was sent here."

"You weren't sent here to become a warrior chief, either," he reminded her. "You were sent here—"

"To speak for the Grus. Well, there they are!" Her sweeping gesture encompassed all the avian leaders she'd just met with minutes ago. "The White Winds. The Gray Winds. The Plains Winds. The Snow Winds. . . . They've told me what they want. They want the invaders off their World! *They* don't want to *wait*!"

Taller had told the other leaders of the danger to the World, how his people had been forced from their territory, then Tesa had outlined her plan. It would be dangerous, and perhaps cost lives, but the only other option was to flee. The Grus were unwilling to sit idly by while their enemy forced them off their own World.

"You were sent here to speak for them, sure," Jib agreed, "but you were also sent to *safeguard* their culture! What you're planning will change them forever, will teach them things they would never have needed to know. It could affect all their traditional interactions. And it will be *your* doing! Don't do it, I beg you. Take them out of here. Go west, away from the invaders' settlement until the CLS—"

"The Grus don't *want* to wait for the CLS!" Tesa insisted, but doubt crawled across her mind. She had suggested taking the flock away, even though she feared the CLS would arrive so late, the invaders would be too entrenched to uproot. Had Taller read her doubts in her body language? He'd argued against relying on any outside force. She'd thought it was his own need to free Weaver immediately . . . but now she wasn't sure.

She changed the topic. "And the *Singers* can't wait for the CLS. I'm not just here to speak for the Grus, but for *all* intelligent beings on Trinity. I'm *obliged* to help the Singers."

The Maori seemed resentful, as if he suspected she had used that argument to convince him. Every day he grew more withdrawn, and they grew further and further apart. Now, when Tesa needed him, needed the only human friend she had for comfort, for advice, all they did was disagree. She tried to blame it on the TSS, but she didn't know anymore. The Indian woman feared he would end up being a hazard to her, to her plans—plans she was afraid to discuss with him. She felt a stab of guilt, then ignored it. She had no time for guilt, no time for hesitation.

"This is a mistake," he predicted.

A wing curled protectively around her, and she realized her cohort had clustered around her tightly. Taller held her as though to ward off Jib's signs. Tesa dropped her lance to return his embrace. The young man turned away, then finally walked off, settling himself on the ground to stare off toward the River.

"I don't understand him," Snowberry signed peevishly. "If he'd lost *his* parents, *his* home . . ."

"Isn't he our friend anymore?" None-So-Pretty asked.

"Of course, he's our friend," Tesa assured the young female. But Lightning, Thunder, and Flies-Too-Fast seemed uncomfortable, as if they felt sorry that Tesa didn't realize the truth about Jib. "He argues with me . . . because he's afraid for your safety."

The youngsters gazed back and forth between the two humans, then finally foraged discreetly, allowing Tesa to be "alone" with Taller. "He really does care," she insisted to her partner.

"We don't need him to care about us," Taller signed gently. "We can care about ourselves. *You* need his caring more. And he can't give it to you. Do you understand why?"

In Jib's mind, her plans with the Grus leaders weren't the kind Interrelators were supposed to make. Interrelators were supposed to help different people interact *peacefully*. But Bruce was gone. So was Meg, Szu-yi, K'heera, her grandparents. She might never know what had happened to the *Brolga*. And Weaver. And without Weaver, Taller had no heart. And without Taller, what did Tesa have, but a job. . . just a job. . . .

She moved closer to the huge white avian, feeling his heat, the softness of his feathers. Taller and Weaver were her partners. Their pain was hers. She didn't think Jib could understand that. She didn't know if any human could.

"Good Eyes," Taller explained patiently, "Jib can't help you because the River Spirits have taken his soul. He *hears* them all day, he calls to them in his sleep, he turns in their direction like a plant toward the Sun Family. You tell us that the Spirits are benign . . . but they have taken his soul. He can't share his heart with you because his heart is in the River . . . and always will be. I'm sorry, Good Eyes. I know you love him."

Tesa watched Jib as he faced the River and realized her partner was right.

Why did this have to happen to him? Why did the Singers have to be telepaths? Why did the Anurans have to find *this* World? Why weren't there any other solutions for her and the Grus? Her head pounded as the endless questions chased themselves around her brain.

As two of the three Suns hovered over the horizon, Tesa gently extricated herself from Taller's embrace, then held her hands out in prayer. *Another answer,* she beseeched the Wakan Tanka of the World, *there must be another answer*. But there was nothing else written on the wind for her.

She could not know when, or if, help might come from the Cooperative League of Systems. So, she would start tomorrow.

For millennia, the Grus had never fought anyone but each other, one on one, in small territorial squabbles. Tomorrow, they would learn to work together, they would learn sabotage and deception. The Grus, who enjoyed perfect harmony with their World, would learn to destroy, even kill. Tomorrow, Tesa would start teaching the Wind people of Trinity the guerrilla warfare techniques her own people had used in centuries of combat.

She picked up her lance, holding it out to the Suns. *In a sacred manner, we pray,* she told the Wakan Tanka. *With clean hands, we pray. Show me the way. Please . . . show me the way.*

Beside her, Taller lifted his head and called to the Suns, sending his own prayer aloft with hers. The cohort picked up the cry and sent it on through the flock until a thousand voices joined her silent one, the vibrations of their call raising goose bumps on her skin.

Tesa swallowed as she remembered an old Lakota war song, and as the Grus sent their boisterous prayers to the heavens, she signed to the Suns as her ancestors had done long ago.

"This World is *ours*. They cannot harm us. They cannot harm one who has dreamed a dream like mine."

# CHAPTER 16
## ♦
# Steal the Horses!

K'heera took the cover off the purifier and peered into the machine. Its efficiency had dropped to sixty percent, and she had to find the problem. A few more hours here at the hatchery's water treatment facility and she'd leave with Arvis for his home, where she'd assist in light housekeeping or appliance repair, be fed, and sleep in a pleasant environment. Her days had taken on a reliable sameness that she found comforting. Her hair was growing in, and she'd convinced Arvis, through the crude sign language she'd taught him, not to have it depilated again even though the short, bristly fur itched constantly. The constant pain from her teeth was something she'd learned to live with.

At least her diet had improved. She couldn't have lasted much longer on the highly seasoned animal products they had been feeding her. Arvis provided her vegetable foods once he learned she needed them. K'heera knew her status was somewhere between a pet and a slave, but she didn't care much.

All that mattered now was doing her job well enough to avoid punishment. She'd even found an odd comfort from her deafness—it kept her from being constantly assaulted by the twittering alien voices. Yet, K'heera still heard them in her dreams, where shift after shift of hairless amphibians brutalized her like an insensate slab of laboratory muscle.

Pulling out the filters, she found the malfunctioning one, using a diagnostic tool to analyze the problem. Some tenacious water mold had adapted itself to the filter's organic filaments, slowly breaking it down. The filter would need further repair, so she replaced it with a new one.

Moving around the large, featureless work area, she slid the malfunctioning filter into a more sophisticated analyzer and initiated its repair program. In spite of the press of aliens, she ignored the other workers. They had no way to communicate, and they were all dull-witted, even more so than Arvis. Most of them did repetitive tasks, while K'heera did complicated tasks. She didn't think less of them, she was simply indifferent. She feared, in time, that she would become just like them, terrified of the supervisors and too vapid to have an original thought.

Halfway through her repair, the Simiu youngster felt a tap. She turned to see the female alien who had been her trainer. And beside her stood Bruce.

They stared at each other wordlessly, stunned by each other's altered appearance. K'heera was shocked to see how thin and haggard he'd become. The trainer spoke to him and then, to the Simiu's surprise, Bruce signed to her in Grus.

"They're assigning me to work with you," he told her. "They want you to train me on these filtration systems. They're aware we know each other. They want me to be your translator, since you . . . can't hear their translating voders."

She noticed the nullifiers around Bruce's neck. The aliens had learned their lesson since she'd been deafened.

The trainer spoke to Bruce again.

"She's reminding us," he signed, "that we can also act as each other's persuaders, if our work is not acceptable."

The trainer showed them the rod, and K'heera squatted and signed rapidly, "I understand, I understand," a simple gesture the aliens now recognized. It was a fitting way for an honorless person to end up, she thought, groveling before some nameless creature, wanting only to be fed, given employment, and kept free of pain. Bruce stared at her, his complexion sallow.

The trainer left them and K'heera turned back to her filters, to begin Bruce's training.

"K'heera," he signed, his hands trembling slightly, "it's so good to see you! I've been so worried about you."

The Simiu stared at him in open amazement. He was *happy* to see her? She'd thought he would hold her in total contempt for her submission. After all, wasn't it her capture that had alerted the aliens that there were other sentient beings on Trinity they could enslave?

"I'm so sorry about your hearing," he apologized. "Don't worry. When we get out of this, Terran doctors can fix that."

K'heera blinked slowly. *When we get out of this?* That kind of talk could get *her* punished. Didn't he understand that?

"Let me show you this diagnostic machine," she signed.

Bruce's brow furrowed, but he watched attentively as she went through the tutorial. "K'heera, are they drugging you?"

Why did he insist on talking about things that weren't part of their training?

"They tried to drug me," he told her, "but I was allergic, so they used fear conditioning instead . . . pretty effective, but it doesn't dull my mind. Are they drugging you?"

"No," she signed finally. "I . . . had a long conditioning. They felt drugs were not necessary." Even talking about that time made her tremble.

"You poor kid," Bruce signed, his face grim. "Don't worry, those bastards'll get theirs."

She glanced around for the trainers. Seeing one eyeing them, she had Bruce go over the tutorial. As he did she tried to make it appear that her signs were correcting him. "You mustn't say things like that, Bruce. We could both be punished."

"You're right," he admitted, "we'll have to be careful. But we're not alone, darlin'. And every passing day brings hope."

Her throat tightened. Hope? Was he joking? "You mock me, human."

"There *is* hope, K'heera! Tesa and Jib are still free. They're with Taller!"

The Simiu trembled. "Don't you understand what'll happen if there's resistance? Don't you know who'll be hurt?"

Bruce nodded. "Whoever they think will be the most effective persuader. I'm ready to take my lumps."

"You don't know what you're saying!"

"Yes, I do. I watched them brutalize Szu-yi"—his hands shook—"when I couldn't tell them where Jib and Tesa were. But we'll be careful, so they won't discover anything *we* do. And if they do catch us . . . we'll just have to take what they dish out, till we bring this system down."

K'heera had to fight the urge to call the trainer and confess Bruce's intent. "You can't do this. . . ."

"We *have* to! We have to resist, little by little, like water striking a stone. We can't lose hope. We'll make it, day by day. We'll have to be clever, but we're *good* at that, being clever." His eyes shone. "You were right about the alien probe, kid. I followed your lead, removed its power cell, and used it to transmit a warning to the *Brolga*."

A flash of nearly forgotten pride surged through K'heera. He'd followed *her* lead? He'd sent a warning . . . ? Reality crashed in again. New Terrans had been appearing on the work crews for days. She'd even seen one of the formerly haughty drum dancers among them. The *Brolga* had clearly been captured.

Bruce understood her expression. "Yeah . . . they got the ship . . . but it still had time to boost our warning and send it out to the CLS! Don't you see, K'heera? You and I being teamed together is incredibly fortunate. Separately, we might've done a little damage, but together . . . ?" A wry smile creased his face, "Honey, we're going to give these guys a hurtin'."

K'heera shut her eyes, blocking out Bruce's traitorous signs. But her conscience insisted, *Pay attention to this human. This is how a being with honor talks.*

She blinked the voice away. Time was growing short; Arvis would be here soon, and she'd taught Bruce almost nothing. Pulling his attention back to the task at hand, she explained the filter system, including the recent problems she'd been having.

"Molds?" Bruce signed, fingering the damaged filter.

"The molds in this river are especially tenacious. Once the biochemists learn enough about their life cycle, they'll be able to introduce growth inhibitors onto the filters to eliminate the problem. But as for now, only vigilance and repairs . . ."

"These organic water filters . . . they'd be ruined if these molds were just allowed to . . . grow?"

"At this time, yes. But it is a temporary problem they will shortly resolve. In the meantime . . ."

"Must be fail-safes in this system . . ." he signed, glancing over the myriad banks of equipment. "Warnings . . . alarms . . ."

"An alarm indicates *someone* has not done their job monitoring the filters," K'heera signed tersely. "An alarm is an announcement that someone will be severely *punished*." It had never happened to her, but she'd witnessed it once. That had provided sufficient motivation for her to have a perfect record.

Bruce nodded absently, not really paying attention to her warning. "But this hatchery . . . feeds them their own native food. . . . And it depends on this treated water. . . ." He smiled, an expression that struck terror in K'heera's soul.

He turned to her. "They let me keep my equipment. I told them I needed it to keep everybody's sound nullifiers charged and working. They glanced through the stuff, and took some out . . . but they missed chips I took out of the probe and hid. Think we could adapt them to bypassing that alarm system?"

K'heera blinked. How could he just assume she would do such a dangerous thing? And the results . . . the hatchery would be *ruined*. Eggs would die. Her perfect work record . . .

*You're thinking just like an honorless slave,* she realized, horrified at how indoctrinated she'd become.

"I just wish we could find some way to get *their* workers to help us," Bruce signed.

"They'd never do that," K'heera told him. "They're terrified of the trainers, and they're mentally stunted."

"That doesn't mean they can't be organized into a work slowdown or passive resistance. Made any friends among them?"

She scowled. Simiu were not good at that.

"The trainer told me . . . you go to the home of the Anuran leader at night. She said . . . it was a very . . . *prestigious* thing."

K'heera watched him choose his signs carefully, so as not to insult her. She knew very well the trainer held her in contempt for her relationship with Arvis. He was, as far as any of the Chosen were concerned, just another Industrious who had not tasted the rod nearly enough. Bruce's attempt to discuss this without increasing her humiliation, in fact, his entire conversation with her, had been the first time any sentient being had shown her *respect* since she'd been taken captive. The dignity he granted her nearly overwhelmed her with gratitude, and she found herself forgetting some of her fears.

Bruce glanced around and signed, "Is there any way you could use your influence with the leader's son?"

*To do what?* she wondered, but didn't dare ask, for fear the respect he'd shown for her would vanish. Also . . . she didn't want to admit that it felt wrong to take advantage of Arvis . . . and that she was afraid of losing her position in his home. Yet, every night, she stayed with the son of the First and had never even *considered* using that to her advantage.

"Think about it when you're over there," Bruce suggested. "Is this him now?"

Arvis padded over to them, signed a greeting to K'heera, then asked if she was hungry. She indicated she was, and with a final glance at Bruce, she left him to follow Arvis home. As she strode along beside the red and blue alien, he laboriously signed to her in their primitive communication. K'heera's thoughts raced. What could she really accomplish in his home? She rarely saw his father. And then there was Lene, the one who had helped in her own capture. She burned with shame thinking of that. It was ridiculous to think she could effect any change on Trinity.

Suddenly a shadow sailed over the ground. The Simiu stared as an Aquila wheeled gracefully in the air. The avian's carefree freedom made K'heera's breath catch in her throat, overwhelming her with the sudden desire, the need to fly. If only she had wings she could escape these monsters—but Weaver had wings and she was just as much a prisoner as K'heera.

The avian dipped her wings. With a shiver, K'heera realized it was Thunder. The Simiu found herself hoping vainly that the avian might light on a nearby tree . . . somewhere where K'heera could see her, maybe even surreptitiously sign to her. . . .

That thought shocked her. She would be caught signing to the avian and punished severely, brutally. These aliens might even kill Thunder if they caught her.

But that thought wouldn't go away. Perhaps she could communicate with Thunder. Perhaps she could get word to Tesa. Even though she was terrified, K'heera's inner voice murmured, *That is what a being with honor would do.*

"First," Tesa signed, "we steal their horses." She paused, realizing she'd used an ASL sign that only Jib understood, and he was sitting on the other side of the clearing, his back to her. The cohort of fifty young Grus merely blinked, confused.

The Indian woman waved her hands, indicated she'd made an error. "I meant *sleds*. First, we steal their flying sleds. Do you all remember what you have to do?"

There were affirmative signs throughout the cohort. She tried to feel confident, but Father Sun would rise soon. The time was upon them. Peering up into the tall, bronze-colored tree where

Thunder perched, Tesa watched the dark shadow of the Aquila cock her head. With a quick move of her long fingers, the avian updated Tesa on the small group of Anurans.

When Thunder had first spotted them, Tesa was afraid that they might be hunting for her and Jib. But they were so far from the River of Fear that herd animals lived here in comfort, though the Gray Winds only visited. The Aquila female learned that these Anurans were studying a herd of grazers. There were ten of them . . . and they had seven flying sleds.

The electronic readings of Terran sleds would be easy to trace. She needed *their* sleds, whose readings matched their own. But stealing horses would be a hell of a lot easier.

The Moon Family had already set, leaving the tiny Child Star as their sole illumination.

"You're really going through with this?" Jib asked finally, approaching.

She frowned. It was the first thing he'd said to her in twenty-eight hours. "With flyers, we can liberate the *Singers*."

He turned away again.

She turned her attention back to her task, and started out for the Anuran camp. She could find it easily, even in the dark. With lights posted all over it, the small outpost sat like a beacon in the surrounding darkness.

Tesa ran through the night, a figure in black and white in her hooded Grus shirt and black leggings. She'd coated her face with black charcoal in an hourglass design that ran from the temples, narrowing around the nose and mouth and broadening back out around the chin. Her cheeks and throat were plastered with a stark white clay. Above her blackened eyes, she'd painted a semicircle of bright red clay that ran from her forehead into her hairline. The colors were traditional war paint—the design emulated the facial markings of the Grus.

When she arrived at the camp she waved at Thunder from behind tall grass, then watched the Aquila relay her signal. Within moments, the young Grus lifted into the sky, flying toward her. *Remember,* she thought at them fiercely, *no calling!*

The flock circled the camp, alighting around it, and among the herd of grazers. Larger than American bison, with longer legs, they were mottled roans. The males had racks of blue, fan-shaped antlers on their heads. The herd lay in the dry grass, many chewing cud, but most still slept. Flies-Too-Fast led his group among them, but the grazers ignored them. The White Wind people were a normal part of their World.

Tesa's regular cohort, including Lightning, surrounded her. With Tesa hiding in their midst, the cohort casually ambled over to where the seven sleds were parked. The Grus probed the ground, acting as though they were simply settling here to forage.

The floodlights the Anurans had perched on their small, portable dwellings gave Tesa all the illumination she needed to study the flyers. They were different in design, but there were recognizable similarities. She wondered about security systems. On Earth, security codes were installed in flyers sold in urban areas, but sleds used on exploratory missions to other worlds rarely had them.

Lightning kept one eye on her, and the other on the Anurans' dwellings. It was his job to inform Tesa if the sleds made noise when she powered them up.

There were a minimum number of switches on the machine, but the control pad was set up oddly. She reached into her pouch and pulled out the crude box Bruce had built. It was one of the last things he'd accomplished before they'd had to leave him. Part Terran circuitry, part Anuran space probe, Bruce hoped she might be able to use this makeshift diagnostic tool to "translate" their electronic equipment. This would be its first field test.

Tesa placed it on top of the control panel and turned it on. English lit up half the screen, and incomprehensible symbols the other. She punched in a series of simple commands Bruce had set up. After a few seconds, the screen showed her a diagram of the sled's schematics. Unfortunately, only parts of the diagram were in English. She scanned the image, getting enough information to proceed. Picking a switch at random, she pressed it, while watching the interactive diagram.

Immediately headlamps flared on, lighting up her dark corner. Slapping her hand down, she shut it back off, then glanced at Lightning. He was on tiptoe, wide-eyed, wings spread in surprise, and she had to bite her lip to keep from laughing.

She glanced at the diagram and tried another switch. Telltales lit up the control panel, and she could feel vibrations in the platform. Lightning assured her of its silence. The diagram flashed, pointing to another switch, so she pressed that, and the machine lifted off the ground and hovered.

Grinning, she sat on the sled and held on to what the diagram indicated was the control bar. She pushed it forward slowly, and the machine lurched. Pulling it back made it reverse. Okay . . . now where was up and down? The diagram was no help at all.

She found a likely control on the handle, but before she could test it, all the Grus snapped to attention, their heads lifting on their impossibly long necks. She turned, alarmed.

An Anuran emerged from a dwelling and wandered around. *Who the hell is that?* she thought, peering through a forest of stalklike legs. *The damn cook?* Lightning stood in front of her, spreading his massive wings in a Grus warning pose. Other cohort members did the same, effectively blocking Tesa from view.

Tesa didn't have time to finish testing the controls. She'd have to turn them on, send them west, and catch up with them later. *Hope they don't run into anything,* she thought, moving from machine to machine, activating them.

The Anuran wandering around camp *was* the cook, she realized with surprise. He peered into containers, then began assembling meals, while Tesa crept from sled to sled behind Grus wings.

Finally, the human cupped her hands around her mouth, letting out a lung-busting Grus alarm call. "B-B-B-B-R-R-R-R-A-A-A-A-A-A," she yelled, over and over, and the others joined her.

The Anuran cook jumped in surprise, dropping one of the containers. Food and liquid burst out. The grazers, surrounded by raucously calling Grus, leaped to their feet, nervously searching for the predators they were sure the Grus were warning off. Flies-Too-Fast bounded through the herd, flapping his wings and calling, the other Grus imitating him, warning the herd of imminent danger. The lead male grazer circled, seeing nothing—but the Grus' calls were too frantic to be ignored. His broad flat muzzle lifted, tasted the air.

Flies-Too-Fast's panicked cries were finally too much for the herd, and they took off running. The Grus chivvied them onto the path they'd selected.

Tesa crossed her fingers, hoping she hadn't adjusted the flyers' speed too high. She sent the sleds into the sky one by one, then watched the Anuran cook react as his sleds flew away of their own volition. His huge eyes widened, and his already brilliant green and gold coloring flared until he was almost luminous. Then he spun to see the herd bearing down on him.

The sleeping Anurans must've felt the drumming hoofbeats through the ground. They came barreling out of their tentlike dwellings just as the fear-crazed grazers pounded through the camp as though it weren't there. While aliens leaped and ran for safety, their supplies and buildings were pounded into the turf.

Tesa called again, leaping onto the last sled. She soared into the air, Lightning and her cohort surrounding her, as they chased after the fleeing sleds. Below her, the Anurans stared, pointing. Shaking her lance at them, she whooped triumphantly.

*Yeah,* she thought gleefully. *First, we steal the horses.*

"Well, of *course* they're resisting!" Atle told his Third-in-Conquest, Amaset. "It's a natural part of the process. We must anticipate it, and stamp it out swiftly." He watched the Council members who'd gathered in his home to discuss their concerns. "Our ancestors met with such resistance and *persevered.*"

"But, Glorious First," the Third protested, "this *one* human destroyed an entire scientific study camp."

The First turned cold eyes on Amaset. "Those biologists should've never been sent out without soldiers."

"It won't happen again," the Third agreed.

"It wouldn't have happened in the first place if *I'd* been in charge," Dacris sang out.

"That's enough," Atle snapped. He turned back to the Third. "Henceforth, all exploratory excursions will be accompanied by a squadron. I very much want this human, and her companion, captured *unharmed*"—he turned flashing eyes on Dacris— "something I could not expect from you." He faced the nervous Councillors. "Think what a persuader *she* will make! Whoever captures her will have their own territory, regardless of their class or standing. Make sure the soldiers know this." He signaled to the Councillors that the meeting was over. "Dacris. Stay behind."

As the others left, Dacris stood stiffly.

"I know you feel you're being unjustly punished," Atle sang. "While your feelings in this matter don't concern me, your contempt for my orders does. Still, I have not demoted you. Removing you from command of the space station and not allowing you to take the captured ship Home should have been punishment enough. But you still defy me. This is my last warning. You are now in charge of the hatchery. . . ."

Dacris' color flushed brightly. The assignment would humiliate the Second, which was exactly what Atle wanted.

"You'll no longer be involved in these Council meetings," Atle continued, dulling his own color. "It's been too long since you've given me any practical advice, and your criticisms erode confidence in me. That's something I can't allow." He stared hard at Dacris. "You may throw down a challenge. I'll be happy to wrestle you. You're much younger than I. You might win."

The green and gold Troubadour glared defiantly, but sang, "I decline. I'll serve my First in whatever capacity you desire."

"Well sung," sang the First. "That will be all."

As Dacris left the First's home, Atle sagged. The humans' resistance he could understand, but Dacris' . . .

Arvis and Lene entered with the Simiu servant. Atle watched the female Chosen with mixed feelings. He was still angry about her using hormones to seduce his son, but her scheming had been successful. Arvis had been granted citizenship. Now gravid with his grandchild, she was beautiful, Atle thought. So did Arvis.

The promise of a grandchild made the stresses of the new colony easier for the First to bear. He anticipated seeing his grandchild hatch, swimming free on their new planet. And Lene, to mollify him, had promised to name the child after his deceased son or daughter. She was clever. It mollified him well.

Suddenly Atle spied Dacris watching Lene and Arvis through an open window. They did not see him, but Atle saw him watching them, saw the naked hatred in his eyes. Then Dacris boldly met the First's gaze. The Troubadour's color gleamed and he blinked his lower lids slowly, contemptuously, finally turning away as if nothing in Atle's home was of any concern to him.


# CHAPTER 17

◆

# Javier


Javier First-Light-of-Day stood hip deep in the river harvesting red, gold, and teal-colored leaves from the swaying reeds. He was methodical, stripping the oldest, driest leaves, collecting them in a fist-sized bunch, then using the longest of them to tie the others into a neat bundle. Then he stacked the bundle end up in the long, colorful basket hanging on his back. The job reminded him of collecting wild rice in Michigan. He only wished he could enjoy this as much. However, a squat, brown alien with a punishing rod stood on a hovering sled not twenty yards from him and the other humans working nearby.

He'd ended up in a work crew with Carlotta Estafan, Chris Bartus, Moshe Rosten, Noriko Imanaka, and, to his great relief, Martin Brockman, who he'd thought had been killed. They'd been joined by an elderly Lakota, the Interrelator's grandfather, Old Bear. The old man was in good shape, straight and strong, but the Chosen kept him heavily drugged. The rest of his companions ranged in their alertness, but none of them were drug-free.

The leaves were for Weaver and the women working with her, for the baskets and mats they produced, using traditional Grus weaving techniques. Baskets were needed as storage containers and the mats were bedding for humans. These aliens made sure that their captives were self-sufficient.

Javier's long fingers snatched bright red and orange leaves off a vine trailing up one of the reeds. He stripped it so quickly the Anuran guard never noticed. Another swift hand move crushed the leaves and brought them to his nose. He inhaled sharply, lingering a scant second over the scent before gathering more reed leaves. His brow furrowed over his hooded, black eyes as he tried to recognize the compounds that produced that smell.

Many plants, even alien ones, had similar properties that could be identified by aromatic essential oils. Javier needed something irritating enough to make him vomit. The headaches he suffered testified to the drugs in his food. Whatever they were giving him caused him to hesitate over important decisions. He didn't dare attempt an escape while under its influence.

And Javier had every intention of escaping. He hadn't given up a satisfying career on Earth to be made a slave on what was, no doubt, the most beautiful world he'd ever seen.

Running a hand through his thick black hair, he glanced at the platform where Weaver and her companions worked. The pain of seeing her there was still raw to him.

He'd waited so long to meet the legendary avian, to discuss her artistry. . . . To find her forced to produce bare essentials so he and his fellow humans could be more conveniently enslaved broke his heart. He could barely believe what was happening to her, to her people. He *had* to do *something*.

His basket was full, so he waded to the platform to empty it. It was the only part of his day he enjoyed. While he deposited his leaves, he and Weaver could exchange a few signs. Yesterday he'd told her he could graft feathers onto the stumps of her cut ones. The technique was called "imping," and he'd learned it while working with a Hopi raptor expert years ago. Rehabilitators did it so that otherwise healthy birds could fly for exercise. Weaver might not achieve much altitude that way, but it could help her to escape. That discussion had cheered her, and her crown had brightened.

But first, they had to get feathers. Javier had talked to as many of the humans as he could, but no one could help. The Grus, for some reason, had never lived on this river, so there were no discarded feathers to be scavenged, not even old, worn ones. Meg, working on the platform with Weaver, let him know that one of the Simiu would send information out that night, and tell the Interrelator of their need. But when, or if, feathers would come, no one knew. Messages had been going out for days, but so far, nothing had come back in.

Javier put his basket on the platform and greeted Weaver and her human friends politely. Meg sat beside the avian, with Mrs. Lewis on the other side, assisting with the weaving. Dr. Li sat behind Mrs. Lewis, and sorted leaves. The women's faces were slack, whether from drugs or broken spirits, he didn't know.

Turning his attention to Weaver, he unloaded his bundles.

"The weather is good today, First-Light," she signed. She loved his name because it meant something. She'd told him it made her think of the dawn, that she thought of that whenever she saw him and felt hopeful.

"It's a good day for catching fingerlings," he agreed, as five fat silver-blue fish slid out of his basket. She eyed them speculatively. "It's hard to catch such quick fish without a net or a bill. You wouldn't let my efforts go to waste?"

Her crown flushed from its typical dull plum color, and she downed the fish one after the other as he sorted the bundles from his basket. The women seemed pleased. Weaver was not eating nearly enough to stay in condition and they all worried about it.

"You know, First-Light," Weaver signed while the last fish traveled down her long neck, "it is not seemly for an unmated male to present a mated female like myself with courting gifts. What would my friend Taller think if he knew?"

Javier smiled at her teasing. "It'll be our secret." He hoisted the empty basket and started to wade toward the reeds. Just then a shadow swooped over the water, and he lifted his head. It was an immature Aquila, circling low over the colony. Suddenly another Aquila dropped down from the upper atmosphere and joined the first, then another appeared, and another. Soon there were dozens of the creatures circling.

Everyone in the colony—the Industrious, the humans, the Simiu, even the Chosen—stopped to watch the gathering of beautiful raptors, like so many mystical Thunderbirds.

But Javier watched Weaver, who only stared calmly at the sky, as though her old enemy held no fear for her now that she knew the Chosen.

Something fell from the Aquila-filled sky. Like a bizarre parody of autumn, multicolored leaves drifted to the World from opened nets held in the Aquilas' talons. As the leaves settled on land and water, Javier realized there were *messages* scrawled on them. He collected the nearest ones.

"Don't give up!" one read.

"The CLS knows!" read another.

"Watch the skies!" said yet another.

"Work slower!"

"Watch for Iktomi!"

"Don't let the bastards get you down!"

Javier laughed as the Interrelator *leafleted* the colony.

Everywhere, humans picked up leaves and smiled. He saw a man on the shore explain the messages to Kh'arhh'tk, and the drum dancer stared into the heavens.

Then Javier examined an odd-shaped leaf that said "We can do it!" It was triangularly shaped and a rich golden orange. Impulsively, he crushed it and smelled a familiar, sharp odor. His dark eyes shone. The smell was similar to *Oleum ricini*—the castor oil plant. He tasted the leaf's blood on his palm. Yes. The juice of these leaves should be a strong emetic. On Earth, castor leaves had once been used for narcotic poisoning. He found others and tossed them into his basket.

The Chosen irritably ordered humans and Industrious alike to gather the leaves, but the humans responded with so much fervor, they quickly decided that wasn't the best tactic.

Suddenly the cloud of raptors parted, and a mass of startlingly white Grus mixed thickly with them. Javier's hearing ear was off, but he could feel the vibrations from their calls travel over his skin. Around him, humans adjusted nullifiers. Then he spotted her.

Ptesa' Wakandagi, the Interrelator of Trinity, appeared in the eye of the storm riding one of the Chosen's own sleds, garishly dressed and in full war paint. Wildly, she brandished . . . he stared—a Clovis-tipped war lance? Hell, if it wasn't! She called with the Grus as they spiraled lower.

Weaver leaped to her feet, crying out to the skies.

*She must see her mate, Taller*, Javier realized.

Their guard moved toward the female Grus threateningly. Without thinking, Javier darted between them, ready to take the rod for her. Old Bear was right beside him; Martin moved quickly to his other side. Soon Carlotta, Chris, and Noriko joined them. The guard hesitated, glancing at the knot of defiant humans. Impulsively, Javier threw his head back and imitated Weaver. Old Bear followed his lead, as did Martin and the others.

Humans nearby copied them, and soon every captive in the colony was yelling like a Grus, even the Simiu, who howled to the sky. All of them sent their voices soaring up to a woman who could not hear. The guards appeared confused as they moved among the humans, plainly wanting to discipline them, but not knowing where to start. Finally, they gave up.

Javier watched Weaver standing tall, head thrown back, crown blazing a fiery red, her clipped wings drooping in the classic pose of her people. The Grus calls ripped through his body and he relished the feeling of their terrible cacophony.

Just then, a squad of Chosen soldiers flashed through the air, pursuing the Interrelator. Shaking her spear, she took off, her avian escort forming a wall between her and the Chosen soldiers. Javier's heart tightened in fear, even though he was thrilled by her reckless courage. Soon they were gone.

He glanced at Old Bear.

"That's *my* granddaughter!" the old man signed, his eyes shining with fierce pride. "Some woman, huh?"

Javier smiled and nodded as they moved back to the reeds. *No exaggeration there*, he thought. *Some woman.*

He glanced at his companions, knowing that only Carlotta could understand the old man's signing. He pointed after Tesa and made the universal sign for "okay." They all smiled, as Martin gave him a clenched fist, and Chris a thumbs-up.

Weaver had settled back onto her hocks and resumed her work, but when she caught his eyes, she lifted her head, turning it to flash her bright red crown at him.

*Yes, beautiful one*, Javier thought at her, *I saw your lover calling to you. I saw him.* As he stripped the leaves from the reeds, he noted the bright expressions on Meg's and Mrs. Lewis' faces. They moved deftly, their features animated, their bodies alert. He would've felt hopeful then, but for the doctor. Szu-yi rocked on her knees like a sick child, hugging herself and sobbing. Setting his jaw, Javier planned his next move.

*Damn, these things are slow!* Tesa thought, trying to force the alien sled to go faster. The Grus and Aquila blanketed her, but speed was critical as she aimed for a narrow bottleneck where the

River curved between two overgrown forested banks. The trees there formed a natural canopy over the water. If she could just get through that narrow junction . . .

*Fetterman's Fight,* she thought. It had worked hundreds of years ago for Chief Red Cloud and his war party. It *had* to work now for her—and for the people of Trinity. She signaled to the avians and they peeled away from her in pairs, diving to hide in the dense forest that surrounded the River.

The bottleneck was dead ahead.

*Hurry up!* she urged the pokey sled, wanting to kick her heels in its sides. The squad of aliens gained on her. She shook her lance at them brazenly, whooping, then slid under the canopy, through the narrow pass.

The aliens followed in a wedge. As soon as they emerged on the other side, the sky above them darkened. Hundreds of waiting Aquila, including the ones who'd leafleted the colony, launched themselves from the trees, taking the soldiers by surprise.

If the sleds had protective shields on them as human sleds did, none of the soldiers had a chance to engage them—or to use their weapons. The Anurans quickly spun around, trying to retreat, but the Aquila snatched them off their machines, dropping them into the River.

Tesa knew few of the invaders would survive. She'd worked on the attack for days, negotiating with the Hunters, begging them for the kind of cooperation they'd only given once before. Now, as the Aquila yanked the aliens off their sleds, dropping them to their deaths, she felt sickened.

Then the Grus surrounded her, calling victoriously. The human remembered the glimpse she'd had of Weaver, and she remembered why she was doing this.

It was all over in minutes, just as it had been for the arrogant Corporal Fetterman. In 1866, he'd boasted that with eighty trained soldiers he could wipe out the Sioux nation, but that wasn't the way things had turned out. Tesa took a deep breath as she wheeled her sled around, assessing the damage.

Many of the bodies had never made it to the River; a few slammed into the trees, and some on the narrow banks. Most of the sleds had crashed in the River, some had hit the trees, and a few were still circling aimlessly over the scene. As Tesa flew over the carnage, she spotted one corpse with an Aquila still perched on it. The avian mantled the body with her wings, the way her people did to hide food from one another.

Tesa waved at her frantically, signing "No! No!" before she remembered that Hunters didn't sign.

Thunder was suddenly beside her.

"I warned them not to eat the aliens!" Tesa signed to her friend. "Remind that one."

The Aquila dropped like a rocket, backwinging to the side of the older avian. Tesa braked her sled and leaped off as Thunder settled as close to the mature female as she dared.

"She's not eating," Thunder signed. "Something's wrong."

The older female's red eyes were glazed. Tesa could see now that she wasn't mantling the corpse; her wings were drooping because she no longer had the strength to hold them up.

Thunder said something to the afflicted Aquila. The sickened avian responded weakly—then slowly pitched forward. Tesa ran over and touched her neck, searching for a pulse.

"Oh, no," she signed, "she's *dead*! What happened to her?"

Thunder ruffled her feathers worriedly. "All she said was 'bad fish,' that the monster was 'bad fish.' "

Cautiously, Tesa examined the dead Hunter. The alien corpse was one of the red and blue types. One taloned foot had hooked into the alien's spine; the other clutched its shoulder. The Aquila's middle talon had punctured a yellow shoulder patch. The patch oozed fluid, and the avian's scaled foot was slick with it.

By now, dozens of Hunters crowded around them. Taller and the cohort settled near, brazenly walking among their old enemies, staring at the fallen raptor. The rest of the Grus cautiously kept their distance on the Riverbank.

"The Hunters are asking what happened to SouthWind," Thunder told Tesa. "Some of them are her daughters."

"I'm trying to figure that out. Tell them . . . I'm so terribly sorry. . . ." Jib's warnings came back to her all too vividly.

"Why are you apologizing?" Thunder asked. "SouthWind fought for the World and her story will be told to every hatchling."

"She will be remembered by the Wind people as well," Taller signed to Thunder. "Ask her daughters if we may take a feather. We will use it to mourn her for as long as it survives."

Tesa was startled by Taller's gesture, realizing he was speaking for all the Grus leaders.

"Our feathers don't decay for many years," Thunder told him. "It's a long time to mourn for someone not of your own."

"We'll mourn SouthWind even if we must pass her feather on to our children," Taller assured her.

There was a ripple of activity among the Hunters as they conferred together. Finally, Thunder signed for them.

"Her daughters are moved by your offer. They would like you to take her feathers, but not for mourning. I have told them of Weaver's need for strong flying feathers. They want you to take SouthWind's primaries, so Weaver can fly to freedom on their mother's wings. That would be a fitting memorial for a Hunter!"

Tesa's eyes caught Taller's. They'd collected shed feathers from the Grus flock, but many were so frayed and worn they feared they wouldn't be strong enough for Weaver.

The Grus leader's feathers stood straight out, his crown shrinking with emotion. Finally, he bowed his head in gratitude, then he and every Grus present pointed their bills to the sky and called, lifting the spirit of SouthWind, urging her good speed on her journey to the Suns. Her voice catching, Tesa joined them.

Finally, the Interrelator turned back to her avian translator. "Thunder, I've got to know what killed SouthWind. These yellow patches . . . SouthWind's talon pierced it. . . ."

Thunder blinked at Tesa. "K'heera was taken by aliens who were this color. She touched one of them before collapsing."

Tesa dug her Swiss Army knife out of her pocket, and snapped open its small cell analyzer. Whatever she could learn here could only help them in future conflicts.

Jib parked his alien sled in a hidden place and approached the bank of the River. He tried not to imagine what would happen if Tesa were killed or captured in her planned raid on the Anuran village. He had every reason to be afraid for her, but even so, he'd be able to control his anxiety better if he'd been getting any decent sleep lately. But that'd been impossible.

He'd been shut off from the mournful music of the Singers right after he and Tesa had left Bruce. One moment a sad but pleasurable background song had hummed in his mind, and then the next it had stopped completely. Taniwha must've been maintaining that tenuous contact, and when the herd realized it, they'd cut him off cold. For Jib, it'd been like losing his sense of balance . . . or even his sense of self. His resulting depression made dealing with Tesa even more difficult, and made their recent disagreements all the more painful.

Then, a few days after that, the new music started. It kept him awake, drifting through his mind just as he skirted sleep, yanking him awake to the unnatural silence of sound nullifiers.

Old lullabies his mom had sung to him, popular tunes he'd been fond of, rhythmic Maori chants he'd thought he'd forgotten. Every morning he'd wake up groggy, with old, persistent tunes running maddeningly through his head. In the last few days, the music had deteriorated into vague instrumental fragments, then chaotic sounds he couldn't recognize. He feared the telepathy withdrawal was making him lose his mind.

Unless . . . it was Taniwha trying to contact him. Jib didn't discuss it with Tesa; she would insist it was just wishful thinking—and he was terrified she'd be right. But, maybe the Singer calf had been touching the memories of music in his mind, growing more and more familiar with that part of his brain until he could once again insinuate his own music without startling the human. But why? Could he be trying to communicate with Jib without his people knowing? That made some kind of sense.

So now he stood on the Riverbank, searching with his mind. But no matter what his mind craved, he could not initiate contact.

While Tesa had planned her raid on the Anuran colony, Jib had resolved to search the western end of the River until he found the Singers. He'd taken one of the stolen Anuran sleds and followed the waterway until he'd found a patch of the Singers' favorite water plant. Now he left the bank to stand in the water; trying to relax, he opened his mind. It was the only thing he could do.

That . . . and sing. He sang of the Land of the Long White Cloud, and the changing sea around her, of the Lovers Papatuanuku and Ranginui—Mother Earth and Father Sun. He sang of the Waikato River, the longest river in New Zealand, whose full Maori name was *Waikato-taniwha-rau,* "the flowing water of a hundred water monsters." For generations that river had ruled Maori lives, just as this River ruled the lives of the Singers. He sang from his heart, his fingers keeping time on his brown thigh.

Jib grew homesick for his beautiful country, his family and loved ones. That was a feeling he never thought he'd have, but singing of his people and their land made him feel more alone than he ever had in his life. Tesa and he were constantly at odds with each other these days. K'heera and everyone he'd come to care about on Trinity had been enslaved, maybe even killed. There was little the young man could do to make any difference in the terrible situation they were now in. He felt helpless. Hopeless. As desperate as Taniwha had been the night he'd been stranded on the sandbar. Jib clutched his greenstone tiki as his voice rang out in sorrow.

Closing his eyes, he felt despondency washing over him like a tide. He remembered the night Tesa had *heard* music, the night they'd worked together to free the calf and send him back to his parents. A night before the World had changed forever.

Still, the silence in his mind was absolute.

*Give it up, mate,* he thought bleakly. *The Singers will never trust you again. They'll die, and there's not a bloody thing you can do to help them.*

Swallowing a lump in his throat, Jib turned to leave the River. As he placed one foot onto the shore, something massive jostled him, knocking him into the water. His arms flailed as the tepid water covered his head. He inhaled some, just as a powerful body shoved him back up into the air. Sputtering and thrashing, the Maori scrambled. His fingers felt familiar, slick skin, a round back, a wide body.

And then it happened, the jolt of mental contact directly into his brain. He shuddered, opening his mind, his heart pounding frantically.

Taniwha pulled him through the water like a ski board out of control as Jib clung to the powerful flippers, grinning wildly.

Atle's colors flared with outrage. "Twenty-five *dead*? That was the entire complement! Against a *lone* human and a group of primitive hunter-gatherers! It's not possible!"

"The Third, Amaset, was found dead with his company. . . ." the Fourth-in-Conquest, Leuth, sang.

Atle sank down on his haunches. Another defeat like this and he'd be forced to give up command, to hand power over . . . to Dacris. Could the Second be right about these beings? Would he be forced to meet their ruthlessness with senseless bloodletting?

The First blinked slowly, collecting his thoughts. Perhaps the years without conquests had dulled his people. The ease of using their own stunted children might have atrophied the skills they needed to conquer these new people. He had to *do* something— something to convince himself they were still the conquerors of old. Something decisive. Something clever.

"Bring me the original crew stationed on this planet, and the elders who are related to the Interrelator," Atle ordered.

"I never believed Thunder was actually *there* until now," K'heera told Bruce, trying to stop from trembling as she added more new chips into the filtration system's computer. "I just signed to the trees."

"She's there," Bruce assured her.

As K'heera installed chips, he rerouted the alarm system into them, adding new commands and instructions. The hard part was doing it so that it appeared to their "overseers," as Bruce sneeringly called the trainers, to be routine maintenance. This was the last thing they'd be able to tamper with. Most of the water filters were seriously infected with the water mold. The Simiu estimated that in two days the entire system would break down.

"Without you, K'heera, Tesa would've never been able to plan that little surprise this morning. You can't see Thunder, but she can see you in your lighted room. You just keep feeding the information to her like I've told you, but *don't get caught*."

*Don't get caught,* K'heera thought. She'd developed a sudden need to use the bathroom at night, and had clumsily fallen into Arvis' and Lene's pool twice as she walked around the room in darkness. After that, they'd moved her in with Arvis' sister, who slept with a night-light. Once the Industrious female was asleep, nothing woke her, and K'heera could sign silently for hours. It was dangerous, she knew, but honorable. She only wished she could shake the notion that she was betraying Arvis.

"Did you get any more of those nuggets?" Bruce asked.

"Yes," K'heera answered, glancing around. She dug into the pockets of her vest, pulling out the hard, round, colorful balls so Bruce could hide them in his "bank" under the console. The nuggets were pure protein and their smell alone was enough to gag the Simiu.

But the overseers used them as a reward, so Bruce had pretended to like them to get some. He'd urged K'heera to do the same at Arvis' home, and she had, though eating them to prove her interest had made her sick.

Bruce used them to ingratiate himself with their Industrious coworkers, sneaking them nuggets and murmuring softly, even though they couldn't understand him. She didn't believe there was any point to it, but lately, she'd seen the workers stare longingly at Bruce when they weren't being watched.

The Simiu couldn't imagine how that would possibly ever help them, but decided it couldn't hurt to go along with it. She didn't realize it consciously, but little by little, she'd come to regard Bruce as a true uncle, accepting his guidance, trusting his mature judgment. Even when it endangered her. Even when she was afraid. Because she knew what they were doing was right. And honorable.

"Tonight, tell Thunder Tesa's raid was a big success," Bruce signed. "Tell her it really cheered us up. Be sure and tell her about the hatchery, that in two days it'll fail. She might want to plan something important for the same time. . . ."

Suddenly he touched her lightly the way he did when they were being watched. Soldiers had entered the building and were marching straight toward them. K'heera's heart thudded. They knew. They *knew* she'd betrayed them. They were coming to take her, torture her again. She began shaking from head to foot.

"Easy," Bruce signed. "Take it easy, K'heera. Just don't say anything. It'll be okay."

One of the Anurans gestured at Bruce, and K'heera realized he was speaking to the human through a voder. Bruce replied, then the soldiers took him by the arms roughly and led him out of the building, leaving K'heera standing foolishly alone, ashamed of the rank fear she'd felt only for herself.

Bruce glanced back at her, nodding quickly toward the filter system. Now she'd have to take care of it alone. In two days it would fail, and if Bruce had not returned only *she* would be responsible. Blinking her vivid purple eyes, K'heera stopped shaking. It *would* fail. She would see to that.

As she forced her attention back to the machine, she noticed every Industrious in the building watching her. She thought she could see worry in their eyes, and realized they were worried for Bruce, that as his friend, they were transferring their concern for him to her. So when the trainers finally turned away, she handed out protein nuggets, murmured soft sounds, and patted the moist alien skin as comfortingly as she could.

# CHAPTER 18
◆
# Tesa's Raid

The elevated walkway that led from the hatchery to the home of the First seemed to Bruce like the last mile. He was familiar with the route from watching K'heera taking it, but why he was being taken there, he couldn't imagine. He didn't want to, either.

Out of long habit he searched the cloud formations, felt the direction of the air. It would rain tonight. Yeah, a real gully-washer. He hoped he'd be alive to see it.

Finally, the Anurans ushered him through the building's front portal into a large open room. To his surprise Meg, Szu-yi, Nadine Lewis, and Old Bear stood nervously around it.

*Put all the bad eggs in one basket,* he thought.

They'd been responsible for the clandestine communications among the humans. And they'd been responsible for keeping morale up, by telling tales of Trinity as it had been *before.*

Szu-yi stood in the shelter of Nadine's strong arms, trembling as if with fever. This did not bode well for her. He couldn't bear to think he'd have to watch her be punished again because of what Tesa had done earlier. He moved to the doctor's side.

"Shhh," he soothed her, "it's going to be okay, honey."

She stared at him, eyes wide, disbelieving. "I sent messages to K'heera . . . about them . . . and they've found out. . . ."

Bruce glanced at Nadine's worried face. "Don't say that, darlin'," he begged the Asian woman. "Let us do the talkin'."

Szu-yi nodded rapidly, eagerly, brushing tears from her eyes. Nadine hugged her tight.

Just then, all the guards turned toward the front entrance as the First entered, his large eyes scanning the ragged group. The guards squatted, pulling the humans down with them.

The First sang something, and then the mechanical voice of his voder chimed in. "Am I correct that *you* are the senior member of this group?" He was talking to Meg.

She stepped forward. "Yes. That's correct." One of the guards nudged her hard, reminding her of something. Her jaw clenched as she amended, "That's correct, *Glorious First.*"

"We know you all have a personal relationship with the Interrelator . . . the person who attacked our colony today."

*Here it comes,* Bruce thought. *The bad news.* Had they captured Tesa? Had they killed her?

"We understand this Interrelator is charged with the welfare of the avians you call Grus and Aquila, avians you believe to be intelligent." The First walked around, and when he came to Szu-yi, patted her arm consolingly. The doctor turned her face away.

Meg said nothing, waiting.

"Her ability to obtain the cooperation of these avians has impressed us enough that we are reconsidering our historical prerogative. Our people understand only conquest and cultural assimilation. *Your* people have found another way. Perhaps it is time for us to examine your philosophy."

The humans glanced at one another warily.

"We differ in many ways," the First sang. "The way we wage war, for example. You *destroy* your enemy, and if you suffer fewer deaths than you commit, you say you have 'won.' We, however, would say that you had lost. Every individual death leaves you one less who could serve your state."

The First waited until they absorbed this. "When the Chosen fight, few die. Each death, to us, is wasteful, a loss. A First that loses too many soldiers does not remain a First for long. And I've lost many today." He paused. "I will lose no more. I am ready to negotiate with your Interrelator, to meet, as both our peoples do, at a table, and discuss mutually agreeable terms. And to learn how we may become as you are, people of peace . . . perhaps even members of your Cooperative League of Systems."

He wanted to *negotiate* with Tesa? Bruce blinked. It was too easy.

"If what you say is true," Meg said suddenly, her voice surprisingly strong, "then release everyone you've captured. *Then* we'll talk about negotiations."

"If I did release everyone, what protection would *my* people have?" the First asked reasonably. "You humans have been known to enact terrible vengeance. Your Interrelator might destroy us for revenge, hesitating only because you all *are* here."

"Our records have shown you that the CLS forbids us to have weapons on this planet," Meg insisted.

"If you had secreted weapons here for your protection, that is not information you would have left in your records. All nations keep defense secrets."

He waited until Meg grudgingly agreed, then went on. "Besides, some of your people have been given important jobs. You can't be replaced overnight. While negotiations go on, we can retrain others to take your place, ease you out of our system. And finally, your presence in our colony protects us against punitive measures from your CLS, until our negotiations with the Interrelator are concluded."

Meg nodded curtly. "How are we supposed to tell the Interrelator of your interest in negotiations?"

"I'll release you"—he nodded at Meg—"and you." He pointed to Old Bear. "We'll give you a flyer. Your Interrelator is everywhere—*she* will find *you*. Tell her I will meet her wherever she pleases, with trained negotiators."

"You must think we're as dumb as a mud fence," Bruce blurted. "You just want them to *lead* you to her!"

The First turned, his yellow arm patches brightening. "You assume that we do not know where she is. She is northwest of here on a grassy plain, surrounded by thousands of Grus, with more converging every day. We could capture her today if we chose to use *your* methods. But that is not our way."

The weatherman's blood chilled at the First's announcement.

"Still, Bruce has a point," Meg said, regaining the Anuran's attention. "Even if you don't follow us to capture her, when Tesa shows up to negotiate, you can pounce on her then."

The First considered her words. "Point taken. To ensure the Interrelator's safety, we will negotiate with her *emissary*. We sincerely wish to end these hostilities."

Bruce felt uneasy. Szu-yi shook her head slightly.

"But . . . to ensure the safety of *our* negotiators," the First said, "we will keep you three"—he indicated Bruce, Szu-yi, and Nadine—"in a separate facility. Then we can negotiate in good faith, and trust the Interrelator to end her bloodthirsty attacks against us." He glanced out the back wall at the waning light. "It's time for you two to go and find your Interrelator."

Guards led Meg and Old Bear out of the First's home. The weatherman watched their apprehensive expressions, while Nadine muffled Szu-yi's quiet sobs against her chest.

Tesa had mixed feelings about the rain, as she stood in a thicket of reeds on the marsh surrounding the River. It was nearly midnight, and the sky was black and featureless as the torrential downpour blanketed the Anurans' colony. She wore nothing but the remains of her old, black StarBridge jumpsuit, cut down to a camisole. Her hair was tied back severely, and her skin was streaked with a black paint that wouldn't easily wash off. She wore no white tonight. The heavy downpour would hide her, covering her sounds as she moved about the River. But it would hamper her own vision, and could completely ruin her only weapon.

Her old sinew-backed bow and a quiver of arrows were wrapped tightly in waterproofed leather, and strapped securely to her back. But the wood, the sinew backing, and the gut she'd used for the bowstring all responded badly to humidity. It wouldn't be the strong, reliable weapon she was used to. If the sinew backing got wet enough, the bow might even crack if drawn too hard. She wondered if she'd even be able to hit anything with it. At least she'd dipped her arrow points in that dead alien's yellow poison patch, so accuracy might not be that critical. She tied the leather package high in the reeds.

Touching the collection of tools clustered on a technician's belt around her waist, Tesa made sure they were all still there. Then she slung a lightweight oxygen-maker she'd taken from the *Demoiselle* around her neck. It would break down water into needed oxygen and feed it to her face mask, so she could swim underwater. The rain would mask her wake of bubbles. She reviewed again the layout of the colony so painstakingly drawn for her in sign by Thunder, who'd gotten it from K'heera.

Peering into the darkness, she eyed the varied buildings. Their artificial lights seemed to urge her on. Smiling grimly, the Interrelator settled the breather mask on her face, then slipped into the River's dark water.

Tesa had a sudden, sharp memory of her bloody dreams, then blanked them out as she swam through the inky fluid.

Finally, she came up under a long, low, rectangular building, several stories high, that stretched out over the water on stilts. She peered overhead at the soldiers' barracks. Pulling off her breather, she glanced around, letting her eyes adjust. It was darker than night under the belly of this building, but somewhere there should be telltales. . . . She saw them finally, at the far end of the structure.

The multicolored telltales shone brightly against their dark machinery. Tesa reached overhead, grabbing hold of the catwalk-type ladder that perched there for servicing. Hauling herself out of the water, she sat on the walkway and stared at the alien apparatus. Pulling out the plastic-encased schematics she'd drawn from K'heera's signed instructions, she squinted in the dark, using the telltales to read by. She recognized the power converter, but ignored it. What she wanted was the small water-processing plant each building had.

When she found the neat, spare units, they weren't half as big as she'd expected. They filtered River water and processed it to be safe for the residents, then treated the used water so it would be sent back to the River as clean as when it had left. *Neat,* she thought. She studied the incoming and outgoing pipes. If Jib hadn't recounted the story of the eleven-year-old computer whiz at StarBridge who had reversed some Simiu's toilet as a prank, she'd never have thought of this.

According to K'heera, to get inside the little units, you only had to press this lever. . . .

The system opened like a magic flower. Tesa grinned, then checked her drawing one more time. The Anurans used a simple color coding for all their machinery, so their dull-witted servants could handle the repairs.

*The blue pipe is for clean water,* she read. *The red for waste. This button shuts the system off, this one turns it back on. Okay. Here we go.*

She turned the system off, and disconnected the incoming water pipe; however, when she attempted to remove the outgoing waste pipe, it wouldn't budge. She struggled with it for several seconds before giving up. She couldn't waste time on one uncooperative unit. She replaced the water pipe the way it was and turned the system back on. After closing the unit back up, she slipped into the water again.

There were five soldiers' barracks. She still had four more she could sabotage.

The others all cooperated nicely. On each one, she removed the waste pipe and attached it to the water intake. Each barracks had a water holding tank that held hundreds of gallons in reserve. Tesa figured it would take half an hour for the waste pipe to contaminate the holding tank enough so that fouled water would start seeping into the soldiers' sleeping pools. Then, it would be another ten minutes before anyone figured out what was going on. She planned to be back at her starting place in the reeds before that last ten minutes was up.

Her sabotage completed, she slapped on her breather, then headed for the long, low, roofed platform that sat in the middle of the River. This platform, open on all sides, was where the human and Simiu captives were kept at night . . . except for K'heera.

Swimming beneath the facility, she peeked out from under it. At opposite ends, on sleds parked in midair, hovered two Anuran guards. The open platform was surrounded by powerful, invisible force-fields that kept the humans from escaping. The guards were just an added precaution. They couldn't be discounted, but the rain would reduce their visibility.

Fortunately, the fields did not go past the platform itself, nor did they affect the catwalk constructed around the water treatment facility. Tesa had considered damaging the platform's power plant, which would disable the force-field and enable all the humans to make a break for it, but realized that would alert the guards instantly. Besides, most of the humans were too drugged to take advantage of it.

Perching on the catwalk, Tesa felt overhead for the outline of the trapdoor that led to the floor above. The nearly seamless door, set flush with the prisoners' platform, could not be opened from their side, but there was a handy latch on Tesa's side. This allowed maintenance staff access to the platform without disabling the force-field.

Carefully, Tesa opened the trapdoor and peeked through. Prone bodies lay side by side before her in long rows. She peered around for the guards, waiting until they were both turned away from her, then hoisted herself up through the door. After jamming a piece of wet fabric between the door and its frame to keep the catch from engaging, she lay flat so she'd seem like another sleeping body. Cautiously, she peered around for the mass of white that would be Weaver.

Of course, the avian was at the farthest end of the building. Tesa poked the person lying nearest her, but there was no response. She crawled on elbows, belly, and knees, creeping foot by foot down the row of sleepers. Meg and the others would be closest to Weaver.

Twice she had to crawl in between sleepers to hide from the guards. Several captives awoke, eyes widening when they realized who she was, what she was doing. She signed them to stillness, and they obeyed as she traveled down the line. When she found the three Simiu drum dancers, shorn and thin, they were so far under that she could get no response from them at all.

Finally, she lay down next to Weaver's gleaming, white form as casually as if they were back in their own nest shelter. The avian's head was tucked under her wing, so Tesa carefully pulled the wing over her own head, bringing her face as close to her partner's eye as she could. She jostled Weaver, waiting for the eye to blink open. Tesa's heart trip-hammered. What if Weaver was too drugged to fly? What if she couldn't rouse her?

Finally, the sleeping bird's lids separated, her nictitating membrane uncovering the round, golden orb. She blinked, then her eye dilated and her crown stretched as she realized who was bold enough to crawl beneath her wing. Tesa breathed a sigh of relief as they pulled their heads out from under the wing.

"Move slowly," Tesa signed. "Make your gestures natural. They can see you so easily." The Interrelator peered around the avian worriedly. "Where are my grandparents? Where are Meg, Bruce, and Szu-yi? Why aren't they with you?"

"They were taken away after your raid," Weaver replied.

Taken away. Because of her raid? *Oh, no. . . .*

"Only First-Light is here now, Good Eyes," Weaver signed.

*Who?* Tesa wondered, not understanding. She finally noticed strange, hooded, dark eyes watching her from over Weaver's back. She turned her attention back to the avian.

"Did they clip only one wing?" Tesa asked her.

"Only one. But all the feathers, even the tertials."

"I've brought Aquila feathers, slivers of wood, and surgical glue." She pulled the waterproof package out of her camisole and opened it, checking SouthWind's feathers for damage.

The man on the other side of Weaver crept around her. "You have the feathers?" he signed.

"Yes," Tesa signed back. "Who are you?"

"I asked for the feathers. I've done imping before . . . the feathers have to be seated just right."

Tesa nodded. "We don't have much time to get this done before the shit, literally, hits the fan. Stretch your wing and act like you're preening," she instructed Weaver, who instantly obliged.

Each feather had to be matched to the hollow stump left from a cut feather. Then, the new feather needed its shaft trimmed to allow it to be slid into the stump. Thin wooden slivers were glued deep into the stump, then the new feather glued over the sliver, lending stability to the mating. The feather had to overlap its neighbor to allow correct airflow.

The Aquila feathers were all the wrong size, so they had to be trimmed. The two strangers worked quickly as Tesa mentally counted down the time they had left. When she slid the last feather into place, she signed to the man, "Why aren't you drugged?"

"I was," he signed back, "but some of the leaves you dropped were emetics. I've been emptying myself ever since. I'm a little wobbly, but clearheaded."

"And the others?"

"Martin Brockman, beside me, he's clearheaded. Carlotta Estafan behind you is okay. Moshe Rosten, Chris Bartus, and Noriko Imanaka near her are fine, too. We all work together."

"And you are . . . ?"

"Javier First-Light-of-Day."

"I'm . . ."

"He knows who you are," Weaver signed quickly.

"Right. I brought hollow reeds. You can follow me out the service door, but I can't wait for you. I'm here for Weaver."

First-Light nodded, even as he checked the feathers for looseness. "I'm not leaving without her, anyway," he signed.

That was when Tesa finally noticed the way he interacted with Weaver and realized they'd developed a relationship. *So, Rob sent good people, just like he promised.* She gazed into Weaver's golden eyes. "Are you still strong, my friend?"

"Strong enough," the avian assured her. "And Taller?"

"His strength is here with you. He needs you, Weaver."

"But how can I leave?" she asked. "We're enclosed by invisible walls that are painful to touch."

Tesa nodded toward one of the guards. "They wear a device on their belts that neutralizes the field so they can pass through it. To free yourself . . . you'll have to lure one of them in here . . . then . . . take the device from him. Can you do that?"

"You're asking me if I can kill one of these un-Worldly creatures?" Weaver asked coolly. "Easily."

"It will have to be fast, before the other one can react," Tesa told her. "Take the device from his belt and slip it over your neck. Once it's on your body, you can pass through the field without fear. Fly west." She pointed to a clump of reeds. "The other guard will call for reinforcements, but they'll be busy dealing with another problem. Head for the forest. Thunder will take you to Taller. Don't wait for me."

"Suppose she can't get the field neutralizer off him?" First-Light interjected. "I'll stay with her until she's out of here."

"No," Tesa said, handing Weaver a small stone knife on a thong. "If you can't unfasten the alien's belt, use this to cut through." She gazed at First-Light. "You won't be able to get away unseen if you wait for Weaver. You have to come now."

First-Light watched Weaver, his face drawn, concerned. Tesa was startled by the depth of emotion he had for her.

"This is not my first time in combat, friend," Weaver assured him. "Soon, I'll be with Taller . . . and then you'll have to give courting gifts to someone else, First-Light."

The man smiled. "My best gifts will always be for you."

To Tesa's surprise, her partner enveloped the man under her wing briefly. Then she turned to the Interrelator. "Take care of him, Good Eyes. He's been a good friend to me."

She nodded. "First-Light, have your people follow you one at a time. If they're spotted crawling out . . ."

"We can handle it," he assured her as she turned to go.

Tesa glanced back once, saw him sign to Carlotta.

Once under the platform, Tesa counted seconds as five humans exited through the trapdoor and slipped into the inky water. First-Light was the sixth and last, closing the door behind him.

The small group clustered under the trapdoor so that the bright lights of the telltales could illuminate their signing.

"I was afraid you might disobey orders," Tesa signed to him.

He lifted an eyebrow, but didn't comment. She started signing, but he stopped her. "Martin, Moshe, Noriko, and Chris don't know sign language. They're crew from the *Brolga*."

Tesa groaned inwardly. "*Tow* them if you have to," she signed, handing him the short lengths of hollow reed. "Strike out for that area"—she pointed to her reed blind—"but don't lift your heads above water." She checked her chrono. "We've got four minutes." She nodded at the wet, nervous people, attached her face mask, then disappeared beneath the waves.

Tesa waded into the center of the reeds only moments in front of Martin Brockman. He grinned, giving her a thumbs-up. She returned the gesture, then reached for her bow. Moving to a high spot, she knelt and unwrapped her weapon.

She unpacked her arrows from their dry pouch, handling them carefully as Brockman watched with undisguised curiosity. Carlotta finally joined near them, then Moshe, Chris, and Noriko, followed, at last, by First-Light.

Weaver lay still on the quiet platform, trying to give her human friends the time they needed to swim to cover. Finally, she stood and walked to one of the water stations, scooping up a cool drink in her long bill. She peered around. A guard was near, the other at the opposite end of the structure. Suddenly she dropped her head and coughed loudly, as though there were something wrong with the water. The nearest guard turned, curious. She coughed again, violently, pawing at her bill, tossing her head. She staggered around the platform, carelessly stepping on several of the prone humans.

The nearest guard lowered his sled until it was level with the floor of the platform, then stepped off it, moving easily through the field. He approached Weaver cautiously, just as the second guard moved around the building to get a better look.

Weaver lurched, placing her large body between the guard approaching her and the one behind her, blocking his view. When the near guard was close enough, she drew herself up and drove her powerful bill straight into his eye. He went down, thudding against the floor and twitching, as Weaver lunged for his belt. Glancing back, she saw the second guard moving his sled closer. Her long fingers fumbled with the belt catch futilely, so she took Tesa's knife and severed the material in one swipe. Knotting the belt deftly, the Grus slipped it over her head. The second guard lowered his sled for a better view.

Only the invisible barrier stood before her and freedom. The first time she'd been brought here, they'd shoved her against the transparent walls, demonstrating how painful an escape attempt would be. Now she would have to have faith in this alien device, faith that it would neutralize the power in that field, that it would not strike her down in agony.

She swallowed, glancing back at the second guard, who was trying to see his companion. Weaver touched the device with her bill, knowing her fate hinged on this bizarre, un-Worldly thing. With a deep breath, she spread her mismatched wings.

Taking two strong strides, she sailed effortlessly through the invisible barrier. Once outside, the rain and wind buffeted her wings, the feathers that weren't hers unbalancing her, the downpour pelting against her, driving her down toward the water. She pumped harder in the one-two, one-two beat that was her people's special rhythm. The waterway dropped away and she lifted, compensating for the borrowed feathers. One-two. One-two. The platform receded as she sailed into the night sky. The rows of soldiers' barracks suddenly lit from within as the guard behind her pursued her on his sled. She could hear him singing, calling for help, but there was no response from the barracks. Weaver lifted over the reeds, gazing down in the darkness, glimpsing her friends hiding there, seeing her partner poised with her weapon. She called to them, urging them safe passage, braying her thanks, even as the guard bore down on her. Weaver heard a twang, saw Tesa release her arrow.

The missile overshot its target and flew harmlessly through the sky. Weaver pumped harder, knowing she'd have to outrun the mechanical flyer now. Then there was a scream behind her, and she turned her head to see the guard clutch his shoulder. Had he been hit? If he had, it couldn't have been more than a scratch. Slowly, the alien stiffened and fell into the black water below. Now, how had Good Eyes done that?

The empty sled soon overtook, then passed her, sailing into the distant horizon, perhaps, Weaver thought, enjoying its own freedom. She pumped her wings, aiming for the forest, surprised to find how eager she was to join with her sisters, the Hunters.

# CHAPTER 19
♦
# Weaver's Plan

Rain and river water streamed into Javier's eyes as he tried to count heads. Martin's blond one was between him and Noriko; Moshe and Chris were standing slightly behind her. The Lakota woman was crouched on one knee in the pelting rain. It took a minute before he realized what she was doing.

As he stared at her stance and the tip of her skyward-pointing arrow, Weaver sailed over, a gleaming beacon in the hellish sky, moving as casually as if her people always flew through a deluge in the dead of night. The avian's call tore through the air, nearly felling him where he stood. Everyone but the Interrelator touched the nullifiers in their ears. To know Weaver was sending that call to thank them, to give them strength, lifted Javier's spirit as nothing else could have.

Suddenly an airborne Anuran guard drew up close behind her and Javier had to will himself to silence. There was no way Weaver, in poor condition and with borrowed feathers, could outfly that machine. He turned to the Interrelator, saw her arrow pulled back, held taut, her arms and leg muscles contracting even as the bow did. She wasn't serious? In the dark? In the *rain*?

She released the missile and it shot through the night sky as the guard passed directly overhead. It was hard to see, but he could make out the light wooden arrow skimming near the sled . . . then over it until it disappeared in the rain.

*Damn!* he swore silently.

The Interrelator had notched another arrow immediately, but the guard was now clearly out of range. Then, just as the Anuran was nearly level with Weaver's tail, he lurched, grabbed his shoulder, then plunged into the river. The Interrelator clenched her fist triumphantly, and he realized the arrow had to have been poison-tipped. It must have scratched the guard. Weaver, pacing the now-empty sled, flew on unmolested toward the inky forest.

The Interrelator quickly unfolded her long legs and slipped back into the water, slinging the bow and quiver across her chest. She waved to draw them close, signing so rapidly in the dark that even he couldn't follow. She was his height, Javier realized dazedly, maybe a little taller.

He felt something shoved into his hands, and took hold. Some kind of rope, so they wouldn't get lost as they moved farther into the cover of the tall grasses. Javier blinked, suddenly light-headed. Low blood sugar, on top of too much adrenaline after a day of purging. If only he could sit for a second . . . Suddenly the reeds, the river, his fellow humans, all seemed to recede as if he were being pulled backward down a long hallway.

He blinked as Martin shook him. *Did I pass out?*

Then Martin was replaced by a pair of lovely light eyes in a dark face as the Interrelator peered worriedly at him. She held his face, and he could smell the sharp odor of the paint on her hands. She pressed something against his lips, pressuring his jaw to make it open. A fibrous wad fell against his tongue and when he bit down a sharp, citruslike flavor flooded his mouth. He smelled oranges and chewed. The tangy flavor revived him.

"You okay?" the Interrelator signed.

She was still touching his face and he focused on that, impulsively reaching up to cover her hand with his. Still chewing, he savored different flavors, unable to categorize them.

She grew aware of their contact and, looking uncomfortable, slowly drew away. He found himself strangely regretful.

"We've got to get out of here," she told him, glancing over her shoulder at the soldiers' barracks. Aliens clustered around the building, gesturing excitedly. He wasn't sure what had happened, but it was obvious sleep time was over for them.

"Too bad we have to go," Carlotta signed, nodding toward the milling soldiers, "looks like the party's just starting."

Tugging the rope, the Interrelator led them deeper into the dark reeds. She must have created some disturbance. Javier thought about four barracks of soldiers disrupted, and smiled.

Repeatedly, through their watery march upriver, they were forced to submerge and wait for troops to pass. It seemed hours before they could leave the tall grass and slip into the even darker forest. By then, his legs were shaking with fatigue.

Once the black forest surrounded them, Javier felt the night enclose him like a fist. He wondered if he was in a time warp, if this was a night that would last two or three times as long as it should. He felt the sky should be streaked with light, when he knew that it was hours yet before dawn.

Now that they were on land, the Interrelator picked up the pace. Just when Javier thought he couldn't jog blindly on for even one more minute, they finally halted. There in the darkness sat four alien flyers, parked as casually as if they were in a public park. Their rescuer hurriedly turned them on, and one by one, the a-gravs hovered. He stared at the woman's dark form, wondering how she'd managed to get them.

She gestured at Martin to get on and he complied; Chris peered at the controls curiously as he climbed on in front of the engineer. Carlotta tugged Javier up behind her and he was happy to let her take the controls. The Interrelator shared her sled with Noriko and Moshe, as they moved forward, single file through the woods, only a meter above the forest floor.

*Clever,* he thought. They'd make better time if they flew above the trees, but they'd be spotted in an instant. No doubt the only thing masking their electronic readouts was all the soldiers searching for them, soaring around on the same machines.

As Carlotta ably handled their machine, Javier wondered what awaited them at the end of the trail.


It was dawn by the time Tesa and her band of exhausted Terrans returned to the savannah where the flocks of Grus waited. The rain had ended hours ago, but she was saturated anyway, and the day promised to be hot and steamy. And now she had to figure out what to do with her new charges.

Maybe she was just tired, but all she wanted was to return to the embrace of her Grus family and leave these humans to one another. Jib could handle them, she decided.

Preoccupied, Tesa stepped off the sled, but her foot dropped into a hidden animal burrow, and she stumbled. A steadying hand caught her arm, saving her from a twisted ankle.

"Thanks," she signed, turning to face her helper.

First-Light nodded curtly with barely masked concern. His shadowed, dark eyes fastened on her paint-streaked face, making her feel self-conscious. She must look like an oversize feral child with her blackened face and arms, clothed in nothing but a worn camisole, bow and quiver slung crookedly across her chest.

*I'm not used to humans anymore,* she decided. Unless it was his eyes that made her uneasy. She was used to the golden eyes of the Grus, Thunder's red ones, Meg's bright blues, or Bruce's gray ones. But this man's were hooded and as black as the ice on a bottomless lake, giving nothing away, no key to his soul.

She pulled her arm gently from his grip. It was the second time he'd touched her, and the second time it'd unnerved her. He turned away, obviously realizing he'd made her uncomfortable.

Before she could worry further, their whole party was surrounded by White Winds as the cohort dropped from the sky. Lightning, Flies-Too-Fast, and the rest pushed past the other humans and surrounded Tesa, enveloping her with their wings. Young Frost Moon nearly knocked First-Light off his feet.

"You're so *rude*," she admonished them gently, losing herself in the warmth of their feathers. "Did Weaver arrive?"

"She flew in with an escort of Hunters just a short while ago," Lightning assured her. "She and Taller have been dancing ever since." He pointed at the pair with his bill. They were bowing, leaping, and twining their necks like two-year-olds.

"They act like new lovers," she signed, and that odd notion made the youngsters' crowns shrink up tight.

First-Light also watched the pair, and Tesa remembered the way he'd cared for Weaver. "She's safe again," she signed, "thanks to your feather grafting."

His mouth turned up slightly.

That was when Tesa noticed the gold ball in his ear.

"Are . . . were . . . you deaf?" she signed. In her surprise, she used American Sign Language instead of Grus.

He paused, then nodded, answering her in the same language. "Yes, but they could only give me hearing in this one ear."

She stiffened, recalling all the arguments she'd had with Rob and her parents, because she'd decided against having that same surgery performed. Those arguments were what had brought her to Trinity. Tesa no sooner wanted hearing than she'd want to be another species. Being Deaf was part of her identity.

The Interrelator had no idea what to say to this man. He was suddenly more than a stranger; he was a person who had once been Deaf, but now no longer was. Did that change explain his expressionless face? Deaf people used their faces in their language—was First-Light's dourness an attempt to put that part of his life behind him? Did he think of himself as Hearing? And why shouldn't he? She stared at the small gold ball, thinking of all the soul-searching and conflict with loved ones that it represented to her.

Her dismay must have been plain on her face because First-Light signed, "It bothers you that I had my deafness corrected." He wore the same casual expression; his face revealed nothing.

"No! Of course not," she lied. "You had every right. . . ." She could see in his eyes that he knew she was lying.

"The first time I met another Deaf person, I was twenty-four," he explained. As he signed in ASL, she realized that signing had not been his first language. "I lip-read. *He* signed. We needed voders to communicate. It inspired me to learn ASL . . . but most of my life has been spent on the periphery of the hearing world." He shrugged, as if it weren't that important.

"A year ago," he continued, "my doctor suggested this reconstruction surgery. On Earth, I worked with people of primal cultures, many of whom weren't comfortable with the high-tech equipment I needed for interpreting. I thought this would be more convenient than the hardware I had to carry around with me. Well . . . it didn't take in my left ear, but it works well enough in my right. All of that was before I saw Weaver's cloak . . . and knew I'd be coming to Trinity. Try not to hold it against me. Our lives . . . were very different, Ms. Wakandagi."

She should say something reassuring to him, let him know he didn't need to justify his actions to her. But all Tesa managed to sign was, "You know so much about my life?"

He gave her a wry smile. "*Everyone* knows about *your* life."

She was embarrassed again.

He changed the subject, and returned to signing Grus. "May I greet Weaver? I'd like to check those grafted feathers."

Tesa nodded, relieved to be on another topic—any other topic. "I'll introduce you to Taller, first. I'm sure he'll want to thank you personally for all your help."

Then she remembered the other Terrans. Turning to the sleds, she found Carlotta deep in discussion with Scorched, None-So-Pretty, and Snowberry. Whatever they were talking about had the humans captivated, as Carlotta scribbled translations in a patch of sandy soil she'd cleared—except for the young pilot, Chris, whose fatigue had caught up to him. He was curled up on a parked sled, sound asleep. Tesa caught Snowberry's eye and asked him to keep the group near the sleds. He waved agreement and rejoined the conversation.

*How long can we maintain such crude communication?* Tesa wondered as Carlotta wrote on the ground. *And what kind of relationship does Carlotta have with First-Light? Could she be his wife? And why the hell should I care?*

Pushing away her jumbled thoughts, Tesa beckoned to First-Light and together they approached her partners. Lightning, Flies-Too-Fast, Hurricane, and Winter Bloom strode along as well, brazenly examining the Terran male, then staring wide-eyed at Tesa. He accepted their perusal good-naturedly, imitating them, gazing back in turn, and exchanging a few signed pleasantries.

As they walked, Tesa found herself stealing quick glances at him, just as her friends were doing. He was interesting, she thought. Not handsome in the limited way humans defined the term, but tall and wiry, with a strong, straight stance that to the White Wind people was much more important. His serious demeanor was . . . different. In some ways, he reminded her more of a Hunter than a White Wind. She was curious, too, about how he'd received the vivid diagonal scar that marred his right cheek.

Taller shot straight into the air, then fanned his wings to drop slowly to the ground. As soon as his toes touched the World, Weaver bounded around him. They danced closer, touching keels, their necks intertwining, then they were in the air again, bobbing, weaving, dancing their old courtship rite anew.

The Grus leader felt like a youngster. The despondency that had crushed him had evaporated when his people announced Weaver's return. Waves of sound had rippled from a thousand throats, as she flew to him under an escort of Hunters. Weaver was free! Free, and his again. Taller wanted to dance for days, as he had when he'd first courted her, so many years ago.

Behind him, he saw other members of his family draw near. Good Eyes moved slowly, weary from her dangerous mission. His son, Lightning, stayed close by her, ready to lend his support. The other member of their odd trio, Thunder, had already returned to their enemies' camp, despite the danger. The Hunter was Good Eyes' sharp-eyed observer, and nothing that had happened tonight could have occurred, but for her. Flies-Too-Fast, who had been as steadfast as a son these last weeks, walked on Good Eyes' other side. Their young companions milled around them in a knot of white feathers and long black legs, signing excitedly to one another, peering at something Taller couldn't see.

As soon as his human partner approached, Taller hurried to drape a wing around her, hugging her in unbridled joy. He buried her under his feathers, calling joyously, while Weaver's voice joined his.

The human's grimy, painted arms hugged him in return, her tiny fingers burrowing under his soft undercoat. She pressed her flat face against the base of his throat in her own alien sign of affection, a sign he'd come to crave once he'd learned to love her. Taller thanked the Suns again for the blessing they'd bestowed upon him by making her his partner.

Finally, she extricated herself. "I want you to meet . . ."

Just then the cohort parted, revealing a strange human male hidden in their midst. To the Grus leader, it was as if he'd appeared from nowhere. The newcomer was as tall as Good Eyes, and dark, with fierce black eyes. The human stepped forward, closer to Good Eyes. Too close.

Taller's hormones were in full bloom. His head spun in the strange male's direction, his eyes widening, his crown flaring red in challenge. But the human was intently regarding Weaver, and he ignored the warning. Obeying instincts as old as his people, Taller's feathers flared in anger, his wings and neck stretched forward threateningly. Impulsively, he attacked.

Weaver bleated an alarm call, but Taller ignored her. Dimly, he was aware that Good Eyes' face twisted in alarm and she lurched forward as if to stop him, but he was too quick.

The enraged avian lunged to strike a killing blow, but the human male finally saw him and reacted. Instantly he dropped to one knee and bowed his head, flaring his elbows wide. It was the most submissive posture a White Wind could assume, placing his life in the will of his senior. The gesture stopped Taller cold. Of all the aliens he had met, only Good Eyes had ever copied the people's postures. Furious and confused, Taller struck the ground, tearing out a divot of sod and flinging it in the air. The human male never flinched, never moved.

With a flash of white, Weaver was suddenly between him and the stranger. To Taller's amazement, she shoved her mate rudely with her body, poking his back hard with her graceful bill.

"What *are* you *doing*?" she demanded angrily.

"Protecting my family from this challenger," Taller insisted, making himself tall. The human was still locked in the submissive stance. He did not seem like a challenger now.

"*This* is no stranger! This is my *friend*," Weaver informed him irritably, giving the sign a special, intimate twist.

Taller's crown blazed red. Her *friend*?

"This is the human who asked for the feathers, who helped Good Eyes attach them. Without him, I would not be flying. And before that, he . . . cared for me when we were separated. He . . . even caught food for me when I had no will to eat, no will to live."

Taller was incredulous. "He caught food for you?" This *male* . . . ? He stared again at the stranger, his crown flaring with jealousy.

"Taller," Weaver signed, "I wouldn't be here if not for *him*. Besides," she moved so that only Taller could see her signs, "he is *different* from other humans; I could see this even in my despair. He understands the World, the people. He has a *real* name. And see how he watches Good Eyes."

*Good Eyes?* Taller felt baffled by the turn in conversation.

"When you and Good Eyes flew over the enemies' colony, First-Light saw her in the sky, flying boldly with her cohort. His eyes . . . lit from within. And then my heart *knew*. Remember? Just a few months ago *you* told *me* to find Good Eyes a human mate!"

Taller stared at his partner with new understanding. He glanced sideways at Good Eyes, then back at the male. "He's not as tall as she is," he signed grudgingly.

"He's tall enough," Weaver replied, closing the subject.

*This is why matchmaking is better done by females,* Taller decided grumpily, having no idea how to save face in this awkward situation. He forced his crown to shrink.

Weaver moved away from him, and touched the Terran on the arm, urging him to stand. Boldly, she draped her wing over him, conspicuously using the wing with the grafted Hunter feathers.

"Taller, my partner," she announced formally, "this is First-Light-of-Day, my special . . . friend."

Good Eyes appeared completely nonplussed when Weaver deliberately treated this stranger as if he were a family member.

Weaver signed coyly to the human male, "I warned you he wouldn't be happy about those fish."

Taller fixed the newcomer with a cool stare, but First-Light gazed back confidently, easily bearing "the look." The Grus leader would never easily accept anyone's interest in Good Eyes but . . . for her happiness . . . he'd have to endure it. But Weaver had better be sure about this. Taller would allow no one, especially no mere human, to cause Good Eyes unhappiness.

"Welcome to the World, First-Light," the leader signed stiffly. "Perhaps someday I may be able to show my gratitude for . . . the help you've given *both* my life's mates."

"You owe me nothing," the human replied. "I did what any friend would do. When our enemy has been driven from the World, perhaps you'll give me permission to study with your people."

Taller stared with one eye. "What can the White Wind people teach a race of beings who fly without wings, and build shelters where there is no heat, no air?" His mate's eyes bored into him, her crown flaring in annoyance, but he ignored her.

First-Light's steady gaze never faltered. "I want to study all the things that grow on the World—which plants are used in healing, which are for weaving, which for food. . . ."

"First-Light," Taller signed, wondering if the human was mocking him, "the study of all the things that grow on the World would take more than your lifetime and mine combined."

The human's expression never changed. "Then, with your permission, I hope to start soon."

Taller lifted his head. This human was asking to live on the World forever! The avian paused, then finally signed, "Let us both hope you can start your work soon." First-Light's eyes softened, and Taller knew he'd just granted this Terran's most heartfelt wish.

The avian glanced back at his human partner. There was so much he had to tell her, so many things had happened since she'd left, but if he shared his news with her now, she wouldn't sleep, and she needed rest more than anything. His news would wait.

"My friend," he signed to her, "it's been a long night. We all need sleep. There'll be stories to tell after our rest."

First-Light was regarding Good Eyes, too. The change in the male's face was more subtle than in most humans', but the Grus leader could sense his concern. Could Weaver really know humans so well?

"You're right," Good Eyes admitted. "I'm beat. I guess we all are." She gazed at the male Weaver had chosen for her as if she only now saw the exhaustion etched clearly around his eyes. "Let's collect the others. I'll show you where we can wash up, then we'll all have to sleep in my lean-to. It'll be tight, but . . . who cares? We'll build more shelters later."

Tiredly, Good Eyes bid good morning to her partners and led First-Light and her cohort away. Taller watched them until the great mass of his people swallowed them up and they were lost to sight. Weaver also watched them leave together, then twined her neck around his, preening the feathers at the back of his head that he could never reach.

"He's the one," she signed smugly. "You'll see."

Six hours later, Tesa cared a great deal more about the close quarters of her lean-to. She woke drowsily, sweating in the humid afternoon air, feeling trapped. Blinking, she glanced around. She was lying on her right side, facing the back of a stranger.

*Oh, yes, Carlotta.* She could see Noriko just beyond her. It was so odd that the first thing greeting her sight wasn't one of her cohort's feathers, that she felt disoriented and stared at Carlotta's back, trying to remember all that had happened in the last twenty-eight and a half hours.

Then she realized someone was holding her. Who had crawled in behind her? Oh, yes, First-Light. Martin Brockman was on his other side, with Chris and Moshe fitting in on the end. First-Light must've slung an arm around her in his sleep and was now pressed tightly against her back, his breath pulsing steadily against her ear. Did he think she was Carlotta? She swallowed, embarrassed and unsure of what to do. She had to have been completely wrung out not to have been startled awake when it had first happened. From the dull ache in her side she guessed they'd been like this for hours.

Tesa breathed steadily, not wanting to wake him, but not wanting to stay like this, either. He'd be embarrassed, too, especially if he was having a relationship with the other woman. She fidgeted, hoping he'd roll over in his sleep, but he only tightened his embrace and sighed. She rolled her eyes.

If it weren't so warm, she might've taken comfort from the friendly contact. It'd been a long time since she'd slept spoonlike with a warm human body. Normally, Lightning and Flies-Too-Fast crowded into the lean-to with her. To have a human's body pressed along her own was unsettling . . . yet rather pleasant. As the seconds ticked by, she grew more and more aware of their odd intimacy—the warmth of his hand, the strength in his arm, his mouth so close to her ear. A blush crept up her neck.

He must've wakened then, because he tensed. Carefully, he slid his arm away, and she was surprised to feel disappointed. Well, there wasn't any point in pretending it hadn't happened. She rolled over to face him, and he smiled sheepishly.

"Sorry," he signed. "That was the first pleasant dream I've had . . . since the *Brolga*'s capture."

She smiled back. "It's okay." She inclined her head in Carlotta's direction. "Did I move into the wrong place?"

First-Light seemed confused, then shook his head. "Carlotta and I only met on the *Brolga*. I . . . uh . . ." He schooled his face, then continued, "I have no partner." He presented it casually, but that simple statement changed things, somehow.

Rays of sunlight splashed across them, making him appear more attractive than she'd first thought. The shadows highlighted the scar on his cheek. The sudden lack of dialogue felt awkward, so Tesa signed the first thing that came to mind. "What other languages do you use besides ASL and Grus?"

"English. Spanish. I can read Navaho, but don't speak it."

"I thought you might be Navaho, but I wasn't sure."

He nodded. "My father was, my mother Costa Rican. That's where I grew up, in Costa Rica, in the city. I fell in love with the rain forest there, with the endless variety of plants. . . . I didn't see the Navaho nation until I was in my teens. But the first time I saw a Blessing Way ceremony, I knew I wanted to study the way native people used plants." He was watching her as he signed, then his expression changed subtly. He seemed surprised, and drew away slightly.

"What is it?" Tesa asked, wondering if she'd gotten all the war paint off. "Do I look *that* bad in the morning?"

His eyes softened, but the odd expression was still there. "No, you look fine. I . . . just never realized how young you are."

*What difference does that make?* she thought, irritated. To the White Wind people, once you dropped your juvenile feathers, age was irrelevant. He moved, and sunlight glinted off the gold ball in his ear. She stiffened, felt her own expression close down. "How old was I supposed to be?"

He shook his head, plainly regretting his words. "I didn't mean that. Look, I've been reading about you, reading the papers you've written. . . . I knew you came here from StarBridge, but I didn't think . . ." He stopped, pulled his thoughts together. "I didn't mean to offend you. I was just surprised. If I wasn't half asleep I'd have never spoken so bluntly."

"We like people who speak bluntly," she signed, trying to hold back her growing annoyance. "It only makes *humans* uncomfortable."

Before he could respond, Tesa crawled out of the lean-to. She had too much to do to be lying around, engaging in idle chitchat. She needed to eliminate, change clothes, and get these people fed. Then she had to find Jib, and make plans to rescue the Singers. There was a war on, damn it!

She had to force herself not to look back at the ethnobotanist as she greeted her cohort. Javier, however, felt no such compunction, and she could feel his black eyes boring into her as she lost herself among wings, long necks, and shimmering whiteness. Why did he bother her so much? Was she so alienated from her own kind that they couldn't even have a simple conversation without reading more into it than there was?

Tesa tried to move away from the cohort, but found herself still surrounded. There were multitudes of Grus here, both white and gray. The people were massing in such numbers, Tesa wondered distractedly how long the food here would hold out. She turned to go in another direction, but the cohort blocked her again, and she lost her patience, nudging Lightning to make him move.

Suddenly the group obliged en masse, and a space opened up in their center. There, in the grassy circle they'd vacated, stood Old Bear, smiling, holding out his arms to her. Tesa stared as if focusing on a hologram. It was him, and yet not him. He seemed leaner, if that was possible, and older, but his skin still had that bright ruddiness, and his eyes the old sparkle. The flood of conflicting emotions inside her spilled over into her eyes.

"Yes, *takoja*," he signed in Plains Indian sign language, "it's me. And Meg's here, too. Give me a good hug. I've missed you so much."

Feeling like the little girl he'd helped raise, she flung herself into his embrace, making sure he was real, not some transmitted spirit from another planet. Maybe the Sun Family had sent her a sign, a reward for all the risks she'd been taking.

Old Bear's embrace was not as strong as it had once been. Finally, she stepped away, and he wiped the tears off her cheeks.

"Don't cry, *takoja*. It makes your eyes all red."

"How did you get here?" she asked, still weeping. "Meg's with you? I don't understand. Where did you come from?"

"It's a long story. We were released a few hours before you rescued Weaver. The Hunters helped us find our way here. We arrived before you, but all we could do was sleep. I'll explain everything over some food. Wake your group up, they need to be part of this discussion."

Tesa nodded, rubbing the last of her tears away. Looking back at the lean-to, she saw First-Light had already roused the others, who were crawling out, blinking sleepily. When they saw Old Bear, they greeted him warmly.

"You took good care of Javier, I hope," the elder signed confidentially. "He's a good man, don't you think, *takoja*?"

Tesa stared at her grandfather. *First Weaver, then Taller, now Old Bear! Does everybody think this guy is a saint?* "I suppose so," she answered reluctantly. "A little old, though."

Her grandfather startled her and the whole cohort by throwing his head back and laughing heartily.

# CHAPTER 20

# Atle's Offer

A web work of walkways stretched over the interior of the Chosens' hatchery like the crosshatched branches of a ladder tree. Below the narrow, railed walkways lay an organized gridwork of rectangular pools, each pool filled to capacity with four Industrious egg-laying females and the Chosen males that would fertilize their valuable product.

The hatchery was working at peak capacity, the machinery pumping in chemically balanced clean water and pumping out soiled water, even as fertilized eggs were sucked out of the pools and deposited into holding tanks filled with carefully monitored nutrient broth. The Troubadour Dacris, formerly Second-in-Conquest but now having nothing to do with conquest at all, stalked the overhead walkways, contemplating the vast mechanical organism that was now his charge. The factory was his only responsibility and the shame of this simple duty burned him.

He paused to watch the Industrious attendants feed the egg-laying females their chemically controlled diets. The egg-layers, considerably more stunted than their attendants, stared ahead glassily, swallowing their meal without a thought, as their bodies pumped a continuous string of eggs into their pool. Behind the females, clutching them chest-to-back in the nuptial embrace of amplexus, were Chosen males who either had not taken enough of the inhibiting hormone to resist the rains, or whose duties allowed them to be free enough to enjoy a breeding season.

Dacris watched the pools where the frenzied coupling and egg production continued around the clock, and thought of his own sleeping pool, ruined last night by their marauding human enemy. He and the others in his barracks had had to sleep in the river. The taste of that water had been all wrong, and he'd been constantly buffeted by its currents. The soldiers that had once been under his charge had gone to find the terrorist, while he'd endured the ultimate humiliation—being left behind. Dacris took a bitter joy in the knowledge that the perpetrators had not been found. Had *he* been in charge . . .

He wondered how Atle justified releasing two humans just hours before the unseen raid that had damaged the water system of four barracks, freeing several humans and the only captive avian they had kept alive. To make matters worse, one of their people, a Troubadour, had been brutally murdered, and another guard killed by a scratch from a primitive projectile weapon tipped with a One-Touch's toxin. In the past, *five* humans would have been sacrificed and eaten to make reparation for each dead soldier. But that was in another day, long gone and, to most, forgotten.

Dacris blinked and slowed his breathing. As far as he was concerned, he was more a true Chosen than Atle would ever be. And when he thought of the creatures they'd discovered here, his anger grew hotter.

These aliens had no fear, no respect, for the powerful people who had conquered them, and why should they? He imagined the hideous creatures being forced to eat one of their own or starve—that would give them some incentive to obey! Dacris glowered into the pools, hating the males who felt free enough to yield to their passion, hating the placid Industrious females who endured their endless, unnatural breeding cycle, hating the four-footed alien worker who just now came into view—but most of all hating Atle with every cell of his being.

Dacris watched the furred slave of Atle's slave move around the pools' edges and lower walkways and raged in silence, thinking of that imbecile, Arvis, being given Chosen status, being allowed to *train* this valuable servant, and worst of all, being allowed—no, *induced*—to breed a female of *rank*!

He struggled to bank his anger as the Simiu went about her work, methodically going from computer station to computer station, checking readouts. If he could only catch her in an error! Then he could vent his rage in her justifiable discipline, but her ability was so far beyond their expectations that he had yet to find an excuse.

She was just another reminder to him of the need for clear-thinking servants, instead of the mindless Industrious drones they were burdened with. His mind traveled to the future, to conquered *planets* filled with her kind. He would train them the old way—it would be his right, no one could stop him. He dwelled on that sweet fantasy . . . until he remembered his demotion.

Would Atle allow him to ever again *own* his own workers? He doubted it. He watched the alien padding around the network of pools and walkways and ached for her to make an error—just one. He swallowed hard, struggling to get a grip on his fury.

To distract himself, Dacris strode to the end of the upper walkway, to the computer station there. The Armored Industrious working at the terminal scrambled off the padded bench and Dacris moved into her place. The graphics on the tank seemed like a child's game, but were actually a functional diagnostic program that the Industrious could use. Someday there would be no need to expend such energy just to keep the State running. He dumped the Industrious technician's work, not caring that she would have to start over from the beginning, and accessed the alien's work.

He wasn't just searching for an error, he was doing his job. Besides, what new shame could Atle inflict on him if he failed even this simple assignment? He scanned the work the Simiu had already done, double-checking her readouts, her responses, her actions. He eliminated the part of the program that was in her language so he could follow her work in his. His eyes moved along the changing data. No errors. A good servant.

His skin felt dry and he moistened it with the odorless oil left there for the Industrious. The poor-quality lubricant only irritated him further, as the computer moved into the work she was currently doing. This supervisor's program would not let her know she was being observed as he watched her manipulate data, correct problems, improve the efficiency of the system. Her perfection frustrated him, and his skin glowed in anger.

Dacris moved to turn off the machine in disgust when something caught his eye, some small change that seemed somehow . . . not right. He moved closer to the tank, watching, figuring in his head. He blinked slowly, his lower lids covering his eyes for a restful moment. She went on to the next station, and his program followed her, this time seeking a similarity. Yes. There it was. An *error*. His skin flushed.

At the next station there was another change, and that made him pause. The mistake was in the same place, changing the same values, but wrongly. He scanned backward, but there was no record of the alteration—and that in itself was incorrect. After a few minutes, he padded away from the station to the walkway to observe her actions. She was deaf and seemed unaware of him. According to the computer, she was making changes and adjustments to the filter stations—changes that should have been *physical*—switching or testing filters, but in reality she was doing nothing but manipulating the program itself.

She made similar, subtle changes at each place on her route. What did it mean? He forgot about discipline and focused on the larger issue. The tiny changes she made in the computer programs were, in themselves, not terribly intricate, but cumulatively . . . they could be significant. The fact that the program had been altered so that he could not review what had been done to it meant that all the automatic saves had been overridden.

Once the alien finished her work here, she would move on to the tanks that nurtured the eggs until the growing embryos were at the optimal age for consumption. Her work affected every phase of production. Was this bold slave trying to undermine the *entire* factory? What ambition! It was worthy of a One-Touch!

If he told Atle this, the First would have to admit his error in disciplining his Second and reinstate him. Because of the scope of the transgression, Atle would be forced to grant ownership of the Simiu to Dacris. He would have to make his own son—that moronic servant!—hand her over to the Troubadour.

Dacris returned to the walkway in time to watch the Simiu move away from her last station. Sensing his presence, she glanced over her shoulder, staring at him before moving away quickly. *I know you're not loafing, good servant.*

He moved toward the exit, imagining Atle's face when he made his claim. He saw the First's expression as he handed the slave over to Dacris, saw the One-Touch explaining the new reality to his dullard son. Dacris only wished he could implicate that silly Industrious in this and successfully claim him as well.

As he neared the exit, his steps slowed. Suppose he *didn't* tell?

If the hatchery was damaged, Dacris would be accountable.

Wait.

Wait.

Suppose he held the critical information until it was too late to correct, releasing the news to the *Council,* not just the Glorious First. He might be able to manipulate this into something more important than the ownership of one slave. It was *Atle* who'd decided this alien could serve the hatchery. It was the First who had permitted her greater responsibility. Her betrayal would reflect not on his Industrious son, but on himself.

Dacris turned away from the exit and prowled the walkway, no longer entertaining dark fantasies of discipline and fear. Could he use this slave's clever sabotage to overthrow the First and supplant his position?

Yes, Dacris thought, that was a much more profitable plan than plotting to destroy one simple slave.

K'heera made the final override adjustment on the last station in the egg-laying room and prepared to leave. Her whole body quivered in fear, she stank of it—how was it no one noticed? The things she did required courage and honor, but she felt neither brave nor honorable, only desperate.

Six months ago, if anyone had told her she would have found herself longing for the company of a human, she would have challenged that fool. But now, as she made adjustments to this complicated alien program, adjustments that were getting harder and harder to conceal, she longed to see Bruce's sly smile, to take heart from his casual confidence, his outstanding courage, and the honor he wore so easily. He was her true uncle, and the fear that threatened her resolve was partly for him. Where was he now? What was he enduring at the hands of these monsters?

*Don't think about that, l'il darlin',* she could hear him saying in her mind, the only place she could hear anything now. *We'll lay a hurtin' on these bastards, you'll see.*

She finished her work and slowed her breathing. It sickened her to think of the countless embryos nurtured nearly to hatching. What kind of a people devoured their own young? In shame, she remembered her sanctimonious criticism of the Honored Interrelator as she consumed a lower form of life. K'heera had thought she understood what was right and wrong then.

She shook her head, needing to be clear-minded now. She owed that to the Interrelator, she owed it to Bruce.

The Interrelator had done her part. Word was that she'd damaged barracks and freed some captives, including Weaver, who had killed a guard. K'heera knew that wouldn't have happened if not for the information she'd given Thunder, and was proud of that. The Simiu knew, too, that the Interrelator had used a weapon to slay another guard and save Weaver's life. She knew it and was glad and paused not a moment at that incongruity.

But that disruption might have meant terrible punishment for Bruce or Szu-yi, or anyone that was close to the Interrelator.

*Don't worry about that, l'il darlin',* Bruce assured her in her mind. *It's nothin' we can't handle.*

K'heera didn't want to think about what would happen when the eggs died. She refused to wonder if the innocent egg-layers would sicken in their pools. She wouldn't think about the soldiers coming for her, as they had for Bruce. She wouldn't let her mind wander—not even for a second—about what they would do to her when they determined she was responsible.

*Stop thinking. Just work.* She moved forward, then felt something odd, and nervously looked over her shoulder.

That's when she saw the new soldier who'd been put in charge of the hatchery. His very presence was enough to terrify the Industrious, and even the Chosen trainers seemed frightened of him. And now he was watching *her.*

*Did he see anything? Does he know what I'm doing?*

The green and gold alien watched her, then casually walked away as if he'd seen nothing of importance. She forced herself to turn and trot on to her next assignment. She longed for Bruce, for his smile, his odd way of signing, his calming adult assurance. But Bruce had been taken away.

*I'll lay a hurting on them,* she told herself. *Their punishment is nothing I can't handle.*

It was too late now to turn her back, either on the job Bruce had left her . . . or on the path of her own honor.

They made quite a procession—Tesa, Old Bear, First-Light, and the other five humans rescued from the Anuran camp. Around them strode the cohort, who were surrounded by a growing mass of curious Grus. The sporadic buffeting of vocal outbreaks was bone-jarring, even for Tesa.

When she finally spied Meg sitting between Jib and Weaver, the young woman had to school her face to keep it from showing the shock she felt at her friend's appearance. The older woman's skin was almost gray, and for the first time, the seventy-year-old biologist seemed frail. Tesa hugged her carefully, and was pleased at the strength in Meg's returning embrace.

"How are the others?" the Indian woman asked. "Have you seen them? Have you . . . seen Bruce?"

Meg nodded. "When I saw him last, he was fine. He'd been working with K'heera, trying to sabotage the food factory."

"Then K'heera's all right?"

The blue eyes saddened. "They took her nullifiers away when they first captured her. She's deaf, Tesa."

*No, she's not, she's Hearing* . . . Tesa thought for a second before she reoriented. K'heera had been *deafened*? With no one there to console her, relieve her pain and fear, or help her adjust to a whole new way of living?

"At least she knows Grus Sign Language," Meg continued. "She's been a big help to Bruce . . . before they were separated."

"I came to rescue you," Tesa signed with a wry expression. "Too bad you couldn't wait." She indicated the group standing awkwardly nearby. "I had to settle for what I could get."

The Russian woman grinned. "*Golubchik,* you brought out the cream of the crop! Javier is a wild foods gourmet! He kept our diets supplemented, and our morale up. . . ." She eyed Tesa's odd expression and trailed off.

"Why did they let you and Old Bear go, Meg?" Tesa asked,

Jib waved a hand at her, interrupting. "There's a whole lot been going on, mate, that you've missed."

His large eyes were brighter than she'd seen them in a long time. His whole expression was different—expectant, hopeful . . . almost euphoric. So, he *had* made contact with the Singers. She didn't know whether to be happy about that or sad.

"He's right. We have a *lot* to talk about, dear," Meg agreed, "but this discussion must be shared with everyone. Some of the Gray Winds helped us clear a 'story' circle"—for the first time, Tesa noticed the wide patch of bare sandy soil near them—"so we can convey the essence of our news with those who can't sign, and learn anything they might want to say."

Tesa nodded, then made herself comfortable between Meg and Weaver, her cohort settling onto their hocks behind her. Taller stood to the side with some of the other Grus leaders. Frost Moon, his cinnamon and white feathers gleaming in the sun, moved around the circle, handing the humans small sticks they could use to write in the sand. The extra effort made the ship's crew smile in appreciation. When Javier assumed the interpreter's job, Tesa nodded a curt "thank you" to him.

Suddenly there was a rustle of activity among the Wind people, then small net baskets appeared and Tesa remembered the *other* reason they were there—to eat! The sight of fresh food reminded her of how hungry she was, so for a while there was no conversation as the humans helped themselves to a variety of Trinity's tropical foods, including greens, fruits, tubers, and freshwater shellfish. They shared the bounty until nothing was left but shells, rinds, and remnants. Tesa caught Taller's eye and acknowledged his hospitality.

Finally, she scrubbed her hands in the sand, as the Grus began to preen. "That'll hold me," she signed. "How about the rest of you?"

Javier conveyed a Grus thank you to their benefactors, and all the Terrans copied it.

Then Jib sat up on his heels and told the story of his latest contact with the Singers. "They're frightened," he concluded, "but they're healthy. They've confused the Anurans with their old enemy, 'the Great Hunger,' and the terror they're living under is . . . terrible."

Tesa rubbed her forehead distractedly, remembering the frightening predator she'd imagined when they'd first found Taniwha stranded on the sandbar. "Jib, this monster they're afraid of, any idea if that thing is a real threat now? I kept wondering about that when we were wading through the River last night."

Javier hesitated in his translation, and for once he appeared unsettled. It almost made her smile. Finally, he scrawled a translation, and she watched the others pale.

The Maori shrugged. "Whenever they think of it, the memories are as fresh as yesterday. But they have no sense of time. Tesa, what are you thinking?"

She shook her head. "Maybe it's extinct, just a memory that frightens them."

"I'll try talking to them again," Jib offered, "but even if I can find out anything useful, I don't see what good it'll do."

"It's the longest long shot," she admitted, "but . . ." She hesitated, not wanting to admit to him she was thinking of something she'd seen in a dream. "I have to wonder . . . if they had anything to do with this monster's extinction. They've driven everyone else away from the River. If they *did,* might there be some hope that they could help defeat the Anurans?"

Jib's euphoria dimmed. "When the Singers tried, they failed. That's rattled them the most, since they *could* affect their old predator, once they became aware of its presence."

Weaver fluffed her feathers out. "The Healer would talk about the aliens when we worked together, remember, First-One?"

Meg nodded, looking pensive.

"She talked about their physical differences," the female avian continued. "How they took in moisture through their skin, how they laid clear, gelatinous eggs that had to be kept moist."

"Szu-yi talked about them incessantly," Meg admitted, "as if she wanted us to know as much about them as she did. We hated hearing about them, but it seemed to help her."

"She said they have two brains," Weaver signed matter-of-factly. "I thought that explained their madness, but the Healer said it was important, their two brains."

The elder woman agreed. "She was obsessed by that, their split brains. One's in their tail, like a big nerve cluster. She kept telling us to get word to K'heera so she could tell Thunder, so we did, but we couldn't see what difference it made."

"Thunder relayed it," Tesa assured her. "Do the Singers know that, Jib? Would it matter to them?"

"When they touch another mind, they study it first, so they might already know, but 'no stone unturned,' eh?"

Tesa sighed, frustrated, and waited for Javier to catch up with his transcribing. "If we attempt to free the Singers from the west end of the River, will they cooperate with you, Jib?"

"I don't know. I'll talk to them. . . ."

She wondered about the price he would end up paying for that contact. She turned to Meg. "So, how *did* you both get away?"

"We didn't *get away,* Tesa. We were released. The Glorious . . . that is, the First, the leader . . . wants to negotiate with you. His society doesn't believe in waging war that causes death. The price is more than he wants to pay. He sent us to tell you he's ready to talk, now."

The Indian woman felt color flood her face, but before she could respond Jib interjected excitedly, "Negotiate? He'll *negotiate*? That's *incredible!*"

The nonsigning humans began gesturing animatedly, talking so rapidly that Javier could not read their lips. It was confusing for them, trying to speak to each other and to him, when none of them could hear.

Finally, when he understood what they were trying to say, he told Tesa, "They're afraid it's a trap for *you.* They . . . *we* experienced how ruthless these people are. None of us believe he has any interest in negotiation, we think he just wants to get hold of you and squash any rebellion you could foment."

"He anticipated that concern," Meg explained. "He's willing to talk with anyone Tesa appoints as her representative. He doesn't expect her to come forward personally."

"I'll do it!" Jib volunteered, before Tesa could respond. "I've had training in negotiations at StarBridge, and I'm willing to take any chance if it will bring peace back to the World."

There was an excited exchange of signs among the Grus leaders and more heated discussion among the humans. Then Taller gave the Wind people's consensus. "The prey can't *negotiate* with the predator! While the prey sets terms, the predator eats."

"That's not always true," Jib signed respectfully. "The Blue Cloud people negotiated a truce with your ancestors, and only recently you made peace with the Hunters."

Taller's crown flared, but he couldn't deny that. It helped Jib's argument that Tesa herself had negotiated that last peace.

"I feel very awkward," Meg admitted, "having to convey the message of these . . . beings . . . who, frankly, I despise. The First has Bruce, Szu-yi, and Nadine separated from the others in a more secure area, *he* says, to protect *his* people from you, Tesa. But, it also puts them in the position of being valuable hostages."

"The very reason we should take up his offer," Jib insisted. "How else can we test his sincerity? If he takes your negotiator— me—hostage, then Tesa, you can do whatever you want in good conscience, since his offer is meaningless. But if it's sincere, we might be able to end this conflict! We might even be able to turn this into a First Contact! By the time the CLS gets here, we could be into a negotiated peace!"

The effects of the Singers' mental contact grew more apparent on the young man as his enthusiasm soared. Tesa caught sight of her grandfather's expression and inclined her head toward him, wanting to know his views.

"It's always tempting to talk peace," Old Bear assured Jib. "And while talking, active hostilities are usually ended. That's good. While they hold our people, we can hope that they'll be treated well. In the meantime, we can count the days until the CLS arrives, so they can bring trained diplomats to continue the negotiations we begin. It could be a good start. . . ."

"But . . ." Jib prodded.

"While we negotiate, they entrench. They still hold our people. They still live on the World, and learn about us through our own records. Years could pass before anything is decided. Time is on *their* side. Negotiating just buys them more."

"But we have to *try*!" Jib insisted. "On Earth, my people and yours fought their invaders well, and still, we lost. Our people died, our land was taken, our cultures nearly destroyed. How long did it take your ancestors to win back the Black Hills? You achieved *that* through *negotiation* hundreds of years after futile conflicts. We have a better choice now, and we've got to *try*!"

Old Bear smiled ruefully. "Your eloquence is a credit to your people, son. They'd be proud to hear you."

"I can do this," Jib assured Tesa, "I know it! Please!" He looked around for support, and spied Taller.

Tesa watched the white avian try to stare Jib down, but he couldn't. Ruffling his feathers, the leader told the human youth, "We want the World free of these beings as quickly as possible, however we must. And we trust Good Eyes to help us find the way to do it."

"*This* could be the way," Jib insisted, but seeing Taller's resistance, turned back to Tesa. "You're not going to let them put this all on you? That's a hell of a thing to carry, mate."

*I'm an Interrelator,* she thought frantically. *My job is to speak for the people.* She struggled with the decision, wishing the choices would go away, wishing she would wake up and this would be just another bad dream she needed to interpret.

"Please, Tesa," Jib implored, "let me have a shot at this."

She rose abruptly, gathering her old star quilt around her out of habit. "I've heard you!" she signed, more abruptly than she'd intended. "I've listened to everything you've all said. I need some time to think this through. . . . We'll discuss it again, when I have a solution."

Tesa felt her head hammering. Her inner soul howled with laughter. Solutions? What solutions? She clung to the quilt and marched across the grassland as the army of Grus parted before her like the Red Sea before Moses. She walked alone, heading for nowhere, feeling as though she understood nothing. A warm wind whipped around her as the eyes of a thousand people and a handful of humans watched her, until they were far behind her on the endless plain. But they were still watching, she knew, still waiting, for the answer only a *heyoka* could find.

# CHAPTER 21

◆

# *Heyoka* Medicine

"Negotiate, *like hell!*" Martin Brockman mouthed.

Javier had to sympathize.

"They've still got the *Brolga*, her Captain, and half our crew! There's no way we'll go along with that decision."

Crouched, Javier wrote, "What can you do alone?"

"I'm not alone. Moshe, Chris, Noriko, *and* Carlotta agree with me. *We're* not negotiating."

"The Interrelator needs our support," the ethnobotanist wrote.

Martin stopped Javier's hand. "If I owe anybody in this place, it's *you*. We all do. You found those leaves that cleaned out our systems, made sure the Interrelator took us along. . . ."

Javier shook his head. He'd only done his part.

"Okay, okay! We'll see what she has to say, and decide then. Good enough?"

Javier nodded grudgingly, but as Martin walked away toward the others, the scientist had mixed feelings.

"Suppressing rebellion?" Meg signed, appearing beside him. Old Bear was with her, his young eyes seeming incongruous in his worn, old face.

Javier shrugged tiredly.

She linked an arm through his, while talking with the other. "Ever regret answering my invitation?"

He remembered how Weaver looked, flying to freedom on his feather grafting. He remembered, too, a dark figure in the water, pulling him to safety. "Whatever's happened . . . whatever *happens* . . . I'm glad to be a part of it. I'm glad to be here."

"I wanted to say something to you about that meeting with Tesa. . . . She's been on Trinity so long she's . . . out of sync with humans. She must've seemed a little rough around the edges. . . ."

"Don't apologize for her," Javier insisted. "She doesn't have to cater to human needs. The Grus are her people now, Meg. She belongs here. She belongs to them. She's very lucky. Believe me, I only wish I could . . . offer her something she couldn't get from . . . her people. . . ."

"What the hell does that mean?" Meg asked bluntly.

He turned away. "If I were ten years younger . . ."

She patted his scarred cheek. "Javier, dear, why don't you concern yourself with something *important,* like, will there be a free Trinity a year from now?"

"Ever try one of these?" Old Bear asked suddenly, handing the botanist a thin, orange leaf. "They're good."

Javier was so relieved to change the subject that he took the leaf and chewed it, barely giving it a glance. Citrus and mint flooded his mouth, the taste surprisingly familiar. The Interrelator had made him eat these when he'd gone light-headed. He'd never taste that flavor again without thinking of her. Why did that make his chest tighten up?

"The Wind people call it 'blood-of-the-World,' " Old Bear signed. "They say the Sun Family sent it, and eating it honors them. When

I first came here, I ate it out of respect. But after a while I realized that eating something makes it part of you, so eating this plant could make me part of the World."

"Don't you miss Earth, Old Bear?" Javier asked. The Lakota, like traditional Navahos, had strong ties to their homelands.

"Yes. I miss my home, the Black Hills, my family." He thumped his chest. "But I brought them with me in my heart."

Javier had nothing of Earth except the memories of other people's lives.

"Know what a *heyoka* is, son?" Old Bear asked.

"Yes, a contrary. You're a *heyoka*?"

The elder grinned, his lined face youthful for a moment. "That's probably what keeps me here, when most men my age would rather be retired, taking it easy. My granddaughter's one, too."

He stared at the elder, surprised. He knew the Interrelator followed the old religion, but . . .

"Worst thing about it is," Old Bear confided, "you always end up approaching everything the wrong way. You say what you don't mean. Walk away from the very thing you should walk toward. Sleep in the arms of someone you never thought of making love to. We can't help it, that's just the way we are."

Javier watched the old man's signs, trying to figure out what he was really saying.

"You'd think Tesa would be out there with a young, handsome buck wrapped up in that blanket with her. But no, she's running this thing around and around her head, carrying it alone. . . ."

It was a huge burden, Javier thought, to be the only Interrelator on an invaded planet. . . .

Old Bear moved away then, and tugged on Meg's elbow.

Before leaving, she stood on tiptoe to kiss Javier's jaw. "Want to know what to offer Tesa? How about your strength?"

The old Lakota looped his arm through Meg's, and together they disappeared into the feathered crowd.

For years Javier had believed there was no point in letting others get too close when there'd always be barriers, physically and emotionally. He'd never been Deaf, and he would never be Hearing. He'd spent his life searching for something he couldn't find, couldn't even name, a sense of belonging, of being *part* of something. It was too improbable that he might stumble onto it on this distant planet, long after he'd given up searching.

Glancing about, he suddenly realized he wasn't alone. A group of White Winds had gathered casually around him. They seemed to vary in ages, one obviously just a yearling, the others of indeterminate years. Except for one. The tallest avian flanking his right had a dusting of cinnamon around his head. "You're Lightning," Javier signed confidently.

"Yes, First-Light," the youngster responded.

"And you are . . . ?" he asked an older one on his left.

"Flies-Too-Fast," the avian signed, lifting his head.

"I am None-So-Pretty," a small female near Lightning told him. "And this is Frost Moon"—she indicated the yearling with her bill—"Snowberry, Hurricane, Winter Bloom, and Scorched."

*Interesting,* thought Javier, as he struggled to memorize their subtle physical differences. This was the Interrelator's cohort, the avians she flew with, her most loyal companions. "It is *nice* to meet *you,*" None-So-Pretty told him.

Frost Moon jostled the little female and stared at her oddly. "How do we know *that*?"

"We don't have to know it," Scorched signed, ruffling the gray tertial feathers that gave her her name. "Good Eyes told us to say it to new humans. It's a human *policy.*"

"You mean *courtesy,*" Lightning corrected smoothly, and they all peered at him, their crowns spreading, acknowledging his superior knowledge.

The group walked together for a while until Javier asked, "Where are we going?" They were clearly steering him.

"Weaver wants you," Lightning signed.

"It's nice to be wanted," Javier agreed, making the youngster's crown shrink.

"Good Eyes said you fixed Weaver's severed feathers," Flies-Too-Fast commented. His signs implied that he'd discounted the story as propaganda. "She said you made Weaver fly again."

"I helped," Javier told him.

"That's good, to be able to fix broken feathers!" the big male, Hurricane, told Lightning, as though this talent had just elevated him into the ranks of sentient beings.

Lightning seemed to reserve judgment, asking instead, "Is your mate dead?" Every member of the cohort stared down at him.

"Excuse me?" Javier responded, nonplussed.

"You're a mature human. You should be mated. Is she dead? Or did you abandon her on Earth?"

"Wait a minute," Javier begged. "I've *never* had . . . a mate. I've had *friends.* . . . You know about human friends?"

"Of course!" Lightning signed haughtily, as the cohort's attention returned to him. "I grew up with humans. I understand their relationships thoroughly. Before I was hatched, First-One-There had a friend, Puff. Now, Old Bear's her friend. And Good Eyes has had *lots* of friends. Jib, for example."

"He still *is* her friend," Flies-Too-Fast reminded him.

"Yes, but at StarBridge, he was such a *special* friend, he and Good Eyes shared a *shelter*! Of course," he addressed this to Javier, "humans share shelters casually. Good Eyes has often shared shelters—with Jib, Relaxed, the Fisher. . . ."

"Really?" Javier asked, intrigued.

"Don't forget First-One-There, the Healer, Teacher, and Old Bear, too!" Snowberry chimed in.

"And what about all those strangers sharing her shelter last night!" Winter Bloom added.

*Oh,* Javier thought, finally remembering how many different relationships the Grus sign "friend" covered.

The entire group suddenly seemed quite disapproving as Lightning stared at Javier. "Usually, only the *cohort* shares that shelter with Good Eyes. . . ."

*Threw you guys out of bed, did we?* He mulled over the Interrelator's many "friends," and wondered if any of them were *really* special. Then he wondered why he should care.

"*We're* Good Eyes' most special friends of all," Flies-Too-Fast insisted. "She *flies* with us!"

"It would be hard to beat that," Javier admitted.

"Haven't you ever flown with anyone?" Lightning asked

"No, afraid not."

The cohort exchanged private signs, probably pitying him, he thought. Never having mated, never having flown with a loved one. He should have been amused as they defined his sudden innocence, but instead he felt surprisingly despondent.

"But Good Eyes says you're *old*!" None-So-Pretty announced with an impatient ruffle of feathers. "You must have had a mate *once*. Don't you know how to court?"

"I thought the people only mated when they found the one partner in all the World that was right for them?" he asked. The cohort agreed that that was true. "Well, humans can be like that, too. That's why I haven't mated."

The avians discussed this among themselves.

"Did the Interrelator ask you to find this out from me?" Javier finally asked them, trying not to seem hopeful.

Lightning fluffed out, shedding a tiny cinnamon feather that drifted lazily toward the ground. "Oh, no! She says humans think we're 'prying' when we ask personal questions. We . . . have a difference of opinion on this."

"Taller wanted to know," Flies-Too-Fast volunteered.

Lightning seemed alarmed. "I don't think you were supposed to tell him *that*."

The older avian seemed confused. "What difference does it make? He doesn't have a mate. That's all that concerned Taller."

Suddenly the youngsters stopped and Javier found himself facing Weaver. Her beauty filled his heart. *Good work, kids.*

Taller preened nearby, as if he had no interest in this human, but the leader's casual actions covered a keen eye that stayed trained on the human.

"First-Light, what a surprise!" Weaver signed, as if she weren't responsible for his arrival here.

Helplessly entranced by her, he dug in his pocket for a gift. Wrapped in a broad, sturdy leaf were two delicate flowers he'd found. Wonderfully fragrant, the tiny, trumpetlike jewels were a rich purple brightly accented with a splash of yellow.

"Oh," she signed, genuinely surprised, "they're lovely!"

Suddenly the entire cohort *and* Taller were staring at them.

"These are too beautiful to eat!" Weaver insisted.

"Not too beautiful for you," he signed brazenly.

As Weaver touched the blossoms, her mate stabbed the ground, flinging sod in the air. Javier pretended not to see that.

"You'll get us in trouble with your courting, First-Light," Weaver scolded halfheartedly.

"I'll be more careful," he promised with equal insincerity.

"You need to turn that romantic charm on someone worthy of your attentions," she told him. "Some *unmated* female."

"You think I give my heart away so easily?" he asked.

Ignoring that, she folded the protective leaf around the flowers. "I know someone who might name this plant for you."

He thought she meant one of the Gray Wind healers as she wrapped her wing around him, then turned them around. When she dropped her wing, he saw that they weren't in the center of the huge flock, as he'd thought, but on its rim. A vast, autumn-colored savannah stretched before him, empty.

No, not empty.

Herds of large animals grazed in the distance. Between the flock and the herd stood something colored like Trinity, but different . . . brighter. With a start, he recognized the familiar star quilt. The Interrelator was out there on that grassy plain, wrapped in her blanket, struggling to make her difficult decisions. Her aloneness tugged at him.

"Good Eyes could name your flower, First-Light."

"Weaver," he signed flatly, "this won't work."

The avian didn't respond, simply stared at him.

"She doesn't want me."

"She doesn't know what she wants," Weaver assured him.

"We're too different. . . ."

"Are human males and females *supposed* to be the same?"

He grew exasperated. "Our ages . . ."

Her head shot up; she was annoyed. "I'd heard humans were peculiar, but really, First-Light, you insult my partner!"

"Weaver, please, try to understand. . . ."

"I understand *this*. Taller and I have lived with Good Eyes, raised a child with her, perhaps our last child. She could not be closer to us if she hatched from our own egg. Her spirit suffers from loneliness and the burden of her station, a condition we can't relieve."

"I know. But . . ."

"And all those days you and I spent together, enslaved, the nights we passed in conversation. . . . Did you think I learned nothing about you in all that time? Do you think that my people are simple because our wings can't leave our World?"

He'd offended her, and that hurt him. "I wouldn't have come here to learn from you if I thought that. . . ."

"Do you find Good Eyes unattractive?"

"No! She's very attractive!"

"And *brave*! Don't you think she's brave?"

He sighed. He had lain in the dark the night she'd leafleted the camp, asking Weaver question after question about the Interrelator. When the woman herself had actually appeared later, he'd wondered what primal magic the avian had called on to bring her to them. "I would be a liar if I said her courage didn't win my heart the first day I saw her."

"I knew that!" the Grus signed triumphantly. "I just wanted to see you say it. Then, why won't you . . . ?"

Suddenly Taller loomed into view. "Friend of mine, are you *begging* this *stranger* to approach our partner?"

"I'll handle this!" she snapped. The Grus leader stepped back, stunned.

*Oh, great,* Javier thought. *With a little more effort I could create both an interspecies crisis and a marital spat!*

Weaver stared at Javier full-faced. "The World could be home to you, my friend, and all the people your family. Or you could live here forever and still be as rootless as the empty man who left Earth not so long ago."

Her words cut into his soul with cruel insight.

"Weaver," Taller addressed her again, this time gently, "come along. You've done what you could."

She stared at Javier for a moment longer, then finally turned her back and let Taller preen her. Javier wanted to say something, make her understand, but as usual, when he most needed them, words dried up on him. The cohort huddled together, but when they saw him watching, they, too, turned away.

Javier gazed around the savannah, at the Grus huddling together in pairs and cohorts, at the humans who had formed relationships and allegiances even under the worst circumstances. The only two beings on this plain who stood alone were himself . . . and the Interrelator.

He exhaled in a rush and stopped thinking, finally allowing his body to do what it had wanted to all along, and walked toward the solitary figure draped in an autumn-colored quilt.

Tesa's head told her to follow Jib's advice. The worst that would happen is that they would lose some time and Jib would be captured. The best might mean a reasonable end to an unreasonable situation. An end without bloodshed. Why did she find that so hard to believe?

*Too easy,* she thought for the hundredth time.

Jib would be a good negotiator, he'd had excellent training. She could picture him standing firm before the invaders, presenting the White Winds' demands, making the Anurans accept their terms.

That's where the image started cracking around the edges.

The Wind people would be waiting for the invaders to leave, but they wouldn't. Not while negotiations were still going on. They'd hold on to Tesa's people, and the days would drag on, with tiny concessions to keep them hopeful, keep them busy.

When the CLS finally arrived they'd take over with more experienced diplomats. *Could* they *make* the invaders leave? How? Sheer force? For all Tesa knew, the invaders were evenly matched with anything the League Irenics might carry, they were just loath to use their power to kill. She couldn't see an end.

*I can't do it,* she thought. *I don't know enough. I can't tell those people how to save their World. I don't know how!* Her chest tightened up so hard she could barely breathe.

Shutting her eyes, she willed her fear away. Blanking her mind, she watched the herd of Quakers she'd been halfheartedly observing as they placidly devoured entire fern trees at the edge of the grassland. Their massive size and the incredible confidence they exuded as they went about their everyday activities helped calm her. *They* didn't care about the Anuran invaders. To the huge orange and tan animals, each enemy was nothing but a bump on the landscape to be trampled.

Tesa imagined the huge herd storming through the Anuran colony, flattening buildings, crushing ships, laying waste valuable equipment, creating chaos and irreparable damage just like the malleable Leaf-Eaters had so obligingly done to the small camp she'd raided. Unfortunately the Quakers weren't nearly as cooperative. They considered anything that interfered with their enormous food requirements an annoyance. Nothing short of an aerial bombing raid would motivate them to move from wherever they were currently feeding. If there was any way to communicate with them, the Wind people had no idea what it was.

*Where do Quakers sleep at night?* Tesa wondered. *Do they take cover in the forest, or just settle down in the open?* The matriarchs stayed on the outside, with the younger herd members pushed toward the center where they could be protected. The few bulls that hovered around the fringes might've seemed like heads of the harem, but Tesa had been watching long enough to know that the matriarchs kept them there, that no male was allowed near a female, except by the oldest female's approval.

*Where does a Quaker sleep at night?* She smiled, remembering the ancient joke. *Anywhere she damned pleases.*

Suddenly the herd lifted their heads to gaze in her direction, so she turned to see what they were watching. A human had emerged from the flock and was approaching her. Tesa was startled when she realized it was First-Light.

*What now?* She knew that the humans she'd rescued last night were dead against negotiating. Had they sent him out here to argue the situation further? She felt the pressure like a physical force crushing her, as heavy as a Quaker. How long had it been since she'd felt buoyant on Trinity?

She turned away from him just as he moved beside her. It was rude, but she couldn't help it, she couldn't stand another litany of complaints, demands, or a new piece of bad news.

When he didn't try to get her attention for several minutes, her curiosity got the better of her. Whatever it was wouldn't go away by wishing it. "What's the matter?" she signed brusquely.

He stared at her as if he had no idea what she meant.

"Why are you here?" she clarified. "Are you bringing a message? Does somebody want me?"

He paused for a maddening amount of time before carefully answering, "I didn't come to bring a message."

She exhaled wearily. "Then why are you here?"

He paused, as if talking to her was harder than anything he'd done in a long time. "I'm here . . . for you."

She blinked, totally confused, completely missing the point.

"You looked like you could use a friend," he explained.

*A friend?* "Is that what you're here for? To be my friend?"

"If you want, Interrelator."

She shook her head; that title was still so foreign to her. "Don't call me that. I don't feel like an Interrelator right now. I feel . . . totally *unqualified* . . . to do what they want me to do. . . ." She stopped herself. She shouldn't be admitting this to anyone. The humans needed to have confidence in her.

"Who would be qualified to deal with invading aliens?" he asked. "The CLS has *never* faced this problem before, so all you can do is what seems right to you. Your best guess will be as good as anyone's."

His simple statement seemed to clarify the problem, if only for the moment. She changed the subject. "Call me 'Tesa.' No one calls me 'Interrelator.' "

"You were named after White Buffalo Woman, from Lakota legend," he signed.

"Yes, that's right," she agreed, surprised that he knew.

"To the Grus you are 'Good Eyes'—because your eyes are like theirs?"

"That started it. I kept the name because Taller said . . ."

His words came to her as though he'd signed them yesterday. *Good Eyes, you see what others can't, you see the truth, even when it's upside down, even when it's backward.*

"He said . . . I'd earned it. . . ." She forced down the lump in her throat, and blinked until she no longer felt on the verge of tears. "But . . . I can't . . . see the answer to this. . . ." Why did she say that? Because he was here? Because the only time she'd felt any respite from this nightmare was a pleasant moment when she'd accidentally found herself in his arms?

"What do you *want* to do?" he asked suddenly, his piercing, predator's gaze holding hers intently.

"I think, probably . . . we should try to do what Jib . . ."

He stopped her. "No. What do you *want* to do? In your *heart*. What do you *see* yourself, all of us, doing?"

Tesa searched inside herself, and her hands answered without hesitation. "We need to hit them hard, take them by surprise on so many fronts they'll be too divided to deal with everything."

"Fight?" He seemed surprised.

"You asked me what my *heart* wanted," she reminded him. "Well, my *heart* remembers old invasions and broken treaties and eloquent leaders who traveled far and spoke for days and died of broken hearts when they could not save their people. My heart doesn't want to talk . . . except to say, 'Leave the World.' "

Javier thought about that.

"I can't just follow my heart," she assured him, sorry she'd been so blunt. "I didn't spend all that time on StarBridge to resort to brute force the first time I'm confronted with a difficult problem. . . . But . . . if we send Jib . . . they'll *take* him, I *know* it. They've already got my friends, my grandmother. . . . Jib's like a brother to me. . . . They'll *use* him. . . ." She was back to the circular argument, like a snake eating its tail.

He'd signed nothing while she rambled on, and finally her signs trailed away. First-Light waited until she was still, then finally asked, "You're a *heyoka*. What does your medicine tell you to do?"

Her medicine?

That simply, it became clear to her. Tesa would have realized it herself, but she'd been too busy trying to be too many different people for everyone who needed her. She was a *heyoka*. Her conflict stemmed from the fact that what she wanted to do— wage a futile war—was the exact opposite of what she *should* do—negotiate. That was the source of her turmoil. His question reminded her of what she should have never forgotten. Why hadn't her grandfather said anything to her? Because he was a *heyoka,* too, of course.

"Do you follow the old ways?" she asked.

"I respect them, but I wasn't raised with them."

"How much do you know about the Lakota?"

"I earned my doctorate studying the use of traditional Lakota medicine herbs."

She glanced at him sideways, the way the Grus did. "You're not an anthropologist?"

He smiled slightly and spelled, "Ethnobotanist."

Yes. She remembered Rob talking about him.

"Good Eyes," he prodded her, "what are you going to do?"

"Follow my medicine," she told him.

He nodded. "Then we'll fight."

A great calm settled over her. There was a lot to do. "*I'll* fight. I have to."

"You won't fight alone, Good Eyes. The Wind people won't let you. And we won't let you, either."

"I can't ask anyone else to follow my path."

They were face-to-face, signing as privately as if they were surrounded. To her left, the massive Quakers moved on, the ground, even at this distance, rumbling beneath her. To her right, the Wind people went about their business, studiously ignoring the two humans, but Tesa knew most of them were covertly watching, especially Taller and Weaver. She stared into the dark eyes of this stranger, noticing again the gold earring.

He'd followed her eyes. "I can remove it."

She furrowed her brow. "Remove it?"

"You can sever the mechanism. It's not hard. . . ."

"But then you'd be . . ." He'd do that . . . for her?

When she didn't continue, he reached up to his ear, but she stopped him, her hand covering his. "No! I mean . . . I don't want you to. It's not important." As soon as she'd signed that, she knew it was the truth. She hung on to his hand, feeling his warmth, the same warmth that had surrounded her last night.

Tesa found herself staring at the jagged scar cutting diagonally across his cheek. Impulsively, she released his hand to touch it. "How did you get this?"

"Eagle," he signed succinctly.

She jerked her hand away as if she'd been burned. *"Eagle?"*

"A Hopi raptor rehabilitator, who was also a medicine man, wanted to release a recovered golden eagle," he told her. "I went with him. When he let the bird go, I was filming. She came at me, right for my face, for the gold patch on my cheek. At least, that's what I thought. She cut me, then took off. The medicine man said the patch had nothing to do with it, that she'd marked me for something special."

"The scar looks like . . . lightning. A sign of the Thunder Beings. . . ." Her dreams of the mythical creatures had made her a *heyoka*. Had they marked him for her?

Javier moved closer. "Whatever your decision, Good Eyes . . . let me be part of it."

She reached for the mark on his face again, then stopped her hand. Her indecision was gone. In answer to his question, she opened her arms, inviting him inside her blanket. He understood immediately what that meant; she could see the surprise, then the delight, on his normally staid face.

He moved inside the circle of her arms, sliding his own around her, pulling her to him in a strong, sure embrace, pressing his lightning-marked cheek against hers.

She wrapped the quilt around them like wings, absorbing the hidden force of his desire, taking strength from it. When his mouth finally joined with hers, the weight that had been pressing down on her changed into energy. Her spirit was electrified, as if the Thunder Beings had given her their lightning power to use against her enemy.

Tesa and First-Light clung to each other in the privacy of the blanket, tracing words on each other's back, sharing something neither of them had ever known, while the gathered flocks of the Wind people and a small scattering of humans went about their business, pretending not to see.

Except for Taller, who called to the skies, proclaiming his mate as the finest matchmaker of all their people. Who else had ever brought about the pairing of such a difficult species?

Weaver joined him, and the others took up the call, pair by pair, until the entire plain vibrated with the power of thousands of avian voices. The other humans reeled under the onslaught, but Javier and Tesa never noticed, thinking only that the strange feeling rocketing through them came from within.

# CHAPTER 22
◆
# By Dawn's Early Light

Atle pulled himself out of his pool slowly, trying not to wake his wife, but he'd barely set foot on the ledge before her eyes were open. "Go back to sleep. It's not even dawn."

"You haven't slept at all," she sang.

He'd dozed, but whenever he did, he heard mournful, alien music and jerked awake, searching for it futilely with his keen hearing. When had he last slept the night through? Oh, yes— before he'd demoted Dacris. Before the humans had escaped. Before he'd willingly released two more.

The First reached for his garment. He'd eat something. He never did get dinner last night, with the emergency Council meeting. . . .

Leaving the sleeping room, he padded quietly into the pantry. The Council had decided to wait twelve hours. If the humans didn't agree to negotiate by then, Atle would have to take action. He didn't mind moving against the humans and their avian allies— he'd anticipated that from the beginning. What concerned him was the willingness of the Council to accept the argument that the humans would only respond to greater force. This time, he would have to kill some.

It'd been hundreds of years since they'd approached war with this attitude. But the humans had opened a floodgate of anger with their wanton brutality, and the Council felt that they had to assert their power now, to make the humans yield.

Atle had agreed, but the escape of the avian and a handful of humans had weakened his position. If he didn't gain it back through strength, he could be removed. Dacris was still his successor. What Atle needed was to successfully subjugate the humans with as few deaths as possible—that would turn this into the success it was destined to be.

The Interrelator could still follow her training and negotiate. That would solve everything. Several prominent members of the Chorus were waiting to begin the negotiations. Once they began, he would have time to pinpoint her position, and capture her. Without her, the avians could not support an organized resistance, and the other humans would lose heart. *She* was the key. The perfect persuader.

When he entered the brightly lit pantry, Arvis and Lene were there, packing food into a case. She was heavy with egg, her lovely back brilliantly colored with the glow of impending motherhood. Both jumped, startled by his sudden appearance.

"Arvis?" he asked. "What are you doing up at this hour?"

His son blinked nervously, and Lene spoke for him. "The Simiu wasn't allowed to leave the hatchery last night. . . ."

"I know," he stopped her. "After the escape, her staying here wouldn't look right."

"Arvis wants to bring her something to eat. I told him he shouldn't worry about her anymore, but . . ."

"That's fine, Lene," Atle assured her. "He's just being responsible. She has special dietary needs, and she's a valuable commodity. It wouldn't do for her to become ill."

He patted Arvis' shoulder. "Go feed your servant, son. Make sure she's well cared for, so she stays productive."

Arvis relaxed. "Father, can I fix something for you? Lene

should eat, too, but she insisted on helping me."

Could this ambitious female have actually developed some affection for his son? Or was she merely trying to keep him out of trouble? She hadn't picked the best house to be allied with, after all. "Why don't you prepare both of us something to eat, Arvis? After all, daughter"—he turned his marbled eyes on her—"your body must stay strong to protect my grandchild."

Happy to be of service, Arvis bustled about the pantry, pulling out fresh eggs and his father's favorite marinade. Lene sat beside the First, obviously pleased to share a meal with him, despite his tarnished reputation.

Tesa opened her eyes in the dark. Her dreams had been remarkably peaceful. There were no bloody Rivers, no floating corpses. Instead, she'd dreamed of music, hearing it inside her mind as clearly as if Doctor Blanket had sent it. There'd been the phrases of popular songs she'd only ever felt the bass to, snatches of symphonies, and of course Mozart. She'd even heard the lilting melodies of the *siyotanka*, the Lakota courting flute. There'd been Navaho chants and, not surprisingly, war dances. What a curious dream.

Easing out of Javier's arms, she peered out of the shelter to see the stars. *Around oh four hundred,* she realized. She should get up soon. She had things to do. Preparations to make.

Glancing outside the shelter, she saw Flies-Too-Fast keeping watch among the clustered cohort, the others either lying on the ground or standing on one foot, heads tucked, asleep. She ducked back inside and edged closer to the only other occupant. She'd been amused when the rest of the humans revealed their own quickly assembled lean-tos, assuring her privacy again. She was sure, however, that her cohort wasn't yet sanguine about her newest roommate. Tesa shifted, trying to settle back down, but finally had to admit she was too wired to go back to sleep.

Javier opened his eyes, then pulled her against him, as if to make her stop moving. "Time?" he signed. She held up four fingers and he grimaced. "I'm too old to get up this early."

She raised an eyebrow. "You weren't too old to spend half the night . . ."

"Never mind," he interrupted, smiling.

"Did you dream?" she asked.

He paused, thinking, then his brow furrowed. "No."

Tesa gazed around the lean-to for a minute, then finally asked, "What kind of predator would the Quakers have?"

He thought about that, then shook his head. "Time. Injury. I don't know. Is that what's keeping you awake?"

"If there was something big enough to prey on the Quakers, we might be able to simulate it. Scare the Quakers into . . . I shouldn't be thinking like that. Just because the Quakers aren't cooperative doesn't give me the right to manipulate them. . . ."

He watched her for a moment, then asked, "You're worried?"

"Shouldn't I be? I'm asking the Grus and the Aquila to do something they've never done—fight as a unified force."

Neither of them said anything for a while, and she knew they were both remembering Jib's warning.

*Tesa, this is wrong! You're changing their culture. That's not what an Interrelator is supposed to do!*

She remembered, too, his final prediction.

*If you go through with this, they'll be killed. It'll be your responsibility!*

She might've backed down then, except for Taller. The Wind people, he'd announced, were ready to take back the River of Fear from the invaders—from the very Spirits themselves if they had to. If Good Eyes refused to lead them, he would do it himself.

"I think we've got a good chance," Javier signed.

*To tweak the giant's nose?* she thought. Everyone except Jib had been enthusiastic, ready to act. Tesa closed her eyes, trying to shut out her regrets. Javier pulled her close again, and she wondered, would they be here, together, in twenty-four hours?

Finally, she sat back up. "We've got to get ready. We can't wait till dawn. . . ."

"I know," he agreed, sitting tailor-fashion and scrubbing his face with his hands. "When this is over . . . is there a chance . . . we might be able to spend some time together . . . alone?"

His optimism raised her spirits and she wondered if that was why he asked. "Depends on what you mean by 'alone.' Without humans? Or without the Wind people?"

He laughed lightly. "I know better than that. I meant other humans."

"Oh, we'll have lots of privacy back home, in the marsh. I have my own shelter . . . it's next to Taller and Weaver's. . . ." She grinned at his expression. "Be patient! Taller will get used to you in time. Next spring, we'll go to the caldera. . . ."

"Where you raised Thunder? I'd like to see that."

*We'll have the whole World to explore*, she thought wistfully, *if we live through today*. Digging around in the corner of the shelter for her small woven basket, Tesa pulled out her battered hairbrush and her face paints. Running the brush through her long, dark hair, she tied it back tight, then laid out her paints. She glanced up, feeling Javier watching her.

"Ever have your face painted?" she asked.

"No," he admitted. "During ceremonies, I just observed."

"You sure you're not an anthropologist?" she teased, and then colored his face, using her own pattern. Except for the scar on his cheek. She painted that white, the lightning mark prominent against the black covering most of his face. Tesa wanted the Spirits to see it, so they would protect him.

Jib stepped off the alien sled, slipping the sound nullifiers from his ears. The sudden rush of River noise was disconcerting and his ears popped.

"I don't like leaving you here," Meg complained in her thick Slavic accent. It would be an hour before sunrise. The Moons all hovered low over the water, painting it with their dim light.

"That makes us even, mum," Jib agreed. "I don't like *any* of this. Isn't there *any* way to change her mind?"

"If Tesa doesn't act," Meg said patiently, "she'll have a hard time holding the Grus back. At least this way, she can orchestrate them, get them to work together. . . ."

"It's not right," he insisted.

She shook her head. "We'll just have to hope. . . ."

"And what'll *you* be doing when everything hits the fan?"

She looked him straight in the eye. "My best."

"Right in the middle of it, eh, mum?" He tried not to sound recriminating, but he couldn't help it.

"It won't be the first time. You're sure they'll come?"

"The Singers . . . ? Yes, they'll come."

"And you'll be safe with them in the west end of the River?"

He shrugged. Tesa wanted him to take the captive Singers as far from the action as he could get them. She was afraid they might panic if things went badly. Their mental emanations might not have any effect on the Anurans, but their terrified thoughts could adversely affect humans, as well as any creature of Trinity.

"They'll go if I urge them," he said noncommittally.

"If we knock out the force-field, we'll let you know, and you can guide them through to the sea."

Another temporary refuge. When winter came, the sea would be too cold for them. They depended on the warmer River, then.

"Jib," Meg said firmly, pulling his attention back.

"Yes, mum?"

"Be careful, dear. I'll be worried about you."

As they hugged good-bye, he thought, *Not as worried as I'll be about you.*


"Bruce! Bruce! Wake up! Please, wake up!"

The voice in his ear was tinny, like bad radio reception. He rolled over on the hard pallet.

"Bruce, *please!*"

He blinked, turned back, felt a warm body, and wrapped his arms comfortably around it. "S'okay, darlin'," he mumbled. "We're not late. Let's sleep a little longer." A sharp pain shot through his thigh and his eyes snapped open. Szu-yi was pressed up against him, staring at him wild-eyed. She'd pinched him to wake him up. "What's the matter?" He peered past the doctor and saw Tesa's grandmother, Nadine, hovering nearby.

"I'm sorry, Bruce, I tried to keep her still," Nadine apologized. "The poor dear hasn't slept a wink all night."

"What's the matter, Szu-yi?" he asked gently. There wasn't much left of the stern, no-nonsense doctor Bruce had once known. He never thought he'd miss that person, but this pathetic, terrified creature broke his heart. He stroked her hair gently.

"They're coming! Oh, Bruce, they're coming! It's terrible, so terrible. They're coming to get us. . . ."

"Sssshhhh," he soothed. Szu-yi suffered from repetitive nightmares. "I won't let them take you."

"Not *them!*" she hissed, then glanced around. The locked, guarded room was empty but for the three of them. "*Tesa's* coming, with the Grus! They'll be killed. . . ."

Nadine and Bruce stared at one another. He'd learned long ago not to discount the power of dreams . . . but a madwoman's?

Suddenly Szu-yi pulled herself together. "Our nullifiers. Will they last? Are they good enough?"

"I checked them yesterday," he assured her. "They're fine."

"Good. Good." She tried to act businesslike. "They're coming for us. . . ."

"Then, we'd better be ready," he told her. She nodded and Nadine did as well.

"Bruce," she said in a childlike voice, "why do I keep hearing music?"

"You mean, like the Anurans' voices?"

She shook her head.

"She's been hearing music for days," Nadine explained.

"It's so sad, it breaks my heart. Beautiful, sad music." Szu-yi turned away, obviously listening.

Bruce remembered *hearing* that music once, a few lifetimes ago. He hugged Szu-yi and made her lie down. "It's the River Spirits, darlin'. They want you to rest."

"The River Spirits? Oh, good. They're from Trinity." She shut her eyes, while Bruce and Nadine lay awake, waiting.

K'heera stood on her hind legs to peer out the narrow windows in the room she'd been sequestered in. It was dawn, and Father Sun was streaking the sky with color. She'd been locked in this tiny room with the once handsome Kh'arhh'tk and his two surviving drum dancers, but she might as well have been left alone. Shorn of their hair and painfully thin from being forced to eat animal protein, the dancers stayed as far from her as they could remove themselves, even keeping their backs to her as they slept. Oddly enough, that didn't bother her. What did bother her was that they'd been brought to work in the hatchery as it was about to fail. They'd be caught in the backlash, and blamed along with her.

Her purple eyes searched the tree line, searching for Thunder, but could see nothing. Desperate, she signed anyway.

"The hatchery has been irreversibly damaged. All the eggs will die. In a few hours, I will no longer be able to hide the problems. This may be the last time I . . ." Feeling a gust of air on her back, she quickly sat down.

But it was only Lene and Arvis. The dancers were watching the two red-and-blues suspiciously, but when the Anurans gestured at them to leave the room, they obeyed. K'heera glanced quickly over her shoulder toward the window, then followed the others.

Their small sleeping quarters must've been originally designed as a storage area, K'heera thought, since it opened up onto the large room where the hatchery's Industrious had their meals. The workers were filing in now, still fastening their clothes, many still damp from their sleeping pools.

Some of the dullest shuffled over to her and she adjusted fastenings on their clothing that they'd attached crookedly. More highly skilled servants brought in meals. K'heera was grateful that the servants' food came from their ship.

Then she saw the collection of vegetables and fruits Arvis had brought her, and was surprised at his continuing concern for her well-being. He urged her to eat through simple signs, and in spite of her lack of appetite she obliged him. The humans had a name for this. Oh, yes, *the last meal*.

The other Simiu were openly staring at K'heera's breakfast, so she asked Arvis to offer them some. If she offered it herself, they would have to refuse.

She could see their hunger as they gratefully took the food. She could see, too, their humiliation at having to eat at her largess, even though the gift didn't come directly from her. Well, that was their problem. If they were going to cling to stereotypes and an ancient honor code that had little relevance here, she wouldn't spend time worrying about it.

The fresh food was wonderful, and gave her an odd sense of calm. She asked Arvis where Bruce was, but he didn't know. The chances of her being able to tell Thunder the location—even if she was still out there—were remote.

Then, without warning, the doors to the dining area slid open, and soldiers rushed in. The Industrious dropped their meals and squatted in terror. The other Simiu backed into a corner, baffled. K'heera knew why the troops were there, and calmly remained beside Lene and Arvis, who seemed alarmed.

The soldiers forced the Industrious and the drum dancers against a back wall, as Lene moved behind Arvis for protection. The soldiers were not armed with punishing rods, but with small hand weapons K'heera had never seen before. She held her honor around her the way Bruce had held his and refused to show fear.

Everyone stopped moving when Dacris entered the room. The Industrious cowered as he loomed over them threateningly. Finally, he stood before Arvis, Lene, and K'heera.

Arvis' throat quivered, and K'heera wondered if the red-and-blue was asking for an explanation. Dacris responded, pointed to K'heera, then produced a container full of eggs. Their foul smell filled the room. Yet Dacris seemed calm, almost pleased. The green and gold Anuran signaled to some of the soldiers and they moved forward to take K'heera.

She was ready, but Arvis stepped in front of her, stopping the soldiers. They paused, hesitant to violate the wishes of the son of their leader. Lene tried to pull Arvis away from K'heera, but he resisted. He sang to the soldiers, to Dacris. It was hard for the Industrious to form complex thoughts, so she understood the effort this had to involve.

Dacris moved toward the servant, angry now, his own throat moving rapidly. K'heera moved beside Arvis while he and Dacris argued. Dacris gestured at Arvis, then at Lene, probably accusing them of conspiring with K'heera. She shouldn't care about that, but she did. Arvis might have treated her like a pet, but he'd been kind and conscientious, giving her the same regard he wanted to be given himself. She couldn't allow him to suffer.

K'heera moved in front of him, trying to get Dacris to see her, but when he did, he acted as if her bid for attention was an attack, and lashed out at her with a punishing rod. The Simiu screamed and fell, struggling to get away, but he shocked her again and again.

Dimly, she saw a surge of movement and suddenly the pain stopped. When she looked up, Arvis was between her and Dacris again—but something had changed between them.

She blinked, peered around. Arvis had knocked the weapon from Dacris' hand. K'heera shook her head, trying to clear it. Arvis seemed different suddenly, bigger. There were spots on his upper arms she'd never noticed . . . oh, yes, she had! She'd touched them by accident once, during her futile "first contact." Those were his poison patches! They were swollen, a brilliant yellow color, and fluid dripped down his arms. Amazingly, Dacris was backing away from Arvis, eyeing the patches.

Arvis turned to her, helped her back to her feet, patting her gently. He stared into her eyes, as if trying to see the hurt there. Then he must've heard something, because his head snapped around. At the same moment, Dacris charged.

K'heera barely got out of the way as the green-and-gold tackled the One-Touch. They wrestled, and K'heera could see how disadvantaged Arvis was. The soldier was plainly experienced, while Arvis had no idea what to do. His only advantage was his poison, but K'heera doubted if he even knew that.

Soldiers stared, while holding the Industrious at bay. Was this their Arena-of-Honor? How could there be any honor in battling such a mismatched opponent?

Lene circled the grappling figures, her throat rippling, and K'heera hoped she was shouting advice to Arvis. Soon it became more than the female could endure and she bolted from the room.

The figures twisted in each other's arms, and suddenly Arvis was in a position of power. K'heera barked encouragement but all the One-Touch did was hold his opponent. He could've poisoned the soldier, but hesitated too long. Arvis was simply too gentle to deliberately injure anyone. Then the moment was gone, and Dacris was on top again.

K'heera realized that the One-Touch was losing strength. Dacris was really hurting him. She surged forward, wanting to help him, but the soldiers threatened her with their weapons, pushing her back. Arvis quickly lost ground. Then the Troubadour executed a powerful hold and suddenly Arvis' head twisted in a direction it was never meant to go. Pain blossomed in his large, marbled eyes as he slumped to the floor.

Dacris moved away from his victim, exultant, singing his own glory. K'heera edged toward the dying Arvis, and the soldiers permitted her to tend her master at his death.

The Simiu's heart filled with pain as she leaned over the prostrate creature. "You fought well," she signed. "You are a being of honor." She'd never thought there could be any honor in losing.

Arvis couldn't move his body, could only blink to acknowledge what she'd said. With a sigh, he died, and K'heera felt his death as keenly as if he'd been her closest friend. She turned her head toward the crowing Anuran who was still proclaiming his mastery. The challenging roar soared up from the bottom of her rib cage and flowed from her throat, filling the room.

All eyes fastened on her. Dacris stared as K'heera bared her blunted teeth in a ferocious challenge. Uncomprehending, the Anuran moved toward her angrily.

She sprang at him, her powerful haunches catapulting her across the distance, her hands reaching for his throat. Shocked, he stepped back. When she hit him, they toppled; he struck the ground hard, K'heera astride him, strangling the life out of his hated body. Then the soldiers were on her en masse, shocking her with their rods until she was nearly senseless from the pain. She rolled away, trying to escape, all the while shrieking in agony.

The pain stopped as suddenly as it had begun, and K'heera glanced up to see why. Incredibly, the large group of Industrious and the drum dancers had broken ranks and rushed to help her. They surrounded her, protected her, as the guards battled them, taken completely aback by their sudden disobedience. K'heera wanted them to stop, knowing they would just bring more punishment on themselves and spare her nothing.

After a few chaotic moments, the soldiers had the upper hand again, and K'heera was grateful she couldn't hear the cries of the punished servants. Then Dacris was there.

Dimly, the Simiu was aware of the mottled patches around his throat where her hands had choked him; she took joy in that. His throat vibrated continuously. He must have been furiously berating her, and that amused her, too, to be deaf to his threats. Then he showed her his weapon. She didn't know what it was, but she could guess its purpose. He raised it to her face, but she refused to flinch, to even blink, and held his gaze steady. She felt no fear, knowing that she'd brought honor to herself, and to her uncle, Bruce. This, no doubt, would be the most honorable death any Harkk'ett had enjoyed in the last fifteen years.

The Troubadour moved to press a membrane on the weapon, while K'heera braced herself for the end. Then the Anuran stiffened and jerked his head away. She peered over his shoulder.

In the doorway stood the First. Beside him was Lene.

# CHAPTER 23
## ◆
# War!

Atle stopped just inside the dining hall and sang an order, bringing the action to a halt. A sharp gesture to the soldiers made them back away. He was relieved to know they hadn't already given their loyalty to Dacris. But he'd have to be careful; the situation could still turn into a coup.

He marched into the room, Lene following in his wake. In the center of the room stood Dacris, *armed*, Atle noted, with a lethal weapon. He held the weapon trained on the Simiu. Marks on the Second's throat testified to the servant's attack.

Near them lay Arvis' body. Astonished, Atle noted the swollen poison patches, the dripping toxin. In the end his son had been Chosen, after all. Grief and pride battled within him, but he masked his emotions with practiced ease.

Lene squatted beside her dead mate, keening mournfully, and the First was surprised and touched to see genuine emotion shaking her body.

He turned to his Second. "Release that servant."

Dacris obeyed and stepped away from the Simiu.

Atle asked the nearest soldier for a report and he complied. Another confirmed the story.

The Troubadour's coloring flowered; the hand holding the weapon twitched. "I defended myself against an Industrious *servant* and a scheming alien who has destroyed our food!"

"Hand your weapon to the nearest soldier," Atle sang calmly. "You've killed. You will be tried according to our laws."

The Troubadour flinched, turned to the soldiers. "Is this the leadership you want? A First who condones an attack on the Chosen by their *servants*? How many Chosen must *die* before he *acts*?" He clutched the weapon, refusing to yield it as he had the last time, aboard the humans' ship.

Atle approached the Second boldly. "Give me that weapon and surrender yourself. Obey the laws you've sworn to uphold."

"The same laws *you've* defied to elevate your *servant* to gain a free grandchild?" Dacris taunted. "Why didn't you just *breed* the virgin yourself?" The Troubadour swung the weapon toward Atle and aimed.

The First's color flamed as he dived for Dacris' knees, knocking him down. The Troubadour recovered without losing his weapon, but Atle grabbed his wrist, blocking his aim, then scrabbled up the Second's body. With a heave, Dacris flipped them over, desperate to avoid the One-Touch's toxin. Atle could see the fear of his own death in Dacris' eyes.

The Troubadour was lighter, quicker, younger, and heady from having already killed one opponent. His moves were swift and painful, and it was all Atle could do just to control the weapon.

The First's arms grew heavy and leaden. For a moment he thought, *Why not give in?* Was this why he'd searched for a new Home? So he could fight for his position against his Second?

Then he heard Lene's keening, and remembered his son. Arvis' unhatched child could be free on this World as Arvis had never been—but not if Dacris won.

With a sudden lurch, Atle toppled the Troubadour. "Release the weapon and surrender yourself," he ordered, gasping.

Dacris' eyes stared wildly at the One-Touch's fatal patches. They wept copiously, the First's garment catching most of it. But one drop hung precariously over the Second's face.

"Yield!" the First commanded.

Desperately, the Second jerked the weapon up, frantically trying to take aim. He fired and the piercing beam went wild, tearing a hole through a wall.

The building shook and Atle's patches sprayed fluid, striking the Second's eyes and face. Dacris screamed and fired again as Atle tried to control the weapon's wild blasts. Everyone hit the floor, and the Industrious' frightened cries mingled with the Second's death call.

At last Atle stepped away from the corpse. Dacris' body twisted in painful contortions, the final legacy of the powerful toxin. The First pulled the weapon out of his grasp.

Slowly, the servants and soldiers climbed to their feet. The Simiu had covered Lene's body with her own, protecting her.

Before the First could restore order, a messenger raced in.

"What is it?" he snapped.

The low-ranked Armored started to sing, but he was drowned out by an explosion. Looking through the window, Atle saw shadows passing over, even as the horrendously loud sound of a thousand avians filled the building. Then came a terrible crashing, tearing noise, louder even than the avian voices, and the entire building buckled, heaving under his feet.

When things settled, Atle found himself on the floor, covered in debris. He clawed his way up from under ceiling tiles to find his messenger dead. The Industrious were panicking, while the soldiers looked to him for order.

The First braced himself on shaky legs, and dimming his hearing to tolerate the deafening avian cries, he barked instructions, sending the soldiers out to join the battle. The Simiu had gathered the Industrious and her own people around her, so he gestured to her to hurry them outside, out of the damaged building. Lene went with them, the Simiu supporting her.

Atle had finally received the answer to his message. The humans had come to negotiate.


"I've never seen animals that weren't afraid of fire," Carlotta complained as she flew beside Martin on an alien sled waving a burning torch.

A large herd of Quakers lumbered before them, at least forty individuals. Forty laconic, impervious, disinterested individuals. Brockman thought sourly that nothing short of the wrath of God could get these critters to even *consider* a stampede.

The blond engineer shook his head. "Tesa was afraid of this. Still, we've gotta try. If it works. . . ." He was grateful to be free of the sound nullifiers for a little while, to communicate with the others directly. In the distance, they could barely hear the joined voices of the Grus as they attacked the Anurans' colony, and the explosions as Tesa and Javier used the aliens' own captured sleds as bombs against them. Chris and Noriko had been up the entire night rigging the sleds for remote control and placing the powerful batteries where they should explode on impact.

"The grass is too wet," Moshe told him, coming up on his left. "It can't sustain a good blaze with all the rain we've had. And when I wave my torch, they just eye me like a mosquito with a smoke trail. What next?"

"One swat from those short trunks and we're grease spots," Brockman reminded them.

"We could try buzzing them faster," Chris suggested.

"At least we've got them *pointed* in the right direction!" Martin said optimistically. But the colony was kilometers away.

"How long can we keep this up?" Noriko asked. "I don't want to play cowboy when we're supposed to be the cavalry."

"A little longer," Brockman answered vaguely. He wasn't sure what other help they could give if this didn't work. "Come on, let's put some heart into it!" He waved his torch and moved his sled faster. "Yeee-HAH! *MOVE IT, DAMN YOU!*"

The nearest Quaker merely shook her head, waiting for him to get within range of her tusks and trunk.

Atle glanced back at the hatchery building once he was outside. The structure had been badly damaged, and that, coupled with the ruined programs and fouled equipment, made it unsalvageable.

"Glorious First! You're alive!" His Fourth was panting.

"What are they bombing us with? The humans have no major weapons here."

"Our stolen sleds. They're sending them down on us with the power housing exposed. Once they hit, they detonate."

Impressive. They might have almost forty of the flyers.

Overhead, the avians blackened the sky, the raptors and the wading birds flying together. Suddenly the flock parted and another sled came whistling down, smashing into a soldiers' barracks. It must've struck the solar batteries because there was a huge explosion.

"First, what are our orders?" the Fourth asked.

"Tell the soldiers . . . to take the humans prisoner. . . ."

"And if they can't?"

"Then they'll have to kill. The hatchery's ruined; we have to eat. And we *must* win." Another sled screamed out of the sky, but missed its target and hit the opposite bank of the river. "Get the colonists out of the buildings, the prisoners, too. Get them into the forest. And call the *Flood*. Tell the remaining crew we need them here, tell them to bring the last two ships, and be prepared to use lethal force."

Tesa leaned over the edge of her sled, trying to glimpse the buildings spread out before her. Her cohort separated for a moment and she counted two hits and a miss. Not bad for someone new to tossing lightning. She tried to figure out which building housed the mechanism for the force-field that kept the Singers prisoner. There was a tiny shed on the bank, far from the other buildings, but even with Chris and Noriko's remote controls, small things were damned hard to hit.

Javier stood behind her on her sled. Around and beneath them flew hundreds of Grus and Aquila, and beside the two humans was the battalion of empty sleds programmed to follow them.

"I've got to ride this next one down," she signed to him.

"You're going to do *what*?"

"Don't worry, I'll have two of them. Once I'm sure of the target, I'll aim one, then step off onto the other and ride it back up. I might be able to knock out the River's force-field if I hit that shed."

He grabbed her forearm. "Tesa, no! The Quakers should've been here by now. They aren't. Without that distraction you'll be too easy a target."

She watched him, waiting for him to realize he couldn't change her mind. He did finally, and his face grew expressionless once more. "I want you to keep sending the other sleds onto the biggest buildings till I get back."

He nodded curtly.

"This'll only take a minute," she insisted. "Then the River will be open." She gave him a quick kiss, and stepped onto another sled, matching it with a mate on its far side. With a whoop, she started her descent.

Jib leaned against the bulk of his friend Taniwha, trying to calm him, but the explosions in the east frightened the herd. The human pictured the west end of the River. There were giant trees there that grew over the water on a tripod of roots. The Singers could swim among those roots and hide. There was plenty of food, yet the herd seemed reluctant to go.

*What's wrong?* he thought at them. *We'll be safe there.*

The images Jib received rocked him. Anguish filled the World, and the humans and Simiu prisoners suffered worst of all. Their pain was so great, the Singers could no longer ignore it. The humans' dreams tortured their sleep, and though they'd sung their finest laments to console them, it hadn't helped. They'd never felt this much sorrow since they'd last been attacked by the Mate Kai, the Great Hunger.

Jib shuddered, as he recognized people he knew, Bruce . . . and

Szu-yi. Her fear was the most profound, the Singers told him, like their own fear of their old predator. Her thoughts were so strong, Jib could smell blood in the water, feel the Singers' raw terror. *Let's swim west,* he begged them.

But they wouldn't go, and finally he realized it was because of him. Deep in his mind, *he* didn't want to go. He hated what Tesa was doing, but even so, he hated more not being there for her. Maybe it was the Maori in him, but he knew running away from the battle was wrong. Taniwha touched those thoughts, brought them forward, and made him face them.

*That's fine for me,* he insisted, *but not for you! It's my job to keep you safe, get you out of harm's way. . . .*

But there was no place on the planet to be safe as long as the Anurans were here.

*But there's nothing you can do, you've tried!*

Yes, Taniwha agreed, that was true. And they were afraid, as afraid as they'd ever been of their old enemy. But generations ago they had driven away the Mate Kai, and after that, any other creature that had threatened their River. Some of the beings they'd driven away, like the White Winds, were now fighting to save not just their River, but their World. How could they let them do that without trying to help?

Jib felt Taniwha's ache for his mother. If Tesa destroyed the field, they could be reunited, along with rest of the herd that had fled to the sea. He saw them suddenly, clearly. They were nowhere *near* the sea, but were hovering around the field, waiting for it to fail. Their hopes had lured the captured herd as much as Jib's desire to help his friends.

Taniwha shoved Jib gently. He remembered, oddly, his great-grandmother telling him he'd always be lucky in water. He touched his greenstone tiki . . . and remembered something else. . . .

*Why don't the Quakers drink at your River?*

Too messy. They wallowed in the water, muddying it, destroying the banks with their huge bodies. We sent them away.

*You sent them away?* Jib thought. *Yes. We'll swim east, to help the others. . . . But first, there's something you must do. . . .*

"Okay," Martin admitted, "I give up. This is useless."

His companions seemed just as disgusted as they stared at the unmovable animals.

"We may as well join up with Tesa and help her. . . ."

"Martin, wait," Noriko warned, pointing to the Quaker matriarchs. They'd lifted their massive heads, as though hearing something. The entire herd suddenly turned completely around, facing the wrong direction, then, amazingly enough, they spun around like trained circus elephants until they faced the direction of the river. Then they started moving forward, slowly at first, then faster. Their ears moved as if they could hear something at a great distance, something calling them.

"What the . . . ?" Moshe mumbled.

"They're picking up speed!" Chris announced.

"Let's not get left behind!" Carlotta cried as the Quakers erupted into a thundering gallop.

Tesa waited until the last possible minute to step off the aimed sled onto the one flying right beside it. She pulled back hard on the controls for lift, while the empty flyer continued on its way, sailing effortlessly into its target. There was an impact and a plume of smoke, then the iridescent power grid that flowed across the River winked out. She was about to give a victory shout when she saw the herd of free Singers surge through the open water, right into the colony.

*What are they doing?* she thought as they entered the battle-field. Then she saw a dark mass coming down from the west. In its midst was a small head bobbing above the waves. *Jib?*

The distraction cost her. She was suddenly surrounded by a swarm of Anuran soldiers. Pushing the sled to its limit, she dodged them, but her flyer was no faster than the soldiers' models, and their experience handling the machines exceeded hers.

A large brown Anuran leaped onto her sled, and she struck him hard with her coup stick. He kept his balance, and when she swung back to hit him again, a soldier behind her grabbed the lance, nearly knocking her off the sled.

Suddenly Aquila appeared, grabbing soldiers, yanking them off their sleds. Two of the Anurans fired, and one of the Hunters was fatally hit, plummeting into the River. Thunder taloned the soldier holding Tesa's coup stick, forcing him to release it. The alien aimed his weapon at the Hunter, but Tesa rapped the stick against his arm, and the weapon and its owner plummeted into the River.

Tesa's cohort had caught up with her, and spiraled around. She signaled them to leave, fearing they'd be shot, when suddenly another arm grabbed her from behind, hauling her off her sled. The sudden action made her drop the coup stick. She swung an elbow hard into her attacker before realizing it was Javier, pulling her to safety onto his sled. They escaped, surrounded by the cohort, leaving the soldiers to fend off the angry Aquila. When the humans were safely above the cloud of massed avians again, Thunder delivered the dropped lance. Tesa signed her thanks, then turned to her rescuer.

"Talk about crazy stunts," she scolded him.

"An old Lakota trick," he reminded her, nursing his side.

"I think it's a little safer on horseback," she insisted.

Below them, the avian cover started breaking up, leaving wide holes in their curtain. Groups of soldiers were firing on the birds, killing and wounding them, causing the flocks to split up in defense. The Aquila attacked the soldiers, but there were four or five aliens aboard each sled now, and even if the avians picked several off, there were still more left that could fire on them.

Quickly Tesa descended, pulling the waiting sleds with her, but she knew now she'd never have time to use them all. "We've got to outfly them," she warned Javier.

She plunged the sled into a spiraling dive and the cohort followed as she directed other sleds into bombing runs. She dive-bombed buildings, sending a-gravs directly into the structures. Anurans were running everywhere, and foul-smelling fires consumed the prefabricated buildings.

*But it's not enough,* she realized as the soldiers closed in on them. She'd put too much hope in the Quakers.

One of the soldiers fired a projectile at them, and they both ducked instinctively and let the sled drop. The missile hit Frost Moon hard and he spiraled to the ground. Javier had to stop Tesa from reaching over the side of the sled after him.

The young avian's death shattered her, but she couldn't mourn now. They were all in too much danger. She gazed around, collected her thoughts, tried to focus on the immediate problem. They were flying too low, she thought, just as a huge swath of trees toppled right in her path; she barely had enough time to swerve out of their way, her cohort cutting sharply to follow. On the ground, Anurans were stumbling, falling, as if hit by an earthquake. Javier gripped her shoulder, pointing. . . .

The Quakers burst out of the dense forest at a gallop. Tesa had no idea that the behemoths could move that fast. Two buildings collapsed just from the vibrations of the ground beneath them. They barreled through, lifting their trunks, trumpeting. Their treelike feet and legs flattened everything beneath them. Aliens scrambled for cover before their assault.

The soldiers forgot about the avians, forgot about the humans in the face of this wholesale destruction. They left their pursuit to fire wildly on the stampeding monsters, but weapons that were designed to kill lesser creatures merely wounded the powerful Quakers. And that only made them mad.

Javier pointed up. "Here comes the *bad* news."

Two large spacecraft loomed over them. Projectiles fired from one of the craft, hitting the stampeding animals. When they didn't fall immediately, Tesa rejoiced, thinking their weapons were useless against such bulk. But the small missiles must have been chemical, because within minutes the huge creatures started collapsing, crushing anything beneath them.

"We've got to get out of here!" Javier insisted.

"No, wait!" Tesa turned back to the River.

She couldn't find Jib, but she could make out the reunited herd of Singers. Back in the forest, she could see a large group of humans surrounded by Anuran soldiers, being marched back to the colony. Grus and Aquila bodies littered the ground.

*It can't all have been for nothing!* she thought.

"Tesa, *now!*" Javier demanded, but it was already too late. They'd been surrounded again by a large group of soldiers. This group had learned their lesson; they kept their distance, aiming heavy weapons. One of the soldiers signaled her to land. She stiffened, searching for an escape, but there was none. She signaled the cohort to disperse, but they hesitated.

Then Snowberry, whose family the Anurans had wiped out in Taller's territory, flew at the nearest soldier. Tesa screamed at him to stop, but he hit the Anuran hard, knocking him from his sled. The young male was immediately struck by at least ten missiles from the other soldiers' weapons. His brilliant crown dulled and he fell from the sky like a stone.

Tesa signaled the others wildly, shouting at them, and finally they obeyed her and left. Above them, the Aquila futilely fought the huge spaceships. Tesa realized they'd gotten too far from their allies. They were cut off. She couldn't face losing Javier, too. There was nothing to do but surrender.

Bitterly damning her foolishness, Tesa raised her hands in capitulation and descended.

Even with the breathing mask, Jib could barely catch his breath as the Singers towed him into the Anuran colony. The closer they got to the site of their slaughter, the more anxious they grew. Still, they could sense the rest of their herd, and their eagerness to be reunited outweighed their fear.

Jib had redonned his nullifiers, but felt as if he could still "hear," since the Singers filtered the sound into his mind. The muffled roars of explosions, the sounds of buildings collapsing, were violent and scary. He had to keep reassuring himself that they would be okay, they would make it. If *he* panicked, there was no telling what would happen to the herd.

The young Maori watched as Tesa destroyed the force-field, and he was soon caught up in the herd's excitement as they remet their loved ones. The mental pull of the Singers was more than the Quakers could resist, and soon they were storming the place. Even from the River, Jib could see the mass destruction they caused, and the effect that devastation had on the enemy forces. He cheered and the Singers did, too.

He urged the herd east, to the sea, but the River was suddenly filled with charging Quakers. The herd was forced to split up to avoid them. Jib clung to Taniwha desperately.

When the ships appeared and began striking the Quakers down, the Singers grew more frightened. Nothing had ever been able to injure the great beasts, not even the Mate Kai. Jib tried to get them unified again, but the moment had been lost.

The water around them churned wildly, and Taniwha yanked Jib into a small side pool as the massive body of a drugged Quaker crashed down near them, trapping them in the tiny inlet. The young calf wailed for his mother and his panic pushed the herd to their limit. Jib tried to ease the youngster's fears, but soon his brain was flooded by his friend's terror. Unbidden, images of the Great Hunger filled his mind. Reptilian, as large as a Quaker, its enormous snout opened to reveal rows of bloodstained razor teeth. Jib could barely breathe, he was so frightened, and could no longer focus on what was real.

*Drive it away,* Jib begged Taniwha. That's what his people had done so many centuries ago. He reached into his . . . no . . . Taniwha's racial memories. He could see the being clearly, see how the herd projected their fear into it, driving it away until it starved. But *how* did they do it?

He opened his mind until he stopped being Jib and became a Singer, until he could feel his big, round body, his paddle tail, his strong flippers. Then he reached into his Singer's memories, and called up the beast again. This time he didn't shy from the image, but examined it. He saw his people die, saw their blood, smelled it in the water. And he felt their panic, *his* panic, felt them project it . . . into the tiny brain of the primitive creature that fed on them. A brain that was so simple, it could register only the basest emotions.

Jib was jerked out of his reverie by the ominous presence of an armed guard. Taniwha swam the length of their tiny enclosure wildly, towing the Maori. The guard fired at the helpless animal and a small projectile buried itself in Taniwha's side. Jib felt as if he'd been struck himself; he screamed as Taniwha's pain flooded through him. Shaking his head, he tried to ignore the horrible sensation and searched the calf's back until he found the missile. He yanked it free, fearing it might be filled with toxins, but that didn't diminish the youngster's pain.

Blinking water out of his eyes, desperate to do *something*, Jib stared at the guard who was aiming again at the young Singer. He fixed the Anuran's image in his tortured mind, and slowly turned it into the Mate Kai. Somehow, Taniwha understood, and projected his fear and pain at the soldier. Jib followed the thought, felt it penetrate the guard's mind, felt it be absorbed harmlessly. The guard fired again. Taniwha leaped in the water, twisting away, but this missile lodged in his flipper.

*What's wrong? What's wrong?* Jib thought frantically, pulling the painful object free. He was flooded with chaotic, panicky thoughts from Taniwha, from the herd, all echoing the same question. Helplessly, he watched the guard take aim as Taniwha, exhausted, surrendered and stopped moving.

Then Jib *heard* a stray thought. . . . A voice he knew . . .

*Two brains. The damned things have two* brains! Tell them, Weaver! It's important! You've got to tell them!

Szu-yi?

Nearly hallucinating with images and thoughts not his own, Jib stared once more at the guard. He saw the alien head, the sophisticated brain there . . . then followed the spine down into the short, stumpy tail. He remembered the ancient predator . . . with its tiny, primitive brain . . . was this brain more like the Mate Kai's?

Taniwha followed Jib's thought and flung his fear down the guard's spinal channel into the separate nerve cluster hidden there. Instantly the soldier spasmed, collapsed onto his sled, and went into seizures.

Jib grunted as the entire herd joined his mind, searching for the image of the tiny hindbrain. The overload was too great for the human. He felt as if he were being killed by ecstasy and lost himself completely as, with one powerful mind, the Singers united against their enemy.

Bruce felt the warning surge of vibration before he heard anything. "Hurry, Nadine, Szu-yi, your nullifiers!"

Their door opened with a rush, and soldiers stormed in, grabbing them roughly, hustling them outside with no warning, no explanation. Szu-yi seemed preternaturally calm, though usually the very sight of the soldiers set her twitching.

*They're going to kill us,* Bruce decided. *We're too much trouble, so they're just going to finally kill us.*

When they left the building, the guards pushed them and other human prisoners toward the forest.

*What the hell's going on?* He searched the sky and saw the great clouds of avians. Then the first bomb hit.

The force of the explosion threw them to the ground. A handful of humans bolted for freedom, and were shot down by the guards. They were playing for keeps, now.

Yanked to their feet, the group was pushed into the forest, but within minutes, something was stampeding toward them, something *big.* The entire group dispersed before the rampaging Quakers, and most of the guards were lost in the shuffle. Bruce grabbed hold of Nadine and Szu-yi and they ran for it, nearly slamming into Meg's sled before they saw her and Old Bear.

"Get on! Get on!" the Russian scientist urged as Bruce shoved the two women aboard, then leaped up behind the Lakota elder.

Meg was waving wildly at the humans as they scattered into the forest, and the ones who saw her followed them deeper into the woods. But within minutes they were surrounded by more Anurans and were forced back toward the River.

He could see Szu-yi plucking at Meg's sleeve, asking her in sign if Weaver had told everyone about the Anurans' brains. She seemed obsessed, the way she often got about odd bits of information these days. Meg patted her, assured her Weaver had told them, but Szu-yi kept signing it over and over, something about the aliens' brains. Bruce was lost.

The Anurans herded Meg and Old Bear east along the River. *Hopeless,* Bruce thought, *but a damned good try.* When he saw soldiers capture Tesa, it broke his heart.

Then, suddenly, the guard nearest him dropped his weapon and blinked dully. Slowly, almost casually, he toppled off his flyer. The Anuran beside him watched in amazement, then collapsed in his turn. One by one the invaders went down, as if the effect were contagious. Some of the fallen ones seizured. Bruce saw a huge shadow growing over them and looked up. The big ships were gliding downward, out of control. They were going to crash.

Waving his arms at everyone nearby, Bruce signaled, "RUN!"

K'heera pulled her wards down the bank of the river, as far from the fighting as she could get. The terrified Industrious, the three drum dancers, and the gravid One-Touch followed her blindly. She turned back in time to see soldiers collapsing, just before Lene fainted. Within minutes, the Industrious fell prostrate, twitching helplessly. The Simiu halted, baffled, then glanced up in time to see the falling ship.

The drum dancers, unaware of the crashing spacecraft, had continued on. They waved at her, urging her to follow them. Desperate to stop them, she raced forward, tackling two of them to the ground. The third stopped to help his friends ward her off, just as the ship sliced off the tops of the nearest trees and demolished the forest beside them. The shock of the crash flung the third Simiu to the ground.

The drum dancers stood dazedly, realizing that the Anurans were helpless, and that K'heera had saved them from being crushed. They glanced nervously at one another, then at K'heera.

She felt the division growing between them again, and would not yield to it. She had no reason to hang her head anymore, and if they treated her dishonorably, she would not tolerate it.

Then, the three dancers faced her. Kh'arhh'tk, the leader, spoke to her rapidly, no doubt in their own language, completely forgetting that she could hear no more than he could with his sound nullifiers. As he spoke, he gestured at his companions, and K'heera wondered what he was saying.

*Could he be thanking me?* she mused. She dismissed the notion. These proud males would never acknowledge being rescued by a Harkk'ett.

Finally, Kh'arhh'tk stopped speaking. He stared at his companions and then, ceremoniously, the three males performed the Mizari honor gesture, a symbol of the highest respect one intelligent creature could have for another. It was a moment before K'heera let herself realize that they'd performed it for her.

# Epilogue

Tesa was warm, and finally safe, so when she felt herself being jostled, she rolled over to avoid it. Brushing against a soft bundle of feathers, she snuggled against it contentedly. Then she was jostled again. She waved a hand, telling whoever it was to stop, but it wouldn't. Opening her eyes grumpily, she saw a familiar, and normally welcomed, face.

*First-Light,* she thought, pulling him down on top of her.

He resisted. "Tesa, not now. We're not alone!"

*What?* She glanced around. They were in her lean-to, Javier kneeling over her. Lightning was on her left, it was his warm feathers she'd cuddled into. Flies-Too-Fast was sleeping soundly on her right, his head still tucked. The sun was bright. Javier must've been up for a while. Whenever he left, the cohort took advantage and resumed their previously privileged positions.

"You've got to get up, Good Eyes," he told her. "The League Irenic Captain, J'karthha, is here to see you."

How did she ever get hooked up with a morning person? Tesa wondered blearily. She'd have to talk to Weaver about that. She sat up, wiping the sleep from her eyes. Then she remembered everything.

It had been a month since the Singers had devastated the Anurans. Two days ago, ships started arriving—Tesa couldn't believe how many ships. Every vessel that had been within range of Bruce's aborted transmission had responded immediately. They'd come from every Known World, freighters, and barges, and every kind of transport, from economy ships to luxury vessels. Fifteen had arrived in the last two days, and many more were still being turned away.

Last night, two armed ships from the CLS Irenic force arrived. The officer in charge, a Simiu female named J'karthha, had wanted to debark immediately, but when Bruce explained that they had everything under control, she was willing to wait until morning. Now, Tesa couldn't put this off any longer.

Javier pressed a cup of coffee into her hand. "Try this. It'll help. Old Bear made it."

She nodded, staring at the cup incredulously. *Where did he get coffee?* Oh, yes.

Two days ago Bruce, Martin Brockman, and his crew had taken the repaired *Demoiselle* back to Taller's territory, to find out what happened to the Anurans who'd been left there. They'd carried the Anurans' own weapons . . . something K'heera had suggested.

The Anurans at the quonset hut were either dead or in the same condition most of the others were in—brain-damaged or so physically injured they were no threat. Like the aliens on the River of Fear, only the Industrious seemed undamaged. They'd wakened from their faint confused, but with no other problems.

*Good thing*, Tesa thought. Without them, they'd never have been able to care for all the survivors.

In fact, the first crew that had arrived had boarded the space station and were amazed to find that the Singers' mental retaliation was so powerful, it had devastated the Anurans even aboard the *Crane*. There were only a few Industrious, but they knew how to operate the food servers and had kept the injured alive.

Bruce and his crew brought the aliens from the Hedford Shelter back to Florida, so operations could be centralized. The weatherman would've remembered to bring back coffee.

Tesa sipped it carefully. It was wonderfully fragrant, and so reminiscent of the coffee she'd grown up with she almost wept.

"You all right?" Javier signed.

She'd always been emotional, but lately it'd been worse. She was tired all the time, and sometimes burst into sobs for no reason. She wondered how long Javier would put up with it; she was getting on her *own* nerves.

"Fine. I'm fine," she reassured him, enjoying the coffee.

Lightning was hock-sitting beside her, and she offered him a sip. He had a hard time getting any out of the cup, but took such pleasure in the taste he did get, she had to smile. He handed her her woven Grus shirt. "I've preened it for you. I thought you'd want to look your best for the Irenic Captain."

"Thanks." Taking the lovely garment from him, Tesa slipped it over her camisole. Was Lightning giving her a subtle hint that she hadn't been taking very good care of herself lately? She found her hairbrush and pulled it through her knotted mop. "Has the Captain been down long?"

"About an hour," Javier signed. "Bruce has kept her occupied, showing her the Anurans' barracks."

Tesa nodded. They'd destroyed three barracks, but two had been untouched. That's where they held the Chosen survivors.

She finished the coffee, tossed her brush in the corner, and crawled out. The small shelter had been built under a copse of trees, next to a pile of massive felled logs that lay strewn everywhere like a giant child's pickup sticks. The lean-to faced the River, and now, the first thing she saw every morning was utter destruction. Crushed and fire-ravaged buildings were everywhere, as were broken trees and foliage. Damaged feathers littered the landscape.

It had taken them a whole day to remove the corpse of the Quaker who'd passed out in the River and drowned, trapping Jib and Taniwha. Tesa had lost count of the a-grav units they'd had to use to lift her. Fortunately, that old matriarch was the only mortality. The other collapsed behemoths had recovered and wandered off. However, because humans had attempted to stampede them, the giant animals held them responsible for their loss. At the first sight of Terrans now, they would attack.

And how long had it taken to remove all the dead Wind people, all the dead Hunters? Tesa remembered holding the body of Frost Moon and sobbing . . . his large body had weighed so little with the life gone out of it. When they'd found Snowberry's shattered corpse, she could not make her voice carry his spirit to the Suns, she could only weep.

Thunder's mother, Rain, had suffered a broken wing, and they weren't sure if it would heal well enough for her to fly again. The Grus healer in Taller's tribe, Loves-the-Wind, had lost her mate and was so grief-stricken they didn't know if she'd recover. Four Singers had drowned before they'd learned their enemies' secret.

At least Jib had been able to convince the Grus and Aquila that the River Spirits were now their allies, that they would never hold their loved ones' souls again. That had been the only relief the grieving avians would have from their war.

Javier squeezed her shoulder, and she returned to the present. He'd been busy since the day of the fight, helping the Grus healers, grafting feathers, assisting Szu-yi. And keeping Tesa together. She patted his hand and turned to see Thunder, who was perched on top of the lean-to.

"Good morning, Good Eyes," the raptor greeted her. "Did you sleep well?".

"Very well, my friend," she signed honestly. She hadn't dreamed in two weeks. "And you?"

"I never opened my eyes once the Suns set. I'm still catching up from all the sleep I missed these last weeks."

Tesa smiled. "Have you eaten yet?"

The avian stretched a wing. "Not yet. I'll wait a little while . . . maybe take another nap."

"I'll bet we can get someone else to find some food for you," Tesa assured her. The colony was ringed with Hunters, the trees laden with them. They would not leave until the last Anuran had left the World.

She followed Javier to meet the Captain, as Lightning, Flies-Too-Fast, and the remnants of her cohort trailed along. Even Thunder hopped off her perch to join them. They'd become obsessively protective of her, since the war.

Many of the Grus had already left the colony for their own territories, except for a core of leaders, their mates, and cohorts who'd also vowed to remain until the last Anuran was gone. A group of young Gray Winds scouted breeding territory along the River. The Singers welcomed them and the Hunters, now.

Javier brought the group to a large building that had been some sort of science station. The humans had turned it into their center of operations. It was the building K'heera had been brought to when she'd been captured. Tesa had never been inside it. She didn't intend to enter it now.

First-Light anticipated that, and went into the building without her and brought the Captain out. Bruce came with her, as well as a Heeyoon male who was her assistant.

The aged female was heavily scarred. Those marks indicated challenges in the Arena-of-Honor and were badges of glory her people considered attractive. J'karthha, obviously, had long ago earned the experience to be in charge of a troop of peacekeeping soldiers. Like most Simiu, the Captain wore nothing but an armband indicating her rank and station. The salmon-colored female's vivid purple eyes twinkled when she saw Tesa and she gave her, first, the Simiu greeting gesture, then followed it with a deep Mizari honor bow. Her assistant copied her gestures regally.

Tesa started to reciprocate, but the matriarch stopped her with a hand. When her mouth moved, Tesa remembered to turn her voder on, something she'd gotten out of the habit of doing.

". . . to greet you is *my* privilege, Honored Interrelator," the Captain was saying. "I am J'karthha, and this is my aide, SwiftPace. You're well? You suffered no injuries?"

Tesa thought of Snowberry and Frost Moon. She thought of Rain. Of Szu-yi. She shook her head. "No, I'm fine, really."

"A terrible thing, what you endured, and all your people," the Captain said, after reading Tesa's answer. Sound nullifiers were perched prominently in her ears. She stepped down from the building, moved beside the Interrelator, and started walking. Everyone followed them. "You know, I've been in the Irenics for many years. It's been an exciting life. Lots of travel. I've dealt with colony skirmishes. A few small civil wars. A lot of diplomatic missions. But none of us has ever had to deal with a full-scale invasion. As you humans would say, we're treading water, trying to figure out what to do."

But Tesa had trod water harder than everyone else.

"Have you heard the *good* news?" J'karthha asked, glancing at Javier. He shook his head.

She stared at him. He had *good* news, and hadn't told her?

"Two Mizari vessels with a squadron of Irenics and some specially trained diplomats have overtaken the *Brolga*."

That *was* good news, and she was heartened by it.

"The Captain and crew were all alive, if a little the worse for wear. It took a few hours to get the Anurans to surrender, but they finally did. Captain Stepp and her people were offered transport to the nearest space station, but they refused. They insisted on bringing the *Brolga* back here, so that's what they're doing. Additional crew from the Mizari vessels have joined them so they can have medical care and rest."

"Martin and his crew will be happy to hear that," Tesa signed to Javier.

"Yes, he will . . . but, you know . . . I don't think they'll be going back with their ship," he told her.

"You mean, they want to stay here?"

"That's what I've heard," the Simiu reported. "You've got a lot to do to repair this damage. You'll need extra hands."

*How odd,* Tesa thought. She'd expected them to take the first ship out of here. She looked up, saw a familiar building, and halted abruptly. "Where are you taking me?"

Javier glanced at her guiltily.

"Take it easy, darlin'," Bruce suggested.

The Simiu touched Tesa's arm gently. "We'll be transferring the Anurans onto our vessels today. We thought . . . as the Interrelator . . . you should speak to their leader before . . . he leaves."

She felt manipulated and shot an angry glance at her lover, then at Bruce. The cohort, including Thunder, read her body language and clustered around her protectively.

"Good Eyes," Javier signed pleadingly, "you need to face him. This one time. If you don't . . ."

She wouldn't heal, he'd told her. He insisted she had Post-traumatic Stress Syndrome. Szu-yi agreed with him. Even *she* had recommended her confronting the alien leader. Tesa had never actually refused, she'd just kept putting it off.

The Captain and her aide glanced at each other uneasily.

Javier moved closer to her. "You can put this behind you," he signed to her privately. "But first you've got to *finish* it. You need to do this, for yourself . . . for *us*. So we can *begin*. . . ."

Tears filled Tesa's eyes, and when she tried to blink them away, they fell in a small flood down her face. She didn't want him to be right, but he was. She swallowed hard, wiped her face, and nodded, then glared halfheartedly at Bruce. "Don't think I haven't noticed the way you two are always scheming against me."

"Who, *us*?" Bruce protested with feigned innocence.

When she turned back to the Simiu, the Captain acted as if she hadn't witnessed her sudden bout of emotion. "Okay. Let's do it." Taking a deep breath, she started up the walkway. Only then did she notice Old Bear, Nadine, and Meg. She stopped to greet them.

Her grandfather pressed something into her hand. She gazed at it. It was a medicine bundle. "I had a dream," he signed, "so I made this. Nadine and Meg helped me put it together."

The bag was woven from the ruddy-colored reeds, and tied with the long stems of blood-of-the-World. It smelled like oranges and mint. "What's in it?" Tesa asked, not wanting to unwrap it in front of the others.

"A charred piece of wood that was struck by a falling sled," he signed. "A sliver of Rain's bone they had to remove. A small bone from a Singer. A few hairs from a Quaker. One of Lightning's cinnamon feathers. A bit of Thunder's down. . . . Some of Snowberry's and Frost Moon's blood."

Clutching the bag in her hand, Tesa felt the power of the sacred things inside it. "Thank you, Grandfather." They kissed, then Meg and Nadine hugged her and they walked away.

K'heera stood by the door of the First's house and opened it as they approached. She greeted the Interrelator formally, the Grus, the Aquila, Javier, then finally Captain J'karthha and her aide. Lastly, she greeted Bruce.

"My honored uncle," she signed.

He returned the Simiu greeting perfectly, then grinned.

The visitors returned the Simiu's greeting with the same honor they'd given Tesa. If it meant anything to K'heera, she kept it to herself. When they were done, Tesa dropped to one knee and hugged her friend, and K'heera returned the embrace with as much hearty enthusiasm as she'd shown when they'd first been reunited.

"K'heera," Tesa signed, "I want you to talk to the Captain about how quickly we can get your hearing restored. Javier said that there were doctors on one of the luxury transports who have the facilities and the equipment and were willing to operate."

The young Simiu glanced at the Captain, then at Tesa. She ran a hand distractedly through her short mane. Szu-yi had been able to eliminate the pain from her teeth, but they were still blunted. "I don't think there will be time for that. . . ."

"Why not? What have we got *but* time?"

"Honored Interrelator," the Captain interjected, "we want the Honored K'heera to join us as we transport the Anurans to their Home. She has so much experience dealing with them. . . ."

"No!" Tesa signed sharply. The Captain stepped back, startled. "She's been through *enough*! She's *not* a diplomat; she's just an innocent person caught up in this mess. I'm not going to let her *endure* another day of dealing with these . . ."

K'heera stopped her with a gentle hand. "Good Eyes, my most honorable friend, please listen. This was *my* idea. I *lived* with these people, with the First himself. I *know* them. I even came to care for some of them. I wasn't at StarBridge for long, but I *did* pay attention while I was there. I can help."

Tesa felt stricken. "But, K'heera, just because you're female doesn't mean you *have* to take on this responsibility. We could use your technical skills here, and on the *Singing Crane*." Gazing at the Simiu, Tesa realized that K'heera had made up her mind. Shamelessly, the human resorted to a personal plea. "I don't *want* you to go."

K'heera was visibly touched. "And I don't want to leave my uncle, or you, or my silent shadow, Thunder. But I must do this. It would be dishonorable for me not to."

"The Honored K'heera could never bring dishonor on herself . . . or her *honored* family," the Captain stated firmly.

K'heera gestured her appreciation.

"Did you both know about this?" Tesa asked Javier and Bruce. Their blank expressions didn't hide their knowledge.

"Good Eyes," K'heera signed, "they only did what I asked. Now, come speak to the First. He is eager to meet you."

*I'll bet!* she thought, and stepped inside the building with K'heera, leaving her entourage outside.

Inside the first room, squatting by a low table, were four of the red and blue aliens. Three were obviously females, one a much larger male. Tesa recognized one of the females as an Industrious. She bustled out with platters of food and fussed over the two elders. The food was dried, not fresh, but attractively presented and came from the Anuran ship's seemingly inexhaustible supply. The third female helped serve the elders. She was plainly expecting a birth before long.

"Good Eyes," K'heera signed the introduction, "this is Sine, daughter of the First. This is Dunn, his wife. This is Lene, the wife of his son. And this is Atle, the First."

None of the aliens stood, and Tesa did not lower herself to their level. She knew that, originally, the leader's full title had been "First-in-Conquest," and that he'd specifically asked K'heera not to use it. His wife and daughter-in-law had no visible scars, but he was paralyzed down his right side.

The alien's throat rippled, and Tesa read her voder. "I have been wanting to meet you," she read. "Have they told you that we are a people who have never known defeat?"

"So I understand," she signed.

"The term 'Interrelator' is supposed to mean one who helps one group communicate with another! How does it feel to have conquered the Chosen?"

Every muscle in the human's body tightened. "You are mistaken, First. *I* didn't conquer you. You were overcome by a people who have never discovered the wheel. A simple people who only wanted their River back, and not to be your food."

He stared at her steadily with his large, marbled eyes. "They struck the killing blow, that is true, Interrelator. But none of it would have happened if not for you."

"If I had answered your call to negotiate," she asked, "would you have sat and talked with me? Or would you have delayed me until you could defeat *my* people?"

"My offer was made in good faith," he insisted. "An offer you never even considered. It was my bad fortune to find a beautiful planet jealously guarded by *humans*—the most bloodthirsty of people." He glanced at his family, then gently touched the swollen back of his daughter-in-law.

Without another word, Tesa turned and left the building, nearly choking on rage. As calmly as she could, she asked K'heera, "Was he telling the truth?"

"Who can say?" the Simiu admitted. "Only he knows what his original plan was. And his mind . . . is not what it once was."

Tesa nodded briefly, then turned to Javier, her eyes glistening. "Let's get out of here."

With a curt nod, he took her elbow and started walking away.

"Excuse me, Interrelator," the Heeyoon aide gestured to catch her attention. "Pardon my intrusion, but Dr. Gable . . ."

"Forgive me," J'karthha apologized. "I forgot. Rob Gable wants to speak to you. We've got a holo-field set up in the headquarters. He's been on hold. . . ."

Tesa groaned inwardly. "Yes, of course. I'll talk to him." Javier squeezed her hand, and Bruce patted her shoulder.

"Good Eyes, wait." Lightning moved in front of her, stopping the small crowd. "Where are you going now?" He knew she was upset, and probably wondered why these strangers were dragging her all over, since he couldn't follow most of the conversation.

"I have to talk to the See-Through Man," she explained.

Every one of the cohort ruffled their feathers, then abruptly exploded into flight, even Thunder.

"What was all that about?" Bruce asked.

Tesa shook her head. "They don't like the hologram." She was glad Rob would appear inside, even if she didn't relish the idea of entering the building.

The holo-field was set up in a private place, and when Rob finally materialized, Tesa nearly burst into laughter, she was so glad to see him. Then, almost immediately, she had to suppress the urge to cry. "Hi!" she signed, trying to seem cheery.

"Hi, yourself. Boy, it's good to finally *see* you, Tesa. I've been worried sick. Kid, you've been through *hell*!"

The last time she'd spoken to him, he'd thought she'd looked tired. She wondered what he thought of her appearance now.

"Well, it's over now. Rob, what are they going to *do* with the Anurans? How big a threat are they to the stability of the CLS?" Unspoken, she was asking, *Will they be back next year?*

"They're going to remove them from Trinity, and the *Brolga*, and take them back to their own solar system. Their ship will be flanked by two of those huge Mizari ships, so they'll make a big display. The Mizari plan to engage the Anurans in discussions about their 'attitude' toward other intelligent beings. They plan to offer the Anurans a semihospitable planetoid in a remote, uninhabited system, and also help them improve conditions on the uninhabited desert world they found themselves in. They figure if they help them with some of their population pressure, they can negotiate with them about their societal problems."

"And if the Anurans aren't willing to change their society?"

"There'll be a permanent outpost in their solar system. They'll never be able to mount an attack without us knowing, so we'll have time to act. And they'll be made to understand that we intend to react *hard* at the first sign of hostility."

At least *that* wasn't her problem. Once the aliens were removed, it would be over for her, really *over*. Tesa would be able to go back to her job as Interrelator, and everything would settle back into the wonderfully boring routine it had once been.

"Tell me," Rob signed, "how's K'heera, and Jib? I know how they are physically, but how are they . . . otherwise?"

She wanted to say, *How should I know, when I don't even know how I am?* but she suppressed it. "K'heera's great. She handled this much better than the rest of us."

"You can't believe what this has done for her family," Rob told her. "If it was possible for a Simiu to achieve sainthood, K'heera's done it, and lifted her whole family up on the same pedestal. It's been a bitter pill for the Harkk'etts to swallow."

"I thought they *wanted* her to gain honor for them!"

"Oh, they did. But the way it's turned out . . . well, now they have to be really *nice* to humans. K'heera's given us all the credit. Did you know she officially named Bruce her *uncle*? She's given *him* her family honor! The Harkk'etts are spinning about it, but they've got to put on a good public face, or lose the prestige she's gained them. It's actually pretty funny!"

Tesa smiled. Then she remembered the other person Rob had asked about. "Uh . . . listen, Rob . . . about Jib. . . ."

"He's okay, isn't he? They told me he was fine. . . ."

"He didn't get hurt . . . not physically. . . . Look, that thing you told me about, that TSS? Well . . . Jib can't leave Trinity. He's going to have to stay here."

"I don't understand. He's got a promising career. He never wanted to be planet-bound, he always saw himself traveling. . . ."

"That was before the war. When he helped the Singers defeat the Anurans . . . they swept him along. They didn't understand that Jib was only human, not even a telepath. . . ."

"Oh, god, Tesa, tell me they didn't destroy his mind!"

"No!" she reassured him quickly. "He's still Jib . . . but, he's *different*. He's not Rewi Parker anymore. The Wind people have given him a new name—Spirit Keeper. They think that all the spirits they believed once resided in the River, the spirits that kept them away, now reside, happily, in Jib. He's . . . part of the Singers now. He thinks like them. He's . . . linked to them. Much more than I am with the Wind people. We had to rig him a special wet suit to keep him from getting hypothermia. . . . But, Rob . . . he's happy."

The psychologist's face fell, and Tesa knew he felt responsible. She understood that feeling, so didn't try to console him with empty words. "Well . . . I've got good news for *him*. Since there's a telepathic species on Trinity, we're sending a telepath to work with them. His girlfriend, Anzia."

"I'll tell him," Tesa promised. "Try not to feel bad. . . ."

"That's . . . not the only thing on my mind, Tesa. I've . . . been trying to figure out how to tell you this." He was very somber. "Please understand that I'm *totally* against this decision, that I fought it. Mahree and Dhurrrkk' agree with me. We're not just sitting idly by. . . ."

*Oh, god*, she thought, *this is* really *bad news*. Groping for the chair she remembered seeing behind her, Tesa eased herself into it. "Rob, what are you talking about? What's happened?"

She saw him swallow. "There have been meetings with the CLS. . . . They . . . want to . . . question you about your actions."

"Sure. Of course. I understand. . . ."

"They want you to appear before the Planetary Councillors . . . in *person*. You'll have to . . . leave Trinity. . . ."

She reeled. "*Leave* Trinity . . . ? For how long?"

Rob tried to move his hands, fumbled, started over. "I don't know. Tesa, they've . . . suspended you as Interrelator. They feel . . . your actions weren't . . . appropriate. They're especially upset about . . . your refusal to negotiate with the Anurans when you had the chance. And they're not happy about the Quakers, either. They've made arrangements for you to be carried on the luxury transport *Brooklyn Bridge*." He paused, embarrassed.

"If I leave, what are the chances of my ever returning?"

He shook his head. "This has become an incredible political mess. I shouldn't tell you this, but if you leave . . . I don't know if they'll *ever* let you return."

Of course not. It was too messy. They'd keep her in hearing after hearing, and delay decision after decision, while her life dribbled away. It would be easier that way—for them.

"Tesa, this is wrong, and I know it. I don't know how to tell you how sick I am about this."

She held up her hand, feeling unnaturally calm. "Don't feel bad, Rob. It's not your fault. I had to make some hard decisions, and some of them were wrong. I can live with that. Look . . . I've got to tell Taller . . . and get ready to leave."

"Okay, Tesa. I understand."

The former Interrelator walked out of the room in a daze. Once outside, she was shocked to find that every Grus remaining near the River had gathered in front of the building. Many of the humans were there, too, and the Simiu, as well as Captain J'karthha and her aide. Was she the last person to know *this*, as well?

Taller stood on the porch boldly, the only one of his people besides Lightning and Weaver that would do so. Thunder stood among them. The sight of her avian family was almost more than she could bear. She stood tall and faced her old friend.

"Taller, I . . . have to leave you. I have to leave the World."

He didn't even act surprised. "Why?"

"Because . . . I've been told to, by the people I work for. . . ."

"By the See-Through Man?" he asked.

"Yes."

Every feather on the avian's body stood straight out, then settled down slowly. His crown blazed brighter than she'd ever seen it. "I'll speak to the See-Through Man, here, in front of the Wind people. He'll explain to *us* why you must leave."

Tesa was so surprised she didn't react, but Bruce did. He tapped Javier, Martin, and Noriko and the four went inside the building. "You want to *speak* to the . . . ?"

"Personally," Taller insisted.

Within minutes, they had a holo-field set up on the porch. Bruce tapped in a code and the words "One minute please" appeared suspended in air. Then the words dissolved and Rob appeared wraithlike in the outdoor light.

The entire flock of Wind people moved away from the porch. All but Taller, who stood his ground. Rob stared into his own field, obviously startled.

"Greetings, Taller," the human signed in passable Grus.

"You have no reason to greet me, See-Through Man," Taller signed. "I have *summoned* you here to tell you that Good Eyes belongs to our people, to my family, and that she will not be leaving the World, not now, not *ever*."

As with one voice, the collected Wind people lifted their heads and called out. The sound buffeted the gathered humans and Simiu, and even Rob reacted to it, even though Tesa knew his holo-device would nullify the danger.

"Taller, please," Rob argued, "this is not *my* decision. Tesa . . . Good Eyes . . . and I both have to obey higher . . ."

"Understand me, See-Through Man," Taller admonished. "Good Eyes belongs to the people, and we will do what we must to keep her here. Who are *you* to choose our Interrelator? We have defeated one invader! Do you think we fear *your* people?"

"Wait a minute, please, Taller," Tesa begged. "The last thing I want is for the Wind people to break relations with the humans. Don't make this worse than it is."

"What could be worse than this?" The Grus leader glanced at Javier. "Especially now. Unless . . . you *want* to leave us?"

It seemed to Tesa that every avian present leaned forward to see her answer. Even the Hunters seemed eager to know. Her eyes swam. "No . . . of course not . . . I never want to leave. . . ."

"Then, you won't," Taller announced. The avian leader turned again to Rob. He indicated the group standing closest to him. "These are the leaders of all the people on this continent. They agree with me. What do you say, See-Through Man?"

Rob, for once, was at a loss for words. "Of course, you are an independent people, and we honor your sovereignty, as we always have. We want nothing but good relations between our people. However . . . if Good Eyes stays with you . . . it can only be as a civilian. She will not be your representative for us."

"Send whatever representative you want," Taller announced. "But to speak with us they will have to go through Good Eyes."

Rob stared imploringly at Tesa.

She returned his gaze. "You think I should leave anyway, don't you?"

He didn't answer, but she saw agreement in his eyes.

"I can't, Rob."

"I understand. Look, Tesa . . . once you make this decision, you'll be defying the CLS. If you ever *do* leave the planet . . . there's a real good chance they'd never let you return."

"You already told me that." She nodded with a wry smile, remembering. "It's okay. This is my home. I belong here."

"Good luck, Tesa," he signed. "And to you, Taller, and all your people."

"We don't need *luck*, See-Through Man," Taller told him. "The Spirits are on *our* side." Then, ostentatiously, the huge avian enveloped Tesa with his wing. Rob signed off.

There was one last raucous chorus, and then, with a great fluttering of feathers, the group dispersed, feeling, no doubt, as if they had conquered yet another formidable enemy.

"That was very courageous," Tesa told Taller.

He preened himself as if it were a matter of little consequence.
"Get some rest, Good Eyes. You seem tired."

Javier appeared at her elbow at the mention of those magic
words and signed, "Good idea, Taller."

The avian leader bristled, but Weaver jostled him, and the
two avians quickly left the porch. Tesa peered around. Even
the cohort and Thunder had disappeared.

"You okay?" Javier asked.

"Stop asking me that," she signed abruptly.

"It's not every day that someone you care about gets drummed
out of her job and nearly out of the human race," he told her. "I
swear, I didn't know about that. . . ."

She stopped his hands. "You know, it might not be such a good
idea for you to . . . be with me."

He stared at her quizzically.

"There could be repercussions to my refusing to leave. They
could try and get to me through *you*."

"I can handle that, trust me."

"First-Light, you don't understand. . . ."

"*Stop!*" he ordered her. "You're *not* responsible for everything.
In fact, as of now, you're not responsible for *anything!* You're not
even employed! No more reports. No more bureaucracy. You'll
probably have to *learn* to enjoy leisure, but . . . I'll help you. And
we've got a lot of plants to catalog."

Tesa wanted to hug him and weep all at the same time. She
would always be responsible for what had happened here. No one
could take that burden away. She'd made the decisions. . . .

Javier glanced over her shoulder, so she turned to see Szu-yi
approaching. It still disturbed her to see how badly the doctor had
changed.

"Tesa," the doctor signed, "I just heard what happened. Don't
be upset. You should be glad to be rid of those fools!"

Tesa blinked, surprised at her vehemence. Then she noticed the
gold balls in Szu-yi's ears. The younger woman touched one,
confused.

"These? Yes, well . . . the doctors on one of the ships did it for
me. I've made some decisions, dear. I'm . . . going to be staying
with Loves-the-Wind. She's lost her mate, you know, and she's
taking it very badly. She needs some company . . . and I . . . Well,
don't be insulted . . . but I want to get away from humans for a
while. I just . . . need some time alone. . . . Loves-the-Wind is a
healer, and so am I. I think we can help each other. . . . And . . .
I . . . keep hearing *them*, you know. . . . So, I asked the doctors

to fix it so I could turn my hearing *off*. When I'm with the Wind people, I can't hear anything. For now, that's better for me. We're leaving tomorrow. I wanted to say good-bye."

"You mean, 'see you soon,' " Tesa corrected, and hugged the frail woman gently. She watched her leave, wondering whether any of them would ever truly heal.

Feeling a damp hand on her shoulder, she turned to find Jib, dripping and grinning, behind her. "I hate it when you sneak up on me!" she complained good-naturedly. She tried to ignore the glazed, not-quite-there look in the young man's eyes.

"You always did, mate," he signed, tugging absently on his greenstone tiki. "Tesa, I overheard Rob talking to you. . . ."

Jib *overheard* almost everything these days. That was hard to get used to. "Then you know Anzia's coming?"

He blinked. "Anzia?"

Tesa felt her chest tighten.

She'd found all the letters Jib had written to the young woman in his backpack. She'd scanned them briefly, and was shocked to see that the changes Jib had undergone were clearly manifested in his writing. The early electronic letters still had his voice, his personality, which grew more and more altered as he came in contact with the Singers. The letters had gradually deteriorated into rambling, disjointed fragments, almost stream of consciousness writings about the River, and the life Jib experienced there. The few lines he'd scrawled on the paper Tesa gave him were almost incomprehensible. She wondered if reading those letters would help Anzia understand.

"She's . . . an old friend of yours, Jib," Tesa reminded him gently. "She's coming . . . to talk to you and the Singers."

"That'll be great. A friend of mine, huh? Well, I came to tell you . . ." He trailed off, suddenly focusing internally. He nodded slightly, as if talking to himself. Tesa had grown used to this; patiently, she waited. "He lied to you."

She faced him, confused. Who? Rob?

"No," he answered her unspoken question. "Sorry. I meant Atle. He never intended to negotiate in good faith. He wanted to capture you and use you as a persuader, or stall you as long as possible and make you ineffective. He lied to you just now. It really made the Singers mad. You'd better make sure he leaves *today*." With a quick wave, he jogged back to the River and disappeared.

"What was that all about?" Javier asked.

A sob escaped Tesa, then a laugh. She leaped at her lover, wrapping her arms around him as hard as she could, nearly knocking them both over. He returned the embrace, writing a question mark on her back.

She released him. "Jib just gave me back my soul," she signed, confusing him further.

"I can see life with a *heyoka* promises to be very interesting," he mused.

She tilted her head. "Big plans, ethnobotanist. Think you'll be here that long?"

"Taller said I could stay. I asked *him* first. I knew *you'd* say 'no.'"

She laughed, feeling genuinely happy for the first time in days. "Ask me now, if you're so smart!"

He stared deep into her light eyes, and she met his dark gaze unflinchingly. "I want to stay with Good Eyes of the White Wind people. I want to belong to her . . . forever!" He smiled broadly, as if he'd just said the strangest thing.

Tesa nodded sagely. "Of course you can stay, First-Light. You belong here. Just like *me!*" She saw the odd expression in his eyes, but before he could get too serious, she grabbed his hand and tugged him toward the lean-to. "Come on, *old man*. You look tired. I think you could use a *nap!*"

Pretending great reluctance, he let her cajole him all the way there.

> A warrior
> I have been.
> Now
> it is all over.
> A hard time
> I have.
>
> Song of Sitting Bull

# Afterword

In some ways, it seems as though I started the StarBridge series just yesterday . . . and, in others, it seems as though a century or so has gone by. Can it be Book Five already?

I hope all of you StarBridge readers enjoyed the further adventures of Tesa on Trinity. At this point you're all probably wondering whether Tesa and Javier will live happily ever after. Or, will Rob and Mahree ever get together again? And will anyone ever go into Sorrow Sector and come out alive? Just how many intelligent species are there in the Orion Arm, anyway . . . and how many of them will be as threatening as the Anurans?

For that matter, will there be more StarBridge books to come?

Well, you never know. There are always possibilities . . .

—Ann C. Crispin
October 1993